Mr de Sousa's Legacy
A Cornish Love Story

ANN E BROCKBANK

*Best wishes and happy
reading*

A E Brock x

Front cover 'Carne' by © R W Floyd. From an original oil painting

ISBN-13: 978-1490930763
ISBN-10: 1490930760

:

For my darling Rob, with love.

Ann E Brockbank

ACKNOWLEDGMENTS

I couldn't have written this book without the help and support of some very special people. Firstly, to my partner Rob, your love and encouragement has kept me writing. To my good friend Wendy, for being the first person to read Mr de Sousa's Legacy and for steering me in the right direction when needed with your astute and sensitive editing. Your honesty and encouragement was always appreciated. Also to Isabel for your time and expertise. Your editorial suggestions are always wise and have improved the book enormously.

The most nerve-wracking part of writing this book is letting it go out into the world, so I'd like to thank every single reader who has spent their hard-earned money on this book. Without each of you, I'd be a very miserable writer without an audience, I am honoured that you selected my story to read. A very big thank you to you all.

Ann E Brockbank

1

CORNWALL 1938

The sudden unexpected weight on her hands shot a jolt of pain through Rachel's wrists.

'Steady,' she urged herself as her arms trembled and her fingernails clawed at the bare floorboards for stability. Her lips curled to a self satisfied smile. It must be twenty years since she'd attempted this gymnastic feat, and felt proud the handstand had been executed with an enthusiastic, albeit ungainly wallop against the walnut wardrobe door. She'd been seven the last time she did this. Without warning, an unwelcome memory jumped into her head.

'Look mummy? Watch me do a handstand.' But her mother's tear-filled eyes looked only at the sea.

Brushing the sand from her hands, she watched intently as her mother rolled her stockings off. Placing them into her black court shoes, she said in a voice almost inaudible, 'Watch mummy's shoes darling.' As her mother walked towards the waters edge, Rachel slipped her own tiny sand-encrusted feet into her mother's shoes.

'Look mummy?' As she stood, the heels sank deep into the sand. 'I'm as tall as you are now!' She looked up, but her mother was nowhere to be seen.

Jolted from her reverie, her left wrist gave way, and she crumpled into a graceless heap, catching her left shin on the brass wardrobe door handle.

On hearing the thump and subsequent cry of pain from the next room, Rachel's stepdaughter Verity paused momentarily as she brushed her long red hair. She smirked slightly, returning to the task in hand, hoping the accident, which had befallen Rachel, was nothing too minor.

*

It was as though the day had forgotten to wake up. A thick penetrating fog had rolled up the Helford River during the night, and now hung like a shroud over the Cornish river village of Gweek. Beneath its silent cloak, the village struggled with its day-to-day tasks. Figures swept soundlessly through the swirling mist, and the only noise was the chink of iron on iron from a distant workshop. It was a day for indoor chores, and locals huddled inside from the chill air, listening with quiet detachment to rumours of war on the wireless.

Adam de Sousa stood silently on the brow of the bridge, tired but jubilant at his journeys end. He'd arrived on the midday bus, no more than two minutes ago, but already felt a quiet attachment for the place. He'd never been to Cornwall before, nor heard of Gweek until five days ago, but there was an air of excitement within him, and he was eager to settle into the village he would call home for the next two months. Placing the larger of his two bags at his feet, carefully avoiding a large mound of horse manure, he balanced a small black leather case on top of the lichen rich granite wall and tried to get his bearings.

'Once off the bus, you just 'ed for The Black Swan Hotel, you can't miss it. It's the biggest building in the village,' his colleague George Bray had instructed over the phone. Adam smiled to himself. It may be the biggest building in the village, but, neither had envisaged the weather would resemble pea soup. The mist swirled around like smoke vapours, giving the place an eerie quality. Shivering inwardly, he picked up his bags and began to walk in the direction of the dull yellow glow of an illuminated building.

*

The Black Swan Hotel was the only public house in the village. It was a square, solid stone building, situated on the main Falmouth road and was the hub of the community. It once served as a farmhouse, with a blacksmiths forge to the rear, until it was converted to a hotel sometime during the last hundred and fifty years. The hotel was run by a young widow, Rachel Pendarves, since the untimely and tragic death of her husband Alex. Though grief had wearied her these twelve months, taking the shine from her eyes and the lustre from her hair, visitors would always receive a warm welcome there.

The bar was busy that lunchtime, with locals opting for the warmth and cheer of the Snug, rather than the cold dank unworkable fields awaiting harvest.

'A pint and a gill Rach, when you're ready,' Charlie Williams said, as he and his wife Lizzy settled down on the bar stools.

Rachel smiled warmly at her friends, but as she reached for a pint glass, Lizzy noticed that her friend winced slightly.

'You alright Rach? You look like you're in pain there.'

Rachel shot her a sheepish look. 'Oh it's nothing.' She waved her hand dismissively. 'I've cricked my neck, strained my wrist and grazed my shin this morning, that's all.'

Lizzy laughed. 'What on earth were you doing to do that?'

'Shush...' Rachel flushed with embarrassment. 'You really wouldn't believe me if I told you.'

Lizzy gave a wry smile. 'Try me.'

Rachel sighed in resignation. 'Well don't laugh, but as you know, when Alex died my life completely flipped on its axis!'

Lizzy reached out to her with a comforting hand and nodded.

'Well,' she continued. 'I've been in total limbo for a whole year, so because it was the anniversary of his death yesterday, I thought I would set the equilibrium right by turning my world upside down.' She grimaced slightly. 'By doing a handstand!'

Lizzy roared with laughter. 'You daft mare. But I must say, I'm impressed. If I did one now, I'd break my flipping wrists. I'm a bit heavier than I used to be.'

'What do you mean a bit?' Charlie Williams prodded his wife playfully.

Lizzy turned to face her husband and pouted. 'I'm all woman Charlie Williams and you know it.'

They exchanged a tender smile. 'You sure are, girl.' He winked.

'Anyway Rach,' she said, turning her attention back to her friend. 'This handstand, did it help?'

Rachel shrugged her shoulders. The flood of memories brought on by the act had unnerved her slightly, though she chose not to reveal this. She gave a dry smile. 'Only time will tell. You know I'll never get over Alex, but I just feel that it's time to move on and get on with my life. Does that sound callous?'

'Not at all.' Lizzy squeezed Rachel's hand. 'Good for you, that's what I think. I can't tell you how good it is to see you out of your black clothes at last.'

Rachel looked wistfully down at the rose print dress she had retrieved from the depths of her wardrobe. She smoothed her hands along the thin material. 'This dress was Alex's favourite,' she said quietly

'Well, you look lovely in it.'

Rachel smiled thinly. 'Would you like to tell that to my delightful stepdaughter?' she said wearily, turning to serve Jinny Noble. As she pulled the pint, she recalled the altercation with Verity earlier that morning, regarding this very dress. Verity, normally the laziest of young women, was already out of bed and making herself breakfast when Rachel had entered the kitchen. Never one for pleasantries, Rachel didn't expect any morning greeting from Verity, nor did she expect the shocking barrage of verbal abuse which ensued.

'What the hell do you think you're wearing?' she'd shrieked, upsetting her cup as she stood up from where she sat. 'It's the day after the first anniversary of my father's death! Have you no shame, flouncing about the place like a painted whore?' She spat the words at her venomously.

Quite taken aback, Rachel began to well up, but standing her ground, she quietly answered, 'I am well aware of the significance of the day. I miss your father as much as you do, and you know that. What I wear is for him, to celebrate his life. Your father loved me in this dress, and I shall wear it with pride, for he bought it for me on our honeymoon.'

Verity's eyes misted red with fury. 'He'd turn in his grave if he saw you now. You're a disgrace to his memory.' With one sweep of the hand, she sent her breakfast crashing onto the floor, and ran from the kitchen.

Standing amongst the debris of broken crockery, considering whether to change her dress, but grim determination won, and she began to make breakfast.

Lizzy watched Rachel's face dim slightly. 'Hey?' She clicked her fingers to raise her from her reverie. 'What words of wisdom came out of her foul mouth then - as if I didn't know?'

Rachel sighed. 'Apparently, I'm a disgrace to her father's memory, dressed like this.'

'Oh fiddlesticks,' Lizzy fumed. 'I could smack her face for her. I have never come across a child so hateful.'

'She's not a child anymore Lizzy.'

'Well she acts like a child!'

'She's just very unhappy. You know how much she loved Alex.' Rachel sighed heavily as she refilled Charlie's glass. 'I do understand how she feels, but I just want to feel normal again.'

'I know my luver. You don't have to explain to me.' Lizzy's eyes crinkled with affection, as Ely Symonds rattled his glass on the bar to catch Rachel's attention.

'When do you think this fog will lift Ely?' Rachel asked, as she pulled the pump.

'It can't come soon enough,' he answered. 'This chill air gets into my bones and makes 'em grumpy.'

Rachel grinned.

'Aye you can laugh young lady, but when you get to my age, and surely you will one day, the fog will make your bones grumpy too. You mark my words.'

Jinny Noble piped up, 'My grandmother always used to say that your luck changes when foggy weather lifts. She said that the damp air mopped up the bad luck and vaporised it away.'

'God I hope she's right - I could do with some good luck for a change,' Rachel added.

*

The damp air hung musty in Adam's nostrils, as he picked his way through the thicket of leaves, brought down by the recent high winds. He halted slightly at the sight of a figure - it was almost like an apparition as it moved swiftly in the distance.

'Excuse me,' he shouted, quickening his pace. 'I'm looking for The Black Swan?'

'You're stood in front of it me 'andsome.'

As a large stone building loomed over him, a strange high-pitched noise, rather musical and not very far carrying, stopped him dead in his tracks. He listened intently, his eyes straining to see through the fog. All was silent for a second, and then he jumped suddenly, as a sound of huge wings thrashed towards him. He stepped back and stumbled slightly and then there was silence again. Hastily he made for the front door, lifted the latch and stepped quickly into a small vestibule. He wiped his feet on the worn mat and glanced down the corridor. To the left and right of the corridor were doors with small brass plates with Snug and Lounge printed on them respectively. Both rooms had a bar, though a crowd of people sat on high wooden stools, huddled around the left hand side one, so Adam joined them.

Rachel eyed the stranger with interest. She noted that he looked tired, but his disposition seemed kind and friendly. She quickly beckoned him into the room. 'I'll be with you in a moment.' She gestured for him to take a seat near the fire.

As Adam moved towards the seat, he noted that the lady gave him an unhurried once over with her pale blue eyes, before continuing to pull a pint of beer, turning once more to converse with her friends, who were huddled around the radio.

As he rid himself of his overcoat, Neville Chamberlain's voice crackled out from the radio, and a hush fell over the room.

'We, the German Fuhrer and Chancellor and the British Prime Minister, have had a further meeting today and are agreed in recognising that the question of Anglo-German relations is of the first importance for the two countries and for Europe.

'We regard the agreement signed last night and the Anglo-German Naval Agreement as symbolic of the desire of our two peoples never to go to war with one another again.

'We are resolved that the method of consultation shall be the method adopted to deal with any other questions that may concern our two countries, and we are determined to continue our efforts to remove possible sources of difference and thus to contribute to assure the peace of Europe.'

The crowd at the bar gave a collected sigh.

'Well, that's the most positive news we've had for a long time,' Rachel said cheerfully.

'I don't know about that,' Charlie answered, scratching his bald spot with his grubby hands.

'What don't you know?' Lizzy scoffed.

'I reckon there'll be war afore long. It doesn't matter what Mr Chamberlain says, I don't trust that Hitler fellow. There'll be war, you'll see.'

Lizzy huffed. 'I don't know Charlie Williams. You're all doom and gloom, you are. First bit of good news we've had for months, and you go and spoil it with your daft ideas.'

Jinny Noble drained her glass and placed it hard on the bar, rousing her husband Eric from his doze. 'Tain't no good you lot frett'n over something yer can't do ought about, I reckon. Yes, tis possible that there may be a war, tis true, but we gotta get on with life. There be harvest to finish off and God to thank for not taking our men folk to war yet. It worries me to death that my two boys will be taken. Let's be positive about the future. Believe what Chamberlain says, and get on with life. I can tell 'ee, I'll sleep a lot sounder in my bed this night after 'earing what he's just said!'

Charlie growled under his breath. 'I'm just telling 'ee, that's all.'

Jinny shook her head indignantly.

'What do you say Eli?' Charlie tossed the question to the ruddy-faced man in the corner. 'You're mighty quiet sat there.'

Eli Symonds pushed his fingers deep into the pocket of his worn tweed jacket, which was tied at the waist with twine. He drew out his baccy tin, and nodded in agreement. 'Aye, there'll be a war rightly enough,' he said, scrunching his face as he concentrated on filling his pipe.

As silence fell among the locals, Adam's stomach gave a loud hungry rumble, causing them all to turn and stare in his direction.

'Oh lord, I'm ever so sorry. I forgot all about you sitting there,' Rachel said, moving swiftly from the bar to stand at his side.

'No matter,' he said, smiling kindly at her.

Rachel smiled back as she took in his lean muscular body. He had lovely hazel eyes, a strong nose, a kind mouth and his dark hair framed a very handsome face. Her lips had parted slightly as she gazed upon him, becoming suddenly aware of her heartbeat as it began to race. She flushed up to the roots of her hair when she realised she'd been staring at him and cleared her throat quickly. 'What can I get you?' she said, lowering her eyes as she pushed her hands deep into her apron pockets for her pencil and pad.

'I'm looking for a room. I was told you may be able to help. Do you have a vacancy?'

She pushed a wisp of her hair away from her face. 'We do sir, yes. How many nights do you intend to stay?'

'Just for a couple of days, until I sort out my lodgings, if that's alright with you?'

His eyes had been on her the whole time she'd been speaking and Rachel found for a moment she was unable and unwilling to break from this dark handsome mans gaze.

'Stay for as long as you like,' she said softly. 'And your name sir?'

'Adam de Sousa.'

Rachel raised her eyebrows. 'de Sousa? That's quite an uncommon name!'

He nodded and smiled, but gave no explanation as to its origins.

'Right then, can I get you a drink?'

'A beer would be nice,' he answered, cursing his stomach as it rumbled again.

Rachel laughed. 'There's a pot of stew cooking in the kitchen, I'll bring you some with a nice wedge of the bread I baked fresh this morning. Otherwise, I fear your stomach rumbles will shake the pictures off the wall.'

He smiled broadly and welcomed her friendliness. 'Thank you. I'm obliged to you.'

The locals watched in silence as the stranger drank his beer with relish. A few minutes later, he tucked into a large bowl of stew - dipping his bread into the rich warming gravy. When he'd finished, he ordered another beer, and settled back down near the fire. With his legs outstretched, he could feel the warmth seeping into his damp clothes.

Charlie turned to face Adam, and they both nodded at each other. 'You're a stranger to these parts?' Charlie asked casually.

Adam smiled. 'I'm originally from Stratford, but more recently my home has been in Kent.'

The locals put their heads together and mumbled to each other for a moment, and then Charlie turned back to him. 'What do you have in that bag then?'

'Charlie!' Rachel banged the basket of glasses she had just washed and punched her fists into her hips. 'It's none of our business what the gentleman has in his bag!'

Adam smiled. 'That's okay, I don't mind.' He patted the worn leather bag on the chair beside him. 'They're instruments.'

'Instruments eh, you be a musician then?' Lizzy asked hopefully, sliding off her stool. She began to sway her curvy body as though music was playing. 'We like a bit of music in the evenings, don't we Rach? We like to dance as well, though there's precious little opportunity to do so,' she added, smoothing her hands down her cotton dress.

Charlie shot his wife a withering look, and she quickly sat back down on the stool.

Adam laughed. 'Sorry, you misunderstand me. They're veterinary instruments. I'm a vet.' He watched their faces as they digested his words.

Presently Charlie said, 'A veterinary, eh? You'll be working with old George Bray then?' He scratched his head. 'Funny, I didn't know he was thinking of retiring.'

Adam smiled. 'As far as I know, he's not. I'm just covering for him while he has a short stay in hospital that's all.' He downed the last of his pint, rubbed the stiffness from his limbs with his strong hands and stood up. 'Would it be possible to see my room now?' he asked Rachel hopefully.

'Certainly Mr de Sousa. Lizzy, watch the bar for me, will you?' She turned and smiled broadly at Adam. 'If you'd like to follow me?'

Adam picked up his belongings and followed Rachel down the corridor towards the stairs, conscious of many eyes following him. He noted that Rachel probably had a fine figure under her oversized, yet pretty dress. Her shoes had seen better days as well, but were clean and polished. She moved with grace, as he followed her up the stairs. Her skirt swished against her legs, which were bare and as pale as the rest of her visible skin. He surmised she was in her early twenties, but he was wrong in that assumption. He also noted she wore a wedding ring, but also had an aura of sadness about her, that he could not fathom. At the top of the stairs, a sudden breeze from the open window blew a strand of her long auburn hair into disarray, and she turned her face to feel its coolness on her face. 'Hopefully, the mist will lift soon. There's a breeze coming up the Helford.' She smiled brightly.

At the door of room three, Rachel gestured Adam in before her. The room was bright and airy despite the dullness of the day. The bed was made up with crisp white sheets, folded over a green quilted eiderdown. A mahogany wardrobe stood in the far corner, pulled away from the wall, to stop the damp Cornish air from mildewing the contents, and a matching dressing table stood beneath the window.

Adam put his bag on the chair by the door as Rachel bent to light a fire. 'I'll do that,' he said, swiftly moving towards her.

'It's alright - it's all ready to take a lighted match.' She grabbed the box of matches from the mantelpiece, struck one and held it under the mound of kindle and coal. She leant forward, blowing gently to fan the flames. When she was content that the fire would take, she leant back on her haunches and turned to smile at him. 'There, you'll be as warm as toast in a few minutes.'

Adam thanked her warmly.

'I'm Rachel Pendarves by the way, the landlady of this establishment.' She held out her hand. As Adam closed his hand around hers, she felt a warm glow from within her body. They stood for a second longer than was necessary, until the stillness of the mist-covered village, was punctured by the roar of a motorbike descending the road towards the village, swiftly followed by a chorus of barking dogs in its wake. He noted Rachel's eyes cloud over and the smile drain from her face, as the sound of running footsteps echoed outside the bedroom door.

Rachel's face flushed. 'If you'll excuse me Mr de Sousa, I must go now,' she said, rushing to the door. 'If you need anything just call, I'm always around. Oh, and the bathroom is the last door on the right, if you need a bath, let me know, and I'll put the boiler on.'

A moment later she was gone, her footsteps descending the stairs in haste. A door slammed downstairs as the motorbike revved noisily, skidding as it swiftly drove off.

'Verity! Verity! Come back!' Rachel's distraught voice screamed into the mist.

On hearing the commotion, Adam ran to the window, pulled down the sash and peered out into the damp air. Below, he could just about make out the outline of Rachel as she threw her hands up in exasperation and cried, 'You stupid, stupid girl.' As the rider and passenger disappeared in the distance

2

It was an uneasy dream which disturbed Rachel's sleep that night, though the latter part had no validity. She had fallen into a fitful sleep once Verity had returned safely home. Quite defiantly, Verity made no secret of her arrival at one-thirty that morning, calling out her goodbyes to her boyfriend Vincent Day, over the deafening roar of his retreating motorbike, and then slamming the back door for Rachel's benefit.

Vincent Day was a tall, unpleasant man with broad shoulders and a self-assured cockiness about him which Rachel hated. He had collar length untidy black hair, dark skin and cruel eyes. A cigarette hung permanently from the corner of his mouth, and he sneered whenever he was spoken to. He had first arrived in the village a year ago, and since then, he had been in and out of employment, working only whenever there were hands needed to pick fruit, vegetables or flowers. He had made his home in a run down caravan, close to Garras, a couple of miles out of the village of Gweek, and to Rachel's despair, he had taken a great interest in her seventeen-year-old step-daughter, as she had to him.

Exasperated, though thankful that Verity was home safe, sleep still evaded Rachel for a while longer. Instead, her thoughts turned to Sam Blewett, her late husband Alex's oldest friend. Sam was a fifty-two-year-old hardworking blacksmith, who drank, but not to excess. He also possessed a short temper, which he constantly vented on his son Harry. Sam was a tall, heavy man with huge shoulders and strong muscular arms. He had a short stubby nose, a ruddy, clean-shaven face with dark wayward hair that grew grey at the temples. Sam was a widower with two children, a son Harry aged twenty, and a daughter, Sally aged eighteen, who Sam's wife died giving birth to.

His children were as different as chalk and cheese. Sally

Blewett was a handsome, sturdy, country built girl, with brown eyes and straw coloured hair. She had a loud, raucous, infectious laugh and could hold her own in any situation she found herself in, be it a fight or otherwise. Though she knew it was snobbish of her, Rachel found her to be a little coarse and outspoken, very unlike her brother. Harry was as thin and plain as his sister was sturdy and handsome. He had unwillingly followed in his father's footsteps as a blacksmith, but Sam despaired of him. He was slow to learn the trade he secretly despised, and felt clumsy and useless at times. Sally was more use in the forge and could lift far heavier things than Harry, making Sam's relationship with his son, volatile.

There was no doubt about it, Sam had been a tower of strength to Rachel after Alex had so tragically died in a fishing accident twelve months previously. Though Rachel couldn't help but wonder if Sam helped her to ease his own conscience regarding Alex's death, as they were out fishing together the day he died. Normally sure footed and well able to take care of himself, Alex had apparently fallen overboard whilst setting his lobster pots. Sam had told her there was nothing he could do to save him. 'He must have caught his hand in the rope. He went down with the anchor like a ton of bricks and never surfaced.'

Rachel shuddered momentarily at the thought of Alex in his watery grave, but it was more than this image which disturbed her tonight. She pulled the quilt higher for comfort, and shuddered as she recalled the altercation she'd had with Sam a few hours ago as she closed the pub doors.

It had been a happy, lively evening in The Black Swan Hotel. Adam had come into the bar early evening, after enjoying his second bowl of stew and a wedge of homemade bread in the lounge. Rachel's mood was still light, and she silently enjoyed the smiles she got from Adam whenever she looked his way. There was something quite extraordinary about Adam, the locals took to him immediately, so much so, he shared several half pints of ale with various people, and none of them would let him pay his way. Sam had arrived just before ten, and five minutes later Adam yawned and retired to his room. His exit suddenly left Rachel feeling very flat, as though a light had been extinguished. She smiled as Sam made small talk, though she barely took in a word he was saying. As the other customers drifted away, Sam had stayed back, as he did sometimes, for one last drink with her after the other customers had left.

He drained the last of his ale and wiped his mouth with the back of his hand. 'You look different today, brighter, you know, without your black clothes. It's about time you were out of those widow's weeds - it did nothing for you, you know.'

Angered, she snapped at him. 'They weren't meant to do anything for me. I wore them out of respect because of how I felt.'

He raised his eyebrows.

'Feel I mean, I wore them because of how I feel,' she corrected herself.

His eyes travelled the length of her body, making Rachel uncomfortable.

'I'll be off then,' he said, with a twisted smile. 'Unless you want me to set up a barrel for you?'

Rachel shook her head, and he rose to take his leave. She relaxed slightly at his impending departure, following him to the door to lock up. 'Goodnight Sam,' she said, as he closed his hand around the handle. He paused momentarily then suddenly turned, flung his coat at a nearby chair, and moved swiftly towards her.

Taken aback, Rachel stumbled slightly as she stepped away from him.

His great hands grabbed her by the shoulders. 'Rachel, marry me.' It was more of an order than a request. The shock drained the colour from her face, as she struggled to be free of him. His grasp tightened on her shoulders, and she felt the dampness of his sweaty palms leach through her cotton dress. 'You know that I've loved you, since the moment I set eyes on you, when you came to work in this bar all those years ago. I did everything I could to make you notice me, but you only had eyes for Alex,' he scoffed. 'I can't tell you how much it grieved me to watch you marry him.' He paused for a moment to judge her reaction, and then continued defiantly. 'I admit it yes, I was jealous of him.' His eyes darkened. 'It's a terrible emotion jealousy you know. It eats you up and tears you apart.'

Trying anxiously to keep her face void of any emotion, Rachel stood very still, though her head spun and she hardly dared to breathe. 'Sam, please,' she protested, but Sam put a hot finger softly on her lips. She recoiled in disdain from his touch.

'No my luver, I don't mean to be disrespectful of my friend. I'm just telling you the truth. I have, from a distance yearned for you, but Alex was my friend, and I would never have made a cuckold of him.'

Rachel flushed profusely, resenting the implication that she would have ever contemplated such a thing. She turned from him - her face scarlet with rage, but Sam took the gesture as excitement at the prospect, and furthered his proposal. 'Rachel, I love you.' He shook her violently. 'Oh, I know you don't love me, but I think you respect me, and I believe we'll fare well together.'

This was too much to bear. She struggled to free herself from his grasp. 'Please stop this Sam,' she protested.

Ignoring her plea, he pulled her to his chest. 'Then marry me woman? The time is right - I want you to be my wife'.

Rachel was beside herself. As she stood tight-lipped, feeling his hot breath on her neck, she closed her eyes tightly and tried to calm herself.

Sam laughed heartily and held her at arms length. 'Okay,

I can see you're shocked by my proposal. I won't press you for an answer yet, I'll give you some time to think. We'll talk again soon, but mind, I won't be taking no for an answer. You *will* be mine, you're out of mourning now, and I'll not stand by and let another man query my pitch.' He released his grip on her shoulders, and the residue of damp hand marks made her shiver with repulsion. He picked up his coat, and cast his eyes over the pub he believed he would soon be licensee of. 'We'll make a good team, you and I, running this place.' He stepped out of the door into the fog and whistled tunelessly as he walked away.

Angrier than she thought she was capable of, she slammed the door, and with trembling fingers, fumbled with the key in the lock. When all was secure, she took a deep breath and poured herself a large brandy and burst into tears.

Now, as she lay in her bed, shuddering at the very thought of him. What on earth was she going to do? She tossed the question about in her head until she fell into a fitful sleep and began to dream of her darling husband Alex.

She waved him off as he sailed away down the river. Within the dream came Sam Blewett sailing back up the Helford towards her. It was dusk. The tide was at its fullest as Rachel stood silently at the head of the river awaiting Alex and Sam's return from their fishing trip. The age old oak woods which flanked the banks of the Helford were dark and vaporous as the small fishing vessel came into view. Rachel ran to catch the mooring rope, to find the vessel held only Sam and his son Harry, whose head was held low. She recalled Sam's cool blue eyes as he spoke. 'Oh Rachel my luver, I'm so sorry, Alex is dead. He went over the side so quick, I couldn't save him.' Rachel screamed, her hands tearing at her hair in desperation. He was lost at sea, there was no body to bury, no closure, no goodbye, no more love, no future. Darkness came now to her dream, as she found herself back in the bar of The

Black Swan with Sam beside her. 'Marry me. I love you Rachel. The time is right for me to tell you, I want you to be my wife.'

'No!' she moaned. 'No, no, no, the time is not right. This is wrong, so wrong.' She was pushing his great bulk away from her. 'Mr de Sousa is here now. He'll love me, not you!'

She woke with a start - her nightdress soaked in perspiration. She ran her tongue over her dry lips, there was a horrible metallic taste in her mouth, then a tap on her bedroom door made her jump. 'Mrs Pendarves?' an unfamiliar male voice called out to her.

She cleared her voice. 'Yes, hello,' she answered, pulling the covers about her.

'Beg your pardon. It's Adam, Adam de Sousa.' The voice hesitated. 'I thought I heard you scream then call out my name. Are you alright?'

Rachel flushed to the roots of her hair. 'Oh, I'm so sorry to have disturbed you,' she said in a high pitched voice. 'I'm absolutely fine.' She laughed in embarrassment. 'Just a silly dream I think.' She could feel her heart pounding as she spoke to him through the door.

'Very well, as long as you are alright?' he said lightly. 'I'll see you at breakfast then.'

Rachel listened as his footsteps retreated, then glanced at the clock, shocked to find she'd overslept by half an hour. She pushed the covers away and rushed to dress.

*

Verity clicked her tongue disdainfully as Rachel hurried into the kitchen. 'You do realise we have a guest waiting in the lounge, and breakfast is nowhere near ready?'

Rachel ignored her taunt.

'It's not like you to be late up. I hope nothing kept you up last night.'

Refusing to be perturbed, Rachel began to prepare the breakfast.

Verity sneered inwardly as she watched Rachel busy herself at the stove. She hated Rachel, always had, and always would. Right from the moment Rachel had walked through the door of The Black Swan, her father had been smitten. She'd arrived to fill the post of chamber maid and ended up making a bed for herself with her beloved father. She would never forgive her for stealing his affection from her. She was his precious only daughter, and he had doted on her after her mother had died. They didn't need anybody else and didn't want anybody in their close knit relationship. They had managed perfectly well until Rachel came and bewitched him.

Rachel turned and her eyes met the steely cold glare of Verity's, recognising the cool hatred within them.

'What are you looking at?'

'Nothing of any worth,' Verity retorted.

Rachel shuddered inwardly at her coldness. 'Could you set the breakfast table for our guest please,' she said patiently.

'I did it when you were lazing in bed,' she answered curtly. 'Who is he anyway? I saw him earlier when he went to buy a paper, he's very handsome.'

'That's Adam de Sousa,' Rachel answered evenly. 'He's a veterinary surgeon. He'll be with us for a few days.'

'A vet eh! I bet he's not short of a bob or two then!' Verity butted in. 'I shall have to go and introduce myself, before you get your claws into him,' she said, tossing her flame red hair defiantly.

Rachel threw her a contemptuous look as she slid an egg onto the plate of sausage and bacon. 'I hope you were careful last night, whatever you did.'

Verity mimicked her words and twisted her mouth into a half smile.

Rachel paused for a moment. 'I'm worried about you Verity.'

'Well don't,' she snapped, and as she did her emerald

eyes flashed. 'Here, give me that. I'll take handsome Adam his breakfast,' she said, pulling the plate from Rachel's grasp.

Rachel reluctantly let go. 'It's Mr de Sousa to you, while he's a paying guest.

Verity screwed her nose. 'It's Mr de Sousa to you,' she mimicked again, then moistened her lips with her tongue and tossed her hair about her shoulders.

An hour later, setting Verity the task of washing up, Rachel walked into the lounge. Adam was sat in the window seat reading the paper. He folded it quickly as she approached.

She smiled. 'Please don't let me disturb you.'

'You're not, I assure you.' He returned the smile, and Rachel felt a warm glow engulf her body.

She moistened her lips unintentionally. The gesture did not go unnoticed. 'Will you be calling on the veterinary George Bray today?'

Adam nodded. 'Yes, I'll see him later, but I had hoped on doing a little sightseeing around Gweek this morning, but...' He glanced out of the window.

Rachel looked over his shoulder at the dull grey mist which had once again shrouded the creek. 'Believe me - Cornwall is normally bathed in brilliant sunshine, even at this time of year. The summer starts in March and ends in October.'

Adam glanced out of the window again and raised his eyebrows. 'I'll take your word for it.'

She laughed. 'Don't worry! The forecast predicts sunshine, give it another hour and it will all burn away.'

Sure enough, after the early morning mist had lifted, the day had become very warm, cooled only by a faint easterly breeze which sighed off the tidal river.

Adam paused for a few minutes on the banks of the Helford. There were several boats of various sizes tied up on the bank. Some were better kept than others, hence the air of decay which wafted into Adam's nostrils. After a long walk, following the wooded banks of the river, Adam returned to The Black Swan around one-thirty, hot and famished. Just as he approached the building, he was stopped in his tracks by a loud squeal, as Verity ran from the washhouse, straight into Adam's arms.

He staggered backwards, momentarily stunned. 'Whatever is it?' he said, shaking her gently.

For a moment, the terror rendered her speechless, before blurting the words, 'Something black...in there, it's in there!' Her long elegant finger pointed to the washhouse. 'Go and get it out, please...'

'Wait a minute, what are you talking about? What's in there?'

'I don't know, it's big and black, it prodded me with a stick or something.' She began to sob uncontrollably

Adam frowned. 'I'm sure it's nothing to be frightened about. Come on we'll investigate.'

Vigorously shaking her head, she sniffed the tears back. 'Not on your life,' she wailed. Nothing would have made her go back in there.

As Adam approached the washhouse Emma Williams, the hotel's chamber maid, came running out of the kitchen.

'Verity, what on earth are you screaming about, Rachel wants to know what all the commotion is?'

'Oh God Emma,' Verity called out in a high shrill voice. 'Be careful, come here, there's something horrible in the washhouse.'

Emma glanced towards Adam as he stood at the washhouse door and immediately followed him.

In the darkest corner of the room, Adam saw a movement and heard the same high pitched bugling noise he had heard the night before. He reached for the light switch, but nothing happened. He stepped back slightly and shouted, 'Can someone get me a torch?'

Seconds later Emma was by his side with a torch. Adam

Ann E Brockbank

re-entered and cast the light upon a very nervous and agitated black swan. He was quick to realise that the animal was in a poor condition, as it hardly put up any fight as he neared it. 'Why the hell is there no proper light in here,' he muttered crossly to Emma, who was standing by the door.

'Verity was just about to change the bulb,' she answered. She turned to Verity and shouted to her to bring the light bulb. Verity shook her head violently. She clicked her tongue in annoyance and marched up to her, grabbed the bulb and returned to the washhouse. With little difficulty, because of her height, she secured it in the socket. With a flick of the switch, the room was bathed in light, and the frightened bird huddled itself into the corner.

'Oh the poor thing,' Emma cried. 'Look he's got entangled with fishing line.' She moved slowly and knelt beside it. 'I'll calm him down if you can get it off,' she said to Adam.

Adam hesitated for a moment as he took a long look at the girl who was clearly unaware of the danger she could be in. He knew swans could be very strong and could use their wings to good effect when defending themselves, but Emma seemed to have a calming effect on the bird. 'Just give me a moment, I'll get my bag,' he said.

In front of a small, enthralled audience, Adam freed the bird with great care and gentleness of almost nine feet of fishing line. It had wrapped itself around one leg, and if left any longer would have almost surely severed its foot. It had cut deep into its left wing, and had wrapped around its body and neck so many times you could hardly see its glossy black plumes on its long and slender neck. The most difficult operation was to free the line from its beak, as the hook, which was still attached, had secured itself deep into its skin. Though very careful not to hurt the bird, the hook extraction made it hiss angrily. As the operation finished, a small round of applause was given to Vet and nurse.

'There, I'm not too sure how he will fare, but at least he

has a fighting chance now he is free of this.' He shook the fishing line in his fist. Both he and Emma moved away from the swan and for the first time Adam took a good look at his assistant. She was indeed extremely tall, probably six foot in her stocking feet Adam surmised. She was a thin plain girl with mousy coloured hair and a long pointed nose, which emphasised the slight squint she had when looking down it at anyone. 'Adam de Sousa, Veterinary surgeon at your service,' he said, holding his hand out to shake Emma's.

Emma took hold of Adam's hand and shook it firmly. 'Hello Mr de Sousa. Mrs Pendarves said you were staying with us. I'm very pleased to meet you. My name is Emma Williams, I'm Lizzy and Charlie's daughter,' she said shyly. 'I believe you met them last night.'

Adam nodded. 'You were very good with the swan, I was impressed,' he said presently. Emma blushed profusely and nodded a thank you.

'I take it you like animals?'

'Oh yes, very much, I love them. I hate to see any suffering in animals. It makes me very sad and angry when I see something like this today.' She lowered her eyes and blushed again when she realised she had spoken with passion.

Adam realised there was a real fire in her belly. 'Do you think you can take care of the swan until he makes a recovery?'

She nodded excitedly. 'If that is alright with Mrs Pendarves, I will?' She looked hopefully towards Rachel.

'Of course it is my dear. But what on earth will it eat apart from bread?' Rachel asked Adam.

Adam smiled. 'Well don't give it too much bread. They normally eat aquatic vegetation from the riverbed. Apart from that, small fish, frogs and worms, grain, such as wheat and vegetable matter, especially lettuce and potatoes. Mind you chop it up fine though. But first I think it will need a long drink. Could you fetch a bucket of water Emma?'

Emma rushed off to find a bucket as Rachel asked how old the bird was.

'He's about three, I would say.'

'He?'

Adam nodded. 'Goodness knows where he's come from though. He's not native to the UK. Do you normally have black swans in Gweek?'

'No, never!' she laughed lightly.

'I just wondered with the hotel being named so.'

'Well I've never seen one before, I have to admit.'

Adam shook his head. 'It's a mystery how he's got here. Come to think of it though I thought I heard a strange noise yesterday when I arrived.'

Well I've never seen him before. He must have followed you here. He probably knew you were a vet and could help him,' she joked.

'Oh gracious me, talking of vets, I'd clean forgotten I had promised George Bray that I would see him just after lunch.' He glanced at his watch, it was almost two-thirty.

Rachel laughed softly. 'Don't worry. George was drinking in the bar until ten minutes ago. He got up and rushed off when he remembered he was meant to be meeting you. I think you have time for a sandwich and drink before you go.'

3

The summer moved gently to a close, and November gales and rain replaced the warm autumn sunshine. Adam found himself to be very busy. He'd been working at George Bray's veterinary practice for over a month now. Initially as a locum vet, while George was in hospital for a routine hernia operation. The stay was only meant to be a few weeks while the old man recovered, but there had been complications with the operation. George caught an infection and had quite unexpectedly died, leaving Adam solely in charge of his veterinary practice, albeit for the time being. Adam found himself in a bittersweet scenario, as he was truly sorry for George's tragic outcome. He'd got on very well with the old vet, but could not help feeling thrilled that his stay in the village was going to be a lot longer than planned.

So it was that Adam moved into the practice and reluctantly moved out of The Black Swan. He'd become very fond of Rachel during the two weeks he'd stayed there. He felt especially protective of her since he'd learned of her tragic loss. He also became acutely aware that she was worried about something, and particularly didn't like to be left alone in the bar at closing time. He took it on himself to help her with the barrel changing and clearing up at the end of the day, then made a point of not going to his room until the bar was closed and the doors secured. He could see in Rachel's face, she was silently grateful, especially as one customer in particular, glowered angrily at her from the end of the bar most nights.

'He's a bit of a disagreeable character,' Adam commented one night.

'Oh that's Sam, it's just his way,' she replied, offering no more information.

Adam left it at that, but a couple of nights before he was

due to leave the hotel to take up his new residence, a very worrying incident occurred. Adam was sat upon a stool near the fire, hungrily enjoying a much needed pasty and pint.

'Had a busy day Adam?' Charlie asked, watching him devour the meal.

'I'll say. One of farmer Trencom's cows escaped and took itself off to the river bank and promptly got stuck in the mud. We've had a devil of a job to get him out before the tide came back up. Seven hours we were at it. I think every bone in my body aches with the pulling and tugging we had to do to get him free.'

'Aye they're heavy buggers to move when they're not stuck in the mud,' Ely chipped in.

'I'll boil some hot water for you Adam. A good soak in a bath will take the aches and pains away,' Rachel said gently as she filled his glass with ale.

Suddenly, Sam, who was sitting at the opposite end of the bar, banged his fists violently on the bar. 'What do I have to do to get a pint in this place?'

Rachel moved swiftly towards him, angrily took his glass, filled it and placed it unceremoniously in front of him.

Sam's eyes burned furiously as he scowled at everyone, creating a frisson of tension, which hung like electricity over the bar.

Presently, Charlie asked, 'What the hell is eating you?'

'What's it got to do with you?' Sam spat back.

Charlie just shook his head and turned away from him, raising an eyebrow in defeat. A log spat in the fire grate, shifted in the red hot embers and fell to the floor, filling the hearth with sparks of red hot embers. Sam was on his feet before anyone else had moved. With his bare hand, he picked up the burning log, and held it aloft, within inches of Adam's face. 'You aren't the only bastard who's done any work today you know,' he hissed.

Adam didn't flinch, even though he could feel the heat dangerously close to his skin. Rachel screamed, and everyone was on their feet.

'Sam!' Charlie shouted.

Sam glared at Charlie. 'What the hell do you want me to do, let the place burn down?' he retorted, throwing the burning log back in the fire. He brushed his hands together, turned on his heel, retrieved his drink, drained it, then with one last scowl at everyone, he turned and left.

'Bloody hot head,' Charlie muttered, 'his elder brother George was just the same. Thank goodness his boy Harry takes after his Ma.'

Adam and Rachel exchanged anxious glances.

Wiping the perspiration from his top lip, Adam rose. 'I'll take that bath now, if that's okay.'

Rachel nodded. 'Emma put the boiler on a while back, so the water should be piping hot,' she answered lightly, trying desperately to keep the tremor from her voice.

Ely was the next to leave, expelling wind from both ends as he moved. Charlie and Rachel watched as his stick tapped along the stone floor. He didn't need any help to negotiate the steps out of the door and experience told them both an offer would be firmly refused.

'Well, tea-time beckons,' Charlie said. Noticing the pale pallor of Rachel's complexion, he regarded her for a moment, then lent forward and closed his hand around hers. 'Are you alright my luver?'

Rachel hung her head miserably. 'Why do all the good men die Charlie? Why couldn't it have been Sam who went overboard that day?' She bit her lip regretfully. 'Sorry, that was a terrible thing to say.'

Perturbed by the remark, Charlie asked, 'That idiot's upset you today, hasn't he?'

'Oh Charlie, it's not just what happened today.' She buried her face in her hands. 'I don't know what to do.' She cried, then in a quieter more serious voice she told him of Sam's proposal.

Charlie sighed angrily. 'I'll have a word with him. I'm

not having this.'

Pushing her hands deep into her dress pocket, she searched for her handkerchief. 'Oh God no Charlie, thank you, but don't do that, I don't want any trouble from him.'

He winked at her kindly. 'There won't be any trouble. You leave this to me. I'll not have you upset.' He drained his glass, and left.

She watched the door close, and as silence in the bar ensued, she hoped with all her heart that she hadn't made the situation worse for herself.

*

As Adam soaked in his bath that evening, he recalled the incident with Sam. Something was amiss there if he wasn't mistaken. Sam acted like a jealous husband towards Rachel. He could see she was disturbed by him and felt her vulnerability. He decided there and then to stay on at the hotel for a week longer than planned.

Though she never said as much, Rachel was visibly thankful for his continued presence. Only when he was sure she was okay and Sam had been conspicuous by his absence, did he make the move to leave. He needed to be in his surgery environment to do the job he was trained for.

*

When the time came for Adam to leave, Rachel felt his departure keenly. Adam had been a wonderful presence in the hotel. He was always kind and in good humour and was the most easygoing man she had met for a long time. He didn't abandon her though, and visited the hotel every day, on the pretence of checking how the swan was fairing.

Emma was doing a grand job nursing the sick black swan. She and Harry Blewett had named him Vicos. A name the Romans gave to Gweek when the quiet little backwater was used by them as a major exporting centre.

Adam found Emma to be very intelligent, albeit very meek and shy. He had found her weeping one day at the back of the hotel, but she would not divulge the source of her plight. He voiced his concern to Rachel about her, and found that Emma had a tendency to weep at the jibes the local boys threw at her about her height and plainness. But Adam could see Emma had a brain and utilised her time very profitably by reading books, which was of great benefit to her. He had an idea, and very tentatively put it to Rachel.

'You want Emma to be your veterinary nurse?' Rachel put down the glass she was wiping and mulled the question over in her mind.

Adam nodded. 'I think she would make a good nurse, but I knew I had to ask you first. I don't want to steal your staff from under your nose, but I really could do with her in the surgery.'

Rachel, slightly put out by the proposition, thumped her fists into her hips and asked, 'Has she approached you about this? Is she unhappy here?'

'No!' Adam laughed heartily. 'I assure you she has no idea I have suggested this. You're the only person I've told. I just thought I'd run it past you.'

Rachel sighed and smoothed a hand across the polished bar reflectively. 'Well, it would be a wonderful opportunity for her, she really is very intelligent, too intelligent to waste her time cleaning rooms here, I admit.'

Adam cocked his head hopefully. 'So, should I ask her?'

Rachel nodded. 'I don't know. Stealing my staff from under my nose, are you?' She smiled warmly. 'Yes of course you should ask her. I think it's a wonderful idea.' Rachel smiled coyly. 'So, if you are looking for a nurse, does this mean you are planning to stay at Brays permanently?'

He looked searchingly into her eyes - they seemed filled with hope, which made his heart soar. 'I'm planning on staying for quite a while, yes.'

Rachel could not conceal her joy. 'Well that's wonderful news, just wonderful.' Then in an unprecedented move, she flung her arms around him and kissed him lightly on the cheek, blushing as she stepped back. They both laughed heartily at the gesture, then feeling slightly awkward, Rachel picked up a glass and began to polish it vigorously.

His eyes twinkled as his grin widened. 'Well, I won't speak to Emma today, I'm in a bit of a hurry, but if you don't mind I'll just use your facilities before I go?'

As Adam disappeared, Rachel heard the roar of Vincent Day's motorbike coming into the village. She glanced at the clock, it was one-fifty. Verity didn't finish work for another ten minutes, which meant Vincent would rev his bike outside until she came. Rachel went about her business trying to ignore the incessant noise from outside, when suddenly the bike engine stopped. A moment later, Vincent pushed the door open with such force, that a picture situated directly behind the door, fell from its hangings and smashed on the floor. Rachel bristled at the sight of him. 'You're not welcome in here, so please leave,' she hissed.

Vincent sucked on the cigarette hanging from his mouth and sneered at her. 'It's a public place. I can come in if I want!' He folded his arms defiantly as he leant against the door.

'I run this public house, and I say who's allowed in here, and you are not welcome here.' Rachel held onto the bar to steady herself as she spoke.

He laughed insolently, but stayed put. Feeling slightly perturbed, she said in a low voice. 'Will you please leave?'

Enjoying Rachel's uneasiness, Vincent looked around the deserted bar. '*Make* me leave,' he mocked, beckoning her to him with his nicotine stained fingers. 'Come on then, throw me out if you can?'

Rachel stood her ground as he moved menacingly towards her. Her blood ran cold, and she felt a sudden sickness sweep over her. She prayed silently. Suddenly Adam entered the bar. Without violence, Adam squared up to his opponent. Day's cigarette smoke stung Adam's nostrils, making him curl his lip in distaste. 'I believe the lady asked you to leave.'

Vincent stepped back, unsure of Adam's character. 'Alright, I'm going,' he sneered. As Day walked slowly backwards towards the door, Adam matched every step.

'I don't *ever* want to see you in this establishment again, do I make myself clear?'

Day twitched insolently.

'Do I make myself clear?' Adam hissed.

'Yes,' he answered, visibly rattled.

Adam watched him until he was reunited with his bike before returning to the bar. 'Are you okay?'

Rachel nodded gratefully, reached for the brandy and poured two generous measures. 'Just to steady the nerves.' She smiled, placing a glass in front of Adam. 'Thank you Adam, I admit, I was terrified.'

'So was I.' Adam grinned, picking up the glass of amber liquid with a shaking hand.

'I hate this job Adam. I can't do it without Alex. Nobody would ever cross him. I'm just not able to deal with people like that.'

'Oh Rachel, I'm always here to help now, you know that, don't you?'

Verity had just finished her shift and was walking from the kitchen, wiping her hands on a cloth, when she stopped short on hearing Adam's voice. He appeared to be talking about her. She skulked back into he shadows to listen.

'You know I don't know what someone as lovely looking as Verity sees in such a lout,' Adam said. 'She could easily have her pick of the boys. Why would she choose him?'

Rachel laughed shortly. 'It's probably because I don't like him. But, having said that, she does seem smitten with him I'm afraid.'

'You know, I think if she just gave him the push, she would soon find herself on the arm of a really decent chap.'

'You mean someone like you maybe?' Rachel teased.

Adam laughed shyly and shook his head.

In the dark recess of the kitchen door, Verity's heart began to race. Adam de Sousa was interested in her! She pulled off her apron, wet her lips with the tip of her tongue, patted her hair and walked into the public bar.

She glanced at Rachel with a look she kept only for her.

'I see you're on the hard stuff already step-mother?' She clicked the roof of her mouth with her tongue. She glanced away and her countenance softened. 'Oh Mr de Sousa, I had no idea you were here. How are you?' she said, her face was strong and enquiring.

Adam glanced at Rachel then smiled softly at the girl. 'I'm very well, thank you Verity. I see you are looking as pretty as always. Are you going somewhere nice?'

'I shouldn't think so.' She sneered. 'Not if Vincent has anything to do with it.'

Adam's smile widened. 'Tell him to take you somewhere nice - you deserve it.'

'Actually I might just tell him that I don't want to see him anymore,' she stated casually.

Adam raised his eyebrows. 'I thought you were smitten with him.'

'What me, smitten with him? Don't be silly. Who on earth give you that stupid idea?' She glanced at Rachel. 'He's just a bit of fun that's all. It's nothing serious.'

A blast of horn came from outside as Vincent grew increasingly impatient. Verity turned her head slightly and rolled her eyes. 'I better go. I'll see you later Mr de Sousa,' she said, pouting her lips. She slung her coat over her shoulder and flounced out of the door, without a by-your-leave to Rachel. Adam and Rachel watched from the window, there was a slight altercation between them, then Verity climbed up behind him, and they sped up the valley leaving a cloud of black smoke in their wake.

'Well, there's a turn up for the books,' Adam said, draining his glass and noting the look of distrust on

Rachel's face. 'You don't look convinced.'

'I'll believe it when I see it.' She'd known Verity long enough now to know she was up to something.

'Well it sounds to me like she's got her eye on someone else.' He picked up his bag and winked. 'Hopefully, you won't have to put up with the likes of Day, much longer!' He stood and rubbed his hands together. 'Now, I must be going. I have a call to make at Dougie Trengrath's farm, he has a sick cow.'

'Dougie!' she exclaimed. 'Well, watch out that he doesn't 'Gweek' you!"

"'Gweek' me! Whatever does that mean?'

'You'll find out if he offers you a taste of his homemade beer.'

He smiled widely. 'Why, are you frightened of the competition?'

'No!' She laughed. 'I'm frightened of what it will do to you.'

*

Later that afternoon, after administering aid to Dougie's' stricken bovine, Adam waited for the medicine to take effect.

'Will 'ee take a glass of ale with me Mr de Sousa? I make it myself,' Dougie said, scratching his stubbly chin.

Happy that the cow was responding, Adam stroked the creature gently and nodded to Dougie. 'I don't mind if I do.'

The Trengrath's kitchen smelt of a mixture of warm bread and cow dung as they passed through to the door which led to the cellar. Dougie held the gas lantern high to lead Adam down into the dank depths of the cellar. The room was full of barrels. He picked up a glass and blew into it to clear the dust. 'Here try this one - I think you'll like it.' Dougie turned the tap on one of the barrels and filled the glass.

Adam took a sip, and nodded appreciatively. 'That's lovely.'

Dougie smiled broadly. 'You'll like this one then. It has more of a kick than the other.'

Once again Adam savoured the amber liquid. 'This is really good Dougie,' he said, taking another mouthful.

'I'm experimenting by making my own cider. Want to try some do 'ee Mr de Sousa? This is my latest batch!' Adam was no cider drinker but before he could protest, Dougie thrust a glass of cloudy liquid into his hand. Adam sniffed it, and then took a tentative sip, spitting the bits out as he did. The apple flavour made his taste buds zing. 'Wow, it's good Dougie,' Adam said in astonishment.

'Aye, it's only apples, more of a fruit drink than anything else!'

For the rest of the afternoon, Adam and Dougie sat on upturned buckets comparing the contents of different casks. When they finally emerged, Adam could hardly walk. He staggered across the yard to the stable to check on the cow, found his treatment had worked, closed the stable door, and then promptly passed out in a pile of clean straw.

The call to Rachel from Dougie came through at around seven that evening. Thinking Adam still lived at The Black Swan, he thought he'd better let them know where he was. Adam was fast asleep, and no amount of prodding could wake him from his slumber.

Unbeknown to Adam, he made the journey from Trengrath's farm to The Black Swan, in the bucket of Charlie William's tractor. With great difficulty, he and Rachel wrestled him up the stairs and into the bed he once occupied there. They stood over him for a while, turned him on his side in case he vomited, and covered him with an eiderdown. Rachel checked on him every half hour, but he was well and truly out for the count. Just before she retired to bed, she sat by his side for a moment and watched him sleep. He looked so handsome with his tanned skin and dark hair against the white pillow. Very gently she brushed her fingers down his cheek, remembering the kiss she planted there earlier in the day. Pausing for a moment at the corner of his mouth, she slowly ran her fingertips across his lips, imagining what it would be like to kiss him properly. He stirred slightly and Rachel pulled away and stood up, but he did not wake. 'Goodnight Adam,' she whispered, as she reluctantly left his room.

He woke in all astonishment at eleven-thirty the next morning, with a monumental headache and absolutely no knowledge of why or how he was in such a state. It was clear to Rachel when she brought him tea and toast that he would be incapable of going to work that day.

'But I must go in,' he protested. But as soon as he moved to get out of bed, the room swam, and he was forced to lie down. He looked at Rachel rather sheepishly. 'I take it I was 'Gweeked'? Go on say it, I told you so.'

Rachel laughed softly and shook her head. 'You're not the first, and probably won't be the last person to fall for Dougie's homemade ale.'

'Oh God,' he said cupping his hands to his face. 'I don't think I will ever drink again.'

'Well I hope that doesn't stop you coming into my bar!' Rachel exclaimed, pressing a mug of steaming tea into his hands. 'Here, drink this, it'll sober you up.'

Taking the mug thankfully from her, he smiled sheepishly. Nothing would stop him coming into the bar, as long as the beautiful Rachel was there to serve him, he thought to himself.

'You had better give me the keys to the veterinary surgery,' she said, holding out her hand.

He lowered the mug and pointed to the chair. 'They're in my jacket I think. What do you want my keys for?'

'Well you're in no fit state for work, and your phone may be ringing, I shall sort something out so that the surgery is manned - just you leave it with me. Now, which pocket are they in?' she asked, lifting his jacket from the back of the chair.

Downstairs, Emma was busy in the kitchen washing up. They had three guests that morning, apart from Adam. Mr

Eric Carne, a bachelor and foreman at the Gweek wood yard who lodged at the hotel every Monday to Thursday, returning home to his parents' house in St Austell on Friday afternoons. A slightly shifty looking travelling salesman, going by the name of Mr Tankard had booked in for one night only, bizarrely bringing his own sheets, knife, fork, spoon and plate, and who had whistled tunelessly in his room into the early hours. The third guest was also a regular, Mrs Caroline Beech, a widow and travelling hairdresser, who would stay for three days every month to cut and style the hair of the ladies of Gweek, Constantine, and Mawgan. It had been a busy morning for breakfasts, Rachel had cooked, Verity had served, and Emma was halfway through the pile of washing up. Rachel stood at the kitchen door pondering for a moment, before saying, 'Leave that Emma my love. I have a little job for you.'

Emma shook the soapy water from her arms and wiped them on a towel as she waited for instruction.

'Mr de Sousa isn't very well today Emma. He has a stomach bug and will remain in bed all day.' Emma nodded. 'These are the keys to his surgery.' She dangled the set of keys in front of her. 'I want you to open up for Mr de Sousa. Answer any phone calls which come in, and use your own initiative if you think the call is urgent or not. If it isn't, jot their name and address down and tell them that Mr de Sousa will call on them tomorrow. If the call is urgent, speak to Mr Head at Helston Veterinary Surgery and explain that Mr de Sousa is ill and could he possibly help out for the day. Have you got all that?' Emma nodded eagerly and took the keys from her hand. 'Now stay there all day and then close up at six okay? I'm sure Mr de Sousa will rest easier once he knows someone sensible is in charge.'

Emma's smiled beamed from ear to ear as she pulled off her apron. 'I won't let him down Rachel.'

'I know you won't.'

*

The next morning Adam surfaced at six-thirty. Rachel cooked him a hearty breakfast, which he devoured with great ferocity, then as he dabbed the napkin to his mouth, he asked to see Emma.

Shyly Emma emerged from the kitchen and handed the surgery keys over to him.

'Thank you for your help yesterday Emma, I don't know what I would have done without you.'

'It was my pleasure Mr de Sousa,' she answered, blushing furiously.

'Was there anything you couldn't handle?'

Emma shook her head. 'I put Ralf Penberthy onto Helston - his mare was in foal and struggling.' Adam nodded. 'He called later and asked if you could come along sometime today to take a look at the foal. All the other calls were none urgent, and I found an old appointment book and put them in there for you to look at. Oh and Dougie Trengrath would like you to take a look at his cow in the next few days.' She finished the sentence with a nod of the head.

Adam groaned inwardly at the mention of Dougie Trengrath's name. 'Well done Emma, I shall make sure you are well paid for your trouble.'

'It was no trouble. As I said, it was a pleasure,' she smiled sweetly.

If Adam hadn't made up his mind about Emma working with him, he certainly did when he saw the surgery. The place had been cleaned from top to bottom and sparkled like a new pin. The instruments were laid out in order in their glass cabinets. Jars of potions had been cleaned and replaced in alphabetical order, and the entries in the appointment book were clear and concise. Emma had done a sterling job, so before he made any of his calls he arrived back at The Black Swan with a job proposition for Emma.

Emma was astounded at his offer, but hesitated in

agreeing.

Adam looked at her with concern. 'What is it? Don't you want to work with me?'

'Oh yes,' she gushed. 'I want that more than anything, it's just...'

He laughed lightly. 'What?'

'It's Rachel. I don't want to just leave like that. She's been very good to me.'

Adam laughed. 'Your sentiments do you real justice Emma, but Rachel knows I've asked you, and she has given her blessing.'

'Really?' Her eyes widened.

'Yes, really,' Rachel said, as she emerged from the kitchen. 'I shall miss you dearly Emma, you have been my best employee, but I wouldn't dream of standing in your way. This is a wonderful opportunity for you, and I for one am really happy for you. Now say yes to Mr de Sousa before he changes his mind.'

'Oh yes, yes.' Emma squealed with delight.

'When do you want her to start?' Rachel asked Adam.

'As soon as possible.'

Rachel smiled warmly at Emma. 'Well then, you had better collect your things.'

4

Rachel decided that Christmas 1938 was to be a cheery affair at The Black Swan. As rumours of war still rumbled across Europe, there was an air of uncertainty for what the future would hold for England. She'd invited Charlie, Lizzy and Emma Williams to join them for Christmas dinner, and also extended the invitation to Adam, which he accepted graciously, much to Verity's elation.

Verity, to her credit, had spent many hours cutting up strips of coloured paper, which she then pasted into streamers to hang across the back room of the hotel. Holly and mistletoe were draped over pictures on the wall, and Adam had brought them a huge Christmas tree, sourced from a neighbouring farm, for which they struggled to find enough decorations to hang on it.

Rachel busied herself in the kitchen in the run up to Christmas, making two Christmas cakes and a Christmas pudding, in which she hid three silver sixpenny pieces.

One of the cakes was for Granny Pascoe. Granny was an eccentric, but much revered woman of indeterminate age, who lived in a small cottage on the edge of the river. She was a tiny bird-like woman, dressed in men's clothing and had taken up pipe smoking in her dotage. Almost everyone in the village felt a sense of responsibility for her welfare. Some took her food, bread, or fresh baked biscuits, and the men folk always put aside a couple of mackerel for her. Granny Pascoe visited The Black Swan Hotel early every evening, except for Sunday, and would sit in the snug beside the fire where she drank the half pints of dark mild, paid in for her by other customers. Rachel extended the invitation of Christmas lunch to Granny, but the old lady shook her head. 'Christmas holds nothing for me now - I'll stay by my fireside and let it pass. It's just another day to me, but I thank you for asking.'

So as Adam didn't spend Christmas alone in his flat above the veterinary practice, and as the hotel was empty over the Christmas holiday, Rachel offered him a room for a couple of nights, for which he accepted thankfully. It was not an entirely selfless thing on Rachel's part, she enjoyed Adam's company very much, and as last Christmas had been a joyless occasion without Alex, she was glad of a male companion to share it with this year. Verity, on the other hand, was planning to monopolise him for herself.

*

As Christmas Eve dawned, Rachel cleared the breakfast plates, trying to keep busy to stop her from thinking about Alex. Alex had always been emphatic that Christmas Eve should be every bit as special as Christmas Day. He, Rachel and Verity would share a hearty breakfast, then they would take a walk up Gweek Drive towards the Trelowarren Estate near Mawgan, stopping at the Ship Inn for a hot toddy, then on the way back they would cut through the woods to collect fallen wood for the Christmas fire. Back at the hotel Rachel and Verity would cook a meal of pheasant and roast vegetables for supper, then after closing time, a bottle of old vintage port would be passed around to herald the Eve of Christmas. It had been such a happy time for the three of them, sitting by the fireside together. The image made tears prick at the back of Rachel's eyes, as she wiped away her tears, she noticed Verity ardently watching her. She smiled thinly. 'I was just thinking about your dad,' she said.

'Huh, it'll be the first time for a while then, won't it?' she retorted.

Rachel baulked at the bitterness in her voice. 'How can you say such a cruel, insensitive thing? I think about your dad every second of the day.'

'I'm sure you do, when you're not swooning over Adam de Sousa.' Her eyes flashed angrily, as she turned and flounced out of the kitchen.

Adam noted that Rachel looked pale and distressed when he arrived just after lunch. 'Are you alright?'

She nodded, said nothing, but her eyes told everything.

His arms were full to overloading. He carried a small suitcase, in which he had a change of clothes, a large ripe cheese and a jar of pickled onions. Under his arm, he held a huge bunch of early daffodils and in his other hand he held a very unusual cargo - an extremely disgruntled female black swan, trussed up in a specially made sling. 'A Christmas present for Vicos.' He grinned. 'I hope he likes her.'

'Oh my goodness, Adam!' Rachel held her hands to her face in astonishment. 'Where on earth have you got another black swan from?'

'Stithians lake, actually!' He beamed proudly. 'I was talking to a colleague of mine the other day about Vicos, and he said there was a lone female black swan over there. Apparently it arrived about the time Vicos dropped in at Gweek. We wondered if they had been together at one time and had been separated by the mist that day. Do you remember how misty it was when we first found him?'

'Yes I do remember that day Adam.' In truth, she would never forget the day he'd walked into her life. 'Oh Adam!' She clapped her hands like a child. 'Wouldn't it be wonderful if she was his partner? Come on,' she said, leaving the bar in disarray. She dragged her coat from the hook. 'Let's introduce them.'

Vicos was now much recovered from his ordeal with the fishing line and divided his time between the hotel and the mud flats of the Helford River. They looked first in the wash-house where he slept sometimes, then walked down to the bridge. Within minutes, Vicos had appeared from down river, so Adam and Rachel walked across the green to meet him. Adam placed the sling, which held the female swan, down onto the ground. The swan cried angrily and attempted to peck Adam on the arm. Vicos, his interest aroused, waddled slowly closer. A short burgling conversation was exchanged between the creatures, and Adam released the swan from her bindings. She quickly flapped her great wings, walked up to Vicos and pecked him crossly on the neck.

This worried Rachel. 'What if they start fighting Adam?' she said, backing away slowly.

Adam put his hand on her arm to assure her. 'Give them a minute - I think they'll be alright.' Vicos stood his ground as the female pecked at him again, and then he reached his long willowy neck towards her and gently rubbed his beak down her slender neck. The female responded by ceasing to peck him and within minutes, she was following him down the mud flats into the Helford.

Rachel was overwhelmed. 'Oh Adam isn't that sweet, Vicos has a mate. I'm so glad for him after the ordeal he's been through. Gosh I can't wait to tell Emma and Harry, they'll be thrilled to bits.' She gazed into Adam's eyes. 'What a lovely thing to do.'

Adam laughed lightly. 'Everyone needs a mate.'

Rachel smiled shyly and took a last glance at the swans. 'Come on, let's get back inside, it looks like rain,' she said, touching his arm lightly.

As they approached the hotel, Rachel noticed Verity watching them from the window. Once inside, Adam took his suitcase upstairs, and Rachel walked into the bar.

Verity gave her a look of cool contempt. 'I rest my case,' she hissed, as she stormed out of the bar.

Rachel felt herself go suddenly cold. It was true. Her feelings for Adam were overtaking the grief she felt for Alex, but that didn't mean she didn't still feel the pain of his loss. No one could replace Alex, but loneliness was a terrible thing, and Rachel missed having a man in her life.

*

Before nightfall, drifting rain moved swiftly over land and by closing time on Christmas Eve, all her customers had to make a quick dash home, so as not to get soaked. When the bar was cleared, Rachel poured three brandies and she, Adam and Verity sat beside the cheery fire, munching mince pies and looked forward to the day ahead.

By morning, the rain was jumping off the road, and a strong wind was pushing up the Helford. There had been a high tide at five-thirty that morning, but fortunately, the river hadn't flooded the centre of the village as it sometimes did in severe weather. At nine-thirty, Charlie and Lizzy arrived to drive them all to Constantine Church. Rachel was not a church goer, but did make the exception on Christmas morning, more out of tradition than any religious motive.

They wrapped up warm and were thankful that they did, for it was bitter cold. Mist and driving rain filled the Helford valley, turning the Falmouth to Gweek road into foot thick mud filled ruts. There wasn't a member of that party that day that didn't worry about getting back to Gweek, the conditions were so atrocious. Sure enough, the weather worsened throughout the service. The south-easterly wind was blowing so hard they could hardly hear the vicar's voice at times. It was a relief to them all to get back into their vehicles, but the journey down the two mile lane became a hair-raising affair. Several vehicles slipped and slid in the mud, themselves included. One or two managed to get completely stuck, and Lizzy had to forcibly restrain Charlie from stopping to help them. Instead, she agreed that once they were all back safely at The Black Swan, he could go back in the tractor to help the stranded vehicles, which he and Adam inevitably did.

Whilst they were gone, Rachel and Lizzy prepared the goose, which Charlie had killed and plucked the night before, whilst Emma and Verity chopped the vegetables and set the table in the dining room. At mid-day, Rachel opened the public bar for a couple of hours, and, as was the custom, everyone was treated to a drink on the house. Sam was her first customer when she opened the door, and the sight of him unnerved her momentarily. He spent a great deal of his time at the Kings Arms in Constantine nowadays, venturing to The Black Swan only once or twice a week. When he did, his presence was felt by everybody as he took to sitting in the far corner of the bar, glowering angrily at anyone who spoke to him.

'Merry Christmas,' he said gruffly.

'Merry Christmas to you Sam,' Rachel said, fighting to keep the tremor from her voice.

'I 'av something for you,' he said pulling a large object wrapped in brown paper from behind his back. 'I made it especially for you.' He placed the heavy gift in her hands. Rachel stared at it for a moment, reluctant to accept it. 'Well, open it then woman.'

Unenthusiastically the object was unwrapped to reveal a weather vane. Rachel placed the vane on the bar and took a deep breath. 'Thank you Sam, but you shouldn't have gone to all that bother.'

'Tiss no bother,' he said, trying to curb his irritation. He picked it back up and thrust it under her nose. 'Look, see. I made it especially for 'ee. It has your initials on it.'

She glanced down at the weather vane, which was of a swan design, but beneath the letters indicating the points of the compass were the letters R B. 'It's lovely Sam, but they're not my initials.'

He grinned knowingly. 'They will be one day, when you marry me.'

Rachel felt a shiver down her spine as Sam leered at her.

'Right then, where's this free drink you're handing out?' he said, rubbing his hands together with glee.

Fortunately Sam left after downing his free drink and Rachel began to relax. She threw the weather vane in the deepest, darkest cupboard she could find, for the sight of it made her feel ill.

Adam and Charlie had pulled five vehicles out of the mud. One of them, they had to do twice! So there was many a free drink paid for them when they finally arrived back at The Black Swan.

Rachel laughed out loud when she saw the state of them both. They were soaked to the skin and covered from head to foot in mud, so before dinner could be served, both men had to take a bath.

Dinner began at three and went on until four-thirty. It was a fine meal, clear soup for starters, roast goose with accompanying parsnips, crispy roast potatoes and carrots, all grown in the hotel's kitchen garden. Dessert was plum pudding and brandy sauce, mince pies and shortbread, all washed down with copious amounts of Lizzy's splendid white wine, she'd made from her own grapes, which she nurtured in her greenhouse. To round off the meal, they all enjoyed a glass of fine cognac, which had just happened to find its way past the custom house at the top of Gweek Quay.

Rachel had worn a dress she had specially made for the occasion. It was an A line red jersey dress with a sweetheart neckline and a knitted cardigan to match. She had put on her best stockings and buffed her old black shoes until they shone. She also wore a light dab of Yardley's lavender cologne behind each ear. Later that evening she would sit at her dressing table, enjoying the bouquet of 'Soir De Paris' parfum by Chanel, which Adam secretly gave to her while the others were exchanging more inexpensive presents.

Adam could not take his eyes off Rachel. She was the most stunning woman he had ever seen. His adoring glances did not go amiss with Lizzy and she watched with interest at the scene before her, hoping with all her heart that Rachel would allow herself to come out of mourning proper and see a new future dawn for her with Adam.

After dinner the presents were opened. Each person had drawn a name out of a hat the week before and bought a gift for that person, that way they could all afford to buy and received an admirable present. Lizzy received a bottle of Je Reviens Eau de Parfum by Worth from Rachel. Verity's parcel included nylons and an assortment of makeup from Lizzy. Emma received Yardley bath salts, and a matching aubergine coloured hat and gloves from Verity. Charlie bought Rachel a new pair of black heeled court shoes, chosen, Rachel suspected, by Lizzy. Adam was delighted with the whiskey Emma had bought him and Charlie puffed away on the pipe which Adam had bought him. It was then that Adam surreptitiously slipped a small beautifully gift wrapped box, into the pocket of Rachel's cardigan. The surprised look on her face was quickly concealed when Adam pressed his index finger to his lips.

When Charlie stretched and yawned from his after dinner nap, he left the party to see to his cows. As the women began to clear the table, it was Verity who noticed first that the rain and the strong south-easterly wind had pushed the tide well up the Helford.

'Oh my goodness, look outside!' she exclaimed, kneeling on the window seat. The others moved to the window to see the river swamping the centre of the village.

'The river has burst its banks by the look of it,' Lizzy said. 'Better check that it's not lapping over the front door Rachel.'

Rachel scrambled to the front door to find the water just a couple of inches from the top step. Quickly, she, Lizzy and Verity ran to the outhouse and gathered up a sandbag each to pile by the door. Not knowing the flood drill, Adam quickly followed their lead. When satisfied with the dam, they brushed the dirt from their hands and retreated to the warmth of the fireside.

'Well spotted Verity,' Lizzy commended. She knew from experience that the water would only raise another two inches before high tide, by that time the whole centre of the village would be flooded. Suddenly, she stood up. 'Oh my goodness me!'

'What is it,' asked Adam in alarm.

'Granny Pascoe,' she said gravely. Her house will have flooded. I'd better get Charlie to go and check on her.'

Adam quickly got to his feet. 'He'll be busy with the cows. I'll go.'

'Wait a minute Adam,' Rachel cried. 'You can't go dressed like that. Alex had some waders in the outhouse. I'll go and get them.'

When he was suitably attired for the flood, he ran out into the darkness towards the bridge.

'Adam, watch where you walk,' Rachel warned, as they approached the water. 'There could be all sorts of debris floating under there. As he slowly picked his way towards the bridge, Adam noticed Vicos and his new mate huddled together by the old water pump at the edge of the hotel garden. Once over the bridge he waded towards the aptly named River Cottage and found the front door swinging open.

'Mrs Pascoe, where are you?' Adam shouted. 'Mrs Pascoe, can you hear me? Are you alright?' Adam realised she would probably not recognise his voice. 'Mrs Pascoe, it's Adam de Sousa the vet.' There was no answer. With growing concern he waded through the house. The few possessions Granny Pascoe had were now bobbing about in the muddy water. Adam frantically searched the front room to no avail, and then waded through to the kitchen. It was there that he found her. She had fallen from the chair she had clambered onto to escape the encroaching water some ten minutes ago, and broken both her legs in the act. Now her head was barely above the water. When she saw a figure approaching her tiny voice cried out in pain. Adam dropped to his knees and gathered her up into his arms, but the movement made her scream in agony. 'I have you,' he tried to assure her, but her arms began flaying desperately, which in turn created a small wave, which washed over her face. She coughed and spluttered then cried out again. He scooped his hands under her and lifted her free of the water. Granny screamed in agony, almost deafening Adam, as he waded out into the night. Rachel stood at the door of The Black Swan and saw him coming. 'Call an ambulance,' he shouted, as he stumbled across the bridge with the old lady. She was only a slight woman, but the weight of her in drenched clothes proved a mighty task for Adam. The wind howled up the Helford, almost knocking Adam off his already unsteady feet, but for all the chill of the water, Adam was sweating profusely, and hot beads of perspiration prickled down his back. His arms felt like lead weights and his back was near to breaking, but his pace quickened as the water became shallower. As he stepped through the door to the hotel, Lizzy, Rachel and Verity took his heavy load from him. Adam fell to his knees exhausted.

Laying by the warmth of the fireside the women fussed over Granny. Verity made her a mug of steaming hot tea, while Lizzy got her out of her wet things. Granny seemed totally oblivious to what was happening to her. All she could feel was pain, terrible pain in her legs. She cried and wailed as Rachel dressed her in a warm nightdress, she wanted to put a pair of Alex's socks on Granny's gnarled feet, but as she was in obvious pain whenever her legs were moved, Rachel thought better of it. They placed a pillow under her head and a warm blanket over her and waited in anticipation for the ambulance to arrive.

At six-fifteen the ambulance came, and thankfully managed to drive through the receding flood. Once in the ambulance, Granny was to be taken to the Helston Cottage Hospital, and as Charlie had returned from milking the cows, it was agreed they would follow in Adam's van to make sure she was settled in safely.

It was nine-fifty-five when the men arrived home with news of Granny's condition, which was not good. She was suffering from hyperthermia, and both legs were broken, one of them in two places. If she got through the next couple of days, it was clear that it would be a long time before Granny Pascoe would return to River Cottage.

A nightcap of hot toddies with warm mince pies was quickly served and by eleven o clock, they all made their way home to sleep off what had been a very eventful Christmas day. Verity hung around for a while longer, but eventually tiredness prevailed, and she too made for her bed.

When Verity was safely upstairs, Rachel turned to Adam and smiled, she took Adam's hand into her own. 'You are a wonderful man Adam,' she said, as she reached forward to kiss him tenderly.

In the rosy glow of the firelight, he turned to look at her. 'I'm just an ordinary guy,' he said.

Rachel shook her head. 'You're a very extraordinary man. What you did for Granny Pascoe today was...'

Adam placed his finger tenderly on her lips and stopped her mid sentence. 'It was nothing. I did what anyone would have done,' he said dismissively.

Rachel smiled softly then she recalled the gift he had secretly passed to her. 'Thank you Adam for the perfume. It was a lovely surprise.'

'I wanted to buy you something special Rachel, to thank you for the past couple of days, you made Christmas very special for me this year,' he said with heartfelt gratitude.

Rachel blushed slightly.

He rose from the chair and tenderly brushed his lips against her cheek. 'I'll say goodnight now. It's been a lovely day. I'll see you in the morning.'

Later, Rachel sat by her dressing table, and gazed at the sifted moonlight through the open curtains. The rain had ceased, the sky cleared and the cold penetrated through the window pane, the weather was turning at last. She dabbed a tiny amount of Adam's perfume on her neck, closed her eyes and recalled the wonderful feeling of Adam's tender kiss. Maybe he would bring and end to her aching grief.

5

Cornwall was in the grip of winter. The normally wet winter had been replaced this year with penetrating frost and heavy snowfalls.

The second week of January 1939 saw the coldest day anyone could remember. The big freeze had started on the Tuesday after Christmas, and no amount of fires could warm the nooks and crannies of The Black Swan. Each morning Rachel found her face cloth had frozen to the bathroom sink, and thick ice had glazed the inside of the window.

It was Sunday lunchtime and business had been brisk. Rachel had sold more hot toddies in the last fortnight than she had ever sold before. Eli Symonds sat in his favourite seat by the fire, filling his pipe with tobacco. He pressed it down with his nicotine stained finger and lit the pipe with a spill from the fire. Three generous sucks on the pipe saw a faint glow appear in the bowl, and for a moment Eli was obscured within a cloud of smoke. Satisfied, he sat back in his chair and said, 'Forecast snow on my radio for the next few days, did yours say anything about it, Charlie?'

Charlie smiled and winked at Rachel. 'No Eli, it gave out wall to wall sunshine on mine.'

'Huh, they aut to make their bloody minds up, tin'd right telling some folks one thing and others another,' Eli muttered, lighting his pipe again as it had just gone out.

*

Sure enough the temperature had raised enough to snow, making the roads impassable for a couple of days. A sharp frost followed, making a bad situation worse. Thankfully the thaw came the following Monday, but the rime hung to the bare branches of the trees for days after.

By the beginning of February, the daffodils finally made their sunny appearance, being almost a month later than normal. The village began to fill with casual labourers employed to pick the fields of daffodils. Sally Blewett and Verity relished the idea of crowds of strong young men in the village, though the latter was more constrained in her behaviour towards the men. She had long since ceased seeing Vincent Day and still hankered after Adam, and was sure in her mind that he was just biding time until she was eighteen, before he made his move on her.

Adam, for his part, turned out to be a hit with more than just Verity. The villagers buzzed with talk about their new vet, all good, which was unusual for a stranger to be so taken to the hearts of the locals with such gusto. His heroic rescue of Granny Pascoe was much commended, and then shortly after Christmas, during the cold spell, he helped June Collins when she unexpectedly went into labour two weeks early. Edna Clayton from the general stores sang his praises for mending her burst water pipe, and for helping her mop up afterward and of course, Eli Symonds had Adam to thank for saving his life when he stumbled into a deep snow drift after leaving The Black Swan one night. Eli had thought his time was up as he struggled exhaustedly to get out of the soft freezing tomb, giving up when the exertion became too much for him. After a few short minutes his body was chilled to the bone, and tiredness prevailed. Fortunately, Adam had refused a nightcap from Rachel and left shortly after Eli. It was a bright moonlit night that night, if there had been cloud, Adam would never have seen Eli's hat lying on the ground, and for sure Eli would have perished. Though Adam dismissed his actions as just being there at the right time, most of the villagers held him in high regard.

With the onset of spring, thoughts of passion weighed heavy on Sam Blewett mind. He'd reluctantly put his offer of marriage on hold after the altercation with Charlie Williams back in the autumn. Charlie had told him, in no uncertain terms, that Rachel was still grieving for her husband, and that he was to leave her alone, but damn it, it had been months now since he'd asked, surely she must be getting over Alex by now, and he didn't trust that de Sousa fellow - they were far too friendly for his liking. He slammed the hammer down on the horseshoe, and hot sparks leaped in all directions. There was nothing else for it. He swiftly and roughly shod the waiting horse, much to its indignation. When he finished, the horse retaliated and bit his shoulder to show its displeasure, to which it received a short, sharp, crack of the whip. Leaving the agitated animal tethered to the outside of his forge, he rinsed his hands under the hand pump and made for The Black Swan. He called at the back door which he found to be ajar. A few steps took him through the back scullery, past the door to the upstairs and into the public bar. The place was deserted. He glanced at the whiskey optic and licked his fat lips. With a swift look about him, he reached for a glass, pushed it under the optic twice and downed the drink in one.

'That will be thrupence Sam Blewett, if you don't mind,' Rachel said, her tone was sharp, and her voice was high trying to hide her nervousness.

Indignantly he fumbled in his pocket for change. 'I've come to see 'ee Rachel,' he said.

She pressed her lips tightly together as she stared at him, feeling her heart race, she knew instinctively what he was about to propose again. 'Sam if you are going to repeat your proposal to me, I'm telling you now, that I'm not interested, I do not want to get married again,' she interrupted him firmly.

He caught her hand. 'Don't be so bloody foolish,' he said in exasperation. 'You can't run this place on your own forever - unless of course, you have someone else in mind to help you?'

She grimaced at the suggestion, and small red spots pricked her cheeks. 'Of course not,' she answered curtly.

He searched her eyes knowingly, and felt the anger rising in him. 'I've heard the gossip you know. Do you think I'm stupid? I've seen you and de Sousa with my own eyes!'

She pulled free of his hand in fury. 'How dare you!' She was so angry she could hardly speak.

'Well, there is no smoke without fire.'

'And there is no gossip without malice,' she retorted. She was visibly trembling, but held her head high in defiance.

He leaned towards her, close enough for her to smell the whiskey on his breath. He dropped his voice to a low hiss. 'I'm watching you,' he said menacingly.

He left slamming the door behind him, and Rachel's heart filled with dread.

Adam missed Sam by only a couple of minutes, when he popped into the bar to retrieve a pair of gloves he'd left there the night before. Softly knocking on the open back door, he called out her name as he stepped through, just as Sam had done a few minutes before him. He found Rachel by the fireside, lost in her reverie, and completely unaware of his presence. Concerned at how pale and unwell she looked, he moved towards her.

'Rachel?'

Startled, she spun around with such force. 'Oh Adam it's you' she said, relief sweeping over her when she realised who it was.

He knelt at her feet and took her hands in his. 'You're freezing cold and you look like you have seen a ghost. Whatever is the matter?'

Feeling the warmth of his hands she smiled and her whole countenance changed. 'I've just had an unwelcome encounter with Sam.'

Adam frowned. 'Sam Blewett? What did he want?'

She forced a smile and said bitterly, 'What he wants and what he gets is another matter.'

'What's he said to upset you?'

She regarded him for a moment then shook her head. 'It's nothing I can't handle,' she lied. 'Really it's nothing to worry about. I'm alright.'

The spring sunlight dappled through the lace curtains, highlighting the glisten of tears on her cheeks. He took her gently into his arms and held her as though it was the most natural thing to do. 'You don't look okay to me,' he whispered, drinking in the soft clean smell of her hair. She wept softly for a few minutes in his arms then gently pulled away, her hair was tousled, and she looked more beautiful for it. Reluctantly, she told him of Sam's visit.

Adam listened with disdain. 'I am so sorry you had to go through this, and I'm sorry there's gossip about us. Lord knows we've done nothing to provoke it. I'd no idea he had designs on you.'

'Well, I certainly have none on him I can assure you of that!' Rolling her eyes heavenwards she added angrily, 'He won't give up on me, of that I'm sure. What am I to do?'

Adam took a deep breath. 'Give me a moment.' He left her side and picked up a pen and a scrap of paper from behind the bar and began to write.

She narrowed her eyes with curiosity. 'What are you writing?'

The deed done, he put the pen back down and moved to her side, he lifted her hand and placed the folded paper in her hand and smiled softly. 'This is normally done on the Eve of St Valentines, but as it's only a few days away it shouldn't matter,' he explained.

When Rachel unfolded the paper, her name was beautifully written upon it. She looked at him quizzically.

Carefully, he took it off her and placed the paper into the top left hand pocket of his shirt and grinned boyishly. 'It's an old Valentines Eve practice,' he explained. 'Normally, a man draws a girls' name from a box and agrees to protect the girl for a year. He wears her name, in that year, on his sleeve. He took her hand and pressed it to his heart. 'I'll wear your name next to my heart Rachel. I shall endeavour to look after you, for as long as I'm able. You are not alone in the world anymore.'

Tears overwhelmed her. She felt such a bond between them, it frightened her. 'Thank you,' she said, her voice choked with emotion.

He held her hand for a moment longer. 'Having said all that, I must go. I'm late already for an appointment.' He gave her a crooked smile.

She nodded and laughed lightly and watched as he picked up the gloves he had come in for.

His smile reached his eyes. 'I'll look after you Rachel, I promise.'

As he left, Rachel's heart soared.

*

Adam checked his watch as he clambered into his car. With a little luck, he would be at the hospital before visiting time finished. Adam made a point of visiting Granny Pascoe almost every day since she was taken in. At first, it was touch and go that she would survive such an ordeal, but presently she had improved and was making good progress, until yesterday, when the doctor informed him that she was suffering from pneumonia. When he arrived the nurse told him that she was gravely ill, and granted him access to her, beyond the visiting hours.

As he walked slowly towards her bed, he thought she was asleep. But he knew that for such an old woman she had a keen sense of hearing, and if she was just resting, she would inevitably open her eyes to see who was there, which she did.

'Hello there. I understand you're not feeling too good today?' he said, reaching for her hand.

She scrunched her face up. 'I'm dying Adam,' she said stiffly.

Adam shook his head and gently kissed her bony hand. 'They can treat pneumonia, you'll get through this. You must keep fighting.'

She smiled thinly. 'You're an extraordinary man Adam

de Sousa.'

Adam shook his head.

'Oh yes you are,' she continued. 'I might be old and frail and can't get about the same as other folks, but I hear things, I know what you're like. I see what you do for people, how you help them. You make a difference. You give and never take from people. That's a rare quality in a person.' Adam smiled shyly as the old woman cupped her soft hand around his. 'You are what my grandmother would call a joy bringer - a man of good will and fine sentiments.'

'I just like to help, that's all.'

'Well, I want to give you something,' she said.

'That's not necessary.'

'I'm going to, whether you want me to or not,' she said, pointing to her bedside table. 'Open that door and pass me that white envelope,' she instructed. But as he passed the envelope to her, she began to cough. Adam watched for a moment, but the cough worsened to a hack, her breathing became laboured and a great rattling noise emerged from her throat. He ran for the nurse, but five minutes later, Granny Pascoe passed from this life to the next. He sat at her bedside for a long time holding her withered hand. Presently, he sighed and stood up, and as he did the white envelope fell to the floor. He tentatively flipped it over in his fingers, glanced at the old lady before slitting it open. Granny Pascoe had left her cottage deeds to him. With it was a note, it read:

To Adam.

For someone who always gives, here is a gift for you, to do with as you please. I know in my heart you'll put your legacy to good use.'

Amelia Pascoe.

Astounded, he read and re-read the note, but couldn't believe his own eyes. Presently, he bent down and kissed the old woman on the forehead. 'Thank you Amelia, I shall not waste your gift. Goodnight and God bless. As he pulled away, he was sure a ghost of a smile was on her lips.

*

A week after Granny Pascoe's funeral, the Gweek Parish Council held an extraordinary meeting, to discuss the gift Adam de Sousa had given to the village. Adam had handed over the deeds to Granny Pascoe's cottage to the parish council for them to rent out on a peppercorn rent to whoever they seemed fit, on the proviso that the cottage was kept in good repair, and the revenue was to go towards the upkeep of the village.

6

It was late afternoon one sunny March day, but although the sun shone warm through the veterinary surgery windows, outside there was a slight hint of frost in the air. Emma was on her way to Barleyfield Farm to re-dress the infected paw of Robin Ferris–Norton's Labrador. She was given many jobs like this now and loved every one of them. Adam could plainly see that she was born to nurse sick animals.

Barleyfield Farm was situated west of Gweek, standing a little way back from the main road, but commanding fine views of the Helford River. She rattled the brass door knocker which was dull from lack of polish and as instructed, let herself into the kitchen at the side of the property.

'Hello there. Mr Ferris–Norton? Good afternoon, it's Emma from the veterinary practice. Mr de Sousa said you would be expecting me,' she called out in a sing song voice as she slipped her Wellington boots off.

'In here,' a friendly voice shouted back. 'Come through, I'm in the lounge, second door on your left.'

Emma picked her way through the dark and dingy kitchen and pushed the lounge door open. The warmth of the fire put a rosy glow on her cheeks the moment she walked into the cosy room. A Labrador stood and barked as she entered.

'Quiet Tally,' his master ordered. The dog came to heel and fell silent. 'Hello Emma. Come in my dear.' He felt the cold air that she had brought in with her and his nostrils picked up the smell of lavender oil which was pleasant to his senses.

'Thank you,' Emma said, as she walked towards the two of them. Robin was a twenty-three-year-old, good looking man, fine boned, but Emma thought, a little too thin. He wore a green check shirt under a blue V neck sweater with leather patches at the elbow, and dark blue sturdy wool outdoor trousers. His hair which was brown, needed combing, but he was freshly shaved and smelt of soap.

His eyes, though he suffered the affliction of congenital cataracts, seemed to look right at her when he asked, 'Would you like a drink? There's a rare chill out there today.' He put his hand on the arm of the chair as though to get up. 'Would you like tea or coffee?'

Emma hesitated. 'I don't want to put you to any trouble.'

'It's no trouble,' he said rising from his chair. He reached for his stick. 'So, what's it to be, tea or coffee?'

'Tea please,' she said as she undressed Tally's paw. She had almost finished when the tray Robin was carrying bumped the door open, spilling the tea into the saucer. 'Clumsy me, have I spilt much?' he asked.

Emma got to her feet, inspected the tray and told him that he hadn't.

He gestured for Emma to take a seat, and as they drank their tea, Robin said, 'I vaguely remember you Emma. You don't mind if I call you Emma, do you?'

'Not at all,' she said with a smile.

'Yes, you were the tall girl, who worked at The Black Swan weren't you?'

'Yes, that's me.'

'So, how do you like working for Mr de Sousa?'

'I absolutely love it,' she answered passionately.

'That's good to hear. 'Tell me, how are things down at The Black Swan nowadays. How is that young widow coping? I'm afraid I don't get out much anymore to find things out for myself. My eyesight seems to have deteriorated with every year that passes. There's no clarity to anything, so I'm afraid I don't feel confident to go further than my own back yard, unless someone is with me.'

Emma told her that Rachel was coping, though she suspected she was very lonely.

'Ah yes. ' He sighed softly. 'It's a terrible thing, loneliness. I hope she finds happiness someday soon - she's too young to be on her own.'

They chatted for almost an hour before Emma told him she must dash to lock up the surgery, but she made arrangements to come back in two days to check on Tally.

She rose and he gave her a grateful smile, then walked with her to the back door and bid her a fond farewell. He stood for a while at the door, the wind blowing in from the Helford cut through him like a cold knife making him shiver, then when he thought she was out of view he stepped back into the warmth. She had certainly brightened up his dull day; there was no mistaking that. Later that night, as he laid abed his mind was in turmoil as thoughts of Emma dominated him.

*

It was the end of March when Adam approached Emma as she returned from lunch. 'Mr Ferris-Norton was asking about you Emma. He says he misses your company now Tally is well and you have no need to visit. It seems to me you made quite an impression on him.' Adam looked steadily into her face as he spoke and noted that Emma blushed furiously. He decided to drop the subject for now and said brightly, 'I have several calls to make so I'll be away for the next three and a half hours. I'll see you in surgery this evening alright?'

Emma nodded and as soon as he left, she closed her eyes tight and leant on the surgery wall in a dream. She too had missed Mr Ferris-Norton's company. He had been the only man apart from Adam who had been interested in who she was. It was then she decided, she would take the bull by the horns, so to speak, and visit him the next chance she got.

Sunday was Emma's day off. She'd been up with the lark as usual and had been out picking wild flowers long before anyone else had stirred from their bed. Her bouquet consisted of wild daffodils the colour of sunshine, and sweet scented primroses. As she approached her home, she carefully placed them in a jam jar behind the wall of the old shippon to be retrieved later on that day. At two-thirty that same afternoon, after washing the dinner plates, Emma stole away from the house, picked up her flowers and made her way up to Barleyfield Farm. As she approached the farm gate she could see Nick Kellow in the distance, he was sitting in Mr Ferris-Norton's front garden, smoking a cigarette and reading the newspaper, whilst his lawn-mower ran idly at his side, he was obviously pretending to work.

It was not in Emma's nature to dislike anyone, but Nick Kellow was the exception to the rule. He bore the nicknamed the slug man, because he was employed to pick off slugs and snails from Mr Ferris-Norton's crops. This name though, Emma thought, matched his persona perfectly. He was quite an unsavoury character, with a ruddy pox marked bloated face and a large bulbous nose, which continually dripped. He was quite tall in stature with heavy stocky legs and moved slowly giving the impression that his feet almost never left the ground. Apart from his odd jobs at Barleyfield Farm, he found other employment, digging drainage ditches and mowing lawns. He especially preyed on vulnerable old women, befriending them when they became widowed. It seemed Nick Kellow could smell bereavement in the air, and missed nothing if it meant financial gain. Having said that, he would only befriend people who could give something to him, he would never put himself out to help anyone who could not pay him. Emma thought him a man not to be trusted.

She slipped round the back of the house without being seen, knocked hard on the knocker and entered the great kitchen. Here, there was no smell of Sunday dinner, no warmth from the kitchen range, and the kitchen looked gloomier than ever. 'Hello,' Emma called out. There was no answer. 'Mr Ferris-Norton, it's Emma'

A pained moan came from the front parlour. She placed her flowers on the telephone table and turned the handle of the heavy oak door, but it was wedged shut. She pushed harder, but something heavy against the other side prevented her from opening it more than an inch or two. She heard the moan again, followed swiftly by a rapid panting noise. It was Tally. He barked hoarsely and whined at the sight of the gap in the door. Emma pushed again with all her strength and managed to make the opening wide enough to squeeze her slight figure through. Robin was sprawled behind the door amidst a pile of books, which were strewn about him. His legs were trapped under the great weight of the fallen bookcase. A large open wound of congealed blood to his forehead told Emma he had been there for some time. She quickly phoned for the doctor, before calling Adam for assistance, then rushed to the bay window, pushed the sash up and called out to Nick Kellow for help.

He jumped as if electrified at the sound of her voice and quickly scrambled up and began to push his lawnmower down the lawn. Clearly angry that he had been caught skiving, he ignored her shouts for several seconds until she pushed her way out of the parlour and ran out into the garden.

'For goodness sake man, why didn't you answer my calls?'

He looked at her, his eyes narrowing. 'Who the hell do you think you are Emma Williams to be shouting at me?' he said indignantly.

In a deep authoritative voice Emma said, 'Mr Ferris-Norton is laying injured inside for your information. A bookcase has fallen on him and I need your help to shift it. That's why I'm shouting at you.'

'Oh, well I don't know about lifting any heavy furniture, I've a bad back,' he said, lifting his hat slightly so as to scratch his greasy bald head.

'Oh,' Emma was so angry she could hardly speak. 'Well, you haven't got a bad back from hard work,' she spat the words venomously at him.

He watched angrily as she ran back into the house. 'Cheeky little mare,' he muttered under his breath. No sooner had he stopped the lawn mower to reluctantly go inside, Adam de Sousa arrived, swiftly followed by the doctor.

Nick Kellow hated Adam de Sousa, he'd spent years doing odd jobs for Granny Pascoe so that she would leave the cottage to him, but instead that interfering vet had done one thing, just one thing, to help the old woman, and she left the bloody cottage to him. It just wasn't fair! Disgruntled, he reluctantly followed the men inside the house to offer his help.

Half and hour later, Robin was in his bed, suffering from nothing more than mild concussion, two badly bruised legs and a raging hunger from spending over twenty-four hours trapped under the bookcase. As the doctor attended him, Adam had built a fire in the bedroom grate, and Emma was now busy making a pot of vegetable broth. Adam came up behind her as she cooked. 'It was good fortune that you came and found him today Emma.'

Emma nodded. 'It's only what you said the other day that prompted me to visit Mr Ferris-Norton. I thought he might like a bit of company.'

'Well, it's providence that brought you here today, that's for sure. Well done Emma.'

Emma smiled shyly and returned to her cooking. When the doctor and Adam left, Emma set a tray of steaming broth and a mug of strong tea and took it, along with the flowers she had picked, up to Robin's bedroom. She knocked softly and entered. The room was warm and cosy, Tally sat at the foot of the bed content now that his master was safe.

Robin sniffed the air as Emma placed the tray on his lap.

'Mmm, what a delightful aroma Emma, I smell broth, and...'
He sniffed the air again. 'You have lavender oil on again,
and I smell something else?'

'Primroses, she admitted, smiling inwardly that he had
remembered the perfume she used. 'I've put them with
some daffodils, though I believe daffodils don't really like
to share a vase with anything. I'm afraid there aren't many
fragrant flowers in bloom at the moment, they were all I
could get,' Emma said softly.

He turned his face towards her voice. 'How charming,
to have all this and your company too. I confess I've missed
you Emma.'

'I've missed coming to see you and Tally too.' Emma
blushed as she said it. 'Eat your broth while it is hot.' She
glanced at her watch. 'I'm afraid I shall have to go shortly,
father will need me.'

'You *will* come back though,' Robin said, with a degree
of urgency in his voice.

'Of course, I shall call before work in the morning to see
that you are well. Oh and don't pay Nick Kellow,' she
added. 'He's a lazy so and so and is fooling you about the
work he does.'

Robin smiled. He reached out for her hand, which she
gave willingly. 'Thank you Emma, thank you for everything
you have done for me today. It's appreciated more than I
can say,' he said, as he kissed the back of it tenderly.

His hand, though large, felt warm and soft. Emma let
him hold her for a few moments more. 'My pleasure,' she
said as she made to leave.

Emma skipped brightly along the path towards the river.
Her affection for Robin filled her heart with delight and
happiness radiated from her. No more would she care that
she was tormented by the local boys, nothing could
diminish this wonderful feeling Robin had given her as he
kissed her hand so lovingly.

7

Verity dragged the sheets from the bed indignantly and threw them into a pile by the door. She hated changing the guest beds, there was something quite unsavoury about other peoples bedding. As she began to unfold the clean sheets, she glanced out of the window. The sun was shining and the day was warm for the end of March. Feeling the heat, she pushed a wisp of hair away from her hot face, and walked towards the open window for air. She broke into a broad smile as she caught sight of Adam entering the village store. Quickly abandoning her chores, she rushed to her bedroom, brushed her hair and quickly dowsed herself with a copious amount of perfume. As she crossed the landing towards the stairs, she collided with Rachel unapologetically, sending the pile of clean linen she was carrying, fluttering to the ground.

'Verity,' Rachel shouted crossly. 'Where are you going? You haven't finished the bedrooms yet!'

Verity ignored her and ran down the stairs.

As Rachel watched her go, her senses picked up the scent Adam had bought her for Christmas. Leaving the pile of tangled linen where it had fallen, she rushed to her room and pulled out the drawer where she kept the perfume and gasped, the bottle was half empty. 'Oh how could you,' she cried. The bottle had been almost full last night when she had dabbed a tiny drop of the precious scent on her neck before bedtime, a ritual she did most nights.

Feeling the anger rising within her, she marched into Verity's room and found quite blatantly on her dressing table, a whisky glass containing her precious perfume. As Rachel very carefully decanted the perfume back into its original container, Verity was downstairs by the front door waiting for Adam.

As he stepped out of the village store with his arms full

of groceries, he blinked in the bright sunlight and was glancing in the direction of The Black Swan, hoping for a glimpse of Rachel.

'Looking for me, are you?' She smiled brightly as she skipped across the road to join him.

He inadvertently sniffed, recognising the perfume immediately. 'Oh! You're wearing 'Soir De Paris' Chanel!' he regretted his comment instantly.

Verity noted his uneasiness with interest. 'How do you know that?'

Adam smiled at Verity. 'It's my mother's favourite. You have good taste,' he added.

Verity's eyes narrowed, unsure of what she had stumbled on here. 'It was Rachel's actually. She'd thrown it out, said it made her stink like a skunk.' She waited for his reaction, but before he could answer, a commotion outside Blewett's forge caught his attention.

'You stupid good for nothing idiot,' Sam roared, as he grabbed his son Harry by the scruff of his neck. Can't you do just one simple thing right?' He raised an iron bar to the boy and yanked the boy inside the forge.

'Hold these.' Adam pushed his shopping into Verity's arms and was at the door of the forge as fast as his feet would carry him, but Sam had brought the bar down with a sickening thud across Harry's shoulders.

Harry cried out in pain. 'I'll give you something to cry out for, you useless lump,' Sam said, raising the bar again.

'For Christ sake man, what the devil are you doing? Leave the boy alone,' Adam yelled as he lurched at Sam, grabbing at his arm.

Sam pushed Adam aside with such force he fell hard against the anvil. 'You mind your own business,' he snapped angrily, as he pushed Harry nearer the forge fire.

Adam scrambled to his feet and dusted the dung soiled straw from his clothing. 'I'm making it my business. I'll not stand by and watch you beat this boy, just because you have

72

a short temper. Now leave him be.'

Harry cowered by the forge like a frightened animal, the heat from the fire made him sweat profusely. His eyes darted from one man to the other, fear blocking out the searing pain across his back. Sam's mouth curled into a wry smile, he turned to face Adam, tapping the bar menacingly across his own palm. 'And... if I don't?'

'I'll be forced to make a citizens arrest,' Adam answered sternly.

'A what?'

'You heard me. I shall arrest you.'

Sam sneered in his face. 'You're a bloody vet, not a policeman. You can't do that,' he hissed.

'Just try me,' Adam said darkly.

The two men sized each other up. Sam eyed him cautiously, as he seethed with anger. He wasn't sure about Adam or the authority he had to arrest him, all he knew was that he hated him with a vengeance. He was sure he had something to do with Rachel's reluctance to take up his offer of marriage. 'Get out of my forge de Souza, you interfering bastard,' he said, his voice was low and filled with the bitterest contempt.

'I want your assurance that Harry will not be beaten again,' Adam said.

Sam moved towards his cowering son. 'Get up and get out, you useless lump of rubbish,' he snarled. He pushed the boy with great force towards Adam. 'Here's your assurance, I don't want the idiot here at all. He can go and find his own way in life, and we'll see how long he lasts without me. Go on, get out.' He kicked the boy hard on the backside.

Adam moved forward to his defence, as Harry scrambled to his feet and ran behind Adam for protection.

Sam roared with laughter. 'It looks like you're lumbered with the waste of space de Souza, let's just see how long it takes you to want to beat the living daylights out of him.'

He turned his back on them both and began to pump the forge.

'Come on son.' Adam put a protective arm around Harry and walked him slowly back to his surgery, forgetting the groceries he'd left with Verity. There he helped him off with his shirt, and was appalled at the sight that beheld him. Psoriasis covered eighty percent of his body. He checked for any broken bones and placed a cold compress on the huge blackening bruise on his right shoulder. He had a slit across his right eyebrow, and his eye had swelled, but apart from that, his face would not be disfigured. 'Has your father beaten you before?' he asked softly.

Harry nodded sadly. 'It's… it's true,' he stammered. 'I'm useless in the forge. I hate the work there. I love animals and I love being outside in the fresh air. I'm useless at making things. I just like to look after things.'

'Like Vicos?'

'Yes.'

'Well, we'll have to see what we can do for you.' He smiled gently at the boy. 'I'll get some cream for your skin - how long have you suffered from this skin affliction?'

'All my life,' he answered sadly.

'And have you seen a doctor for any treatment?' Harry shook his head. Adam nodded, just as he thought, the condition had been brought on by fear. He'd seen it before in children with violent parents. 'I'm just going out. You can stay here in the spare room for as long as you like, so there are no worries there, okay.'

'Thank you so much Mr de Sousa,' Harry said happily as tears welled up in his eyes. This was the first act of kindness he'd ever experienced from a man.

*

As Emma breezed into the surgery one morning, Adam asked, 'How's Robin?' It was no secret Emma spent a great deal of time with Robin nowadays, and the change in her was astounding. She walked with her head held high, and a happy air of confidence surrounded her.

Emma blushed slightly. 'He's fine, except for being worried about what he is going to do with the farm.'

Adam paused from packing his case with potions. 'Why, what's the matter with the farm?'

Emma sighed. 'He found out today that Danny, the farm hand, has enlisted in the army this morning. He leaves at the end of the week. There's no one to look after his livestock. He fears he will have to sell the farm lock stock and barrel.'

'That's a bit drastic surely there are other farm hands to take his place?'

She shook her head. 'That's just it you see, everyone we know is already employed.'

Just at that moment, Harry came through the surgery with a bucket and mop, whistling a merry tune.

'Can I clean in here before surgery starts?' he said brightly.

Harry had been at the surgery for nearly a week and was willing to do any job for his keep.

'Course you can Harry let me get out of your way.' Emma smiled at him, and then glanced at Adam - they both thought the same thought. Out in the hallway Emma whispered, 'Harry would make an excellent farm hand, he's so good with animals, it would be a perfect job for him.'

A few minutes later Harry stepped out into the hallway with his mop and bucket, he glanced between Adam and Emma, and his face paled. He swallowed hard. 'Oh no, you're not going to sack me are you?'

Adam placed a protective hand on Harry's shoulder, 'Stop worrying old chap. We've just had a brilliant idea.'

*

At four-thirty the next morning, Harry accompanied Danny as he brought the cows in to be milked. By the end of the week, there wasn't a single job that fazed Harry on the farm. He slipped into the role of farm hand as though he had been born to it.

*

On the twentieth of April, Adam received a letter from his parents. With the rumours of war escalating, they wrote requesting his help, which in turn would take him away from Gweek for at least three weeks. The thought of leaving Gweek, and particularly Rachel, saddened him, he had become increasingly attached to her over the last few months, and being parted from her would be intolerable. He broke the news to Rachel later that day. The look in her eyes when he told her left Adam in no doubt about her feelings for him.

'Where are you going?' Her voice was almost a whisper.

'Tuscany. According to the papers the German army has occupied the remainder of Czechoslovakia. I'm afraid that the Munich Agreement intended as a guarantee of peace, is now in tatters. If Germany declares war and Italy were to take Germany's side, Italy would be a hostile country. We leave quite a lot of things, some valuable, in the villa, and my parents have asked if I can go and retrieve them. If war comes there is no guarantee the villa will be safe and could be stripped of everything.'

Rachel was shocked. 'You're not going to be in danger?'

He touched her hand reassuringly. 'No, not if I go in the next few weeks.'

'Well, I shall not rest until you're back with us,' she declared. He smiled broadly at her. 'What are you smiling at?' she asked.

'I was just thinking that you would love Tuscany. When I was small, we spent most of our holidays there. Oh for those wonderful summer days of long ago. I remember being sixteen and in love for the first time, her name was Anna,' he said wistfully. 'I can visualize it now, it was wonderful. Standing there, in the baking sun, overlooking the vineyards, where rows of vines, laid out in formation, reached out into the rolling hillsides with snaking rust coloured roads between them. As you look further into the distance, green cypress trees dominate the hill tops and red roofed farmhouses nestle in the valleys below. Anna and I picked fruit from the orchard and ate it in a sunflower field at sunset with a bottle of wine stolen from my father's cellar. Heady wonderful days,' he mused, and then added, 'She left me for Massimo three weeks later. It broke my heart.'

'Oh dear,' Rachel smiled sympathetically.

'I got over it,' he said, feigning hurt.

She laughed warmly. 'You make it sound so lovely.'

'It is.' He paused for a moment then said, 'Come with me Rachel.'

She regarded him for a moment to see if he was joking. 'Me?'

He nodded. 'Come with me and drink wine at sunset in a sunflower field.'

Rachel bit down on her lip. She could hardly believe her ears. He was asking her to go on holiday with him, her, he really wanted her to go with him!

Adam studied her face. 'Are you worried about what people would say?'

'I'm worried about what Verity would say. She's very taken with you, you know. I think she hoped you would be taken with her one day.'

He smiled gently. 'I like Verity, she's a nice looking girl, but it's you I'm taken with, not her. I fell for you the moment I saw you.'

Rachel's heart was pounding. 'Oh Adam,' she breathed.

'We could go without anyone knowing we've gone together, if you want. You could maybe say you are visiting relatives for a couple of weeks. Do you have anybody you could pretend to visit?'

Rachel thought for a moment and nodded that she did.

'Well then we could set off separately, then meet up, say in Truro, and go on to Plymouth from there. It would only take us a few days to drive over. Oh say you'll come with me Rachel, please. I'm not asking for anything other than to strengthen the friendship we already have. If you come with me, I shall respect the fact that you are still grieving for Alex. I just want you to come and see the place, before Hitler does his worst.'

She looked deep into his eyes. Her heart was racing, unsure of what to do. 'I have relatives in Yorkshire,' she whispered, her voice almost inaudible.

He watched her in earnest.

'Maybe a visit to them is overdue,' she smiled warmly at him.

'So, you'll come?' he said quietly.

She cleared her throat before answering. 'I will.'

He took her in his arms and feeling the softness of her body against his, he knew he was falling very much in love with her. 'We'll arrange to go at the end of the month,' he said softly.

Rachel pulled away gently and nodded, and then her countenance changed suddenly. 'Oh no, I can't!'

Adam's heart sank. 'Why?'

'It's Verity's eighteenth birthday on May the first.'

'Then we will go shortly after that.' He smiled and kissed her gently on the lips, and as he did he inhaled 'Soir De Paris' perfume. 'You smell delicious.'

'Oh I love it Adam, I normally only wear it at bedtime.' She blushed slightly at this revelation. 'I dabbed a little on this morning. Verity stole it the other week you know? I was so angry with her, but unable to scold her about it, otherwise I think I would have betrayed our little secret.'

A door slammed shut at the back of the hotel, causing Rachel to jump as if electrified. They quickly pulled away from each other, just as Verity walked into the bar.

She regarded them reproachfully for a moment. 'What's wrong with you two, you look like you're plotting something.'

There was a silence while Rachel composed herself enough to answer.

Verity took this as guilt and felt an anger rise within her. She felt that something was going on here with these two, she was certain of it. She glanced at Adam, but he didn't speak, he just stared at her. She pressed her lips tightly together as she stared back at him. 'Tell me what's going on?' Her voice was high and demanding.

Rachel felt the panic rising. 'Well?' Rachel hesitated momentarily. 'You'll have to wait until your birthday to find out,' said quickly.

'My birthday!' As suddenly as her anger started it stopped again. 'Oh, I see,' she said, as her eyes darted from Rachel to Adam.

It was Adam who finally broke the silence. 'Rachel tells me you will be eighteen in a couple of weeks Verity.'

'Yes I will Adam,' she said authoritatively. 'And it'll be nice to be treated as a grown up for once.' She shot a withering look in Rachel's direction.

8

Rachel could hardly contain her excitement about her trip to Tuscany, though the thought of arranging Verity's eighteenth birthday tried its best to dampen her spirit. It was not a task she was looking forward to. She was sure whatever she did for Verity, it would not be appreciated, but she knew she must do her best for the girl, after all, Alex always made such a fuss of her birthdays, and Rachel intended to carry on the tradition. Verity had made numerous remarks over the last year that her eighteenth birthday was something of an important milestone to her, though normally one would have saved that occasion for ones twenty-first. However, Rachel would endeavour to play to her wishes.

To start the celebrations, Rachel had invited a few people over to have a drink at lunch time with Verity to celebrate. As she came downstairs to the bar, she was greeted with a chorus of 'Happy Birthday', and she blushed slightly when she saw Adam joining in.

'What would you like to drink Verity?' Rachel asked.

She glanced at the pint of ale in front of Adam and said, 'I'll have what Adam's drinking.' She knew full well that Rachel didn't approve of women drinking pints. Rachel bit her lip slightly then nodded. 'A pint it is then.'

Lizzy stepped forward and kissed her lightly on the cheek. 'This is from me, Charlie, Emma, Verity, happy birthday my lover,' she said, handing her a package containing a black suede handbag with fringing on the bottom.

'Oh thank you,' she squealed. 'I've wanted one of these for ages.'

'I know,' Lizzy beamed. Rachel told me which one you wanted. Verity's smile dropped as she cast an unpleasant glance at her step-mother. Suddenly, the bag didn't hold the same appeal to her. Rachel refused to be perturbed by her behaviour and handed her two more parcels, one from her and one from Adam. Saving Adam's gift until last, she very reluctantly opened Rachel's package and lifted the cherry red cardigan from its wrappings. It was just what she'd wanted to go with her cherry print dress, but wild horses would not make her wear it now, without a word, she discarded the garment to one side.

Rachel laughed inwardly at the gesture - she expected nothing less from her.

'Oh what could this be?' she said, shaking the package from Adam. With nimble fingers, she began to unwrap it carefully, to reveal a green box. 'What is it?' she asked, smiling brilliantly at the box in her hands.

'Open it and see,' Adam urged.

She turned it over in her fingers, savouring the moment, before gently opening it, to reveal a silver bracelet. 'Oh gosh Adam, it's lovely, I love it, thank you,' she gushed. 'Can you fasten it for me?' She moved swiftly towards him with her wrist extended. As she stood up, the cardigan slipped to the floor with the discarded paper. Her cheeks were tinged pink with joy as she stood up close to Adam. The catch was delicate and for a moment Adam had trouble fastening it. Verity moved closer to see if it would help. She could hear Adam's breathing as he concentrated.

'There,' he said triumphantly, but before he could take a step back from her, Verity kissed him full on the lips. Adam pulled away glancing at Rachel in alarm, but Verity moved closer and wrapped her arms around his waist and laid her head on his chest.

'Oh thank you Adam, it's the most beautiful present I have ever had.'

Eventually, Adam pulled away and nodded an acknowledgment for her thanks.

Admiring her bracelet sparkling in the light, she pretended not to hear what Rachel was saying to her.

'Verity?' Adam said softly.

She looked dreamily at him. 'Yes?'

'Rachel is speaking to you,' he said firmly, but with kindness in his eyes.

She sighed heavily. 'What?' she aimed the question at Rachel, but didn't look her in the eye.

'I'll be making a small buffet for you and some of your friends this evening. You can have the back room all to yourselves if you want.'

Verity gave no response.

'What time do you want to bring them?' Rachel asked.

She shrugged insolently. 'I don't know.'

Rachel tried to hide her irritation. 'I'll make it for seven then, okay?'

Verity gave a short nod and turned to pick up her presents. Thank you for my presents she looked at Lizzy and Adam as she spoke. 'See you later.'

As she left the room, Rachel noticed the cardigan discarded on the floor, all other presents, cards and even the wrapping paper had gone. It hadn't been left by mistake.

When the bar closed, Rachel busied herself all afternoon producing a beautiful iced birthday cake with eighteen written on top. She made a selection of ham, cheese, and egg sandwiches, along with sliced sausage and pickled onions, and to finish off, a large fruit trifle. Lizzy came around about six to help decorate the room with ribbons and flowers and as the clock struck seven, the room was ready for a party. Rachel glanced out of the window to look for Verity before leaving the room to open the bar. She surmised that most of the guests would arrive via the back door as most of them were still underage, and if they needed anything, she was sure Verity would come and demand it. Lizzy returned to the hotel at seven-thirty and commented to Rachel on how quiet they all were.

'They are a bit, aren't they,' Rachel said, pulling a pint for Ely. 'Be a love and go and see if they have everything they need will you? I'm just a bit tied up here at the moment,' she said as a group of walkers entered the bar.

A second later Lizzy came back. 'There's nobody there yet. You did say seven, didn't you?' At eight still nobody came, by nine thirty, Rachel covered up the sandwiches which were starting to curl around the edges. By closing time, Verity still hadn't arrived and Lizzy patted Rachel on the hand. 'I don't know why you bother with that girl, she's so ill-mannered. I could hit her!'

'Oh it doesn't matter Lizzy,' she mumbled.

'It does matter Rach, she needs to be taught a lesson.'

'I'm not her mother, and it's plain to see that she doesn't like me, she never has and never will.'

'But look at all this trouble you've gone to and she can't even be bothered to turn up.' Lizzy was flushed with anger now. 'She is the most insolent, self-centred person I have ever come across. I don't know why you put up with it.'

Rachel held her hands up to calm her down. 'Lizzy, Lizzy listen, I do things for her out of memory of her father. God knows though, she must take after her mother, because Alex was never like her.' Just as she spoke, the bar door opened and Verity walked in as bold as brass. Lizzy marched over to her and grabbed her by the arm. 'Where have you been?'

Verity looked down at where Lizzy was pinching her arm. 'Ouch, get off, you're hurting me,' she whined, while trying to shrug her off, but Lizzy squeezed tighter.

'Rachel spent all afternoon making things for your party and you couldn't even be bothered to turn up.' Verity stood in silence. 'Well?'

'Well what?' Verity said, finally freeing herself from Lizzy's grasp.

'Why didn't you come?'

'I forgot, that's all,' she answered insolently.

Lizzy was so angry she grabbed her again in fury. 'How dare you?'

'Lizzy leave it, it's not worth it,' Rachel intervened.

Verity pulled her arm away indignantly and flounced out of the room stifling a laugh as she glanced at the table of food. Once in her bedroom she slammed the door behind her. Who the bloody hell did Lizzy think she was, giving me a lecture about coming home late. She moved to pick up the red cardigan Rachel had placed on her bed and tossed it into the waste bin. Her stomach rumbled, she hadn't eaten all day and she was famished. She thought of all that food downstairs, but nothing would possess her to eat any of it. Hell would freeze over first. She would wait for breakfast, it wouldn't harm her.

The next morning Rachel was nowhere to be found, Verity opened the cupboard in the kitchen to make breakfast, but there was nothing there, no bread, no porridge, not even an egg in the larder, though she knew the hens would have lain this morning. She looked at the fruit bowl not a single apple was there either. Her stomach rumbled loudly as she walked from the kitchen to the back room, where her buffet was still laid out on the table. It had all been uncovered now and was dry and almost inedible. She walked slowly around the table, and had to admit that Rachel really had gone to a lot of trouble. Silly cow, she thought, if she thinks for one minute that I am ever going to like her, she has another think coming. She lifted a dried ham sandwich from the plate turned it over between her fingers then threw it down. 'I won't. I won't eat this,' she spoke softly to herself. She didn't care how hungry she was. She had no idea where Rachel was, but she knew she must be somewhere in the house and shouted out to her. 'I know you are here somewhere, and if you think you're going to make me eat this rubbish, you are very much mistaken.' Without noticing that she was no longer alone, she picked up the dish of pickled onions and tipped them into the trifle, dropping the dish on top of the sausages. She briskly brushed the palms of her hands together as though it was a job well done, then without kicking her shoes off she stood on a chair and reached for the ginger jar where she knew Rachel kept some loose change. 'I'll buy my own breakfast then, with your money' she muttered to herself.

'You won't find anything in there.'

Verity spun around to find Rachel and Adam standing at the doorway.

'Not exactly how you would expect a 'grown up' to behave, is it Adam?'

Verity glanced at Adam and smiled, but Adam stared at her coolly. 'No it's not,' he said softly, and she noted the criticism in his voice.

Verity shot a look of hatred at Rachel for bringing Adam here to witness her outburst. She got off the chair and swept past them both. 'You bitch,' she hissed. Her voice was low and filled with the bitterest contempt.

'It takes one to know one,' Rachel couldn't help herself saying.

*

Rachel had arranged for Lizzy to take over as the temporary landlady for the duration of her time away. She was the most competent person she knew and Lizzy was the one person she could trust to keep an eye on Verity. She had told Lizzy that she had to make a journey up to Yorkshire to help a sick relative who was due to have an operation. Lizzy on hearing this news, had agreed to help out, but Rachel noted a look of mild suspicion in her eyes.

For Lizzy's part, Rachel was a good friend and as far as she was concerned, what Rachel was really up to was none of her business, but she knew in her heart that Rachel would not be travelling north. And that the handsome Mr de Sousa had something to do with her departure.

*

May the tenth, which was a Wednesday, dawned warm and sunny. Rachel said her goodbyes to Verity, who replied with a disinterested shrug. She was still not speaking to Rachel over the buffet incident. With Vincent Day now well out of the picture, Rachel had no qualms about leaving Verity under Lizzy's watchful eye.

Verity could hardly contain her excitement at Rachel's departure. As soon as she was out of the way, she planned to make her move on Adam. It annoyed her greatly that he hadn't asked her out yet, and that he seemed to want to spend a great deal of time talking to Rachel. She had tried every which way possible to put herself into his personal space. Granted, he was always attentive towards her and complimented her on her appearance, he just needed a nudge in the right direction, she decided. Once Rachel was out of the way, she would make her move. That was if she could find him, he seemed to have disappeared these last few days, though the van he had inherited from George Bray was parked near the surgery, Adam was nowhere to be seen. Emma, when asked, just told her he was out on appointments.

Adam had arranged for Head and Head to cover his rounds and specifically asked Emma to not divulge to anyone in the village that he was away. Emma had no idea why he was so secretive, but felt it was none of her business to ask.

Rachel's bus was at nine-forty-five. It would take her first to Falmouth then onto Truro, from there she would catch the train to Yorkshire she'd told Lizzy. In truth though, she would wait in Truro for Adam to pick her up. He had left Gweek over a week ago, taken the train up to Kent to see his parents and to collect the family car. Much as George Brays van was a reliable old work horse, Adam had serious reservations about its ability to make it all the way to Italy and back. Adam was to travel back down to Cornwall during the night to collect Rachel from Truro. From there they would go on to Plymouth to catch the ferry.

Lizzy hugged Rachel warmly. 'Have a good time,' she

said.

'Oh I..,' she stopped mid sentence.

Lizzy smiled knowingly. 'Go gently Rachel.'

They looked at each other for a long moment, and then Rachel nodded. 'I will.'

Lizzy helped Rachel on the bus with her luggage and once settled she waved her on her way. Verity stood at the window of the hotel and mumbled, 'Good riddance and don't hurry back.

*

As Rachel waited on Lemon quay in Truro, she felt both nervous and elated. She wondered what this holiday would bring, what would happen in that far away hot country? She had wild romantic ideas of making love under the Tuscan sun, but in truth, she and Adam had only ever kissed. She knew he had deep feelings for her, as she did for him, but there had been no talk about a relationship other than the friendship they shared. She was deep in reverie when Adam drove up and sounded his horn. He made her physically jump.

'Sorry, I didn't mean to startle you,' he said, jumping out to gather her bags. 'In you get.' He gestured, opening the car door for her.

For the first couple of miles, there was a strong nervous silence between them, and then they both spoke at once.

Adam laughed. 'Sorry, you were saying?'

'Your parents are well I hope?'

'Yes thank you. Mother is so grateful that I'm going to collect the things she wants. I shall have to take them back to her on my return, so I may have to put you on a train in Plymouth if that's okay?' She nodded, not really wanting to think about her return journey.

There was another pause, and then she asked, 'And you were going to say?'

'I was just about to say, did you get off without any problem?'

'Yes thank you, though I suspect Lizzy had put two and two together, what with you being away as well.'

'Did she say anything?'

'No and she won't. She's a good friend, I trust her implicitly.'

'But you didn't tell her?'

'No! Oh if Verity finds out, I don't know what will happen, it will kill her.'

'She won't.' He reached over and patted her on the leg. His touch sent shivers down Rachel's spine.

*

Adam had booked two rooms for them that night in a small hotel on the outskirts of Plymouth. They dined early, took a short stroll, before getting an early night. They were due to sail at nine the next morning. Rachel was too excited to sleep and was up and about at six the next morning. The voyage was quite uneventful, and the sea was mercifully calm. They sailed into Roscoff eight hours later and found a couple of rooms for the night. The next day they drove for eight hours, before stopping to stay in a small hotel for the night. This was a pattern they repeated for two days before crossing the border into Italy.

As Adam had said, Italy was an outstanding country. They drove through the most wonderful countryside Rachel had ever seen, until they finally came to Lucca. It was late in the afternoon as they drove through the village of Pratolino, stopping off to buy provisions in the local store.

Rachel was amazed at how many people greeted Adam like an old friend, and found Adam to be thankfully proficient in the Italian language. He introduced Rachel to everyone he met and she in turn was welcomed warmly.

With their car loaded up with groceries, they set off up the long steep hill towards the villa which was situated in a medieval hilltop village. It was surrounded by olive groves and vineyards, and as they drove, they passed newly planted fields, which would be filled with sunflowers in the summer. They looked at each other and smiled, the dream had come true at last.

Adam pulled into the drive at the side of the villa and watched with mild amusement as Rachel stood open mouthed at the vista before her. The garden was on several levels linked by worn trodden steps. There were terraces of roses, wildflowers and pear trees, and the smell of thyme on the breeze filled Rachel's senses.

'Oh Adam it's beautiful,' she gasped, as she stood on the panoramic terrace, overlooking the rolling Tuscan hills

He touched her lightly on the shoulder. 'Come and look at the villa,' he said, leading her through an array of terracotta pots, which in late summer would bear an abundance of citrus fruits.

The villa was like stepping back in time. It had a country style kitchen, living room with an open fireplace, three airy bedrooms and a huge bathroom. He showed her to her room, which overlooked woodlands of oaks, cedars, pine and plane trees. It's cooler in this room,' he explained. 'The other room has a better view, but get the full force of the Tuscan sun throughout the day and can become extremely unpleasant at night.'

Rachel eyed the room with pleasure. The bed was dressed simply with cream and white linen, an array of subtle floral cushions, which matched the full length curtains, were placed upon the pillows to compliment the room perfectly. Scraps of driftwood and sea shells adorned the windowsills and faded sketches and photographs covered the walls. 'This is beautiful Adam, it's just perfect.'

'I'll let you settle in and freshen up a little. We'll eat at sunset if that's okay by you.'

She nodded. 'Can I do anything to help?'

'No, you just relax.'

An hour later they came together and dined on the terrace with the heady perfume of early jasmine hanging in the air. With a glass of Chianti, they enjoyed a meal of tomatoes ripened under the Mediterranean sun, sprinkled with freshly picked basil and drizzled with olive oil, followed by chicken and pecorino cheese. They sat mesmerised by the sheer spectacle that is a Tuscan sunset.

'So, Mrs Pendarves, who are these relatives you are meant to be visiting?' Adam asked light-heartedly.

'I've never actually met them to be truthful. Aunty May is my mother's sister. I get a letter from her every Christmas, but apart from that I've had no contact with them. My father wouldn't speak of them at all, apparently my mother, who was renowned for her gregarious personality, changed dramatically after a visit to them. Father could never find out what had happened, but she went from being a carefree happy individual, to a sad and depressive woman in the space of a few weeks. Father was sure something happened to her, either during her visit or on the journey home, because Mum never recovered her vitality and in the end...' Rachel paused, recalling that awful day she had watched her mother drown.

Adam placed his hand on her arm. 'Are you alright?'

Rachel nodded. 'Mum drowned herself, while I was playing handstands on the beach - I was seven-years-old.'

'Gosh Rachel, I'm so sorry.'

'It was awful Adam.' Her voice began to thicken with sadness. 'It was a dull, windy day and I remember her crying, which was not an unusual occurrence. I wanted her to watch me doing a handstand, but she just took herself off to the water's edge. She wore an emerald green wool coat that day and bright red lipstick, she looked beautiful. She took off her shoes and stockings and pulled the collar of her coat up against the wind. She asked me to look after her shoes, and I took my eyes off her for a few minutes, when I looked up, she was gone.' Rachel's eyes look to the ground and she took a deep sigh. 'I did a few more handstands to pass the time until she came back, but of course she didn't. A fisherman found me hours later, sat by my mother's shoes. I remember being very, very cold. My father brought me up from that day, but he was a broken man, his heart never mended.'

Adam wrapped a protective arm around her shoulders. He wanted to know more about her life, and she seemed willing to indulge him. Presently, he asked, 'How did your parents meet?'

'Mum was a Yorkshire woman and was very artistic. She always told me she longed for the sea, so Yorkshire held nothing for her. She longed for the day she could leave school and set off to St Ives. She'd heard that the light at St Ives was perfect for artists, and she was fed up with the cold dark Yorkshire days.'

'It's not always dark and cold in Yorkshire you know!' Adam laughed. 'I've holidayed in the Dales many times.'

'I'm sure it isn't, but that's how Mother always described it. Anyway, she left school at fifteen, packed her bags and set off for Cornwall - broke granny's heart apparently. My father was a carpenter. They met when she asked him to frame some of her paintings.'

'Oh so she made it as an artist then?'

'She did for a time, but when she married my father, she moved with him to Falmouth, had me and then her days were filled with looking after us both. They were very much in love, and I had the most charmed childhood until we lost her. Father did his best, but I sort of took over the cooking and cleaning, and we looked after each other the best we could, until he died of a heart attack when I was sixteen.' She sighed. 'Oh dear sorry, look at me getting all maudlin, you'll be starting to regret bringing me if I go on anymore.'

Adam reached out and took her hand in his. 'No I'm glad you're telling me. I wanted this holiday to get to know you better. How did you come to live in Gweek?'

'When father died, I was just out of school. I couldn't afford the rent on the house in Falmouth, so it was lucky that an old school friend told me about a job in Gweek in

The Black Swan. I've been there for the last eleven years. I worked first as a chambermaid, then barmaid, and then about seven years ago I fell in love with Alex, and the rest they say is history.'

Eventually, weariness from the journey overtook them, and they reluctantly retired to their respective rooms, but as tired as they both were, the heat of the night made sleep almost impossible. Rachel glanced at her watch for the umpteenth time - it was still only three in the morning. She pushed the cotton sheets from her hot body, slipped her feet into her sandals and reached for her dressing gown. Very quietly she walked down the stairs and through the kitchen and drew a glass of water from the tap. With the glass in hand, she tentatively opened the French doors and walked out onto the terrace. The air was slightly cooler outside, but still a balmy twenty degrees. She plumped a cushion up on one of the wicker chairs and sat down to drink her water. She had hardly taken her first sip when she heard a sound from the garden. Without a moments hesitation she walked over to investigate. The noise, she decided, was coming from the pool on the lower level of the terrace. On closer inspection, she found that the terrace was lit by lanterns as far as the swimming pool, there she found Adam naked, floating on his back in the pool, she turned quickly to walk away, but the movement caught Adam's eye.

'Rachel is that you?'

Rachel stopped in her tracks. 'Yes, I'm sorry to intrude, I just thought I heard something and found it was you.'

'Don't go.' There seemed to be a hint of urgency in his voice. He swam to the edge of the pool, climbed the steps and pulled a towel around his waist. 'Come and share a glass of wine with me. I take it you can't sleep in this heat?'

She pulled her gown about her and walked down the steps to the pool terrace. 'I can't believe how hot it is. I'm not used to this heat at night,' she laughed. 'Cornwall can get very hot during the day, but the nights are rarely warm like this.' She tipped the water from her glass onto the scorched earth, and Adam replenished it with Chianti, he refilled his own and chinked her glass. 'Salute!'

She smiled and took a sip of the soft fruity wine. 'I can't believe I'm here, it's like a wonderful dream. I've never experienced anything like it before.'

'I can't believe you are here either, but I'm glad you are.' His eyes crinkled as he smiled at her. What do you say we cool off a bit,' he said, placing his drink on the table. 'The pool is lovely and refreshing if you fancy a dip.' He raised his eyebrows.

Rachel looked longingly at the water. 'I don't have my costume on.'

'Neither do I,' he answered cheekily. 'I won't look if you won't look.'

Rachel hesitated for a moment, she felt so hot and the pool looked so cool, she took a deep breath. 'All right,' she whispered, shedding her gown as Adam looked away. The pool felt like cool silk as it enveloped her hot body, a moment later Adam was beside her. In the coolness of the water and under a huge vault of stars, they gazed at each other. Nothing was said, but both had realised that Rachel was taking the first tentative steps towards falling very much in love with Adam.

They slept late the next morning and breakfasted at ten-thirty on the terrace. Adam had made the short journey to the village to collect fresh bread and cheese and they sat in the glorious late morning sunshine to eat. There was closeness between them now, not quite intimacy yet, but an understanding and a feeling of well-being, of excitement and of wonder.

Though it was a little late in the day, they decided to take the hour drive to Pisa to experience its medieval leaning tower, which Adam told her tilted even when it was being built. There were few people there that afternoon, mainly due to the heat and perhaps the ongoing rumours of war, so Adam and Rachel enjoyed the sights in relative peace. Rachel found that it was not just the famous tower, but all the other Romanesque buildings on Campo dei Miracoli the Field of Miracles were tilting a little. This was because of the unstable ground Adam informed her. Adam was a hive of information, and as they sat on the grass beneath the shade of the tower, he explained to her that they were built in the city's Golden Age, the 12th and 13th century, when Pisa was still a port, and one of the most powerful cities in Italy. Along with Genoa and Venice, Pisa protected the Mediterranean from Muslim domination. The buildings on Campo dei Miracoli were paid for with what was captured in the battle of 1069 against the Sicilian Saracens. Then in the 15th century things went downhill, he explained, Pisa came under Florentine rule in 1406, and the harbour silted up.

'I can't believe this was once a port,' she exclaimed. 'Are we not miles from the coast?'

Adam nodded. 'We're about ten kilometres would you believe.'

She laughed softly. 'It's a bit similar to what happened in Gweek. It existed as a thriving port for Helston for several hundred years you know.'

'So I heard.'

'Unfortunately, it's silting up fast, and I imagine in a few years the larger boats won't be able to get up to Gweek. She smiled knowingly. 'It used to be a prime spot from which to carry on the trade of smuggling you know. I believe brandy, lace and other goods found their way into the villages of the area, despite good policing from the Customs House,' she said with a glint in her eye.

'Does it still go on?' he asked cautiously.

'What, smuggling in Cornwall! Of course not, what a notion,' she answered, curling her lip slightly.

On their way home, they stopped off at Camposanto,

The Holy Field; a late 13th century cloistered cemetery. Adam specifically wanted to show Rachel the impressive Gothic arcades and sculptures. It was so peaceful there. There was hardly a sound that late afternoon. It was a blessing that they were not to know, that very soon, most of the frescos would be destroyed in the oncoming war.

Once they were back at the villa, they both bathed away the dust of the day. Adam took himself off down into the orchard to check on the blossom and surmised there would be a good harvest when the fruit ripened, he was just returning to the villa when he noticed a man approaching, herding a goat.

Rachel stepped out onto the terrace, towel drying her hair, just as the man came to the gate. She looked at him with mild curiosity. He was undersized and pug-faced, with skin as yellow, dry and withered as an autumn leaf. She glanced at Adam enquiringly.

'This is Giovanni and his goat, I'm not sure what the goat is called,' he joked. 'I won't be a moment.'

Rachel watched as Adam walked towards the pair, they seemed to exchange a few words then Adam bent down to rub the goat's belly. The old man reached into his pocket and produced a wine bottle, which he handed to Adam. Adam nodded and the old man and goat walked slowly down the rust coloured road. He walked back up to the terrace, placed the bottle on the table and screwed his nose up. 'I'd advise you not to drink any of that, it's homemade wine and it will blow your head off.'

'What was it given for, is the goat ill?'

He shook his head. 'Giovanni believes that I have a magic touch. He brings his goats to me whenever I am here for me to rub their belly. Giovanni believes that it makes the goat fertile.'

'And does it?'

He shrugged his shoulders. 'It's never failed yet,' he said, as he disappeared into the kitchen. A moment later he emerged with a bottle of wine and two glasses. 'I stole this from my father's cellar,' he said softly.

Rachel remembered the story he had told her about Anna, and said, 'Why don't we take it to the sunflower field?'

He raised his eyebrows. 'And drink it at sunset?'

Her smile said it all.

He placed the wine and glasses in a basket and reached out for her hand. 'It's a bit early in the year for sunflowers, but the field is still there.' He grinned as she tentatively slipped her hand into his and walked towards the field, which although devoid of flowers was bathed gold with the late evening sun. Adam laid a rug on the ground just as the sun, as red as a wound, was setting in a sky. He guided her gently to sit beside him, pulled her round to face him, and his touch was a light as a butterfly as he kissed her yielding lips.

Afterwards, the heady wine and warm sunshine lulled them both into sleep. Bees hummed softly above their heads, a lone woodpecker called and a soft breeze whispered through the fields. Rachel opened her eyes and glanced at the man at her side and was filled with happiness, the dream was real. She lay silently for a long while and watched as Adam slept, with his tousled hair and silky dark eyelashes, he was truly handsome, even when asleep.

Later that night, under the stars, they talked candidly about their future together. Tentatively, they made plans, even though it was early days in their relationship, but despite that and the onset of war, they realised that normal rules of life seem to no longer apply. They decided that they must bide their time for a while, live for the day, take whatever life throws at them, even if it did mean eventually breaking the news to Verity.

They spent the most idyllic few days, not travelling much, but just relaxing and enjoying their new found intimacy. Rachel didn't want the holiday to end, but on May the twenty-second, three days before they had planned to leave, Adam returned from the village with worrying news. Mussolini, the Italian leader had signed an alliance with Hitler, which would commit Italy and Germany to military co-operation and support in the event of a war. The mood in the country Adam loved was changing. Maybe it was time to leave.

With the car and Rachel ready to leave, Adam stood for a moment in silent prayer that the villa would withstand the coming war and that the world would be at peace as soon as possible. He secured the villa the best he could, locking the shutters to the windows, padlocking the outhouses and draining the pool. He bid the old place goodbye then jumped into the car and made for England.

9

As Rachel stepped off the bus at Gweek, she pulled her collar up against the rain, as it came up the Helford in squalls. Low, dank clouds raced up the valley, pouring down upon the already drenched village. Soaked by the time she made the few short steps to The Black Swan, she shook the rain from her coat, and was greeted warmly by Lizzy.

'Welcome home.' Lizzy kissed her friend, noting the tanned skin of her face. 'You look like you had good weather in Yorkshire,' she said with a wry smile. 'Is everything okay?'

'Everything is fine, thank you.' There was an awkward moment as though Lizzy was waiting for a revelation. 'How has Verity been?'

'Positively furious I'd say. She hasn't been able to locate Adam these past two weeks.' She grinned wickedly. 'Our Emma keeps saying he is out, but I think he's gone away, because I haven't seen hide nor hair of him either. I don't suppose you know where he is Rachel?' she asked, with a glint in her eye.

Rachel shook her head. 'Not at the moment, no,' she said hesitantly. 'Why is Verity looking for Adam?'

'She's set her hat at him, big style I reckon.'

Rachel shivered inwardly at this disclosure.

'Goodness Rach, but you look frozen to death, let's get these wet things off you, and we'll have a cup of tea and catch up on all the news. You'll have heard the rumours about Hitler and the Italian leader I take it?'

Rachel nodded. 'It's terrible, it's just terrible.'

*

Over two weeks had passed since Rachel had returned from Tuscany. Adam had waved goodbye to her at Plymouth railway station before taking the car back up to his parents in Kent. Every time she thought of Adam, a rush of shivery excitement passed through her body. She'd had the most wonderful time with him in those few short days away and could hardly contain her happiness. More than anything so wished she could have shared her wonderful secret with Lizzy, but for now, she thought it best not to say a word, and just longed for Adam to return home so she could be in his arms again.

On the fifteenth of June, at three-twenty, just as Rachel was closing the door to the bar, Adam arrived home. Without saying a word they were in each others arms, and out of the blue, great tears welled up and Rachel began to weep.

Half an hour later, when Rachel had tidied the bar she stole away to meet Adam, who was waiting for her along Gweek drive. They drove away along the St Keverne road, turning off at the sign for Helford Passage. At Helford village, they parked George Bray's old van, and took the woodland path towards Frenchman's Creek. It was mid afternoon. The clear blue June sky winked periodically through the dense branches of the trees which flanked the path, which itself had become uneven and carpeted in a thick layer of bluebells. Rachel knew where to go where they could be together in private. She and Alex had picnicked on a small patch of open ground, high up from the path overlooking the tranquil river and had always found it to be quite private. At the clearing, Adam laid down his tartan car blanket. Rachel took the pins from her hair, shook it loose to fall at her shoulders and then they fell into each others arms and made love.

It was Rachel's evening off, so they lingered until early evening. The air had turned chilly and Rachel wore the rug as a shawl as the sun set behind them. Adam looked deep into her eyes, as he kissed her, and very gently pushed away a stray wisp of hair from her face.   'You are the most beautiful woman I have ever known,' he whispered. 'I could think of nothing but you while I was away.'

She nestled deeper into his embrace. 'I thought you were

never coming home.'

'I know, I'm sorry, mother can be so demanding at times. She hadn't seen me properly for so long she was reluctant to let me go. How have you been?'

'Oh Adam, I've been so terribly lonely without you.'

'Never mind, we're together now. I won't leave you again. We shall have to make some firm plans soon though. I want to be able to wake up each morning with you by my side.'

Her face was radiant as she turned her smiling eyes onto him. 'I can't wait.'

Adam sighed. 'I feel so guilty, being so happy especially when there is going to be a war soon.'

She inhaled deeply and shuddered. 'Oh God Adam, will you have to go away and fight?'

He cleared his throat before answering. 'I'll be thirty at the end of October, so I may miss the first wave of recruitment, but I'll serve my country, if I'm called.'

'But surely they need vets! What about the animals?'

He gently placed his fingers on her lips to quieten her, and smiled warmly. 'Don't worry.'

When the last streaks of daylight left the sky, Rachel and Adam packed up their belongings and began to prepare for the uncertainty of the coming months.

*

There was an air of disquiet in the village. Everybody was worried about the unease in Europe, so as midsummer approached, Adam suggested they hold a dance to put a smile back on everyone's face. Some of the locals were more enthusiastic than others, but this didn't deter Adam from going ahead and arranging it. The dance was to be held in Charlie Williams's barn, the refreshments would be supplied by The Black Swan, and everyone was invited.

On June the twenty-first, a local dance band boomed out on a makeshift stage, and fresh flower arrangements adorned the barn walls.

The dance was in full swing when Rachel arrived, and the room was heady with the smell of cheap perfume, wild flowers and tobacco smoke.

She watched for a moment as the girls in tightly fitted floral dresses and freshly styled hair, danced with the farm boys they had made eyes at for months. Across the dance floor, a group of girls lined one side of the room - the same eternal wallflowers, longing for just one dance. One wallflower was missing this year, Rachel thought to herself, as she spotted a blossoming Emma Williams by the bar, with her new man Robin Ferris–Norton. Rachel began to make her way towards them, stopping to chat to people as she went.

As she walked across the floor, Sam Blewett stood at the far end of the bar in his ill-fitting Sunday suit, clutching a pint of ale. His eyes watched Rachel intently as she flitted about from one person to another. He drank his courage from a glass and approached her.

'Evening Rachel,' he said, catching her arm as she walked past. 'Not speaking to me, eh?'

Rachel pulled her arm gently from his grasp. 'Sorry Sam I didn't see you there.'

'Fancy a dance?'

Rachel shook her head. 'Not at the moment thanks. I've only just arrived.'

'Have a drink with me then,' he persisted.

Again, Rachel shook her head. 'Later perhaps, please excuse me Sam I'm on my way to meet someone.' She brushed past him and made for Emma and Robin.

Not to be dissuaded, Sam grabbed her arm and spun her round.

Rachel's face flushed furiously with resentment. 'Watch what you're doing, Sam will you. You almost ripped my dress,' she said, inspecting the sleeve.

Sam looked at her coldly. 'It wouldn't be de Sousa you're meeting is it?'

She scowled darkly at him. 'I'm meeting Emma and Robin if you must know, now leave me be,' she said tartly and walked away. This time he didn't follow.

The music was loud and the dancing was lively, as Rachel caught up with Emma's exciting news. She learned they were to be engaged on the ninetieth of August and married at Christmas.

'Oh but, that is the most wonderful news.' She kissed them both on the cheek. 'When was this arranged? Lizzy never said anything to me this morning.'

Emma smiled happily. 'We've just arranged it with Reverend Pearson at Constantine Church today.'

As Rachel offered her warmest congratulations, Emma noticed her friends at the far side of the dance floor.

'Oh Robin, you must come and meet Sally and Verity,' she urged. 'Please would you excuse us a moment Rachel?'

She smiled and bid them goodbye and they took off across the dance floor. As she watched them go, Adam came up beside her.

'Drink?' he said, offering her a glass of punch, which she took thankfully. 'I thought you weren't coming.'

Rachel explained she'd been settling a late visitor into one of the rooms at The Black Swan.

'Well, you're here now. Would you like to dance?'

'I'd love to dance,' she said placing the drink he had just given her on the table behind her. As he took her by the hand and led her onto the dance floor, Sam watched them with growing antipathy.

Sally and Verity were laughing raucously at some crude joke when Verity spotted Emma and Robin approaching. 'Oh, don't look now, but Emma Williams seems to be heading straight for us with a man in tow,' she said through clenched teeth.

'Oh yes I heard she's been seeing Mr Ferris-Norton,' answered Sally. 'Didn't he go blind?'

'He'd have to be blind to go out with her. I always knew

whoever she caught would have to have a white stick,' Verity exclaimed. They both laughed heartily, but the comment was well within earshot of both Emma and Robin.

'As it happens, yes I do have a white stick,' Robin said coldly. He moved his head slightly. 'Tell me Emma, who is that I am speaking to.'

'Verity Pendarves,' Emma said, scowling coldly at her.

'All well, Miss Pendarves, let me tell you something. Being blind enables me to see the inner beauty which is projected through ones persona. You, I believe are renowned for your beauty Miss Pendarves.'

Verity beamed with delight at his comment.

'But, I fear your inner self is quite ugly. One day, your beauty will fade, and then you will have nothing. Come Emma, I'd like you to meet some of my friends, whom I'm sure will greet you with a certain degree of respect, which is I fear lacking here.'

Sally sniggered insolently, as was her way, but Verity blushed indignantly as Emma shot her a withering look and flounced off.

Rachel smiled happily as Adam waltzed her around the room. 'You dance well,' he said.

'I appear to have an excellent partner,' she answered breathlessly.

Without seeing him approach, Rachel's hand was grabbed roughly by Sam. With his arm wrapped tightly around her tiny waist, Rachel found herself being lumbered across the room in a most ungainly fashion. At that same moment, Verity grabbed Adam and pushed her body into his forcing him to dance with her. Rachel tried unsuccessfully to pull herself away from Sam's grip, but he pulled her tighter towards him. His large sausage like fingers crushed her own slight hand, and the smell of his beery breath turned Rachel's stomach. She tripped over his size eleven feet and stubbed her toe, but still he dragged her around the dance floor. In a last ditch attempt to free herself from his grip, she stopped dead, but he yanked her to move again, this time she lost her footing and stumbled, but still he held his grip firmly. 'You will dance with me. I asked you first,' he hissed angrily.

The singer crooned a song of love and moonlight into a microphone, as Rachel struggled to free herself from Sam's unwanted advances. She looked wildly around the room for help as he stamped on her toe again. 'Let me go Sam, you're treading on my feet.'

'No,' he growled.

Adam had seen enough. He made his excuse to Verity and pushed his way through the crowds of dancers. 'The lady is tired,' Adam said crisply as he stepped between them.

'Push off de Sousa, you interfering bastard,' Sam said, taking a swipe at him. Within seconds Sam was overpowered by Charlie Williams and Adam pulled Rachel away. They watched the altercation between Sam and Charlie, then Sam threw a punch at Charlie, which fortunately missed, but for which he was promptly thrown out into the yard.

'Are you okay?' Adam said, noting the tears welling up in Rachel's eyes.

Rachel nodded. 'I'll be okay in a moment I think,' she said looking down to inspect her broken toenail, which was bleeding profusely. 'I'll just go to the ladies to clean the blood away, if you'll excuse me for a moment.

Adam watched as she limped away and his heart went out to her. She was so lovely, he could well understand Sam for trying his luck with her, but the man was a fool, if he thought for one moment she would have ever considered him. It would be like the beauty and the beast. Besides, she belonged to him now.

Charlie Williams outside toilet was being used for the ladies convenience, which was located at the back of the house. The men had the back of the barn to relieve themselves. Rachel took her handkerchief out of her handbag and ran it under the cold tap then dabbed the blood from her toe - it stung like crazy. 'The big clumsy oaf,' she uttered under her breath.

A shadow fell across her, as Sally loomed over her. 'That's my father you're calling a clumsy oaf, if you don't mind,' she said, thumping her fists into her ample waist.

Rachel knew better than start an argument with Sally, she could hold her own in any unpleasant situation, so she chose to ignore her and dropped her gaze to inspect her toe again.

Sally moved a step closer and hissed, 'You think you're too good for my father, don't you? You think you are bloody Mrs 'high and mighty' giving him the run around like that? You make me sick. I hate people like you. You think you're better than everyone else,' she spat the words venomously at her.

Rachel, refusing to be perturbed, stood up and said, 'I'm not interested in what you think of me. I couldn't care less,' she interrupted her acidly. 'Excuse me.' She made to walk towards the door, but Sally pushed her with such force, she fell against the wall. Stunned for an instant, Rachel picked herself up and shook her head at Sally.

'Is the toilet free, I'm bursting,' a voice came from outside as the door began to open.

Sally turned on her heels. 'Stuck up bitch,' she hissed at Rachel as she left.

By the time Rachel regained her composure and returned to Adam, the dance was almost over. 'I think I would like to leave. Do you fancy a last drink at the Swan?' she asked, trying to conceal the tremble in her voice.

A small crowd followed them back to the hotel and business was brisk for the next half hour. Then at ten-fifteen, Verity arrived back with Sally in tow. With more front than Penzance, Sally banged her palms on the bar and asked for two glasses of light ale.

Rachel pulled one glass and handed it to Verity to which she took a long thirsty drink from, and then she turned to Sally and said quietly, 'I'm not serving you.'

'What do you mean you're not serving me?' Sally asked incredulously.

Rachel ignored her and went about her business.

'You can't do that, this is my local,' Sally protested.

The crowd in the bar fell silent and all eyes fell on Rachel.

'As long as I am the landlady in this establishment, I can ban who I wish from my bar, and you lady, have overstepped the mark today.'

Sally looked to Verity for assistance, but she just stood open-mouthed in astonishment. Bristling with indignity Sally snorted angrily. 'Well, I don't want to drink here anyway. The Ship at Mawgan is a much pleasanter place!'

'Good,' Rachel answered calmly.

She looked around at the other customers. 'Is anyone coming with me to the Ship?' No-one answered. 'Well, think on, this moody bitch could ban any one of you tonight while she is in this frame of mind. I wouldn't give her the chance if I were you. So is anyone coming with me?' Again, no-one answered. 'Suit yourselves,' she said, and walked out of the bar slamming the door as hard as she could.

Verity opened her mouth to protest, but Adam nudged her gently to keep quiet, and because it was Adam, Verity smiled sweetly and backed down, but she would have it out with Rachel later, that was for sure. Fortunately, the unpleasantness did not deter the rest of the customers from having a good time. Sally was a noisy, brash, and sometimes coarse feature in the bar most nights, and a break from her was to be relished. By ten -fifty, the bar was empty, but for Adam and Verity, the latter reluctantly taking herself off to bed without the pleasure of the pending row she was looking forward to with her stepmother.

Rachel pulled the bolt across the front door and made the fire safe for bedtime and then invited Adam to stay for a nightcap.

'I suppose you want to know why I banned Sally?' she said taking a sip of the brandy she had just poured.

'Not unless you want to tell me,' Adam answered softly.

Rachel relayed the incident in the ladies room to him.

Adam shook his head. 'They really are an unpleasant lot aren't they, with the exception of Harry of course.'

'Yes, thank goodness you rescued that poor boy. I hear from Emma that he has worked wonders with the stock at Barleyfield Farm. Robin couldn't manage without him now.'

'Well, I'm glad I could help.' His eyes crinkled into a smile.

Rachel took a sip of brandy. 'He's a funny boy is Harry, he can barely bring himself to speak to me you know, well, not since Alex died. It's as though he's ashamed that he was with him when he died.'

'He's just shy that's all,' Adam answered.

'Well, I don't know, I think there's more to it. He used to never be away from the Swan you know, always chatting and offering to help me. Talking of help,' she added thoughtfully. 'Thank you for rescuing me from Sam tonight.'

'It was nothing.' He reached out and took hold of her hand.

'I believe we've both made an enemy tonight,' she whispered.

Adam cocked his head to one side and looked deep into Rachel's eyes. 'I think tonight has taken its toll on you.'

'I think you're right. I hate unpleasantness - it's so unnecessary.' She closed her eyes. 'Oh I wish we could be back in Tuscany at moments like this. Wouldn't it be lovely to be somewhere warm and peaceful and away from everyone horrible?'

He pulled her close and kissed her warmly. 'I love you, I think it's time we told the world, don't you?'

'Telling the world would be simple. It's telling Verity that I'm frightened of.'

'We'll have to do it soon.'

'I know, I know, let's wait until after Emma and Robin's engagement. I don't want to steal her thunder by announcing our happy news.'

'You're always thinking of others,' he said, kissing her tenderly.

*

Rachel woke with a smile on her face the next day. Nothing could dampen her spirits, except perhaps when Sally approached her late that morning in the grocery store to apologise for her behaviour towards her. Rachel knew the apology had only come about because The Ship at Mawgan was a good half an hour walk from the village and Sally was not one to take exercise keenly. So Rachel being of good nature was willing to let sleeping dogs lie, accepted her apology.

'Does that mean I can come back into the public bar then?' she asked almost insolently.

Rachel nodded, and with her shopping finished, she stepped out into the sunshine, stopping suddenly when she remembered she needed a stone of strong flour. She turned on her heel and stepped back into the gloom of the shop.

Sally hadn't seen her come back in and was busy informing the shopkeeper Edna Clayton, in graphic detail, how she had put Rachel in her place the previous night. 'I told her straight. I said to her, 'who do you think you are Mrs high and mighty'.' She paused for a moment and looked at Edna Clayton. 'What's up with you all of a sudden, you look like you've seen a ghost.'

Edna Clayton gave a weak smile and nodded towards Rachel.

As Sally turned around, she found Rachel stony faced

behind her.

'You really are the most unpleasant person I have ever come across Sally,' Rachel said evenly.

Sally roared with laughter. 'You want to get out more then,' she answered sarcastically, raising her eyebrows to Edna.

With a wry smile, Rachel said, 'You're banned from The Black Swan... forever.' And feeling very satisfied, Rachel flounced out of the store without the stone of flour she had gone back in for.

10

The summer was a busy time at The Black Swan. Rachel had all four bedrooms full most weeks, as holidaymakers flocked to the coast in their droves. It seemed that the threat of war spurned families to take what could be the last holiday together for a long time.

At the beginning of August, Rachel and Lizzy started to make preparations for Emma and Robin's engagement party, which would be held on the front lawn of Barleyfield Farm on Saturday 19th August, weather permitting. Rachel made a cake and she and Lizzy were busy making an engagement dress for Emma. Because the celebration was to last from late afternoon to early evening, they had made her a beautiful calf length silk peach coloured dress with a cream shawl for when the evening chill set in. They all prayed for dry weather, otherwise the party would have been hastily set up in Charlie's barn again. Thankfully when the day came, it dawned bright and sunny. Rachel and Lizzy busied themselves in the kitchen most of the morning, producing a buffet a king would have been proud of. By two in the afternoon they finished laying the spread of food under the shade of a sail, loaned to them from one of the fishermen. Colourful bunting flapped around in the cool breeze which sighed off the Helford. The two women stood with their hands on their hips surveying their work.

'Right let's get changed,' Lizzy said, untying her apron.

As Rachel sat at her dressing table, she felt exhausted. Her head was sore, and her bones seem to ache. She'd felt a little strange when she'd got up that morning, but what with all the hotel guests to see to and the buffet to get ready, she'd shrugged it off. She stood and smoothed down the new dress she had bought herself for the occasion. It was a royal blue and white spotted dress with a tight bodice and flared skirt. It was outrageously extravagant, but she didn't care a hoot. It was time to start thinking about herself. She also wanted to look nice for Adam. With one last pat of her hair she was ready for the party, though in truth, she could have gladly crawled into bed for a nap.

'Who the hell are you all done up for?' Verity said as Rachel walked through the bar. As usual, Rachel ignored the remark. Verity was extremely disgruntled at being left out of the celebrations, even though she knew she had brought it on herself. Emma had been deeply hurt by Verity's unkind remarks regarding Robin, and hadn't spoken to her since the incident at the dance. Verity had shrugged her shoulders with blasé indifference when Rachel informed her that she wouldn't be welcome at the party.

Rachel picked up her handbag from behind the bar. 'I don't think you'll be too busy today,' she said gently.

'That's right, rub it in, that I'll be the only one not at the party,' Verity said coldly.

Rachel stopped and regarded her for a moment. 'You know you could have apologised and told Emma you were very stupid to say such things, she may have forgiven you.'

'And why would I want to do that?'

Rachel shook her head. 'You really are your own worst enemy, Verity. Your father would be very sad to hear how you behaved towards Emma and Robin.'

Verity's cheeks pricked pink at the mention of her father. 'When I want your opinion, I'll ask for it, and leave my father out of it. Maybe you should think of what my father would think of you, all dressed up like a dog's dinner, so soon after his death.'

Too tired to continue with the argument, Rachel walked out without answering.

'The truth hurts,' Verity shouted at Rachel as she stepped out of the door.

Rachel felt weary as she walked up to Barleyfield Farm - Verity's constant unpleasantness was getting her down. Why she was putting off telling her about Adam she had no idea, but somehow she just couldn't bring herself to do the deed. When she reached Barleyfield Farm her mood lifted slightly, and when she spotted Adam, her heart soared with love for him. Conscious of keeping a respectable front, he greeted her with a friendly smile, but noted with concern the look of fatigue on her face.

'Are you okay Rachel,' he whispered.

'To be truthful, I'm really tired, I could do with a sit down.' Adam led her to one of the tables set out on the lawn, seated her and went to fetch a drink. A happy atmosphere prevailed that afternoon, champagne flowed, and laughter resounded in the air. Robin and Emma, happy in their love, passed from guest to guest accepting gifts and well wishes. Rachel felt better for sitting, and joined by Lizzy, Charlie and Adam, they all passed a very pleasant afternoon in the sun. It took an hour to clear the remnants of the party away after the last guests had left, and Lizzy suggested they all gather down at the Williams Farm for a nice cup of tea. Slowly, they all made their way down the track from Barleyfield Farm, chatting about the upcoming nuptials, when the Helford River came into view; they all stopped for a moment to breathe in the salty tanginess floating in on the breeze of the incoming tide. Rachel sighed heavily and dabbed the beads of perspiration on her brow. Her throat felt restricted, and she swallowed to ease the discomfort.

'Are you unwell?' Adam asked, moving closer to her side. Suddenly she stumbled, but Adam broke her fall. 'Rachel, what's the matter?' He tried to help her to stand, but her knees buckled, and she fell to the floor. The rest of the party stopped dead and Charlie rushed back to help, but Rachel's eyes had closed and she appeared to be unconscious.

'How much did she have to drink?' Charlie asked with humour.

'Not a lot,' Adam replied. 'I think she's ill. We need to get a doctor quick.'

As the Williams' Farm was nearer, they decided to take her there. Charlie gathered Rachel's limp body into his arms and ran as fast as his load would allow. She was carefully laid in the bed of one of Lizzy's spare rooms and Dr Daniels was summoned. As they waited for him to arrive, Adam sat at her bedside and held her hand. He was filled with a dread such as he had never known before.

When the doctor arrived, Lizzy and Adam waited in the kitchen for his diagnosis. Lizzy noted the deep concern on Adam's face and assured him that all would be well. After a quarter of an hour Dr Daniels descended the stairs and gratefully took the cup of tea offered to him.

'Well,' he declared, 'she'll need to stay where she is for a few days. She has the flu, which is unusual for this time of year, but that's what it is! She's exhausted, and her breathing is quite shallow, it may be a good idea if someone stayed with her. Make sure she's kept covered and keep the room well ventilated. She has a very sore throat, so lots of sips of hot water with lemon and honey will be beneficial. She'll get worse before she gets better, but give it a couple of days and she'll be on the mend.' He smiled at the relief he saw on their faces. 'I'll see her again tomorrow afternoon.' He put his cup on the table and bid them all a good day.

'Lizzy, would you mind if I stayed here tonight? I'd like to keep watch,' Adam asked.

She touched him lightly on the sleeve. 'Of course you can Adam. You must do whatever you need to do. But what about work tomorrow, you'll be worn out if you sit up all night?'

'I'll cat nap in the chair, it'll be fine. I just want to be there when she wakes up.'

Lizzy nodded knowingly.

'That's kind of him to do that.' Charlie said nonchalantly, as Adam ran back up the stairs.

Lizzy looked at her husband and smiled at his innocence.

That first night, sitting in vigil, was the worst night of Adam's life. Rachel was running a high fever and he and Lizzy constantly tried to cool her forehead with cold damp towels. Through her delirium, Rachel moaned and coughed, gasped and spat out the soothing linctus Lizzy had made for her throat. She fought constantly with them as they tried in vain to keep her covered while her arms flayed and pushed back the sheets. By morning, all three of them were exhausted. Adam managed to grab two hours sleep before work. He relieved Emma of her duties at the surgery so she could sit with Rachel while Lizzy caught up on some much needed sleep. Adam called in on Rachel at lunch time, en-route to help Peter Jenkins horse, who was having difficulty foaling, then again when the equine was delivered of a fine sturdy filly. At Lizzy's request, he shared his evening meal with the Williams before returning to sit with Rachel.

*

Lizzy had popped into The Black Swan the night Rachel had taken ill to inform a very disgruntled Verity of the state of affairs. Verity was told she would have to run the hotel on her own. Fortunately they had Janet the chambermaid, who had been employed to replace Emma when she left, and Mary the kitchen helper offered to do some extra hours so the paying guests would be well looked after. It was arranged that Lizzy would run the bar at lunchtime and Verity would have to do the evening shift.

Over the next couple of days, Lizzy was stopped constantly by members of the community all asking about Rachel. She even had a visit from Sam Blewett! He'd knocked so loudly all the dogs in the yard had started barking. Lizzy was quite taken aback when she saw him.

'I hear Rachel is ill and staying here,' he stated. Verity told me and sent me round to see her,' he added.

Lizzy swallowed hard, on tenterhooks that Adam should appear at this inopportune moment. 'Oh Sam!' She smiled warmly. 'That's very kind of you, but the doctor says she's not to see anyone for at least a week, because of the fever.'

Sam stepped back in alarm. 'Fever you say?'

'Yes. It's best to be careful with things like this,' she added confidently.

'Right, well, you tell her I called.' It was an order rather than a request.

'I will Sam, thank you.' She closed the door and turned to Charlie, who was just finishing his dinner.

'That's my girl. You can certainly spin a pretty yarn when you need to.' He grinned as he mopped the gravy with the last piece of bread.

As Lizzy went about her business she cursed Verity for sending Sam round, when she knew Rachel would not want to see him. Lizzy fizzed with anger about that girl. Not once in the three days Rachel had been incapacitated, had Verity asked about her well-being or felt the need to visit her. Lizzy was thoroughly disgusted with her behaviour.

*

When Rachel opened her eyes and scanned the unfamiliar room, she had no idea where she was, and uncertain of why she was in bed. The sunlight dappled through the lace curtains, and a quiet peacefulness enveloped her. She felt rested at last.

'Good morning.'

Rachel turned her head sharply to find Adam smiling brilliantly from the chair by her bedside. She instinctively reached for his hand. 'What happened? How long have I been here?' she whispered.

'Three days, you've been really poorly.' His voice faltered. 'Oh god Rachel, I thought I'd lost you.' In an instant, he was laid by her side.

Rachel savoured the feeling of his arms around her. His body against hers, felt so wonderful.

Suddenly the door opened and they pulled apart. Lizzy eyed the scene before her and smiled. 'So, you're back with us, I see.' She placed the cup of tea she'd brought for Adam on the bedside table while Adam assumed his position back on the chair. 'You've had us all worried sick. Adam has barely left your side,' she said as Rachel and Adam exchanged embarrassed glances.

*

When Rachel was strong enough to get up, Lizzy insisted she stay with them for a few more days until she was back to full health, to which Rachel gratefully accepted.

When she finally decided she must return home, Adam came for her in his van, although it was only a short trip to The Black Swan, Rachel was still a little unsteady on her feet. Carefully, he helped her into the front seat and when he came back into the kitchen to retrieve her belongings Lizzy said, 'Here.' She dangled a set of keys in front of Adam.

Adam took the keys and gave a quizzical look. 'What are these for?'

'They're for Pond Cottage - our hideaway cottage on the river. I think you two need a few nights away together.'

Adam swallowed hard and smiled weakly.

'Don't worry, your secret is safe with me, I've told Charlie I'm lending the cottage to Rachel, I haven't mentioned that you'll go with her. The cottage is clean, I gave it a once over a week ago, you just need to take some supplies.'

Adam took the keys gratefully. 'How long have you known about us?'

'Since she told me she was going to Yorkshire. I'm a wily old bird you know? Nothing much gets past me. I've seen the looks you give each other. I can't understand why you're keeping your relationship a secret though.'

'It's Verity. Rachel doesn't want to hurt her.'

Lizzy shook her head. 'That insolent little bugger wouldn't think twice about hurting Rachel.'

Adam nodded knowingly.

'Anyway, off you go, a few days alone will do you both

good, and try and persuade her to tell Verity. You can't keep this a secret forever, and you two belong together, anyone can see that.'

*

When Adam presented the keys to Pond Cottage to Rachel, she knew it was time to divulge the extent of their relationship to Lizzy. That evening in the kitchen of The Black Swan, Lizzy and Rachel had a very long chat about Adam. She told her all about Tuscany and the stolen moments they had managed to have since their return.

'I'm sorry I didn't tell you about us,' Rachel said sheepishly. If Lizzy had been disappointed that Rachel hadn't confided in her, she hid it well. 'I didn't want you to have to lie for me, and you would have had to, in fact your having to lie for me now!'

Lizzy laughed. 'I don't care you daft mare. You're my friend, and friends lie for each other.'

Rachel lowered her eyes. 'Do you think I'm awful?'

'What on earth for?'

'Well, for falling in love, so soon after Alex's death!'

Lizzy's face lit up with a homely smile. 'Don't be daft. I think you're very lucky to find someone like Adam' She raised her eyebrows. 'If I wasn't married, I could fancy him myself.' She grinned and Rachel smiled back, but her eyes looked distant. Lizzy took her by the shoulders and shook her gently. 'You deserve to be loved again Rachel, you cannot grieve forever. Alex wouldn't have wanted you to be lonely.'

'He wouldn't want me to hurt his daughter either,' she answered sadly.

'Verity is eighteen. She's never given a fig about you. Don't let that dreadful girl get in the way of your happiness.'

'What happens when Sam finds out?'

'Huh, that oaf! He's all mouth and trousers him!'

'Oh I don't know, I think he can be a dangerous man

when he's riled,' Rachel said fearfully.

'Oh Rach, you can't think like this. This is your life. You shouldn't give a flying fig about anyone else. Do you hear me?'

Rachel nodded.

'So, are you going to tell the world you love Adam de Sousa?'

Rachel's face contorted as she let out a deep sigh. 'Soon,' she said evasively.

Lizzy laughed and shook her head. 'Well, your secret's safe with me until you're ready. I'll hold the fort at the Swan for you while you're away.'

'What on earth am I going to say to Verity?'

'You leave her to me.'

*

As expected, Verity snorted insolently when Lizzy told her Rachel needed to go away for a few days to regain her strength, but after considering it for a few moments she realised that Rachel's absence was Verity's opportunity to make her own move on Adam.

Adam pulled up outside The Black Swan to take Rachel to Pond Cottage, but before he could even open the van door, Verity had done it for him. Momentarily shocked he looked up and smiled at her. 'Hello Verity, you made me jump there.'

She spread herself against the van provocatively. 'Sorry, I just saw you drive up, and I wanted to ask, if you fancy a drink with me when you get back from dropping *her* off.' As she spoke she twisted her hair between her fingers.

Adam winced at the emphasis on the word 'her'. 'Oh sorry Verity, I'm not coming back tonight.'

She eyed him suspiciously. 'Why not?'

Adam could see the fury rising in her eyes and had to think fast on his feet to give an explanation. 'I have business in Plymouth.'

This news irritated her. She was sick to death of not

being able to spend time with him. It had been an ideal opportunity when Rachel had gone down with the flu, but no, she'd seen nothing of him this past week. Now Rachel was going away for a few days, and she could really get her claws into him, he was going to bloody Plymouth!

'When *will* you be back?' she snapped.

Adam raised his eyebrows at her interrogation.

Verity checked herself. 'I mean, I'll look forward to you coming back so we can have a drink then. When *are* you coming back?'

'I'll be back on Wednesday,' he answered nonchalantly.

Verity could hardly contain her disappointment. 'But that's when *she's* coming back!'

Adam was losing patience with her now. 'If by 'she' you mean Rachel, yes, I shall be bringing her back with me. I shall pick her up on my way home,' he added. He could see the frustration in her face. 'We'll have a drink when I get back,' he said to pacify her.

'Will we really?' she whined.

'Yes, when I get back.'

When Verity saw Rachel and Lizzy emerge from The Black Swan with boxes of groceries and a small suitcase, she turned on her heel and flounced off.

*

They approached Pond Cottage from the north side of the Helford, and Adam wore a look of sheer concentration on his face as he negotiated the unfamiliar roads which were tight and twisty. Eventually, the road forked and they took the right turn to Pond Cottage. Adam parked the van at the rear of the property, jumped out and helped Rachel from the passenger seat. They picked their way past the outside privy and around to the front of the house which overlooked the Helford River. A small rowing boat was pulled up the beach, the rowlocks and oars where inside Lizzy had told Adam, should they need them. There was a small picket fence surrounding a small front garden and this being late summer it was a blaze of colour, with an array of beautiful roses, pink dianthus, and sumptuous clematis, which scrambled over the front porch. They exchanged smiles then made their way up the path.

Rachel stepped through the front door and cast a speculative eye over the living room. 'Oh Adam, look at this, it's beautiful.' The room was beamed and whitewashed. A large comfy sofa was positioned beside the fireplace and a radio stood on the dresser on the far wall. They made their way through to the kitchen at the back of the cottage to find a large wooden table in the middle of the room, along with four mismatched chairs. A marmalade jar on the windowsill was filled with cornflowers, a little feminine touch from Lizzy no doubt and the window was framed with gingham curtains pulled back with matching ties.

'Have you ever been here before?' Adam asked.

Rachel nodded. 'A couple of years back, shortly after Lizzy inherited it when her mother died, but oh Adam, I can't believe the transformation. Lizzy's mum was a fiercely independent woman who wouldn't let anyone do anything for her, so consequently the cottage was in a poor state of repair when I last saw it. I knew Charlie had been renovating it, and Lizzy had been gathering bits and bobs to furnish the place, but what with Alex dying and being so busy at The Black Swan, I never came back to see the end result. Come on let's look upstairs.'

They next made for the bedroom which overlooked the river, where a large double bed was dressed with crisp white sheets and a simple patchwork quilt. Walking to the window to admire the view, Adam pushed the sash open and in flooded a cacophony of birdsong. They turned to face each other smiling, and then laughed and fell into each others arms.

*

Rachel had slept for an hour after making love, awakening only when she felt Adam stir and leave her side. She listened to him padding softly around the bed and heard him descend the stairs. Rachel languished in happiness. The afternoon was warm and her skin felt hot. As she stood by the basin and splashed water on her face, Adam called up to her.

'I've made tea. It's waiting in the garden.'

As she emerged from the house in simple cotton, apple green dress, Adam smiled with love. He stood and kissed her before guiding her to a chair, and pouring her a refreshing cup of tea.

'Gosh this is lovely.' She sighed, as two white swans glided elegantly and majestically across the sunlit river, bowing their long willowing necks deep into the water to feed. They came parallel to where Rachel and Adam were seated, slowed to a halt then with a flap of wings they took themselves off towards the peace and solitude of the other side of the river. The afternoon passed in a tranquil haze of wellbeing as they sat and held hands, watching the splendour of the beautiful Helford River.

They decided on a light dinner of chicken, new potatoes and fresh vegetables. Rachel took herself off to the kitchen. The room was dark and cool after the brightness of the sunshine. As she busied herself cooking, Adam laid a tablecloth outside and opened a bottle of cider.

Soon the early evening sky was shredded with scarlet rays as the sun dipped slowly behind the ancient oak trees. Clouds of midges danced in the twilight, and Rachel shivered slightly at the coolness that descended. Once inside, they both rubbed their hands together in unison. 'A little warmth is needed I think,' proclaimed Adam, as he knelt before the fireplace. She watched as he carefully built the sticks and coal onto the screwed up newspaper, he struck a match and held it until it took, then leant forward and blew gently to fan the flames. A moment later he leant back on his haunches and turned to smile at Rachel. 'That should take the chill off.'

They snuggled up on the sofa listening to the radio until Adam yawned noisily, and the fire had collapsed into a pile of grey ash.

'Come on let's take a last look at the river before we retire.' He held his hand out to her. Outside there was no moon, and not a breath of wind. The surface of the river was like an oily mirror. They stood at the water's edge and listened to the night sounds of the river. As the water licked at their feet they both stood back a step and noticing glowing footprints where they had stood.

'Look at that!' Rachel exclaimed, pointing to her feet.

'Oh my goodness, it's phosphorescence, I've heard about it but never seen it.' He bent down and selected a smooth flat pebble and skimmed it across the still river. It splashed in a brilliant cloud of light, leaving a distinct trail lasting for almost a minute, until it gradually faded. Rachel was mesmerised, she had never seen anything like it in her life. It was magical.

'Quick, go and get something warm for us both to wear, we'll take the boat out. We can't miss this opportunity. I'll fetch the rowlocks and oars.'

A couple of minutes later, Adam had pushed the rowing boat across the pebble beach, and they both climbed aboard, pulling their coats about them. As soon as they hit the water they laughed out loud at the beautiful sight around them. Each dip of the paddle caused a swirl of luminescence, and in the wake of the boat, a gleaming trail was visible for at least fifty yards behind them. Every stroke, every motion through the water brought it alive with green & blue phosphorescence. Rachel dipped her hand into the cool water and scooped a handful of light. The splashes she made sent thousands of diamond jewel-like droplets.

'What on earth is it Adam? It's unreal.'

'I think it's a combination of the warm water and algae bloom, but I'm not sure. I'm just so privileged to have seen it for myself.'

Much later that night as they lay entwined in each others arms, Rachel marvelled at the beautiful sights she had witnessed with Adam, not only the mesmerising phosphorescence, but of all the wonderful sights she had shared with him in Tuscany. He was the most inspirational man she had ever met and she loved him with all her heart.

The night had been still, only the murmur of the river could be heard through the open window, and then a lone bird began to sing to break the dawn. They both rose early, the excitement of the previous evening still buzzing within them, urged them both to return to the waters edge.

The water was warm on their toes, but the luminosity of the night had gone. Now mist lay entwined within the branches of the great oak trees that flanked the river. The magic of the night before was replaced with a different kind of magic. The empty shingle cove embraced the gently lapping waves as they rose and fell against it. After breakfast, when the mist had lifted, the day had become very hot, cooled only by a faint easterly breeze. Packing a picnic, they slowly climbed the steep coast path high above Pond Cottage, stopping regularly for Rachel to catch her breath. Once they reached the top they looked out across the countryside, across and out to the glittering sea. In the distance, they could see a ship on the horizon.

'Here's a good place,' Adam exclaimed laying the rug on the ground. They lunched on cheese, pickles and crusty bread, followed by crunchy apples and soft juicy pears.

'I've been thinking,' he said, stretching his long legs out in front of him. 'I've been here a year now, I love it here, but I know you are worried about what Sam will be like when we announce our news to the world. So, why don't I try to get a posting somewhere else in Cornwall? We could move away, Verity can come with us if she wants, and we'll be out of Sam's way, but close enough for us to see our friends.'

Rachel shivered at the thought of telling Verity and Sam. Adam leaned over and kissed her softly. 'We'll have to tell them soon Rachel. I want it to be like it is now, every day.'

'Oh Adam, so do I, but I'm frightened.'

Adam sighed. He knew this was a difficult thing for her to do. 'So, what do you think about moving away?'

'I'd go anywhere with you Adam, you know that.'

'Right that's settled then, I'll make arrangements to find another post and when we settle on somewhere we both like, we will tell Verity, okay?'

She nodded happily.

The next couple of days flew by, and soon it was time to go back home. They loaded up the van and locked the door of the cottage, then stood at the waters edge for one last look and remembered.

'I don't want it to end.' Rachel said, wiping a stray tear from her eye.

His fingers entwined around hers. 'It's not the end, it's the beginning Rachel. Soon, everyday will be like it's been these last three days.'

11

Sunday, the 3rd of September 1939 dawned with glistening sunshine. Rachel had been up since the crack of dawn, busying herself, first in the kitchen, then the bar and finally with the washing. She was preoccupied as she sorted the washing to peg out. She was still on a high from her few days away with Adam, but worried sick about the news that Hitler had invaded Poland. This must surely mean war. She looked up at the bright blue sky above her. Why couldn't people just get on with each other and live in peace? She had just about finished pegging out the washing when Verity appeared in the yard, her face flushed with excitement.

'Hey Rachel,' she called. 'You had better come inside quickly, there is going to be an important radio announcement. Everyone has to listen.'

Rachel took the pegs from her mouth and secured the remaining sheet to the washing line. This could mean only one thing she thought, with a sick sensation in her stomach.

Verity's voice jolted her from her reverie. 'Come on, it's starting,' she yelled.

Rachel wiped her hands down her apron, and made her way into the bar, glancing at the clock as she swept by, it was ten past eleven. She sat on a bar stool along with Verity in silence. At eleven-fifteen a.m. Neville Chamberlain began his speech:

'I am speaking to you from the Cabinet Room at 10 Downing Street.

This morning the British Ambassador in Berlin handed the German Government a final note stating that unless we heard from them by eleven a.m. that they were prepared at once to withdraw their troops from Poland, a state of war would exist between us.

I have to tell you that no such undertaking has been

received and that consequently this country is at war with Germany.'

Rachel sighed heavily, eased herself off the stool and continued to prepare the bar for opening.

The pub was extremely busy, which amazed Rachel. She thought everyone would stay at home after the news, but it seemed everyone wanted to put their views for and against war, and so they did with much altercation.

The days following Chamberlain's speech, Rachel was kept busy sticking brown paper tape to all the windows of The Black Swan, having been told this would prevent the glass from splintering and being thrown all over the room in the event of a nearby bomb explosion. She busied herself making the blackout curtains from the heavy black material that was made available to everyone, though some of her customers told her she would be better to make light wooden frames to fit the windows, and then stretch the black material across the frames, so that no chink of light was visible. In the end decided to try the curtains first.

Thankfully, nothing happened those first few weeks of the war. Apart from being told to take gas masks everywhere, there were few visible signs that England was at war. Life in Gweek carried on as though nothing had happened.

*

As soon as the announcement had been made by Chamberlain, Adam took himself off to see his parents and then to try and sort out a new veterinary posting. He was confident that at the age of thirty, he would not be called up for conscription, but he had made a few calls to the war office to inquire, just to be sure. The last thing he wanted was to settle Rachel in an unfamiliar place, and then to leave her to go to war. He was gone almost four weeks, which caused Rachel to fret constantly about his whereabouts. He returned on the 1st October with news that a veterinary posting was available in Portloe a few miles up the south coast. With Lizzy's help, they managed to steal away for a few hours to make plans and spend some much needed time together. They were to take up their new post at the beginning of November. Rachel was to give notice to the brewery as soon as possible as she had to work a month's notice. As for Verity, well, for the time being, nothing was to be said to her on the subject. They would leave it as long as possible and broach it to her with a great deal of diplomacy. So everything was decided, even though the world was in turmoil, life would have to go on and they were determined to live their life together.

*

Come the middle of October, Cornwall was basking in what some called an Indian Summer. Rachel still hadn't told anyone except Lizzy that she was about to leave The Black Swan, but she knew she soon would have to, as the replacement landlord was due to arrive in five days time to take over the reins from her. She was just pulling a pint for Eli when Verity passed her.

'I'm going out,' she said, skipping through the bar, her cherry print dress swishing as she passed, 'to find Adam,' she said under her breath. She had made it common knowledge that she had set her hat at a certain veterinary surgeon and made a point of telling people that he had set his sights on her, why else would he spend so much time at The Black Swan?

'Gas mask Verity,' Rachel shouted after her.

Verity gave an exasperated sigh, turned on her heel and grabbed the boxed mask from behind the bar. As she slung it over her shoulder the box fell to the floor. 'Oh for Christ sake! Damn this bloody thing,' Verity bawled, as she held the string from which the box had been attached to. 'It's bloody snapped again. These bloody things are useless.'

'Mind your language Verity,' Rachel warned.

Verity shot a look of contempt toward Rachel then

tossed the box and contents behind the bar and flounced out of the pub.

'Verity, you can't go out without it,' Rachel called after her, but her words fell on deaf ears. She threw her hands in the air. 'Oh that girl, I just don't know what to do about her.'

Lizzy broke into a broad smile. 'Leave her, she'll do as she pleases, you know that. But I must say she has a point about these damn boxes. She's given me an idea. Have you got any scraps of material?'

Rachel thought for a moment. 'Yes, I've some in my sewing bag, why?'

'After closing time, we'll get your sewing machine out. I've an idea that'll make us some money,' Lizzy said, with a gleam in her eye.'

Once outside Verity laughed out loud, she loved irritating Rachel - it was what she lived for. She checked her watch, two p.m.. Adam would just be making a snack for his dinner if she called now. She had caught him twice over the last couple of weeks, though not by accident. She had sat behind the William's piggery wall and watched for him to come home. Both occasions he had seemed pleased to see her and had made her a cup of tea, though he always seemed to be in a rush to go back to work, which annoyed her.

Adam had just put the kettle on to boil when he noticed a flash of red hair near the William's piggery, he knew instantly it was Verity. She was obviously watching for him to come home, but today he was working at the Saunders farm all day near Tolvan cross and instead of driving back had walked over the back fields and entered the house by the back door. He quickly made a brew of tea and a sandwich and took his snack upstairs to eat in peace. Verity was becoming a bit of a nuisance. She constantly preened herself in his presence and pouted at him provocatively though Adam gave her no encouragement at all. He knew he was getting into a dangerous situation with her, this could not go on. He decided it was time to urge Rachel to tell her about them. He glanced at the tiny velvet pouch on the table which contained an engagement ring he had bought for Rachel weeks ago. He had decided that the day she told Verity would be the day he would put a ring on her finger and announce his love for her to the world. Preliminary inquiries told him they could be married within the week by special licence and be husband and wife when he took up his new position in Portloe. He popped the ring into his pocket and set off with fervour to finish his job at Saunders Farm. This evening he would propose officially to Rachel and tell everyone their news.

*

After a very productive afternoon with the sewing machine, fabric gas mask bags were soon on sale at The Black Swan for tuppence each, and they sold like hot cakes. Adam walked into the bar after work flushed with excitement.

'Hello,' she said happily. 'Lizzy and I have got a fantastic cottage industry going, selling gas mask bags. We've completely sold out, haven't we Lizzy?'

Adam smiled warmly. 'Isn't there one left for me then?'

'Sorry all gone for now,' Rachel answered with a sparkle in her eyes. 'But I have some khaki material somewhere, which will make a fine one for you. I'll make one up for you tomorrow. Do you want a drink?' she asked gaily as she poised ready to pull a pint.

'I could murder a cup of tea, if it's no trouble,' he answered, hoping to entice her away from the bar.

'Come into the kitchen then, I'll make you a cuppa.' As she walked past him she could hardly contain herself from touching him. 'Lizzy would you mind looking after the bar for a moment?'

Lizzy nodded and took up her position and smiled as she began to stack the clean glasses on the shelf. She was so glad they had made plans and would soon be together, though she would miss her terribly when she had moved away.

As Rachel filled the kettle at the sink, Adam slipped his arms around her waist and kissed her gently on the neck. 'I want to ask you something, Rachel.'

She turned and their lips met with urgent passion. Lost in their love, they never heard the door open.

Verity, angry and disappointed from yet another unsuccessful attempt to see Adam, stormed into the kitchen and stopped dead in her tracks. Her mouth dropped in shock. 'What the hell is going on here?'

Startled, Rachel swung round still in Adam's embrace. They quickly pulled away from each other.

Verity stood motionless, her mind working furiously. She vigorously shook her head at the scene before her. Her face began to contort as though she was about to burst into tears. 'You rotten bitch,' she hissed.

Panic nearly led Rachel into complete denial, but she could see that no matter what she tried to say to Verity, nothing could cover up what was plainly obvious.

It was Adam who moved towards her first. 'Oh Verity,' he said, frowning, as if following her thoughts.

Verity shot Adam a sharp look. 'And you're no better,' she snapped as she turned and ran.

'Verity, wait.' Rachel ran into the bar after her. She was making for the front door. 'Verity please, let me explain?'

The crowd in the bar turned to see what the fracas was about.

Verity stopped, and spun around. 'Go on then,' she spat the words at Rachel. 'Explain to me why you and he were making love in the kitchen. Go on, explain yourself. You reckon to be grieving for my dad, but you're nothing but a whore. You make me sick.' She could not contain the tears which ran down her flushed face.

'Verity that's enough, now calm down.' Rachel moved towards her stepdaughter, under the uncomfortable gaze of the bar crowd.

'Don't you dare come one step near me, do you hear me? Don't dare.' Verity hissed, as she held her hands out to distance herself from Rachel.

Rachel withdrew.

Verity had never felt so humiliated in her life. All her hopes and dreams of a future with Adam had all gone, in a flash. She felt stunned, devastated, angry and oh so stupid, why hadn't she seen what was so clearly under her nose?

Adam appeared behind Rachel and placed his hands gently on her shoulders just to add insult to injury.

'And you.' She scowled darkly at Adam. 'What the hell do you think you were doing, making up to me like that? You made me think that I had some sort of chance with you! You must have been having such a laugh at my expense. Well are you happy now you've made a fool of me?'

Adam squeezed Rachel's shoulders for a moment to give comfort, for he knew how upsetting this was for her as well, and then moved forward.

The bar crowd was silent and all eyes fell on him now.

'Verity, I am so sorry if my attention towards you has been perceived as anything other than friendship. I would not wish to hurt you for the world. I think you are a lovely girl, who will find a lovely man very soon, but I have never encouraged you. I have never led you to believe that our relationship would be anything other than friendship. I am so sorry that you read more into it than was really there.'

Verity stared at him, her eyes blazing with fury. 'Have you forgotten how you encouraged me to give up my relationship with Vince? Have you forgotten that you said I deserved better than him. Have you forgotten how you flattered me and made up to me and told me that I deserved a better man? You even bought me jewellery!'

Adam smiled gently. 'No I haven't forgotten.'

'Well then!'

131

Adam took a deep breath. 'I didn't say those things so that I could have you for myself. I said them so that you would believe in yourself, so that you would find a good man to love. Vincent Day was bad news. He would have brought you down to his level, and you are better than that. You are so much better without him. Don't you see? As for the bracelet, that was just a birthday gift, that's all.'

She shook her head as she backed out of the door. 'I hate you and especially you.' She directed her scorn to Rachel. She turned to leave slamming the door behind her.

'Verity.' Rachel made to follow her, but Adam caught her by the sleeve. 'Leave her, she'll calm down by herself.'

Rachel was distraught. She glanced at Lizzy and asked softly, 'Can you watch the bar for me for a while longer?'

Lizzy nodded, as Adam took Rachel back into the kitchen.

'Well I never, who would o thought it eh, Adam de Sousa and Rachel Pendarves,' Jinny Noble announced.

'Well, I think Rachel deserves a bit of happiness after losing her beloved husband in such tragic circumstances,' Lizzy spoke up.

'Ah but, what about that poor girl of hers? Eh?' Jinny said. 'We all knew she was smitten with the veterinary. Poor girl's heartbroken, so she is,' Jinny added.

Charlie observed his wife coolly. 'Did you know about this?'

'No,' she lied.

'You don't seem so shocked that's all.'

Lizzy looked sternly at Charlie. 'It's none of my business to be shocked, and none of yours, or any of you for that matter,' she said indignantly as she began to collect the glasses from the bar.

'I know someone who'll be interested in this little snippet of gossip,' Eli Symonds said, puffing on his pipe furiously. They all thought of Sam and nodded. 'He's not going to be very happy with 'em, either of 'em, if you ask me. I reckon he'll do for 'em if he gets hold of 'em.'

Lizzy was furious. 'No one is asking you Eli and don't you be spreading gossip and making things worse for folks. Just you remember it was Mr de Sousa who saved your life!'

'Huh,' Eli said, and puffed again on his pipe.

Charlie leaned forward and whispered to his wife, 'He's right though.'

'I know. I know,' Lizzy answered agitated.

Back in the kitchen, Rachel was inconsolable. 'I'm so sorry Rachel,' Adam said softly.

'No, it had to come out in the end. I just knew when it did it would be hard on Verity,' she sobbed.

'I never encouraged her Rachel, I swear.'

'I know my love.' She reached up to kiss him tenderly. By the time she'd composed herself enough to go back into the bar, she found it to be empty. Lizzy was just clearing the last of the glasses and turned suddenly when Rachel appeared.

Lizzy looked at Rachel's pinched face. 'Don't you take on so. Verity will get over it. She's a spoilt little madam if you don't mind me saying so. She just doesn't like it when things don't go her way.'

The two women hugged each other for a moment, and then Rachel wiped her tears. 'I'll finish clearing up. Thanks for looking after the bar.'

'It's my pleasure.'

'Was anything said?' Rachel asked, her voice hesitating slightly, knowing full well that it had.

Lizzy laughed heartily. 'What do you think?' she answered, reaching under the bar for her handbag. 'We'll come back after milking and give you a bit of moral support.' She gave Rachel a wry wink, and then she was gone.

It was eight-thirty and Verity still hadn't come home. Rachel was visibly worried. The bar was unusually busy for a Monday. Rachel guessed that word had got around. There were a couple of people whose manner was decidedly cool towards her, mostly old friends of Alex's. But there were others who nodded and winked at her knowingly. As with all fresh gossip, this would be a seven day wonder, Rachel had no option now, but to ride the storm. Adam arrived at nine-fifteen, and the bar crowd fell silent. He ordered a pint and found himself a stool at the bar. Lizzy and Charlie came in five minutes later, and both patted Adam on the shoulder.

Rachel smiled at Charlie. 'Pint?'

He nodded and gestured for her to come closer. 'I don't want to alarm you, but Verity was seen with Vincent Day a couple of hours ago. They were messing about at Mawgan on that there motor bike of his.'

'Oh no!' She sighed. 'I knew she'd go back to him.' She glanced at the clock. 'Where is she? She's normally home long before now.'

'I reckon she's just making you sweat that's all. You know what she is like when she's with him,' Adam said, reaching over to place his hand on hers. The gesture raised a few eyebrows around the bar.

*

Later that evening, Harry Blewett walked without a care in the world, and such was his happiness and such was his joy, he whistled loudly and tunelessly as he went. With his coat slung over his shoulder, he sauntered down Riverside Walk, past Corner Cottage, Eli Symonds rundown place, then Rose Cottage, which was still vacant since old Dan Trerice had passed away. With a skip in his step and a feeling of well-being, not even passing the Forge worried him now. He was well shot of his violent father and was glad that Sam had decided to disown him. Yes, life was good. He loved the job at the farm, and enjoyed the comfort of his very own place to live, albeit a converted cow shed, which sat within the parameters of Barleyfield Farm. He would be forever grateful to Adam de Sousa for all the help he had given him.

He was just about twenty yards from the forge when he saw Sally running up the lane in great haste. She entered the forge slamming the door behind her as she always did. As Harry drew nearer, raised voices could be heard from within the forge. He faltered slightly - the sound of his father's angry voice still made his blood run cold.

'I'll bloody kill the bastard,' Sam shouted at the top of his voice. Harry shrunk back from sight and dipped into the side lane which ran beside the forge. 'I'm going to finish de Sousa if it's the last thing I do! Rachel Pendarves is mine, do you hear me? Mine!'

Sally's brash voice answered, 'Well, don't stand there ranting at me, go and sort them out.'

With that, Harry made no hesitation, he turned on his heels and ran towards Barleyfield Farm as fast as his legs would carry him, to call the police.

*

By closing time, Rachel was clearly agitated that Verity had not come home, so Adam decided to stay behind until she arrived. He was just seeing Charlie out when Sam burst through the door, knocking them both flying.

'So, you're both here in your bloody love nest, are you?' Sam seethed like an angry bull.

Rachel grasped the bar to steady herself. Her heart was pounding as he moved to the bar. Her eyes darted towards Adam and Charlie as they picked themselves up from the floor. Sam leaned forwards and leered at Rachel's face, his face darkened with rage. 'Don't think you're getting away with this.' He spun around as Adam got to his feet. 'Nor you,' he yelled, as he threw a punch full into Adam's face. Rachel screamed as Adam's nose split, splattering blood across the wall.

Momentarily stunned, Adam wiped the blood with the back of his hand, and then lunged at Sam, but Sam was a bigger man than he and the second punch sent Adam flying over the table towards the fireplace. Sam leant forward to grab Adam and Rachel ran towards him screaming for him to stop. Charlie too tried to grab Sam's arm to pull him away, but Sam was kicking Adam, who had curled himself into a tight ball. Charlie tried to get in-between Sam and Adam, but Sam was hell bent on maiming Adam. Rachel grabbed at Sam's hair and pulled with all her might, dragging great handfuls of it out. For a moment, Sam ceased kicking Adam, as he swiftly turned and smacked Rachel resoundingly across the face. The force sent her reeling across the floor. Rachel lay in a crumpled heap for a moment as she gathered her wits and attempted to get back on her feet, only to be grabbed by her own hair. When she looked up, Sally was leering into her face. She tightened the grip on Rachel's hair and slammed her head down on the bar with a sickening thud.

'That will teach you to mess my father around,' Sally hissed.

Rachel wasn't sure what happened next, but all she knew was that Sally had released her grip on her hair and the bar was full of police.

Sally and Sam were unceremoniously pushed into the waiting police car and carted off to the police station, to be charged with grievous bodily harm the next morning.

As one officer helped Rachel to her feet, another was attending to Adam. Charlie too had suffered a severe kicking from Sam in his attempt to help Adam, so he was sitting by the fire, his arms hugging his torso to ease the pain.

'Oh thank goodness you lot arrived,' Rachel said, shaking the dizziness from her head. She glanced around the room and felt sick to the stomach. Adam was still down on the floor, and Charlie was in obvious pain. She shook her head, all this, because she'd allowed herself to fall in love again.

One of the policemen touched her on the arm gently.

'I've rung for an ambulance. It'll be along shortly,' he said. Rachel nodded in thanks. 'We have some disturbing news Mrs Pendarves - I'm not sure where to start,' the officer said, shifting uneasily in his seat.

Rachel felt a cry escape from her throat, as she thought the officer was going to say Adam was dead, but instead he said, 'The Blewett's will be charged in the morning.' The officer cleared his throat. Rachel watched him intently for a second. Oh God, Adam must be dead, she thought. 'Is there something else?' she asked shakily.

The officer cleared his throat for a second time and nodded that there was. 'Harry Blewett has made some accusations regarding his father, which we feel we need to follow up.'

'Harry?' Rachel knitted her brow. 'What sort of accusations?'

'Harry is saying his father killed your late husband.'

For a moment she didn't register what he had said and then suddenly her blood ran cold. 'Sam killed Alex?' she whispered, her voice almost inaudible. 'But they were best friends.'

The officer nodded. 'If Harry's allegations are true, there will be an underwater search at first light tomorrow.'

Rachel felt the colour drain from her face as she grasped for the bar to steady herself. 'Sam killed my Alex?' the words swam around in her head. The officer brought her a chair to sit on which she slumped on. She glanced at Charlie then at Adam, who was being made ready to go to hospital. She felt as though she was in a dream, a nightmare. A siren could be heard in the distance and the officer tending Adam blew a sigh of relief. Ten minutes later they lifted Adam into the back of an ambulance. Rachel was just about to climb aboard to accompany him, when another police car pulled up outside the hotel.

'Mrs Pendarves?' The officer called, adjusting his hat. 'I need to speak to you.'

Rachel glanced at Adam then back to the officer. 'I'm sorry I'm just going to the hospital. Can it wait?'

'I don't think so,' he answered, his tone sombre. 'It's rather urgent.'

Torn between the two, she said softly, 'I'll be along shortly Adam my love.' But there was no response from him. Sighing heavily, she reluctantly stepped back out of the ambulance. The doors were closed behind her, the blue light flickered on, and the ambulance sped off along the Falmouth road.

Charlie, having been patched up by the ambulance crew, made to leave. 'I'll get Lizzy to come down, and then if you want to go to the hospital, I'll take you in my car.

'Thank you for being here Charlie.'

'No problem, I just wish I could have stopped Sam, but he was too much for me.'

Rachel shuddered at the mention of Sam's name. Then the realisation of what she had just been told, washed over her again like a wave.

'Mrs Pendarves, I have some grave news,' the officer said, as he urged her to sit.

Rachel nodded. 'About Alex? I know!' she answered flatly.

The officer shook his head. 'It's about your stepdaughter Verity I'm afraid.'

Oh this was too much. She hadn't the heart to care or to be bothered with what that girl had been up to. She sighed heavily and asked, 'Verity, why, what has she done now?'

The officer paused for a moment. 'I'm afraid….. Verity…. is dead.'

Rachel's face was void of any expression. She couldn't believe what she was hearing. This couldn't be true, it was a joke, it must be some kind of sick joke that Verity was playing on her, to get her back for loving Adam. She grasped the seat of her chair to steady herself, and stared blindly ahead. Her chest tightened and for a moment she felt as though she was going to have a heart attack. The door to the bar opened, and Lizzy rushed in. Rachel saw her, stood up, but her knees buckled and she collapsed.

After helping her back onto the chair, Lizzy poured her a stiff brandy, Rachel trembled as she curled her fingers around the cold glass.

The policeman pulled up a chair next to her and spoke very gently to her. 'We've interviewed Vincent Day,'

Rachel's eyes widened at the mention of his name,

'Day, what's Day got to do with her death? He didn't...'

The policeman interrupted her. 'Kill her? No, he didn't kill her. But he did tell us that she came to him this afternoon, pleading with him to go out with her again. Apparently, Day has a new woman in tow nowadays and sent her packing, but he said she wouldn't go, and that she was in a very strange mood. Day said she was almost hysterical. He said he just left his motorbike for a moment while he went to relieve himself behind a tree, and she just climbed aboard and rode off. He ran after her, because she had never ridden the bike alone before, but he couldn't stop her. He jumped onto the back of a friend's bike and they followed her.' The policeman paused for a moment and then cleared his throat. 'Verity rode the bike over to Helzhephron, lost control and by all accounts rode it straight over the cliff edge.'

12

The week following Verity's death ranked amongst the most appalling time Rachel had ever known. Not only was she taken to identify Verity's broken and bruised body, but two days later, police frogmen recovered the blacken swollen body of her beloved husband Alex from the mouth of the Helford River.

On information that Harry had given the police, they learned that Alex had been struck over the head by Sam Blewett with a small anchor. He was then tied up and weighed down with the self same anchor, all this had been watched by a terrified Harry. Sam had threatened his son that the same would happen to him if he bleated a single word about the murder to anyone. It appeared that Sam wanted Alex out of the way, so that he could make a play for Rachel. The poor lad had lived with his terrible secret for two years. It was only on account of Harry overhearing his father threatening to kill Adam that made him realise he must do something to stop him, even if it meant risking his own life. Harry's life had been ruled by fear of his father, but he had a great respect for Adam, for he had done more for him in the year he had known him, than his own father had ever done for him. Fearful or not, Harry was not going to let anyone harm Adam, prompting him to make that heroic call to the police.

Thus it was that Sam was charged with murder, and Sally beat her brother to a pulp for his betrayal.

*

Rachel buried her husband and stepdaughter on the 3rd of November. The weather had turned cold and damp - summer had been swallowed up by the oncoming winter. A great number of villagers turned out for the double funeral, though there were some divided in their feelings towards Rachel. Those who knew and loved her, supported her, but there were some who blamed her for Verity's death. One person in particular, someone she hardly knew, spat at her feet as the funeral entourage walked slowly through the village on their way to Constantine Church.

Lizzy had been a tower of strength to Rachel over the past few days, especially as Adam was not there at her side. Rachel had no idea where Adam was, or what was happening to him, only that because of the head injuries he sustained, his parents had had him transferred to a private hospital somewhere in London. Rachel had tried without success to find his whereabouts, so had to endure this terrible ordeal without the man she loved beside her.

As they followed the coffins into church, Lizzy and Charlie walked with Rachel. Behind them, were Emma and Robin, along with Harry, who sported a broken nose, two black eyes and three cracked ribs! Dougie and June Trengrath had come. Jinny Noble and her family followed Eli Symonds, behind them, was Edna Clayton from the shop, with her husband and eight children. Bringing up the rear were neighbouring farmers and farm labourers, fishermen and their wives and licence proprietors from all the surrounding public houses, to pay their last respects to a fine man and his beautiful daughter. Even Vincent Day was there, hidden from view amongst the masses. The sound of all these people singing in the church was almost too much for Rachel to bear. When the service came to an end they all shuffled out into the graveyard to commit the bodies to the ground, Rachel was overwhelmed at the amount of people there.

Rachel was the first to arrive back at The Black Swan, Lizzy and Charlie having dropped her off to take the car home. The bar looked grey and chilly as Rachel walked through. Perhaps it was because there was no fire, or perhaps it was because it was devoid of life now. Everyone had gone. Alex, Verity and Adam - there was nothing left but memories. She shivered. The silence was profound. She thought of Verity, cold in her grave, and wept bitterly. The relationship between them had always been a traumatic and volatile one, but this did not mean she did not feel her death deeply. She knew she was responsible for it, just as Sam Blewett had killed Alex, she had surely killed Verity. For that she would never forgive herself.

The other mourners arrived at The Black Swan, but Rachel sat alone by the now lit fire, her eyes lowered, studiously observing the flames, as her fingers were arduously fiddling with a loose thread on the hem of her skirt. Lizzy passed around the ham sandwiches, as Emma followed her with the teapot, occasionally glancing at Rachel to check on her. Suddenly, a great sob engulfed Rachel, and the tears began to fall uncontrollably for the loss of her beloved Alex and Verity.

With that, the mourners quickly took their leave, and Rachel sighed with relief as the bolt went across the door. The pub would remain closed until the new landlord's arrival.

'What will you do now Rachel?' Lizzy asked with a degree of concern.

'Do?' Rachel looked up at her friend.

'Yes, where will you go? Will you stay on to work in the pub, until we find out where Adam is?'

'No. I'm to move out,' she said softly.

'Then you'll come and live with us, won't she Charlie?' Charlie nodded in agreement.

Rachel smiled weakly as tears rolled down her face. 'Thank you Lizzy. Thank you Charlie.'

'Ooh,' Lizzy hugged her tightly. 'It'll be a pleasure to have you stay my luver.'

Much later that night, Rachel sat at her dressing table. Her bags and suitcases were packed and ready to go by the door. Heavy rain had set in as night fell and was now bouncing ferociously on the roof tiles. She fingered the bottle of perfume Adam had given her almost a year ago. A lump rose in her throat, tears welled up, and she cried out his name. Rubbing her tired eyes, her speechless aching grief tugged at her empty heart. 'Why oh why, does everyone I love leave me?' She sobbed.

*

The next day Charlie settled Rachel into the farmhouse, and it was clearly evident to both he and Lizzy that she was in no fit state to do the handover to the new landlord Daniel Trewin, so Lizzy stepped into the breach and spent the next couple of days showing him the ropes.

First impressions of the new landlord were not favourable in Lizzy's eyes. Daniel was a short burly fellow with bow legs and a tobacco stained smile. His wife, who looked much older than him, was small and thin with a sharp nose and small beady eyes. It went without saying that their first customer on the day he took over was Sally Blewett. Within a week, she was made barmaid.

*

Rachel didn't venture out of the William's farm for many days. Instead she just sat in silence in the room she had recuperated from the flu only a few short weeks ago. Occasionally, she would glance at the chair by the bed and imagine Adam sitting there, and then her gaze would return to the window. Silently, she waited for word from Adam which never came. She wondered what on earth she was going to do, especially as her monthlies had stopped and she'd realised that she was carrying Adam's baby.

*

November was a dreary depressing month, especially with the war news and the black-outs. Lizzy began in earnest to make enquiries about Adam, first asking Edwin Head the vet from Helston if he could glean any information, but all Edwin could find out was that Adam de Sousa would not be taking up his post in Portloe due to health reasons. Next she contacted the ambulance men, who took Adam away that night, but they too had no other information, except that he was immediately transferred to London then onto

143

some private hospital. From there the lead went dead. Her last resort was to contact Adam's parents, who Rachel said lived in Kent, and as the name was so uncommon Lizzy had no trouble finding the number through the operator, only to be told the line was out of action as the occupiers had moved. Angry and defeated Lizzy just couldn't understand why Adam had not sent word to them to say where he was, her heart went out to Rachel in her despair.

It was a chilly foggy day in the middle of November, when Lizzy realised Rachel had finally ventured out of the house, though she knew not where she had gone. She had stolen away before anyone had woken that morning and walked the three miles to Constantine Church. No one saw her standing in the cold damp graveyard. She stood for a long time, not praying, just staring at the mound of ground which covered Alex and Verity. At eight p.m., she caught the bus to Maenporth Beach and climbed the steep coast path high above Maenporth, and at the top, she stopped for a moment to catch her breath. The fog had lifted, replaced by cold dank air as she looked out across the grey sea. In the distance, she could just about make out a ship on the horizon, slightly obscured by a band of rain skirting across the water. She continued to walk, following the coast road until the mouth of the Helford River came into view. This is where my lovely Alex met his death, she thought. For a whole year he'd been anchored down in his watery grave. She shivered uncontrollably, her clothes were soaked and the wind blowing from the sea cut like a cold knife. Mist and driving rain now filled the Helford valley, but nonetheless, she sat and stared. The cliff crumbled slightly underfoot, but nothing mattered anymore.

'Hey you?'

Rachel jumped as if electrified, twisting her head to see a member of the home guard high up on the cliffs. His voice sounded alarmed, and he was clearly agitated at the scene unfolding before him.

'Yes you!' he scolded. 'Come away from the cliff edge. It's not safe!'

Rachel looked down at the loose soil tumbling down to the sea.

'Come on now, I haven't got all day,' he shouted, hoping and praying that she wouldn't just plunge down the cliff.

Like a scolded child, Rachel stood and picked her way slowly up the slippery cliff to the safety of the coast path.

The home guard sighed with relief. Rachel was shivering, her lips were blue and her hair hung in damp clumps down the back of her coat. He noted the empty sadness in her eyes and without further ado put his arm around her shoulder. 'Come on my luver, my station is over there. Let's get a warm drink into you.

The home guard station was a small wooden hut high above the cliff top, though slightly hidden from view. There was a stove in the centre, and Rachel felt its warmth as soon as she stepped inside. The home guard pushed a pile of papers from the seat nearest the stove and gestured for her to sit, while he filled the kettle.

She sat and pinched the bridge of her nose with her finger and thumb to try and ease the throb in her head. The kettle boiled, and he handed her a mug of steaming tea. Rachel cupped her cold hands around the mug and took a sip of the strong sweet liquid.

He smiled kindly. 'So, are you going to tell me what you were doing on that cliff?'

Rachel lowered her eyes and wept.

'Now, things can't be that bad, can they?'

Rachel nodded once to say that they were.

'What sort of worries could a pretty little thing like you possibly have? Sweetheart gone away to war and you can't live without him, eh?' Suddenly, the station door opened and another home guard came in.

'Hello Nick. Quiet shift?' he enquired, then he saw Rachel. 'Goodness me Rachel, what on earth happened to you?'

Rachel stared at Bob Trevaskis as he spoke. He'd been a good friend of Alex's before he moved further down the coast. She stood up. 'It's nothing, nothing. I just got too near the edge that's all. Thank you for the tea …Nick, is it?'

Nick nodded.

'I must go,' she said, picking up her bag before scooting out of the door. As the door closed behind her the two guards looked at each other.

Nick rushed to the door and shouted, 'Can I give you a lift somewhere?' But Rachel was running back along the coast road and his voice was not heard.

Nick closed the door and rubbed his hands together for warmth. 'Don't quote me on this Bob, but she was all for doing herself in. If I hadn't arrived when I did, we'd have had a dead body at the bottom of those cliffs.'

Bob nodded. He knew of her despair and relayed the sad story to Nick. He made a mental note to have a word with Charlie Williams in the morning, unaware that Rachel would have packed her belongings and left Cornwall before then.

*

Rachel was sitting on a train bound for Yorkshire by the time Lizzy found the note she had left. She had struggled all night about her decision to leave. Her despair was so great she knew she could no longer stay in a place filled with so many bad memories.

Dearest Lizzy, Rachel had written through her tears.

Please forgive me stealing away like this, but I don't think my heart can stand another goodbye.

I pray that you will understand my decision to leave Gweek. You alone know the grief which has overwhelmed me. I must go and seek a new life away from here. Please, always remember that I love you all dearly, and I shall never forget your kindness and friendship. I don't really know where I am going or what I shall do in the future. But I

feel it in my heart that to make a life with Adam would now be hopeless, how could we ever build a life together on such a tragedy? If you should ever see him again, do not berate him for his desertion of me, for I know there must be a good reason, but thank him for giving the people of Gweek hope, and setting them out on their new lives, mine included in that. Take care, Lizzy. Thank you for being my friend. I'll keep in touch,
Love Rachel. x

Rachel had of course concealed the main reason for leaving. She was deeply and utterly ashamed at being pregnant out of wedlock. She could not face the village gossips when they found out, and knew this was the only option.

Lizzy cried as she folded the letter and pressed it to her heart. 'Oh Rachel, you silly girl, you didn't have to leave the people who love you.' She looked around her kitchen, which was large and warm, but her heart felt cold and empty at the loss of her friend. She re-read the letter. 'Go gently Rachel wherever you go, I hope with all my heart you and Adam will meet again someday, for you are made for each other, whatever you believe at this moment,' she whispered. As she pushed the letter into her apron pocket she glanced out of the window and saw Robin and Emma walking down the lane towards the house. Their love made her smile, and she wiped a stray tear from her eye.

*

Skipton railway station was deserted when Rachel stepped off the train. The town stood at the gateway to the Yorkshire Dales, but there were no rolling hills or dry stone walls here, only a large depressing cotton mill and a smelly cattle market greeted her as she walked out of the station. Her journey from Cornwall had taken almost twelve hours, and she was emotionally and physically exhausted. She took the slip of paper from her pocket and checked the address, then asked a guard for directions. Fortunately, it turned out to be only a fifteen minute walk, for which she was thankful, as it was snowing in the wind. Rachel had sent a telegram to her Aunty May before she set off, explaining her troubles and asking if she could come and stay with her for a few weeks. She hadn't waited for a reply and hoped that all would be well when she turned up on the doorstep.

Aunty May's house was a small dingy mid-terrace house, situated on a steep hill in the centre of Skipton. Rachel was exhausted by the time she had walked the half mile from the railway station with her heavy bags, but there was to be no respite on her arrival. Though Aunty May was a kindly warm-hearted soul, she was much put upon by her hard drinking husband Jack. It was he who wrenched the door open when she knocked that day. He stood at the door glowering at Rachel for a good few moments. He was a huge man, without looks or charm. His short sandy hair was Brylcreamed back from his forehead. He was collarless, and in his shirt sleeves - the thin white material bulging at the button holes from his distended stomach. A burning Woodbine hung from his whiskery mouth. He belched before he spoke, the stench of tobacco intermingled with beer turned Rachel's stomach.

'Oh aye, it's you, is it?' His eyes rapidly scanned her body, eventually settling on her breasts. 'Well, I know why tha's here, and I'm not happy about having a fallen woman in me house, d'ya hear me?'

His voice was flat and cold and held a thick Yorkshire accent, which Rachel struggled to understand.

She remained silent as he carried on ranting. She was tired and fatigued and could well do without having to stand in the cold whilst being denounced.

Thankfully, a small voice from within the house shouted, 'For goodness sake let her in Jack.' It was her Aunty May.

Jack belched again, stood aside and said, 'Well, don't think thas here on any holiday lady, 'cause you're not. Tha'll work for tha keep, d'ya hear me?' Rachel nodded wearily and stepped into the front room which stunk of acrid tobacco. 'And use t'back door, in future.' Jack prodded her in the back.

Aunty May smiled thinly and greeted Rachel with a kiss on the cheek. As she took her coat, she patted her reassuringly on the back of her hand. 'Ah, you look just like our Jean, same bonny face,' she said, gently stroking her cheek. 'I'll be making supper soon lass, you go and take your bag upstairs, and I'll call you when it's ready.'

'She'll do no such bloody thing,' Jack said brutally. 'She can get some wood in from t'yard afor supper, that's what she can do! Then afterwards, she can make a start on that there ironing.' He pointed to the pile of laundry on the table.

After a meagre meal of thin stew and stale bread, Rachel set to work on the ironing. It was twelve-fifteen before she was able to get ready for bed.

The toilet, she found, was out in the backyard, empty except for cobwebs and squares of yesterday's news, hanging from a rusting nail on the back of the mouldy wooden door. Not a place to linger for any length of time. A minute later she climbed the steep dimly lit stairs to her sparse bedroom, closing the blackout drapes before she lit the paraffin lamp. She washed quickly in a basin of ice cold water, before climbing exhausted into a cold bed. She was asleep instantly, but was woken by voices half an hour later.

'No please Jack, the girl is only next door, she'll hear us.' Rachel heard her aunt plead. A short, sharp, slap silenced her aunt, followed swiftly by animal grunting noises, as he demanded his marital rights. Rachel covered her ears with her hands and buried her head under the blankets in disgust.

Rachel was awakened the next morning by the ferocity of her bedroom door being pushed open. Jack stood over her glowering. 'Gerup. Tha's a job to go and see about. Tha's to report to Mr Hardacre at t' Mill at eight o clock sharp. D'ya hear me? He knows about tha condition, so don't think tha going to lie abed and shirk work, tha's months of work in tha yet, so, gerup!' He slammed the door as he left.

Rachel shivered as she slipped her feet into her slippers. She washed quickly and dressed warmly. Downstairs, there was a pan of porridge, stiff and grey in colour, made with only water and salt, she forced a mouthful down, but balked at the taste, she had never liked porridge, but there was nothing else in the house to eat.

She had a little bit of money left after her train fare, so she bought a loaf of bread on the way to the mill and the warm smell it emitted made her stomach rumble, prompting her to tear a piece from the crust and eat it on the hoof.

Dewhurst Mill was a huge daunting building, half a mile from Aunty May's house. As she approached, the noise from winding machines became almost deafening. She found Mr Hardacre's office on the ground floor of the main building. She knocked on the door, but there was no reply. She knocked again. 'Alright, alright, don't break t'door down,' she heard a gruff voice from within. She stood for a moment, unsure of what to do until the voice shouted, 'Well, come in then for Christ sake.'

She entered, and her eyes swept over the dingy office. The room was sparsely furnished with a large wooden desk, a telephone and two wooden filing cabinets. The windows were grimy, laced with cobwebs and the place smelt of stale sweat and tobacco.

'When tha's finished gawping tha can sit down,' Hardacre hissed.

Rachel promptly sat. Hardacre was a truly unpleasant human being. He was ugly and bald headed except for a strip of hair that was combed over and stuck to his head with its own grease. He had a greedy mouth and small piggy eyes which leered at her. His clothes were black and stained with food, and he was probably in his fifties Rachel surmised.

'So, tha be Jack Taylor's niece ista? Well tha better get used to hard work lass, there is no soft option here for you southerners tha knows. I know tha's up the...' He paused for a moment and smiled thinly, 'in the family way, but that doesn't give you the right to slack. Do I mek myself clear?'

'Crystal,' Rachel said nonchalantly.

Hardacre regarded her reproachfully. 'Any trouble from you lass and tha'll be out on your ear. Be here at seven-thirty sharp tomorrow. You'll be inspecting and boxing reels of cotton.'

*

Arriving for her first day at work, that cold grey November morning, the huge stone built factory walls loomed high and foreboding. The factory's siren pitched loud and piercing into the morning sky, warning workers to get to their work stations. Rachel quickened her step, her uncovered legs feeling the chilly air. Oh how she longed for Cornwall and its warm wet winters. After reporting to the works office, Rachel was shown into the changing room, where crowds of women of various size, shape and age were clad in brown overalls and turban-tied scarves. A moment later, Rachel was led out onto the factory floor, and the white cotton dust and deafening din of the huge winding machines attacked her senses. It was awful, but a means to an end, soon she would save enough money to find somewhere of her own to live. She cradled her tummy - she knew she needed somewhere safe to bring up her little one. At the end of her exhausting first week, her dream was shattered as she waited in line for her pay packet, only to be told it had been collected by her uncle.

*

The early part of the winter seemed endless. With mid December came the rain which lashed the Yorkshire moors for days on end, streams became rivers, fields became quagmires, roads impassable with floods. After the rain, came the snow, a thick blanket of white stretched over the whole county of Yorkshire, then the frost, hard and biting, lasted through Christmas until early January.

Day after day, Rachel trudged through freezing rain, hail and snow all through that long winter of 1939/40. The first Christmas in wartime was a miserable affair for Rachel. She would walk home from the factory in the run up to Christmas, trying to catch glimpses of Christmas cheer through chinks in the blackout curtains. It seemed that not even the war would put a halt to the festivities, except of course for Aunty May and Uncle Jack's house. Their house remained void of any Christmas fare. There was no tree, or Christmas dinner, just the same meagre meal that they always ate. It was all Aunty May could produce on the sparse housekeeping money she was given by Jack, even though he earned a good wage working as a gardener and handyman for the Davenports at Stone Field Manor on the outskirts of Skipton. As for the money Rachel brought in, well that was spent by Jack in the Rose and Crown. She was allowed no money, and it grieved her that she couldn't afford a wedding card to send to Emma and Robin. This was her lot for the time being, her only other option was the workhouse.

13

In complete contrast to the Yorkshire weather, Christmas Eve in Cornwall dawned bright and warm. The daffodils were already showing their yellow petticoats along the road verges, which painted a pretty picture as the newly married Emma and Robin Ferris-Norton rode into Gweek by horse and carriage, kindly lent to them by Dougie Trengrath. Emma was the picture of happiness, dressed in a long white gown with a matching cloak and hood. Though she could never be looked on as particularly pretty, with her rosy cheeks and shining eyes she was undisputedly handsome on this her wedding day.

There was no doubt, Robin would have sold his soul to the devil for one glimpse of his happy new wife, but he remained content that his future would no longer be dark, empty and lonely, now that he had been blessed with his wonderful Emma.

As the carriage rattled through the village, people turned out to cheer and throw rice. The young children from the village ran after the carriage all the way to Barleyfield farm, where they waited noisily for Robin to throw hot pennies at them, which was the custom on such occasions. There were squeals of pain as many burned their fingers in the brawl, and many an old score was settled, as the inevitable punch-up evolved. Emma winced as she watched from her front door, but a penny was a penny, whether it was hot or not, and remembered doing the self same thing not so very long ago.

The wedding breakfast was laid out in the vast dining room at Barleyfield farm. There was a roaring fire lit and mulled wine to greet the guests before they all sat down and ate a hearty early Christmas dinner, washed down with copious glasses of champagne, Robin had had stowed away in the dark recesses of his cellar.

Everyone commented on how fine the farm looked now. It no longer looked stark and uninviting.

'Everything you see is all Emma's work,' Robin commented, making Emma blush slightly.

Emma had painstakingly scrubbed and painted the rooms. Now they shone as bright as sunshine. New furniture had been purchased and rich warm drapes now hung at the windows.

'And I have never been so well fed and looked after as I am now,' he added, as he patted his stomach. Emma thoughtfully laid her hand upon his arm, he covered it with his own and with unseeing eyes he looked straight at her. He scraped the chair back and stood to raise a glass to his young wife. 'To you my lovely wife, I thank God and Adam de Sousa for sending you to me.'

Everyone stood up. 'To Emma, God and Adam de Sousa,' the guests repeated, before draining their glasses.

As they all settled back to the table, Robin enquired, 'Tell me Lizzy have you heard anything from either Adam or Rachel?'

Rolling her eyes heavenwards she said, 'Not a word from either of them.'

'Do you think they are together?' Harry said hopefully.

'I'd like to think so Harry, but I think Rachel would have written to tell me.' In her heart, Lizzy was dismayed that she had not heard a word from her friend. It annoyed her a little as well if the truth be known, that Rachel hadn't contacted her to let her know she was alright. There hadn't even been a card sent congratulating Emma and Robin, though Lizzy knew full well that Rachel knew of the forthcoming wedding before she upped and left like she did.

Emma watched her mother's countenance with interest, knowing how much she missed Rachel - a lot more than she would admit. With that, Emma stood up and raised her glass. 'May I propose a toast, to absent friends?' Again, a resounding chorus followed. 'Absent friends.'

As the day progressed the men folk retired to the front parlour with their brandy and cigars, as Lizzy and Emma, who had insisted on helping with the clearing, were in the kitchen washing the dishes. As the last of the plates were stored away in the cupboard, Lizzy turned to her only daughter and smiled. It was quiet in the kitchen, Emma laid her teacloth on the Aga and looked deeply into her mother's eyes as if she knew she was about to say something profound.

'Will you be alright tonight?' she asked with love.

Emma smiled shyly. 'I'll be fine mum, don't worry about me. Robin is a good and kind man. I know he will be gentle.' She blushed as she spoke.

Lizzy gathered her daughter into her bosom and held her so tight Emma feared she would suffocate. Finally, she let her go and kissed her lightly on the forehead. 'You looked beautiful today child, the most beautiful bride I have ever seen.'

Emma smiled warmly; she knew she could never be classed as a beauty. 'I think you are a little biased mum.'

Lizzy shook her head. 'Beauty comes from within, and you my dear, dear girl are a truly beautiful human being.'

'I'll second that,' Robin's voice filtered through the kitchen. They both turned and Lizzy wiped a stray tear from her cheek.

'Forgive me for intruding,' Robin said happily. 'But Charlie is getting the coats.'

There was a flurry of kisses and hugs, goodbyes and well wishes as they all piled out of the door into the chill evening air. As they stood at the kitchen door and waved their goodbyes, Robin wrapped his arm around Emma to ward off the cold. When Lizzy and Charlie were out of sight, they closed the door and walked hand in hand up the stairs to Robin's bedroom, where they tenderly and gently started their married life together.

14

The onset of spring in Yorkshire gave no respite to the cold weather, whereas in Cornwall, Rachel knew the sun would be warming the ground, and summer was just around the corner. The first spell of hot weather came on June the first and lasted all but two weeks before it broke with a terrific thunderstorm on the eve of Skipton town holiday closedown. This was also the day her baby Fiona entered the world.

She was delivered safely and noisily by caesarean operation, which was performed ten miles away at Keighley Victoria Hospital. Five days later Rachel and baby were transferred to the Maternity Hospital in Skipton where she was to recuperate for the next nine days. It was a happy time for Rachel, happy to be away from the everyday drudge of life at Aunty May's house, but the happiness was to be short lived.

Seven days after giving birth, Rachel fell ill with Scarlet Fever and was separated from her baby when Rachel was sent to an isolation ward. It was to be the last time Rachel saw her baby. During her illness and while she was unable to function properly, her Uncle Jack had pushed some papers under her nose, telling her to sign so the child could be taken home to be looked after until she was well enough to leave hospital. Ten minutes later under the canal bridge, some two hundred yards from the hospital, Jack handed the tiny bundle, still with the name tag on her wrist, which read, 'baby girl Pendarves', over to a smartly dressed man. A hundred pounds was handed over, which Jack stuffed into his inside pocket.

Fifteen miles away in a large country house, a wet nurse and nanny was making ready a nursery, as Daphne Davenport waited in the drawing room for her husband Cedric and her new baby to arrive.

When the car pulled onto the gravel drive of Stone Field Manor, Daphne stood up and walked to the fireplace. The child was placed in the arms of a wet nurse, and Rachel's baby was taken upstairs to the nursery.

As Cedric entered the drawing room, Daphne asked, 'Is everything alright?'

Cedric poured two glasses of whisky. 'The child's mother died, there should be no repercussions,' he said, as he handed a glass to Daphne. 'You'll have to think of a name for her.'

She took a sip of whisky, feeling it burn the back of her dry throat. 'She will be called Helena,' she announced smugly. 'Aunt Helena will be flattered that we have named her after her. They exchanged knowing glances. Suddenly, her eyes narrowed. 'You did give the money to the poor girl's family didn't you?'

'Of course.' He gestured with his free hand 'One hundred pounds, as promised.'

Daphne thought for a moment about the girl dying to give her this gift, sighed happily and chinked glasses with her husband. At last all their worries were over.

They could hear the baby cry in a distant room. Daphne rolled her eyes. 'I hope that noise doesn't go on all night,' she said.

*

Two weeks later, Rachel recovered enough to leave hospital. It was raining when she stepped out of the hospital door. There was no-one there to pick her up, but then she hadn't thought there would be. Dressed in a dowdy beige raincoat, and flat brown sandals, she tied a headscarf around her hair and stepped out into the rain. It was a good mile and a half walk to the centre of Skipton and though all she carried was a small scuffed leather suitcase, she was exhausted by the time she reached the bottom of Aunty May's street. She sat against a stone windowsill and caught her breath for a moment. Conduit

Street was the steepest of all the rows of terrace houses which sat high above Skipton town centre. It was almost a one in four gradient and consisted of sixty two houses on each side - Aunty May's house was number forty two. Rachel was tired, but the growing excitement of being reunited with her baby, her little daughter, who she had named Fiona, urged her to pick up her suitcase and start the steep ascent of the street. Minutes later she stood at number forty-two and knocked exhaustedly on the shabby door. She waited before eventually knocking again. Keen to gain entry she knocked harder then lifted the letter box and shouted, 'Aunty May, it's me Rachel. Can you let me in please?'

'Oh Rachel is that you? Thank God. Tha'll have to come round t'back luv. The front door is locked and I can't get up to open it,' she said, in a small frail voice.

Rachel sighed exhaustedly and set off up the steep hill. By the time she rounded the top of the hill and picked her way down the slippery cobbled back street to Aunty May's back yard, Rachel was soaked through to the skin. She turned the handle and pushed the heavy wooden door open. The house was dark and foreboding and all the curtains were pulled shut. 'Aunty May where are you and why are you sitting in the dark?'

'I'm here, down here,' said a frail voice.

Rachel spun around and found Aunty May at the bottom of the stairs. 'Oh my goodness, what on earth happened?' she cried.

'I fell yesterday,' May wailed. 'I think I have twisted my ankle and wrist.'

'Yesterday! And you mean to tell me you've been there since then? Where is Uncle Jack? Why hasn't he helped you?' Panic rose into her throat. '..And the baby? Who's been looking after the baby?'

'Baby?' May shook her head, slightly confused at her question. 'I don't know where Jack is - he didn't come home last night. He appears to have come into some money, so he's been out drinking most nights.'

Rachel could hardly contain her anger as she dragged a chair towards her aunt and gently lifted her onto it. She shook her head pitifully when she realised her aunt weighed nothing. 'Jack would have done better to buy some decent food for you to eat, instead of frittering his money on drink,' she said to May crossly.

May cried out in pain when Rachel checked her ankle and wrist. 'I'm going to call for the doctor, but first I must see if the baby is okay. Where is she?'

Again, puzzlement crossed May's face. 'Your baby isn't here Rachel.'

'What?' Rachel was puzzled now, though slightly relieved that she was somewhere else being cared for. 'Well, where is she then?'

May, looked at her blankly.

Rachel felt a cold chill run through her body. 'Aunty May, where is she?'

May swallowed hard then croaked. 'She's been adopted. You sent her for adoption!'

Rachel felt as though she had been stabbed. She reeled back against the sink. 'Adopted? I never sent her for adoption! I wouldn't do such a thing. She's my baby, my precious little daughter. Why would I have her adopted?'

May looked as though she was going to faint. 'Jack said you signed the papers.'

'Papers?' She searched desperately through her mind as to what she had signed while she was in hospital. She shook her head. 'No, no, I signed my baby's release form that's all. Uncle Jack said the baby would be better at home until I recovered from the fever.' A moment later the colour from May's face drained and she promptly fainted.

As Rachel held her aunt in her arms, she felt her own world collapse. Plunged into a misery so raw her body ached with the grief which engulfed her. It was only the painful squeak of Aunty May's voice which brought her back from her wretchedness, as the old woman cried, 'Rachel, I'm sorry, but please could you help me. I need a doctor.'

The doctor arrived two hours later. He was a short grumpy little man, who didn't even try to hide his disgust at the terrible state of the house. He barked orders at Rachel to help him get May upstairs, refusing to hear her protests, that she had just given birth and shouldn't really be lifting anything heavy at the moment. 'Just get on with it,' he shouted. 'You lazy good for nothing girl - you should be ashamed of yourself, letting this house get into such a state, so that your poor mother falls and injures herself like this.'

'But....'

'Hold your tongue,' he snapped.

Aunty May tried to retaliate in Rachel's defence, but she was swiftly told to lay quiet while he strapped her ankle and wrist. Rachel stood silently seething behind the doctor until he had finished. 'Right, my dear woman, you must stay there and rest, do you hear me? This is the second time you have fallen! Did you go for those tests I sent you for last week?' May nodded.

'Right, I'll speak to the hospital when I get back to the surgery.' He swiftly turned on Rachel. 'And you.' He stabbed a finger into her shoulder. 'Get off your lazy backside and get this hovel cleaned up. I can't abide sloth in anyone.' He picked up his bag and stormed out of the bedroom, leaving Rachel flabbergasted.

'Oh Rachel dear,' Aunty May cried, 'I am so sorry for his rudeness, he had no right to say anything like that to you.'

Rachel shook her head and knelt at her bedside, tucking the thin torn eiderdown about the old woman. 'It doesn't matter Aunty May. I'll make you a cup of strong tea and then I'll have to go out and get some groceries. I don't suppose there is anything in the house to make even a broth is there?'

May shook her head. 'I haven't got any money to buy

anything, but you might be able to get something on the tick from Mr Inman the greengrocers,' she answered sadly.

'Don't worry Aunty May, I'll sort something out, but then I'm sorry I'll have to leave you for a while. I need to go and see what I can do about my baby.' As she said the words, they choked in her throat.

'What do you mean do?'

'Well, there must be someone I can go to, to find out where she is. I have to get her back, I just have to!'

*

The next few hours were a living hell for Rachel, as she tried without success to find out where her baby had been taken to. Her meeting with the adoption agency drew a blank. There were no official adoption papers for her child - it seemed that Jack had made a secret deal with someone. With this information, Rachel went straight to the Police Station. The sergeant listened to Rachel's allegation.

'Jack Taylor you say?'

Rachel nodded.

'Kevin,' he called to the officer who was standing behind him.

'Yes sarge?'

'Don't we have a Jack Taylor in custody?'

'Certainly do,' he answered. 'Came in last night, drunk as a lord he was, fighting drunk at that, he took a swing for me you know?'

'Put him in the interview room, Kevin. You can sit over there until we've had a word with him.' He gestured towards a hard wooden chair in the corner.

Jack who was nursing a sore head, roared with laughter at Rachel's allegations. He shook his head. 'You don't want to be listening to her, the girl's simple. She's always fantasizing about having a baby. She does it all the time, goes around telling everyone I keep selling her babies. She's more to be pitied than scolded. It's no wonder I turned to drink.' He grinned.

When the sergeant appeared, Rachel stood up. 'Right you, out.'

'What?'

'You heard me, get out. Just think yourself lucky I'm not charging you with wasting precious police time. I haven't got time to deal with simpletons like you who make up stories, so go on, get out and if I see you here again I'll have you thrown in the cell.'

Rachel stood and looked at him incredulously. 'You're not going to believe a drunk over me, are you?'

'I said get out. Now.'

'But you don't understand. He sold my baby!'

The sergeant moved around the counter, grabbed her by the arm and forcibly moved her out of the door. With a sharp push, he sent her flying down the steps. Rachel fell heavily and grazed her knees. The sergeant stood for a moment with a self-satisfied smile on his lips, brushed his hands together and returned inside.

Rachel sat for a long time on the roadside, hugging her knees to her chest, sobbing at the hopelessness of her situation.

*

By eleven that evening, Jack had not arrived home and Rachel's anger had still not alleviated. She made sure Aunty May had all she needed before she began the steep climb up the stairs to her dingy bedroom. Closing the blackout drapes, she sat at her dressing table in the dim light of a paraffin lamp. She sat for a long time, staring into silent shadows, her eyes bloodshot with conflict and confusion, listening for the moment when Uncle Jack would finally reel home. She was just about to climb into her bed when the slam of the front door shuddered throughout the house. Rachel felt her pulse race as she heard him climb the stairs to the first floor, then her heart leapt into her throat as he began to climb the second flight of stairs. A moment later he stormed into her bedroom, slapped his cold drunken hands across her tear-stained cheek, and then grabbed her by the shoulders, his dirty fingernails cutting into her flesh.

'You stupid bitch. How dare you try and get me into trouble after all we've done for you.'

'What *you've* done for me?' Rachel screamed incredulously. 'How dare you. You've done nothing for me, nothing, except steal my baby.'

He slapped her hard again across the cheek. 'You didn't think for one minute that you were going to keep that brat did you?'

'She's my baby! Tell me where she is? You had no right to steal her, she's mine!' Her voice was high pitched and the words came out in great sobs.

'Oh, I have every right. Anyway the brat was lucky to find such a good home. A good god fearing family it's with now, so you should thank me.'

'Thank you!' Rachel cried. 'Thank you! How *dare* you, I curse you for what you've done, may God, strike you dead for what you've done, she was mine.'

'Do you really think I would have somebody's bastard under my roof? It's bad enough having a whore living here, I'll be damned if I give her bastard house room as well. So my girl, you are going to pay for what you did today. You're going to earn your keep, and not just at the Mill.' His eyes glinted as they fell upon her breasts. 'Or it'll be the workhouse for you.' Intent on taking her, he moved onto the bed, Rachel opened her mouth to scream, but Jack covered her mouth with his grimy hand, the weight pushing her down, embedding her head and shoulders into the straw mattress. 'Let's see if you're owt like as good as yer dear mother. She fought like 'ell with me as well, but by god I took 'er in the end. She came 'ear, wi 'er fancy ways, putting stupid thoughts into our May's 'ed. Flounced around all dolled up like a dogs dinner. But I showed 'er what for. She was gone the next morning, taking her stupid ideas with 'er.'

Rachel could not believe what she was hearing. Her

poor beloved mother had killed herself because of what this monster had done to her. The suicide made sense now. With all her strength, Rachel fought him, flaying at his sweating flesh with her fists, until she felt his weight upon her, and she could fight no more. As he fumbled with her nightdress with his rough hands, Rachel mustered up all her strength and pushed him with her hands, bringing her knee up to his groin, sending him crashing from the bed. His great hulk thrashed about moaning on the threadbare carpet for a few seconds, but by the time he'd managed to scramble to his feet, Rachel had leapt from the bed and was stood over him. With sheer anger in her eyes, she held the standard lamp upside down with the iron base in readiness to administer what would be a murderous thud to his skull if he dared to touch her again.

He weighed her up for a moment, then stood and spat at her feet. 'Get out of my house,' he barked.

Rachel held her stance.

'Be gone tomorrow night or else,' he threatened. With that he stormed out of the bedroom, slamming the door behind him.

Rachel ran to shut the door and for good measure, she pulled the worm eaten sideboard to wedge it shut. Her heart was racing so that she could hardly breathe. She sat on the carpet and wept. She wept first in relief, then the tears fell from her face in great swollen droplets for her poor dear mother, then the baby she knew had gone from her life forever, and finally for Adam. 'Why did you abandon us Adam, why?' she cried.

Rachel lay on the carpet all night, sleep having overcome her by the early hours. She was woken by a loud thump on her bedroom door as Jack banged his fist against it. 'See that you are out of my house today, you whore, or else,' he growled.

Rachel's heart began to race again at the sound of his voice, but the fear subsided when it was clear Jack was descending the stairs. She waited, listening intently for the front door to bang shut, and then glanced out of the window and watched Jack march down the street. Once the bedroom door was clear of the sideboard, she slipped downstairs and knocked on Aunty May's door. Aunty May was crying.

'I won't leave you here Aunty May,' Rachel said, kneeling at the side of her bed. 'I'll find somewhere for us both to live today. I won't leave you here.'

Aunty May shook her head. 'Don't you worry about me - I shall not be here after today.' Rachel furrowed her brow. 'You see, I'm ill, some blood disorder the doctor told me when he came back yesterday afternoon, that's why I fell you see. I have to go into hospital today, and..' She paused for a moment. 'I won't ever be coming out.'

'Oh, Aunty May.' Rachel kissed her bony hand and wept.

'Don't cry for me Rachel, you must see to yourself now. I am so sorry that Jack has told you to leave, I can't persuade him otherwise, he won't listen to me, and in truth I suspect you don't really want to stay under his roof for much longer anyway, do you?'

'To tell you the truth, I can't wait to get out of here.' She regarded her aunt for a moment. 'Did you know what he did to Mum?'

'What do you mean?'

When Rachel explained, May responded by being physically sick. Rachel quickly cleaned her up, but her aunt was inconsolable. 'Oh my god, I'd no idea. I thought it was me. I thought I had done something to upset her. She just upped and left that day without a by-your-leave. The next I heard, your father wrote and told me she'd drowned.'

Rachel put her arms around her aunt to comfort her, and they lay there in shared grief.

Presently, May blew her nose and said, 'What on earth will you do, Rachel?'

Rachel shook her head. 'I really don't know.'

'The Salvation Army might help.'

Rachel nodded. 'I might try them yes. I'll come back this afternoon to get my things before Jack gets home. I take it he has gone to work?' May nodded that he had. Rachel stood up, kissed Aunty May goodbye. 'Will you still be here, when I get back?'

May nodded. 'If you're back before three, yes I will. The doctor said he would call at three, and I suspect that the ambulance will call shortly afterwards.'

'I'll be back before three, I promise.'

Her first port of call was indeed the Salvation Army, but as she was about to step through the old wooden doors of the dark ominous building where they operated from, her eye caught sight of a poster. It was a woman dressed in shirt and breeches, holding a pitchfork. The heading read:

'FOR A HEALTHY HAPPY JOB, JOIN THE WOMAN'S LAND ARMY.'

Rachel traced her finger along the small print and jotted the address of where to enlist on the back of a scrap of paper.

*

Just as Rachel was making her way towards the WLA recruitment office to enlist, Adam de Sousa was taking his first tentative steps around the grounds of the rehabilitation centre he had spent the last ten months in.

The beating he had sustained at the hands of Sam Blewett had almost cost him his life. It had indeed cost him dearly. His speech was impaired, though improving daily, and the kick to the head had caused a blood clot in his brain, which although had been successfully operated on, had left him weak down his right side and unable to walk unaided - until this bright sunny August day.

Slowly but surely, Adam was getting stronger each day. The one thing that kept him going was the thought of Rachel, he was determined to return to Cornwall and find her. For the first five months, Adam had been barely conscious, but as soon as he was able, he had enlisted the help of one of the nurses, who painstakingly deciphered his muffled slurred words, in order to write a letter to Rachel. In it, he explained what had happened, and where he was, he also sent money to her so that she could join him. This was sent to The Black Swan in April, and Adam had waited in anticipation, but no return letter came. He surmised that she must have left the hotel, as was their plan. As soon as he was strong enough to make the journey, he would go in search of her.

The letter had arrived, but Sally Blewett had picked up the envelope which bore Rachel's name, opened it, read it, laughed, pocketed the money and burnt the letter in the fire.

*

After Rachel's medical at the WLA, she was shown into a small office and asked to take a seat opposite a woman dressed in WLA service uniform. Her eyes swept over the room. It was drab and dingy, like everything in this war.

The administrator flipped open a folder, scanned the pages for a brief moment then leant forward slightly and clasped her hands together. 'My papers say you are Rachel Pendarves. You are twenty-eight-years-old, widowed, with no children. Is this correct?'

'Yes,' Rachel mumbled.

'Speak up girl, we need to hear what you are saying,' the woman said jovially. 'Your address is forty-two Conduit Street, Skipton, is this correct?'

'Yes, but I shall be leaving tonight.'

The administrator looked up. 'To go where?'

'Not sure, but I'll let you know.'

The administrator nodded. 'Living relatives?'

Rachel paused for a moment. 'An aunt and uncle, at that address.'

The administrator smiled softly. 'We can't promise you

will be billeted near Skipton.'

'I don't want to be.'

The woman raised an eyebrow.

'I want to be as far away as possible,' Rachel continued.

She broke into a broad smile. 'Well Mrs Pendarves, you will attend a short training course where you be taught a number of farming issues, such as milking cows. On most farms, your duties will include, threshing, ploughing, tractor driving, reclaiming land, drainage, etc. What we don't teach you, you will learn on the job.' She added a smile. 'You will be paid one pound twelve pence a week after all deductions have been made for your lodgings and food. This wage is set by the Agricultural Wages Board,' she added.

Rachel nodded.

'Welcome to the WLA Rachel, you will be invaluable to your country.'

'Thank you.'

Minutes later Rachel was issued with a WLA day-to-day uniform, which consisted of brown corduroy breeches, two fawn short sleeved shirts, one pair of brown brogues, two pairs of fawn knee-length woollen socks and a green v-necked pullover. One bib and brace overall, one pair of rubber boots, one long Mackintosh for the winter and a brown wide brimmed hat. She was also issued a service uniform which was to be used for special occasions.

*

Later that afternoon, she knelt by Aunt May's bed. The old woman reached out a work worn hand and gently touched Rachel's cheek. 'You are ready to go then? I heard you emptying your wardrobe and chest of drawers.'

Rachel nodded.

'Have you found somewhere to stay?'

'Yes,' Rachel lied, for she had no idea where she would stay tonight. 'I've joined the WLA. I'm not sure where I will be billeted.'

Aunty May smiled gently. 'It's perhaps what you need

Rachel. What was done here was not done well, and I think you need to go and rebuild your life. The WLA will be a challenge, I have no doubt, but I know you girl, I know how strong you are, both physically and in here.' She pressed her bony hand on Rachel's heart. 'You will come through this Rachel, you may not have your child with you in person, but she will always be here in your heart. You will always be her mother. I pray the hurt will fade as the years pass. And I pray that you will find love one day and start another family. I also pray that you will forgive me for not being able to help you keep your little Fiona.'

Hot tears tumbled down Rachel's cheeks. She held her Aunt's hand and kissed it. 'I am so worried about leaving you Aunty May, what with you being so ill.'

May shook her head. 'I don't want you to fret for me. Do you hear me? Yes I am ill, and in truth, I'm not long for this world. My tired old body is giving up, I know that, but I've had a hard life with Jack, and if my time is up, death does not pose any great worry for me.' She grinned slightly. 'I'll be glad of the rest to tell you the truth.'

'Oh Aunty May,' Rachel cried as she nestled into the bedclothes.

'Come on my child, no more tears. I want you to do something for me.'

'Anything,' Rachel said ardently.

With a bony finger, May pointed to the curtains. 'Take a look inside the hem of the left curtain.'

Rachel looked puzzled, but did as she was told. Her hand came upon a package which she grasped and brought out. 'What is it?'

'Bring it here,' May beckoned. With trembling fingers, she opened the brown package. 'Ah, just as I thought,' she said. 'I saw Jack hide this last night.'

'What is it?' Rachel asked again.

'If my guess is correct, this is the money he got in return for baby Fiona.' Rachel looked horror stuck as May quickly counted its contents. 'Sixty-one pounds,' she said in a self-satisfied tone. 'Here girl, it's yours,'

Rachel reeled back. 'I don't want his dirty money.'

'It's not his, it's yours,' May insisted, pressing the money in her hand.

'No, I can't, it's wrong... my baby,' she whispered quietly. 'How could you think I could take that money when it was gained in such a terrible way?'

'Rachel, be reasonable, what is done is done. This is yours, even if you don't spend it. It's yours to save for the day your daughter comes looking for her real mother.' A shocked look flashed across Rachel's eyes. 'Oh yes Rachel, she will come looking for you. It's natural to want to know. I'm not saying it will be soon. Oh no, it could be years from now. But she will come, you mark my words.'

Rachel was shaking her head. 'She won't. She doesn't know who I am. She never will. It was all done illegally - she'll never be able to find me.' The tears once again streamed down her face.

'Rachel, listen to me, you must go back to the adoption agency and register all your details with them, the date she was born, who you are, and more importantly where you are living. But make sure you always update your details if you ever move on. That way, Fiona will stand a chance of finding you, and you will get your daughter back. Now take this money, even if you take it so that Jack cannot benefit from it, put it in the poor box if you must, but take it.' May's tone was darkly serious, and Rachel very reluctantly took the dirty money from her hand and pushed it deep into her jacket pocket.

Satisfied, May nodded. 'Now go girl, before that doctor has a chance to verbally abuse you again.'

Rachel laughed softly, kissed her gently on the cheek, picked up her belongings, of which there were few, and left number forty-two Conduit Street forever.

15

The Women's Land Army was made up of girls from every walk of life. Rachel was fortunate in more ways than one. First she was billeted with two of the nicest girls she could ever expect to meet. Secondly she got her wish to be as far away from Skipton as possible, finding herself posted to Runstone Manor Farm on the far outskirts of Widecombe-in-the-moor, in the heart of Dartmoor.

Runstone Manor Farm was run by John Hewbey and his wife Katie. There had been a couple of farm hands there until they enlisted, hence the need for help. Rachel arrived at the railway station two weeks after the other two girls and John Hewbey was there to greet her.

His heart sank when he saw her. He had hoped for some burly country girl, especially since the other two girls didn't seem to have a muscle between them, but this one seemed even scrawnier.

Rachel could read the disappointment on his weathered handsome face as she approached with her brown suitcase. She held out her hand to shake his and Hewbey noted how strong her handshake was. 'I'm very pleased to meet you Mr Hewbey,' she said smiling. 'Please don't be alarmed by my slight appearance, I'm stronger than I look. I'm a good worker and not afraid of hard work.'

John raised his thick dark eyebrows in amusement. 'Let's hope so,' he said dryly.

Rachel made the journey to Runstone, cramped in the back of a Standard Fordson tractor, and every now and then John would glance at her and mouth the words, 'Alright?'

Rachel smiled and nodded that she was. She was glad that he was so friendly and could tell in his eyes that he possessed a kindly disposition. He was not a tall man, probably only five feet eight in his stocking feet, but he was stocky in build. He had a mop of dark dusty, untidy hair, which was partially hidden under a well worn flat cap and a smile which sported a partially missing front tooth, which in Rachael's opinion, slightly spoilt his rugged good looks. She surmised that John Hewbey was probably in his early forties. Twenty minutes later, the tractor entered the village of Runstone and Rachel got her first view of Runstone Manor Farm. It was a fine looking fifteenth century building, with a thatched roof and an arched porch at the entrance to the front garden. Inside, Rachel cast a speculative eye over the kitchen. The room was large and warm, with a table at the centre which stood upon a stone floor. Rachel was introduced to Katie, a large jolly looking woman, with a huge bosom who was busy baking at the table.

'Take a seat my love,' Katie said kindly. 'I'll make us all a nice cup of tea. John, will you stay for one?'

'Too busy today Katie my sweet, too busy. I'll be seeing you later.' He turned on his heel and made for the door.

'I'll be out to help as soon as I have changed Mr Hewbey,' Rachel said eagerly.

John roared with laughter. 'Gosh no. You get yourself settled in today. There'll be plenty for you to do tomorrow. Enjoy your cuppa, and I'm sure my Katie will offer you a slice of her wonderful fruit cake.' He winked cheekily at his wife, and then was gone.

Rachel settled down in the cosy kitchen, warmed by the huge black range. She felt her cheeks turn pink and quickly began to take off her hat and scarf.

'Well now my love,' Katie said, placing the said tea and cake in front of her. 'Eat up. My, but you look as thin as a stick. I shall have to fatten you up, I can see that, though not as fat as me eh?' She laughed, sticking her fists into her generous hips. 'This is with babies. Well, that's my excuse anyway.' She chuckled. 'Got another one tucked up in here, so I have, due any day now. This 'e'll be my fourth,' she said proudly. Rachel looked around for evidence of more children. 'Nay my love, they're not around at the moment. Jake is my eldest.' She sighed heavily. 'Jake didn't really care for farm work, well, in truth he and John were always at loggerheads and never got on. Jake was a gentle sort of lad, always praying he was, never away from the church you know. Now don't get me wrong, I have nothing against praying folk, but twice, sometimes three times a day he would walk up to Widecombe, it drove John mad when he needed him on the farm. Anyway, Jake could take no more of John's dissatisfaction and he left last year to go on a retreat at the Abbey down the valley.'

Rachel's eyes widened. 'To be a monk you mean?'

'Aye my love, to be a monk, would you believe? He converted to Catholicism too! I just hope he's happy in his world now, that's all I ask.' She glanced surreptitiously towards the door her husband had left from a few minutes earlier and said in a hushed tone, 'John won't hear his name spoken, so don't mention that I've told you okay?' Rachel nodded. Katie rubbed her floury hands down her apron, picked up the tray of pies she was making and walked towards the Aga. With a kick of her foot, the Aga door was shut. 'Now then where was I, oh yes, then there was Jamie...' Rachel watched as Katie's eyes filled with tears. 'Jamie died, when he was five, almost twelve years ago now, still reduces me to tears when I think of him,' she said sorrowfully. 'You never forget you know, never,' she added seriously. 'And then there is Jacob. Jacob is still on the farm, you'll meet him at dinner. Now you mustn't be frightened of Jacob. He's a great lummox of a lump, a bit simple, probably the I.Q of a daffodil, but harmless enough and a strong as an ox, John couldn't do without him around the farm.' Rachel couldn't help but smile at Katie's description of her son. 'Oh you can smile, but you'll see what I mean when you meet him at tea time,' she said knowingly.

'How old is Jacob?'

'He'll be sixteen next birthday. The doctors said he wouldn't see his tenth birthday, pha! What do they know? The lad doesn't ail a thing, thank the lord.' Katie seemed to pause for a moment as though reflecting on something. 'Well my dear, we have had to call in the help of the WLA, John may have already told you that all our hands have gone and enlisted. If it was just farming for us, I suspect we would have managed with just one extra pair of hands, but you see at the start of the war the government created committees, known to us farmers as the WarAg. Each area committee has to produce a set amount. We farmers were given orders and told how much wheat, potatoes and sugar beet to grow. I know they have a difficult job to do, Britain needs to be fed, but I must say this has caused quite a lot of problems in some areas, because the ground is just not suitable for certain crops. We're lucky here, the soil is good and we can grow almost anything. I don't think we will starve through this damn war,' she said, offering Rachel another slice of cake which Rachel refused gracefully. 'Right,' she said pointing to the Aga. 'The pies are in, the veg chopped, everything's ready for tea I think, so I'll just show you up to your room before they all descend on me. You'll be sharing with Vera and Peggy, they are nice girls. I think you'll all get on a treat.

They climbed the dimly lit staircase, and Katie pushed open a door and stepped in. 'Come in my love, here it is. I'm sure you'll be comfortable here,' she said, patting the freshly made bed.

'Oh I'm sure I will Mrs Hewbey thank you.'

'Now you must call me Katie, everyone else does and John's John, okay?'

'Okay.' Rachel smiled with gratitude at her kindness.

Katie walked towards the door then stopped and smiled kindly. 'The WLA told us you were widowed my love.' Rachel nodded sadly. 'Was it an early casualty of war?' Katie enquired.

Rachel swallowed hard and shook her head. 'He was murdered. Killed by his best friend,' her words were hardly audible.

Katie held her hands to her face in horror. 'Oh my poor girl, why ever did he do that? Oh no, sorry it's none of my business, I'm sure you don't want to talk about it, sorry I asked.'

'It's alright Mrs. I mean Katie, he killed my husband because he..he wanted me for himself.' She lowered her eyes as she finished the last word. 'The thing is I loathed him from the start. I never gave him encouragement at all. He just got it into his stupid head that I would marry him! Oh but Katie, I've racked my brains to try and remember if I gave him an inkling that I would be interested, but I'm sure I didn't, I'm absolutely sure of it.'

'I'm sure you didn't too my love. It was probably just all in his mind. People do strange things when they think they are in love,' Katie said softly. 'I'll see you at teatime. You get yourself settled in.' Suddenly, Katie pushed her hand into the side of her hip. 'Oh,' she said thoughtfully. 'I think this little one wants to be out, by the feel of things.'

Rachel dropped the handful of clothes she was carrying to the drawer in alarm. 'Shall I go and fetch help? Do you need an ambulance?'

'No, no, it's just a twinge. I shall call on Molly Pratchet when I need her, but I'm sure it won't be before tea,' she said with a chuckle. 'Tea time at six, okay?'

'Okay.'

*

Vera and Peggy breezed into the bedroom just as Rachel had finished unpacking.

'Hi,' Peggy said, extending her hand out to Rachel. 'Did you have a good journey?' She spoke as though she'd known Rachel forever.

'Yes thank you,' she answered.

Then Vera touched her on the shoulder and said,

'Welcome aboard. God, I'm starving. All this fresh air gives you a fantastic appetite you know Rach. Can I call you Rach?'

Rachel nodded her approval.

'Wait until you taste Katie's rabbit pie - it is rabbit pie today isn't it Peg?'

'If it's Tuesday, it's rabbit.' Peggy laughed. 'She doesn't deviate from the menu our Katie you know. At least you don't forget what day it is. Come on you two, look sharp.' She threw the hand towel at the sink and finished drying her hands down her shirt.

'Towel!' Vera said with some authority.

Peggy tutted noisily as she retrieved the towel to place it on the rail. 'She's a stickler for tidiness is our Vera you know.'

'Shut up and get going.' Vera gave her a playful push and they all ran laughing down the stairs.

Katie beckoned them all to sit down, but before Rachel could take the place she was allocated, the back door burst open and in came what Rachel could only describe as a giant. The enormous youth stood at least six foot six in his stocking feet, not only that, he was probably about eighteen stone. His face was plump and running with perspiration. His tiny button eyes looked strange against his chubbiness. His lips were thick and he wore a grin which seemed to spread from one ear to the next. His hair was shaved to a quarter of an inch, which made his large ears more prominent. 'Oh...new girl,' he said excitedly, as he rushed towards an open-mouthed Rachel and grabbed her in a bear hug.

'Rachel this is Jacob, as I said he won't harm you, he just wants a hug and then he'll let you be.'

Rachel felt as though the life was being squeezed out of her, and then suddenly Jacob released her and lurched over to the sink to wash his hands with his father. Rachel flopped into her seat, quite taken aback from the incident.

'Don't worry Rach,' Vera whispered. 'That's the last time he'll do that to you. He only does it to people he doesn't know.' She winked.

Rachel smiled thankfully as everyone settled down to eat.

After tea, John urged Rachel to put on her gum boots so he could give her a tour of the farm. Rachel followed John out into the chill night air. There was a faint glow from the oil lamps which lit the cow shed, and once inside the smell of warm dung pricked at her nostrils. There were six stalls all with bags of hay. At the far end of the shed the buckets were clean and stacked one inside each other and a row of milking stools stood in military precision. 'We have thirty-four dairy cows to milk, and now there are five of us, we should get through them a bit quicker. Have you ever milked before?' he asked in earnest.

Rachel nodded. 'It was part of our training.'

John nodded. 'Are you any good,' he asked raising his eyebrows.

'Time will tell,' Rachel answered softly.

'Aye I suppose it will. It's tiring work, especially as the water to cool the milk has to be carried from the well, some forty yards away. Do you think you are up to it?'

'I told you, I'm stronger then I look.'

'Well, you'll be with Vera tomorrow, she'll show you the ropes, but I need you to pick things up quickly, I can't do with slow coaches around here. Everything needs doing at a specific time - the cows won't wait you know!'

The next morning Rachel was woken, not by the cockerel which Vera told her woke them every morning, but by a baby crying. At first, Rachel thought she was dreaming about her own child, but when she opened her tearful eyes, she realised that the cry was coming from within the farmhouse. She sat up in bed and glanced towards the other two girls, but though it was dark, she could tell they were both fast asleep. Silently, she slipped out of bed, put on her slippers and dressing gown and carefully lifted the door latch. There were voices at the other end of the corridor and Rachel heard a baby cry again. As she moved a little closer, Rachel encountered a rather large robust woman as she emerged from one of the bedrooms.

'Oh my lord,' the woman cried, staggering back against the wall. 'I thought you were a ghost! Whatever are you doing skulking around in the dark girl?'

'Oh, I'm really sorry,' Rachel apologised. 'I thought I heard a baby cry.'

'I, so you did girl. Katie has had a daughter.'

'Molly?' Katie's voice called from the bedroom. 'Who's that you're talking to?'

'It's me, Rachel.'

'Oh Rachel, in you come then. Don't hang about in that draughty corridor. Come and see my new little darling.'

Molly nodded for her to enter and Rachel pushed the door open. Inside the fire was lit, and the room was warm, Rachel's heart lurched as she smelt the familiar smell of a new born baby.

'I'm so sorry I woke you my love,' Katie said apologetically.

'You didn't, I assure you. It was the baby I heard, I can't believe you have just given birth without waking the whole house!'

Katie laughed. 'By the time you have your fourth, there is no point in doing all that screaming and shouting malarkey, it doesn't help a bit, so you might as well keep quiet and save all your energy to pushing the little darlings out. Anyway, what do you think?' She gestured to the cot at the far side of the bed. 'Go on, take a look.'

Very slowly Rachel moved towards the crying child. She was a larger baby than her own had been, but just as lovely. She had a shock of dark hair and a pair of lungs that would put a yodeller to shame.

'Can you bring her to me?' Katie asked. Rachel hesitated for a moment. 'It will be alright. She won't break, just pick her up and bring her to me.'

Very tentatively Rachel reached forward, her fingers curling around the pink blanket. A moment later Rachel held her tightly to her own breast and a rush of emotions flooded her, as great tears fell from her cheeks. Katie watched in silence as Rachel embraced her baby, but did not beckon her over, instead, she let whatever was taking place in Rachel's heart happen. For a long time Rachel was lost in her emotions. The baby had ceased crying now and had settled in her arms, Rachel felt complete. It was only when Molly opened the bedroom door, did Rachel jolt from her reverie. She panicked when she realised that she hadn't handed the baby to Katie, and rushed to her side, pushing the child into her arms. 'I'm so sorry Katie. I don't know what came over me.'

'Hush my love,' she said in a calming voice. 'There is no harm done, you look as though you were born to be a mother.' The child was crying again now. 'You've obviously got a gentler touch than I have.' She grinned rocking her baby back and forth. But Rachel's face was full of empty desolation, where as a moment earlier it had been filled with contentment.

Molly started to fuss around, straightening the bed covers. 'Come on you three, look ship-shape, the doctor is on his way. As she spoke, John pushed the door open to let the doctor in the bedroom.

'I'll go now. Sorry again,' Rachel said sorrowfully.

'It's alright my love, truly it is. You go and get some sleep now, it's an early start tomorrow remember.'

Rachel slipped out into the dark corridor and back to her bedroom. The two girls were still fast asleep in their beds. Rachel slowly climbed into her own bed and lay in quiet sorrow for another hour. She thought she heard the baby again, but it was a cat wailing in the yard and sleep finally came to her, half an hour before the cock crowed.

*

Rachel settled into farm life very well, though the WLA posters of smiling girls working in glorious sunshine in green fields were a far cry from the gruelling hard work and harsh working conditions in all weathers. However, despite all this, there was a great sense of camaraderie amongst the three girls, and a sense of mutual trust between Katie and Rachel, so much so Katie entrusted her with her baby Jenna as she made a slow and laborious recovery from what had been quite an uneventful birth.

*

Christmas 1940 was a cheery affair at Runstone Manor Farm, a far cry from the meagre event the previous year at Aunty May's house. She sighed heavily at the thought of her aunt. She had received a letter just four weeks after leaving Skipton to inform her that she had died. It was a letter Aunty May had written herself, where she had once again apologised to Rachel for Jack's unforgivable behaviour towards her. She wrote that she hoped Rachel would one day find happiness and settle down to start a family again, and that if she could, she would be her guardian angel and make her dreams come true. The letter closed saying that - if you are reading this letter, then my life will have ended. Do not be sorry for my departing, nor should you grieve. This is my rest, my well deserved rest. May had left instruction with the hospital for the letter to be sent to Rachel via the WLA. When she read it she smiled. As for Jack, Rachel would not give him a second thought. She hoped that he would rot in hell.

Christmas festivities began at the farm on Christmas Eve. Rachel was busy in the kitchen as Katie supervised the preparations for the Christmas Eve feast.

Much to John's disapproval, Katie insisted that they would host an open house for the villagers of Runstone as they had always done. She knew nobody came empty handed, but although there was rationing now, eggs and butter were in ample supply at the farm, so Rachel was busy making cakes, bread and biscuits. Katie had boiled a ham the previous week and it was now in the larder being pressed under the heaviest of Katie's baking weights. Potatoes were also in ample supply, so Rachel had boiled a huge pan of them, which were now glistening with hot butter and chives on the kitchen windowsill.

Katie glanced at the clock as it chimed seven, another few minutes and the first of the guests would arrive. By seven-thirty, the house would be full, and everyone would tuck into cold pressed ham, hot potatoes, glazed carrots, steaming broccoli and Katie's homemade mustard, all washed down with mulled wine and a sample of Rachel's baking. After tea, they all gathered in the brightly lit front parlour, safe behind the blackout curtains, to sing around the Christmas tree, which was decorated with red and white ribbons and variegated berry laden holly. By ten p.m. everyone made their way home drunkenly, so by eleven, the pots were washed and put away, and everyone was fast asleep in their beds.

A thin fine veil of frost blanketed the countryside on Christmas morning. Vera and Rachel brought the cows to be milked. Jacob mucked out the cow shed, and John set about milking while Peggy made a hearty breakfast for them.

Katie was late rising - she was late almost every day now. For some reason, she had no energy and the new baby was taking its toll on her. She struggled to lift her legs from the bed as baby Jenna cried for her feed. Rachel had made up a bottle before she had gone for the cows, so Katie was glad she didn't have to walk down to the kitchen to warm the bottle. As she gathered Jenna in her arms, she almost stumbled back onto the bed, causing the child to stiffen and scream. Katie sat and gathered herself together, trying to stop the panic rising within her. For one awful moment, she thought her legs were about to give way. She had never felt like this after the birth of her other children, and just put it down to exhaustion, due to her age.

By nine-thirty, breakfast was finished, and as was the custom, they set off to walk to church for the Christmas service. For the first time though, Katie could not accompany them, her legs felt weak and her heart seemed to palpitate at any exertion. John was understandably worried, but Katie brushed away his concerns. 'I'm fine. You get yourself off or you'll miss the start. I'll make a start on the dinner.' She smiled cheerily.

As they left, Rachel whispered to her, 'Everything is ready for the dinner Katie, there is nothing to do. I've made the fire up in the front parlour, so why don't you and Jenna sit in there and relax?' Her words were not condescending, and Katie knew that, Rachel had a deep concern for Katie's wellbeing, and Katie knew that also. She broke into a broad smile. 'I'll do just that.' She winked. 'Thank you.'

*

January 1941. The whole of Dartmoor was covered in a thick blanket of snow for a good part of the month. Icicles hung from lead guttering, and ice thickened daily on the inside of the upstairs windows. Farm work was hard through those winter months. The girls wore layer upon layer of clothes to keep out the cold, but still they suffered shivers. Katie kept herself busy knitting endless hats and scarves for her extended family - it was almost all she could do. Rachel had taken over duties in the kitchen as well as seeing to baby Jenna. As February approached the thaw came slowly. Rachel ventured out to the top meadow with a flask of steaming coffee for John and Jacob, who were busy mending fences brought down with the weight of the snow. At the top of the meadow, Rachel stopped and turned her face skywards. The sun shone brightly though without warmth, and a chill breeze soughed through the wild gorse moors. She smiled thoughtfully, though still brown and barren, Dartmoor was showing the first signs of spring.

As she poured the coffee for the men, and handed out a large saffron bun each, John asked quietly. 'How is my Katie today?'

Rachel bit down on her lip. 'Not too good I'm afraid.'

John sighed, drained his cup, shook it to empty all contents and passed it back to Rachel, a few seconds later Jacob did exactly the same thing and Rachel made her way back to the warmth of the kitchen.

Monday was washing day, and Rachel pushed her sleeves up and stood over the stone trough sink. There was no hot water through the sink tap, which was stuck on the end of a lead pipe. Hot water had to be boiled on the Aga, which was a laborious task. Washing day was hard work and took all day, especially as there were six of them. Rachel hated this task, the smell of the soap and the wet clothes and steam from the kettle was quite unpleasant. Clothes had to be washed in the sink and rubbed on a rubbing board. Then on fine days it was carried through the kitchen into the back parlour and out across the orchard to be hung out on the washing lines. On rainy days, they had to be dried inside on a clothes rack which hung from the ceiling near the fire. Rachel always disliked her clothes to dry like this, for even though the back parlour fire was behind the kitchen, the clothes always took on the smell of cooking. Ironing was an equally arduous task and seemed to take forever, as the iron had to be heated on the Aga. Rachel lost count of the times she burned herself while testing its heat by licking her finger and lightly tapping the face of the iron.

Katie's poor health worried John so much that in late March he voiced his concerns to the doctor, much to Katie's annoyance. 'I'm fine John,' she said, quite put out that he had bothered the doctor. 'I'm sure the doctor has more important people to see without me bothering him.'

'You're the most important person in the world Katie, and I think you need to see him. So we'll just see what the doctor says,' John answered softly.

The tests were not good, and Katie was quickly booked into hospital for an operation.

'There is something wrong down there it seems,' Katie mouthed the words almost inaudibly to Rachel. She was clearly worried. Rachel gave her a big hug and told her not to worry, and that she was sure the operation would sort everything out.

There was no doubt about it the impending operation threw the occupants of Runstone Manor Farm into chaos. Katie was to have her operation in Plymouth on the 23rd of April and John, as the devoted husband he was, was mad intent on going with her. Nothing would sway him, his mind was made up. Vera, he decided would take over the main running of the farm. He knew she could handle Jacob, so that would leave Peggy to complete all other work on the farm. As only Rachel out of the three girls was competent in the kitchen, she was asked to continue undertaking all household duties, which incidentally was strictly against the W.L.A rules, but Rachel waved away any concerns over that. 'Who's going to tell them?' Rachel said, throwing her hands in the air. 'Anyway, I don't mind being indoors in this weather,' she said, glancing out of the kitchen window at the sleet driving across Dartmoor.

'So,' said John 'that just leaves the baby, we can't take her!' His eyes looked doleful. 'Can we ask you to look after the baby as well Rachel?' It was more of a plea than a question.

Rachel could hardly contain her elation. 'Of course I'll look after her. Now off you go and get better. Everything will be okay, I promise you. Jenna and the farm are in good hands.' Rachel saw Katie sigh with relief.

Michael Bainbridge from a neighbouring farm had offered to drive Katie and John as far as Buckfastleigh - from there they would catch the bus to Plymouth. As Rachel helped Katie with her bags into the car, Katie turned and hugged her. 'I must admit Rachel, if you weren't here, I wouldn't have this operation done. I know Jenna is in safe hands with you. You seem so at ease with her.' Rachel smiled and considered for the umpteenth time, whether to tell Katie her sad story of the loss of her own child, but something inside her stopped her from revealing this. Maybe if Katie knew how much Jenna was filling the void of her lost child, and how much she meant to her, she might think twice about leaving her baby with her. It wasn't as if Rachel would abduct her or anything - that would be unthinkable - it was just that Rachel thought if Katie knew how strong the bond between them was growing, she would be quite alarmed. Jenna was becoming the baby Rachel lost.

As Rachel, Peggy, Vera and Jacob waived the trio goodbye, Rachel hugged baby Jenna to her breast. John and Katie would be gone for a couple of weeks, and nothing could have made Rachel happier than what she felt at this moment in time. The happiness though was to be short lived.

At seven-thirty that evening, Vera ran screaming into the kitchen. 'Quick come and look!' Rachel and Peggy exchanged glances and with a scrape of chairs against the stone floor, they followed Vera into the cold night air. 'Look,' Vera cried. 'Look over there!'

At the top of the yard they turned to witness the flashing lights on the far horizon and the boom of exploding bombs in the far off distance, and all knew in their hearts that Plymouth was taking the brunt of the bombing. Back in the kitchen, the wireless confirmed their worst fears. Plymouth had taken one of the hardest poundings of the war and had subjected her people to one of the most terrible ordeals ever endured by a civilian population. John and Katie were in the midst of it.

*

As Adam de Sousa packed his suitcase he listened intently

to the wireless report of the harsh bombing which Plymouth was in the midst of. The room he had called his own for the last eighteen months look stark and uninviting now it was void of all photos and possessions. He was not a hundred percent well, but enough to leave the rehabilitation centre. Sam Blewett's legacy to Adam had left him with a slight slur to his speech due to a cracked skull. He also sported a limp which in time would ease, but never leave him, and suffered a slight weakness down his right side. He was lucky to be alive. When they had transferred him to London from Cornwall, his injuries were indeed life threatening, and it was feared his brain was damaged beyond repair. It was only on account that his father had contacts at the hospital, that Adam had received immediate assistance and emergency surgery which probably saved his life.

Once the suitcase was packed Adam sat on the bed exhausted. Even the smallest of exertions required a great deal of effort, and Adam wondered if he would ever regain enough strength to return to his job as a veterinary surgeon. He moved the suitcase onto the floor and lay down on his eiderdown and closed his eyes. A moment later he reached over to his bedside table and picked up the photo frame which had sat in vigil throughout his time at the centre. With sadness he gazed at the photo of Rachel as she smiled back at him. It had been taken in Tuscany almost two years ago. It felt like an age ago to him, a distant memory which broke his heart whenever he looked at it. 'I will find you one day my lovely Rachel, I promise I will,' he whispered as he placed the photo on his chest and fell into a deep dreamless sleep.

He said his goodbyes the next morning to the staff and with a little help, managed to get into the back seat of his father's car. They were heading for Yorkshire, as life in Kent had become too fraught for Adam's mother when war was declared, and had reluctantly packed up her things, boarded up the house and rented a house near the rehabilitation centre. Now Adam was well enough to leave, they had rented a house on the outskirts of the Yorkshire Dales.

It took all of eight hours to drive to Yorkshire and was becoming dark when they entered the tiny hamlet of Bank Newton. The rain had been relentless since they had driven through Cheshire and Adam's father was tired and weary with it. The house Newton Grange had been a farm at one time, but now the fields and outbuildings lay empty. It seemed so far away from anywhere, in the middle of nowhere, with only the Leeds Liverpool canal for a neighbour. As the car drew up on the drive, the house looked cold and uninviting, Adam shivered slightly at the cold air which swept in when his father opened the car door. His father must have had the same thought as Adam, as he turned and said, 'You two stay in the warmth for a moment. A couple of minutes later he re-emerged from the house with a smile on his face. 'Come on, it's lovely, the housekeeper has built a fire in the front room and the bedrooms and there is something rather delicious cooking in the oven.

With a full stomach, and a warm bed, Adam slept soundly that first night. When he woke the next morning, he walked gingerly with the aid of a stick, and pulled the curtains aside. He saw before him a sight which was beautiful, as acres of rolling fields lined with great oaks filled his vista. He pushed the window open to hear a lark who was singing high up in the garden tree. To his left he could see the canal winding its way down the valley as the sun shone brilliantly against its still waters.

There was a soft knock at his door and his mother entered with a tray. 'I thought you might like breakfast in bed, but I see I'm too late.'

'Thank you mother, I was just enjoying the view. It's quite magnificent.'

She saw a flicker of happiness in her tragic son's eyes and was warmed by it. 'So it is my boy.' She placed the tray on his table, kissed him tenderly on the forehead and left him to begin the final part of his recovery.

16

On a warm late April morning in 1941, Robin and Emma Ferris–Norton were safely delivered of a baby boy. A month later, a huge party was held at Barleyfield Farm to celebrate the christening of the child, which Robin and Emma named Edwin. Most of the village was invited as was Robin's elder brother Jonathan, his sister-in-law Grace and their eighteen-year-old daughter Rebecca, who due to illness had missed the wedding celebrations. It was a fine party despite the rationing restriction on food. There was always a good supply of mackerel in Gweek as well as copious amounts of salad and vegetables, and Lizzy's homemade wine kept everyone in a jolly mood.

'Hi,' Rebecca said, lowering her eyelashes at Harry Blewett, as he stood quietly by the great fireplace.

Harry stood open-mouthed and turned his head to see who she was speaking to.

'I'm Rebecca Ferris-Norton, Robin's niece,' she said, holding her hand out to him.

Harry swallowed hard and tentatively shook her hand - she was the loveliest girl he had ever set eyes on. He looked in wonder at her creamy clear complexion, long dark curls, which fell about her shoulders and her eyes - the most beautiful blue eyes he had ever seen, were actually looking at him.

Rebecca smiled inwardly at his gaze. 'Well?'

'Eh?' he said, absent-mindedly.

'Who are you then, or has the cat got your tongue?'

Harry laughed slightly and licked his lips.

'So, what's your name then?' she reiterated.

'Harry,' he croaked.

She cocked her head. 'Just Harry?'

'Blewett, Harry Blewett.'

'Ah, Harry Blewett, you're the farm manager now aren't you?' Harry nodded shyly. 'Well, Harry Blewett the farm manager, I've heard a lot about you. I know that my uncle couldn't run this farm without you.' Harry coloured up, but remained silent. Rebecca regarded him for a moment then reached for his hand. 'Come on Harry Blewett, why don't you show me around the farm.'

'Well, I err, oh..okay,' he stammered. 'But you'll have to put some gum boots on,' he said, staring at her black shiny shoes.

'Well, I'm sure Emma has some that will fit. Come on let's go and find her.'

Harry just about managed to put his glass down before Rebecca pulled him out of the lounge into the Kitchen.

'Ah, Uncle Robin, I need some gum boots. Harry has promised me a tour of the farm.'

Robin moved his head to face Rebecca. 'Has he now, well, if they are where they should be, and knowing my Emma they will be, she always says, 'there is a place for everything and everything in its place', there should be a pair in the back kitchen which should fit you. Now go careful now.' He moved his head to where he thought Harry was standing. 'Look after her won't you Harry?'

'You can be assured I will, Mr Ferris-Norton.'

As they rushed out into the yard, Lizzy watched Harry go and noted his face flushed with eager anticipation at the prospect of spending some time with a girl for the first time in his life. She remembered that not so long ago, Harry was a thin, weak, frightened young man, terrorised by years of violent abuse by his murderous father, what a difference in him now. He was fresh faced with a ruddy outdoor complexion and had filled out with good home cooking and acquired strong muscles through sheer hard work. His hair had grown thick and no longer fell out through stress, and the skin on his body no longer flaked and fell away due to psoriasis. In short, he was twice, no three times the man he was when Adam de Sousa rescued him. Lizzy's heart missed a beat at the thought of Adam. He'd been the instigator to so many peoples happiness. He'd given her very own Emma a chance to make a career for herself as a veterinary nurse - a role she hoped to return to part time as soon as she could. It had been he who had introduced Emma to Robin, and love had blossomed for her. He'd also saved Granny Pascoe's life and in return, on her death bed, had bequeathed her house to him which Adam promptly gave to the Gweek Parish Council to do as they pleased. Yes, Adam de Sousa had left a legacy behind him, but he also left Rachel with a broken heart, and for that she had trouble forgiving him for.

Away from the party, Harry quietly showed Rebecca around the milking parlour. She listened as he explained how the cows knew when they needed milking, and not time or tide could stop them from making their way to the top meadow gate in eager anticipation. He led her to the pigsty, telling her to be careful where she stepped and introduced her to Myrtle and her piglets, and then he picked up a bucket of corn from the barn and threw a handful onto the floor for the geese.

'My uncle speaks very highly of you Harry Blewett.'

'Well, I don't know about that,' Harry answered, putting the bucket down on the floor. 'But I do love the animals. I couldn't wish for a better job or a better boss, and I'm not just saying that because he's your uncle.'

Rebecca smiled. 'I know. I can see you are happy here. So, what do you do when you're not milking the cows and feeding the pigs?'

Harry shook his head. 'Nothing.'

'Nothing? Don't you even take your sweetheart out?'

Harry regarded her for a moment to surmise whether she was mocking him or not. 'I don't have a sweetheart,' he answered softly.

Rebecca smiled inwardly. 'Does that mean you might be free to take me out on your next day off then?'

The question took him completely by surprise. 'Take *you*

out?'

'Well, don't sound so shocked. I'm not that bad.' She giggled.

Harry blushed profusely. 'I err, I didn't mean for it to come out like that! It's just that I can't believe you want to go out with me.'

'Why?'

He shrugged his shoulders. 'Because!'

'Because what?'

He frowned deeply. 'Because, no-one ever wanted to go out with me before!'

She shoved him playfully. 'A big, handsome strapping lad like you, I don't believe that for a moment.' She squeezed the muscles on his arm. 'I would have thought the girls would be falling over themselves to go out with you.'

Harry still couldn't make his mind up whether she was teasing him or not.

'So?'

'So what?'

She laughed heartily. 'Gosh you really don't know how to go a courting do you? So, do you want to take me out on your next day off?'

Harry was taken aback. 'Well, if you really want me to, yes.'

'I wouldn't have asked otherwise.' She linked her arm in his.

He looked at her and she looked back and smiled, Harry couldn't help himself, he had to say it, 'You will turn up, won't you?' As soon as he spoke he knew he's sounded pathetic.

Rebecca squeezed his arm and whispered in his ear, 'I can't wait. Now come on we must get back to the party or we shall invite gossip before we have had a chance to make any.' She grinned broadly.

17

Set in the beautiful valley of the River Dart in Devon, was home to a community of Benedictine monks, who were striving to dedicate their lives to the service of God, by living a life in common under the guidance of the Rule of St. Benedict. Jake Hewbey was hoping to become one of them.

A monk's day was punctuated by prayer, which consisted mainly of the recitation of the psalmody, together with readings from Scripture. Each day began with Matins at five-forty-five a.m., and ended with Compline at nine p.m. It was shortly after nine one morning when Jake was summoned to the Abbots office.

'Please take a seat.' The Abbot gestured to him.

Jake sat as instructed in the stark stone room, puzzled by what the Abbot wanted.

'I have before me a letter from Runstone Manor Farm. It was written by a Rachel Pendarves, and from what I understand she is one of three land army women billeted at your farm. Jake listened intently as a frown began to form on his forehead. The Abbot continued, 'I'm afraid the letter bears bad news. It states that your parents were caught up in the blitz in Plymouth a week ago and are feared dead.' Jake felt a welling up in his stomach as his head swam and his heart raced. The Abbot placed the letter on his desk and poured a beaker of water from a jug. He placed it down in front of Jake. 'When you are ready I will continue.' Jake nodded for him to do just that. 'The farm is being run at the moment by the before mentioned WLA women, but they are becoming increasingly worried that they will not be able to cope. There is of course your younger brother Jacob to consider, and a baby, born to your parents last year. It is obvious that your help is urgently required on the farm.'

Jake was speechless. The thought of his parents dead was unthinkable. He thought of Jacob and a baby he knew nothing about, but then again, that was his fault for not keeping in touch.

'Jake, are you decided whether to go?'

'I don't know what to do,' he said, stunned by the news.

'Your family needs you Jake.' The Abbot added.

'But, what about the Rule of St. Benedict, chapter 43? It says, 'Let nothing; therefore, be put before the Work of God'.

The Abbot smiled softly. 'Everything good that you do in this life Jake is the work of God.'

'But if I am to become a Benedictine monk I will have to make three vows as a sign of my commitment to the monastic way of life.'

'So you do. The first is obedience to your superior, and I believe your family needs you at this time. As your superior, I think you should go and help in their hour of need.'

Jake lowered his eyes then quickly looked up and spoke. 'But Stability? That vow requires me to remain attached to the monastery for life!'

The Abbot smiled again. 'You will always be part of us. Your heart will not leave this place if you are truly committed to Christ.'

Jake looked around the room. 'And Conversatio Morum (Conversion of Life) I came here to change my life by following the Gospel and in accordance to the monastic ideals set out in the Rule.'

The Abbot sighed. 'And so you have brother, so you have. You have proved loyal to your monastery and are without doubt going to become a fine monk. But God has put this challenge to you and you should take it. It is God's way.'

*

Rachel was busy in the kitchen when Jake walked through the door. They both paused for a moment. Then Rachel wiped her floury hands down her apron and held out her hand. 'Jake is it? Or should I call you brother? Sorry I'm not sure how to address a monk.'

'I'm only a novice. I am waiting to take my vows, you can call me Jake. I take it you are..' He glanced at the letter. 'Rachel?'

'I am. Thank you for coming. I wasn't sure if you would be able. I am truly sorry to bring you away from your home, but we are in rather a pickle here, to say the least.'

Jake relaxed slightly. Rachel seemed a nice pleasant sort of person, who was obviously sympathetic to the turmoil this upheaval was making to his life. 'My parents, I take it you haven't received anymore news.'

Rachel shook her head. 'PC Daniels said it could take weeks before we know anything. The only thing for certain is that they didn't reach the hospital. So we can surmise that the bus was bombed.' Rachel lowered her lashes, and wiped away a stray tear. 'Sorry,' she said. 'John and Katie were very special to me.'

'But why were they going to hospital and why in Plymouth of all places?'

'Your mum had been very ill since the birth of Jenna. She needed an operation, and they could only do it at Plymouth.'

Jake nodded his head. 'Jenna you say, a sister I knew nothing of.' He smiled weakly.

Rachel touched Jake gently on the arm with her hand then swiftly retracted. 'I'm sorry. I don't suppose you are meant to have a woman touch you.'

He held his hands up. 'It's alright, don't worry. May I see Jenna?'

Rachel gestured to the front room. 'She is in her pram asleep.'

Shortly after Jake had dropped his bags in his old bedroom, he donned his father's gum boots and took a look around the farm. Jacob, on seeing his brother, flung himself against him and sobbed brokenheartedly. Jacob had no concept about what had happened to his parents. He only knew that they were not there, and now that his beloved elder brother was, that made everything better.

At dinner that night Vera and Peggy could not take their eyes of the handsome man sharing their table. He was tall and blond, with deep blue eyes and a sharp nose which emphasised the rest of his chiselled features. At nine, Jake retired to his old room and knelt by a statue of St Benedict for Compline. But half way through Vera and Peggy knocked on his bedroom door to wish him goodnight and the intrusion broke his concentration and the essence of the act had vanished.

Jake tried hard to revert back to being a farmer. He also tried desperately to switch his role from farmer to trainee monk at certain times of the day, but time and time again he would be interrupted by someone wanting this done or someone wanted that done. It was driving him to despair.

Rachel observed Jake's slow decline and fretted constantly about it. She had spoken to both Vera and Peggy about her concerns, but they were both adamant that they were only trying to run the farm properly, though Rachel suspected they were both competing for his attention. Vera had even said there was no such thing as a celibate man, not if she had anything to do with it. Then an idea came into Rachel's head. Once Jenna was fast asleep in her cot, and the dinner was prepared, she took the stairs up to the attic and began to clear the years of dust and junk. She piled as much as she could on the far side of the attic then placed a cupboard with a clean tablecloth underneath the skylight and a rug in front. On the cupboard, she placed the statue of St Benedict along with a candle on each side which she had taken from Jake's room. Satisfied with her mornings work, she dusted her hands together and descended the stairs to begin cooking dinner.

When dinner was over, Jake stood up. 'I'm just going to my room for a short while,' he said, as the others made to go back to work.

'Can you just wait a moment Jake,' Rachel said, noting his shoulders heaving in a deep sigh. She waited until everyone had gone then said, 'Don't worry, I'm not going to keep you from your prayers, I just have something to show you.' She led Jake up the dark stairway and pushed the old oak door open. 'Forgive me for touching your personal things, but I think you will get some peace and quiet up here. I'll see you later.'

As she turned to leave, he caught the sleeve of her dress. 'Thank you Rachel. You don't know how much this means to me.'

She smiled thoughtfully. 'I think I do.'

18

It was 1941 as spring moved into summer Robin settled himself down on a wicker chair in front of the great bay windows of Barleyfield Farm to enjoy the sunshine. He could hear the wireless playing from the front parlour - the music punctuated with news stories of a war that fortunately hadn't encroached too much on the lives of the Gweek residents. Yes, many of the young men in the surrounding valley had left to fight for the cause, and some tragically were lost in action, though none as such from Gweek. Robin sighed as he sat, he wished he could do something to help, but his eyes rendered him useless to the war effort. All he could do was make sure his farm stayed productive in all ways.

He had been sitting for about fifteen minutes when his nostrils picked up the sweet flowery scent of Emma's perfume as she breezed into the garden with Edwin. 'Hello darling?' he said, holding out his hand.

Emma curled her soft fingers around his and bent to kiss him on the lips. 'We have a letter Robin,' she said, hitching Edwin higher up onto her hip.

'From whom?'

'It seems to have a Yorkshire postmark,' she said placing Edwin on the rug by Robin. She settled herself in the chair adjacent to Robin, flipped the envelope over and opened it. Robin waited for a moment, tapping his finger on the chair arm. 'Well mercy me! It's from Adam de Sousa!'

'Adam? Goodness what has he to say?'

She began to read out loud:

Dear Robin and Emma,

Please excuse the terrible handwriting. I'm afraid the legacy of Sam Blewett's boot in my skull has left me with considerable weakness down my right side, causing a tremor in my writing hand. It also left me with a limp and a speech impediment, which unfortunately makes me slur to my words, which to the unsuspecting makes me sound intoxicated and somewhat inaudible, hence the reason I haven't phoned. The latter I am told will diminish over the months with speech therapy, of which I am studiously working on. The limp I'm afraid will remain for some time to come. Anyway enough about me, I am writing first to enquire about your health, and hope you are enjoying married life, it seems such a long time since I saw you and I can heartily say I miss you all. I am also writing with some news which will perhaps interest you Robin.   During my eighteen months rehabilitation, I became very good friends with a Mr Gerald Casidy, a rather splendid and much renowned eye surgeon, who specialises in congenital cataracts. Forgive me for being so presumptuous, but I spoke to him about you, and though he cannot promise anything, he is willing to take a look at you. He has your name and address on file and is awaiting your call if you should wish to take him up on his offer. You will of course have to travel to London, which I suspect is the only drawback. Anyway, I will leave the ball in your court for you and Emma to contemplate. I have enclosed his card in this letter

The other reason for writing is to see how you all are? Lizzy, Charlie, Harry et al, and of course Rachel. Apart from that last night I was there, I have such fond memories of Gweek. I would love to know that you are all well and the war hasn't caused too much inconvenience to the villagers of Gweek. I would especially like some news of Rachel as I think of her often. I wrote to her at The Black Swan twice, shortly after leaving hospital for the rehabilitation home, once enclosing money so that she could perhaps join me, which was, as you know, our original plan, but either the letters got lost in the post or Rachel, for some reason, couldn't write back. I don't know the reason why and this is why I beg you for news of her, and maybe you could show her this letter. I want her to know how very much I miss her and want to see her again. I'm not well enough to travel to Cornwall, my doctor says it will be at least another ten months to a year before I will be back to almost a hundred percent fit and well, but I am willing to send more money if she chooses to visit me, Verity is welcome too, should she wish. Talking of Verity, I hope things settled down after she found out about us and she isn't giving Rachel too much of a hard time. You will see from the address I have moved with my parents to Yorkshire. Fearing for their lives, my parents boarded the house up in Kent and moved lock stock and barrel to West Marton in Yorkshire, safely away from the bombs. Let's hope West Marton along with Gweek manages to keep safe of any stray German bombs eh?

So, I shall close this letter now and look forward to hearing from you.

With great affection, Adam

Emma placed the letter on her lap. 'Oh dear. We shall have to break the news about Verity to him. It will be such a shock. But what do you think about the eye surgeon Robin?'

'Well, I have to agree, it's a wonderful offer, but I can't go to London alone, and it's too dangerous for us all to go, what with the bombing and everything.' He paused for a moment to contemplate the consequences. 'No, I'm afraid it can't be done. Much as I would love to see you and my little Edwin, I fear we must wait until this wretched war is over. Hopefully, he will still be willing to see me.' He reached over to find Emma's hand. 'I'm surprised at him not knowing where Rachel was though. I truly believed she left to find him all those months ago.'

Edwin who was sitting on a rug on the lawn toppled over and Emma left Robin's side to sit him back up.

She sighed. 'If he wrote to The Black Swan, I could wager that Sally Blewett opened those letters and pocketed the money, the thieving mare.'

Robin smiled thinly. 'Well, we can't prove anything on that score.' A shriek of laughter from the top meadow stopped Robin mid sentence. He raised his eyebrows. 'I take it Rebecca is with Harry?' he enquired.

'Yes she and Harry have taken a picnic up to the fields. It's nice to see Harry so happy. Rebecca has really brought him out of his shell.'

'As long as he doesn't neglect his farm duties,' Robin said seriously.

'He won't, you know he won't, so, don't tease him. You'll never find a more conscientious worker. Anyway, going back to the letter, what shall I write to Adam?'

'Thank him for speaking to the eye surgeon on my behalf and tell him that that we'll write to Mr err...'

Emma picked up the business card and read, 'Casidy, Gerald Casidy.'

'Yes, tell him we will write and thank him for the offer, but London is quite out of the question. I'm not prepared to risk my family, not even if it means foregoing my sight for a while longer.

'And about Rachel?'

'Well, we have no idea where she is. I don't suppose your Mother has heard from her, has she?'

'Not a word.'

'Well, you'll just have to tell him she's vanished. Oh and tell him not to send anything to The Black Swan again.'

19

As harvest time approached at Runstone Manor Farm, Jake's time for prayer seemed to lessen with each waking day. He still rose early to take Matins, but time and time again he found himself absorbed in the workings of a very busy farm, and he would forgo the time he had set aside for his religious studies. Rachel tried to ease his workload to help, and he was grateful to her, but he was afraid to admit to himself that God was being pushed to the back of his mind. He had even questioned God when it became obvious that his parents were reported missing presumed dead. Their bodies were never found which left Jake, Jacob and baby Jenna orphans. Why would God do such a thing? He wished with all his heart he could speak with the Abbot, but the work load at the farm rendered it impossible to take the time out to visit the Abbey.

Because none of the farmers were allowed to leave fields fallow, harvest time was extremely busy with the usual crops -wheat first, some oats and barley. Casual labour became vital, as three women and two men were just not enough, especially when it came to a task like threshing, where you needed three or four men, one on the engine, one on the drum, one on the bailer. Fortunately local farmers helped each other and there was a great camaraderie between them.

When it came time for corn cutting, the fields were overrun with rabbits. Jake was, to put it mildly, useless with a shotgun, but Vera, whose father had owned a shotgun, came into her own, one day shooting fifty-seven rabbits from sixty shots without moving from the same spot. There was many a rabbit pie made that week around the village as Peggy sold the rabbits at the farm door for a shilling each.

Runstone Manor farm didn't usually keep pigs but, Jake's forward thinking had urged him to buy five pigs at Widecombe Fair in September, and gave Peggy the job of looking after them. At first, she was mortified at the thought, but soon she got used to them and fed them with skimmed milk, ground barley, and scraps from the kitchen. By mid September, they all had names, and she cried buckets in late November when four of them were sold to the butchers. She was allowed to keep one pig, but was told by Jake in no uncertain terms that the remaining pig 'Billy' would eventually grace Runstone Manor's kitchen table. Peggy cursed him and said she thought him very cruel, especially as he was a praying man as well! Her words cut deep and tugged at Jake's conscience, and not for the first time did he wonder where his gentle self had gone, and if he would ever return to the values the Abbey had taught him. War was making him hard that was for sure.

*

As winter progressed, a northerly wind had got up, which made it bitterly cold outside. Whipping rain had turned to sleet just as milking had finished and was now battering at the windows of Runstone Manor Farm. Inside Rachel sat at the kitchen table after dinner and began to write. It was a letter to Lizzy, a long overdue letter which she had started months ago. The date at the top of the page read March 1941, it was now December, she scribbled it out and wrote the new date, she was determined to find the time that night to finish, so she could pop it into the Christmas card she had selected to send to her. She had thought about phoning, but the guilt of leaving the William's farm like she had weighed heavy on her conscience, and in the end decided a letter could explain things better. She missed Lizzy, more than she cared to admit. Vera and Peggy were good friends to her, but with Lizzy it was more than that, it was a special kind of friendship, that no matter what happened, or how long it was between seeing each other, they could just pick up where they had left off as though the time spent apart hadn't happened. Or so she thought.

*

The onset of December was damp, dreary and windy in Gweek, but fortunately very mild. There had been changes in the village during the past couple of weeks, Daniel Trewin the landlord of The Black Swan had moved to the Ship Inn at Mawgan, taking with him Sally Blewett, but not his wife! She had been absent from the hotel for over a month, allegedly visiting relatives, but the general consensus was that she had left him over his blatant affair with Sally. None of them would be missed. Trewin had been an ignorant, foul-mouthed landlord without any social skills at all. Some would say he and Sally didn't spoil a pair! So, it was with great interest as to who was taking over The Black Swan. The Brewery had put a temporary manager in for the time being, and the new landlord was due to arrive in the middle of December. The other major change in Gweek was the new permanent occupant in Granny Pascoe's cottage. Harry Blewett had wrangled and pleaded with the parish council and finally managed to secure the house for himself and his bride-to-be Rebecca Ferris-Norton.

The wedding was to be held at Constantine Parish Church on the tenth of December, and Lizzy was busy putting the finishing touches to Rebecca's wedding gown when the postman arrived.

'Morning Lizzy,' Stan Clements said as he handed her the letter.

'Morning Stan - do you care for a dish of tea? I've just made one,' she asked brightly.

'Very kind of you Lizzy, but I've got quite a load to deliver today, but thank you anyway,' he said, pulling on his cap.

'Bye then.' She closed the door and pondered on the postmark, Buckfastleigh Devon, and wondered who she knew there as she slit the envelope open with her finger.

My Dearest Lizzy,
I do hope you can find it in your heart to forgive me, first for

leaving the way I did, and for not getting in touch sooner. Please understand that I needed to get away from Gweek and all the memories it held. I am so sorry that I was unable to send greetings to Emma and Robin on their wedding day. I trust all went well, and they are happy together. This last year has been challenging in many ways, I have both struggled emotionally and financially, but I have joined the WLA and have been billeted in a lovely Devon village with a very nice family and I am beginning to see the light at the end of a very long, sad, tunnel.

My dear Lizzy since writing the above news something very grave has happened. You will see from the alteration in the date on my letter it has been over nine months since I started it. In the interim, I am afraid the owners of the farm where I work were caught up in the bombing of Plymouth last March and were killed. We have had to all rally round to keep the farm going, as you can imagine we are all exhausted with the extra work load. All in all it has been a very sad year for all of us. I must close this letter now as dinner will not cook itself, I do hope you and Charlie are well, I think of you both with great affection. Please remember that I love and miss you all very much. Merry Christmas and a Happy New Year.
Rachel x

Lizzy held Rachel's letter to her breast and sighed with relief.

Rachel had said nothing about her baby in her letter, as she was heartily ashamed of the whole affair. How could she ever tell Lizzy, that she had let her baby slip from her hands with no way of ever getting her back? No, it must be her secret forever. She decided it's the only way she could live with herself. So, instead she wrote and tried to make her life sound interesting, tried to make Lizzy think that her going away had all been for the best, but when Lizzy read the letter, that wet December day, she knew this was not the Rachel she knew and loved, her words had been cryptic and deep down Lizzy knew Rachel was hiding some dark secret. Lizzy thought it strange that Rachel didn't mention Adam in her letter, and wondered if she had finally got over the heartbreak. In truth Rachel had written to ask if she had heard from Adam or indeed if he had ever returned to Gweek to fetch her as they had planned, but Rachel had screwed that page up and burned it on the fire. Adam had gone from her life, so too had Adam's baby. She wanted no more heartbreak and fooled herself that she was over him.

Lizzy was dismayed that Rachel had forgotten to put her new address at the top of the letter. The postmark said Buckfastleigh in Devon and all she knew was that she was in a village somewhere nearby, so she couldn't even reply or send a return Christmas card.

Lizzy had just finished re-reading the letter when Emma breezed through the back door. Lizzy could see she was flushed with excitement as she handed Edwin over into her mother's arms. 'Guess what Mum? Robin has had a letter from Mr Casson, you know that eye specialist Adam wrote to him about. Well, he's coming to Exeter the week before Christmas and has asked to see Robin at a clinic he's holding there. Oh Mum, if all is well, he is going to operate on Robin, and he'll be able to see again.' Suddenly, she began to cry.

Lizzy hitched Edwin further up onto her hip and reached out to her daughter. 'Hey now hush, what's this all about, what are the tears for?' she asked as she comforted her daughter.

Emma was silent for a moment then said, 'Oh I don't know what is wrong with me Mum. I'm so excited that Robin will see his son, that life will be normal again for him, it's just that...' Emma looked away as though she was examining the curtains.

'What?' Lizzy asked with a short laugh.

'Oh dear,' she said unhappily. 'What happens when he looks at me for the first time Mum?' she said miserably

'What do you mean?'

'Well, look at me, I'm just a plain Jane, and Robin is the most handsome of men. What on earth will he think when he sees that he is married to someone like me?'

Bristling with indignation, Lizzy said, 'Don't be a bloody fool. I've never heard anything so ridiculous. Robin loves you for the person you are. He fell in love with your kindness and your personality, and you are not a plain Jane! You are my beautiful daughter, look see.' She pushed her towards the wall mirror. 'You have the most beautiful skin. Your eyes shine with love. Your hair is glossy and thick and this is what Robin will see.' She shook her by the shoulders. 'He will see that he has been blessed with a beautiful wife and a handsome son. Now I don't want to hear anymore of this nonsense, do you hear me?' Emma nodded woefully and gave her a grateful smile. 'When do you leave for Exeter?' she asked, trying to calm her annoyance.

Wiping her tears, Emma answered, 'The eighteenth of December. If all goes well we should be back just before Christmas.'

Lizzy countenance softened. 'So, that means I can have my delicious grandson to myself for a whole week.'

Emma's face beamed. 'Oh mum would you? I didn't want to put on you, but then again, I think the journey would be too much with Edwin in tow. I didn't know how to ask you.'

'Away with you girl, of course I'll have him.'

With that Emma took Edwin from Lizzy's arms. 'Thanks Mum,' she said meekly as she waved a happy goodbye to her.

Lizzy glanced out of the kitchen window as the sun peeped shyly and briefly through the heavy grey cloud, then picked up Rachel's letter. She read it through once more then sat at her kitchen table and composed a letter to Adam de Sousa.

20

Adam stood up and shook the hand of Sarah Jenkins, his speech therapist. 'Thank you for all you have done for me,' he said in earnest and with great clarity.

'The pleasure has been mine Adam.' She smiled warmly, her deep lined face crinkling as she did. 'You have been most conscientious in your efforts to regain your speech. I applaud you for it.'

Adam nodded as he accepted the compliment.

'I hope you do as well in regaining your mobility,' she said.

Adam reached for his walking stick and tapped it on the carpet. 'I intend to. I can walk for almost five minutes unaided, without stumbling. I just pray that the feeling returns to my leg. It is quite unnerving to take a step and not feel the ground underfoot.'

'I can imagine it is,' she said as she let him help her on with her coat. 'Do you intend to return to your vocation as a veterinary practitioner?' she asked, as she slipped her hands inside her gloves.

He lowered his eyes. 'It is my dearest wish, though I should think I will only ever be surgery based from now on and not out in the field,' he said slightly dejected.

She smiled knowingly. 'Never say never Adam, you of all people, have the will and strength to conquer anything. One day I am sure you will be the man you were. You mark my words. Don't come to the door, it is bitter cold outside, I shall see myself out. Good day to you Adam and good luck in the future.' She closed the study door and was gone.

He stood for a moment then glanced out of the window onto the frost laden branches of the great oak which stood in the front garden. Beyond that, the Yorkshire fields lay white and crisp in the cold morning mist. He pondered on Sarah's words, 'one day you will be the man you once were.' Physically, he agreed with her, emotionally, he knew in his heart that he would only be half the man he was, because he'd lost his lovely Rachel.

A knock on the door roused his from his reverie as his mother brought him his mid morning coffee. With it, she bore two letters, both with a Cornish postmark. The first was from Robin and Emma with their news, the second, from Lizzy, threw his life into turmoil. It read:

My dear Adam,
I hope this letter finds you well and improving in health. I felt it my duty to let you know that I have heard from Rachel. She is by all accounts working as a Land Army Girl in Devon, somewhere near Buckfastleigh. I am sorry I cannot be more specific as to her whereabouts, as she did not include her address on the letter. What you do with this information is your business. I just thought you should know where she is. I shall leave the ball in your court. Wishing you seasons greetings from all of us.
Lizzy Williams.

Adam returned the letter to its envelope and placed it inside his jacket pocket. He glanced at the weather - snow had been forecast for later and wondered, quite irrationally, if he could persuade his father to drive him three hundred miles to Devon, before the snow came and blocked them in the county of Yorkshire. He picked up his stick and made to find his father.

'Your father has returned to his bed,' his mother informed him, as she filled the heavy stone hot water bottle from the kettle. 'That cough has gone to his chest. I'm just about to call for a doctor. Did you want anything specific? I don't really want to disturb him at the moment other than to put this bottle into his bed. He had a very uncomfortable night.'

Adam shook his head. 'No it was nothing. It'll wait,' he said gloomily. As he returned to his study to drink his coffee, the first flakes of snow fell from the sky.

*

The wind pushed heavy grey clouds across the darkening sky at Gweek that Christmas Eve, but nothing could dampen the excitement the Williams family felt surrounding the triumphant return of Robin and Emma from Exeter. A phone call the previous evening from Emma had informed them that Robin had regained his sight, albeit slightly blurred, and they were due to come home the next day.

It had been a worrying time for Emma while Robin was in hospital, though the operation went well and Robin suffered only a small amount of discomfort, she fretted constantly about the outcome. She also missed home and her darling Edwin, and longed to get back into the bosom of her family. Emma's worst fears however were unfounded. As the bandage had been removed from Robin's eyes, Emma had stood back at first, too fearful to present herself. But through watery eyes he'd beckoned his beloved wife to his side, cupped her face gently in his hands and gazed upon her for what felt like an age. 'Oh my God Emma, no painting could be more beautiful or a flower more exquisitely fragrant than the image you present before me.' Emma's heart had soared.

As they pulled triumphantly into the yard at Barleyfield Farm, they were greeted by Lizzy and Charlie and the newly weds Harry and Rebecca as they all huddled in the doorway.

'Come in quick before you get soaked,' Lizzy beckoned, and they dashed into the warmth of the kitchen. As they shook the raindrops from their coats, Robin's eyes focused on the little boy in Rebecca's arms.

'Oh my son, my Edwin,' he said, dropping his coat in his wake. He scooped the child into his arms as heavy sobs caught in his throat. There wasn't a dry eye in the house, and Christmas was a fine affair at Barleyfield Farm that year.

*

Christmas at Runstone Manor Farm was a quieter affair

than the previous Christmas had been. John and Katie were very much missed by all, and neighbours who normally called, were conspicuous by their absence. Nevertheless, Rachel made what she could of the situation and cooked a fine Christmas dinner for the five of them, before they all had to return to their never ending round of farm jobs. As she washed the dishes, she pondered on what all her friends were doing this third Christmas in wartime, and it upset her a little that Lizzy hadn't acknowledge her Christmas letter. She sighed and wiped her hands on the towel - she probably wouldn't send her one next year.

*

Adam's father was taken to the hospital the day before Christmas Eve with pneumonia. They sat in vigil by his bedside for five days, and Christmas passed by without celebration. On the sixth day, his father's symptoms improved, and he was allowed home for the New Year, but the illness had weakened him considerably. As his father lay abed, he yearned for the warmth of his Tuscan villa. The trip to Devon was never mentioned, and Adam put his reunion with Rachel to the back of his mind and concentrated on improving his own mobility. With luck, he would be able to drive in a few months, if he could only get the feeling back in his leg.

21

After a cold spring, 1942 promised to be the worst summer on record. May ended wet followed by an even wetter June and July. The ceaseless rain battered the crops, leaving them flattened and mouldy. Many fields were flooded and unworkable and Jake despaired at what the harvest would bring. Fortunately, with Jake's forward thinking, he had bought in poultry the previous autumn, both table birds and layers, so they were able to sell the eggs to a nearby packing station. They sent them once a fortnight, in wooden boxes with cardboard slots, and fortunately received a fair price from the station. Eggs were also sold from the farm door for one shilling a dozen, so the poultry brought in a steady albeit paltry income.

By the end of July, Jake was near the end of his tether with the weather, until one morning he woke to brilliant sunshine. He set to work immediately with the others, to salvage whatever they could from the rotting crops. As August moved on, the heat from the now sweltering sun saved the day. September continued in the same vein and harvest time reaped its rewards, albeit smaller than other years.

*

In Yorkshire, Adam stood exhausted under the great oak tree which flanked the front garden of Bank Newton House. It had been a long hard struggle, but Adam had done it, he had set out this morning to East Marton, and followed the canal towpath back to Bank Newton, finally he had managed his goal which was to walk unaided for almost an hour. It had started with five minutes at the beginning of the year and slowly, very slowly, over the next nine months, he had built up enough energy to reach his goal - it felt so good. He now had regained a little more feeling in his leg, which allowed more confidence to be sure footed. Now he was able to arrange his journey to Devon. He had hoped that he would be able to drive, but after trying on several occasions, his foot would just not work as it should, and rendered the task too dangerous to consider. To ask his father to drive him was also out of the question. The illness at Christmas had left him suffering from a chronic lung infection which kept him to his own fireside for most of the time. So Adam knew his journey would have to be by public transport.

The train to Plymouth was teaming with people, and Adam had to struggle to find a seat. He never expected that so many people would be travelling about the countryside, and had to admit that being in the back of beyond in Yorkshire had completely cut him off from the goings on in the outside world. At Plymouth he caught a bus to Buckfastleigh, and began to make inquiries at the post office. All he had to go on was that Rachel was a land army girl, and that two members of the family she worked for had been casualties in the Plymouth bombing. The Post office drew a blank, but put him in touch with the Buckfastleigh Herald, a printing firm who distributed the local paper. The office was stuffy and hot for October when Adam rang the bell for service. A small balding man in his mid forties, sporting a splendid bushy moustache and long black apron, pondered on his question.

'I do remember something about that awful night, we reported on lots of casualties.' He gently stroked the moustache with is thumb and forefinger. 'Jim?' he called through to the back. 'Come here a minute.' Jim, wiping his inky hands on a cloth, appeared at the door enquiringly. 'Do you remember a couple, farmers I think they were, got blown up on a bus in the Plymouth bombings?'

Jim pressed his lips together, thought for a moment, then said, 'From near Widecombe, if I remember rightly. The name Hunstone or Runstone rings a bell. Husband and wife, on their way to the hospital they were, never got there, poor sods.'

Adam smiled broadly and thanked them profusely. He arrived at Widecombe-in-the-Moor early on Saturday evening. After booking in at The Old Inn, he settled himself down in the snug for an early dinner. After a much needed generous portion of ale pie, enquiries to the landlord about Rachel's whereabouts proved fruitless. He was new to the job and didn't know many of the locals yet. He told him there were a great many land army girls working in the surrounding countryside, and suggested if he came down for a drink later that evening, someone might know of her. Unfortunately, the journey had taken its toll on Adam and he had slept right through to the morning.

When Adam stepped out of the Inn early the next morning, Widecombe-in-the-Moor was deserted, except for about twenty wild ponies, which roamed the village quite freely. With his new found ability to walk for up to an hour, Adam set off to find Rachel. This was no easy task, as he walked he found many scattered farms and villages, the fields marked out by hedgerows forming distinctive patterns, connected by a cobweb of lanes. It was only by chance that he arrived at Runstone, though he knew not where he was exactly, as all the signposts had been taken down on the onset of war. With his map in hand he had been making for a hamlet just south of Widecombe, but exhaustion had forced him to rest near Runstone Cross, a large granite outcrop, north of the village. He sat down on the grassy bank and rested his head against the cold granite plinth, taking a sip of water from his bottle. The sun was warm on his face, the birds sang in the clear blue sky and Adam closed his eyes for a moment and was dozing within a few minutes.

A few yards away at Runstone Manor Farm, Jake called out to Rachel, 'The tractor and trailer's on its way.'

Rachel was gathering goods into a basket from the kitchen table. 'I'm coming,' she replied gaily.

A harvest festival had been planned at Widecombe for

the first Sunday in October - an event that seemed unlikely to happen just a few short months ago. The trailer, pulled along by Peter Gee and his tractor, trundled past Adam as he slept against the stone cross. Gee glanced down at the stranger and smiled that the noise hadn't roused him. He pulled up aside the front arched gate of the farm, just as Rachel ran up the path with her arms full of an array of fine vegetables, eggs and loaves of bread. This she added to the other produce in the cart which was making its way to Widecombe Church for the harvest display.

As Jake loaded the sack of potatoes in the cart he shouted, 'That's all Peter, we'll follow you up by foot.'

Peter Gee doffed his cap to Jake and set the tractor going, waking Adam from his nap. Rubbing the sleep from his eyes, Adam glanced down the hill towards where Jake was standing in the road. Adam made the decision to go and ask the man if he had ever heard of Rachel, but just as he made to get up from where he sat, the man was joined by a woman carrying a child in her arms. Adam was dumbstruck, unable to move, he could not believe that the woman he loved and yearned for, was right there, just a few yards from where he stood. 'Rachel', he said out loud. 'My Rachel.' He moved forward then stopped dead in his tracks, his eyes widened and his face took on a look of hopeless despair.

Rachel passed baby Jenna to Jake and he in turn wrapped his arm protectively around Rachel's shoulder. 'I didn't think we would be celebrating Harvest this year he said jovially. Rachel leant her head towards him and patted the hand he had laid on her shoulder and smiled happily back at him. To Rachel and Jake this show of affection was purely friendship, there were no sexual connotations about their closeness, but to an onlooker, the threesome looked like a happy family unit.

Ann E Brockbank

22
1960

Life at Runstone Manor Farm had carried on at much the same pace after the war was over. Food was still in short supply and rationing had gone on for a lot longer than anyone would have imagined, but as always, the farm produced enough food to live quite comfortably.

After the war, Jake continued to run the farm, but during the late forties he returned to the Abbey once a year for a months retreat. These ceased though at the turn of the decade, as Jake found more peace within himself working the land. Life had been very busy during the war years and spending time meditating no longer came easy to him, so in the end, he bid the Abbey a last farewell.

Jacob died in the summer of fifty three, at the age of twenty eight. There was no illness or warning - he just died in his sleep, living almost twenty years past anyone's expectations. The farm was now run by Jake and five local lads, three Barker brothers, Jim, who was forty-one, Samuel, thirty-eight and David, twenty-two. The eldest of the three had been fortunate to come home from the war unscathed and started at Runstone immediately, the latter had been working there since he was sixteen. Also helping, was Tom Hislop and Martin Byers, twenty-four and twenty-eight respectively. Vera and Peggy had left as soon as the war ended, and were both married with a brood of children between them. The everyday running of the household was down to Jenna and Rachel.

Runstone Manor Farm had become Rachel's home, and after the war she took no persuading to stay on there, and though she and Jake never became a couple like so many people thought they would, she was not at all lonely in her life. Jenna had been her pride and joy. She had looked upon her as her own, as Jenna looked upon her as a

216

mother. Jenna had filled the awful void left by the loss of her own daughter, though she never stopped thinking about her baby, or young woman as she would be now. From time to time she still thought of Adam, and wondered what had become of him and if he had survived the war. Occasionally she would dwell upon the time they spent in Tuscany, those heady days of love in the sunflower field, but these thoughts made her cry, and she quickly pushed them to the back of her mind. Yes, Adam de Sousa was in the far and distant past and the most pressing issue now for Rachel was preparing for Jenna's wedding to David Barker, the youngest of the Barker boys.

Romance had blossomed between them almost three years ago, and the wedding date had been fixed for the twelfth of March, which was just two weeks away. The wedding preparations brought it home to Rachel, how much she had missed of her own daughter's life. She wondered time and time again if Fiona would ever contact her via the adoption agency. After much deliberation, Rachel decided to contact the adoption agency on the off chance that Fiona had been in touch and they had perhaps mislaid her address. It was providence that she did, because the agency had no documentation of her ever registering with them. This was swiftly put right, and Rachel re-registered with the adoption contact register. She was not even sure if the adoption contact register could help, after all the adoption had not been a legal one, but nevertheless it was worth a try.

*

It was eight-thirty in the evening and there was already a thin crust of frost forming on the lawn as Helena Davenport drove up the drive at Stone Field Manor in Yorkshire. She shivered with cold. The car had hardly warmed up on the short journey from work. She hated the winter, especially in Yorkshire, for it seemed to go on forever. February, though a short month, seemed to be always colder and longer than the rest of the winter, but nothing was going to dampen her high spirits on this day. She was happy with life, she was to be married in August, and with that a settlement on her marriage would go towards buying the veterinary practice where she and her husband-to-be worked. Everything was working out just fine. As she slid out of the car seat, a figure appeared from the side of the house, it was Jack Taylor the gardener. 'Nanny Charlotte's very ill,' he said shortly. There had never been any love lost between him and Nanny Charlotte, but Helena thought he could have told her in a more caring manner. 'She's dying,' he added without expression.

Helena's heart lurched as she took the information in then slammed the car door and rushed up the stairs into the nursery where Nanny Charlotte lay in the bedroom she had occupied all the years Helena could remember. She looked very tiny lying there in bed. There was a fire lit and the room was warm and stuffy and Nanny was breathing with great difficulty. Nanny Charlotte was eighty-one, she had worked long after she should have done, in fact she was past retiring age when Helena had arrived at the house and given to her to care for.

The old lady sensed someone was in the room. 'Helena is that you?'

Helena sat on the bed and took the old woman's hand and stroked the transparent skin gently. 'Yes Nanny, it's me. Has the doctor been to see you?'

'Yes, he came earlier and said he would call again tomorrow. Oh my darling Helena, I fear I shall miss your wedding, and all the children you will produce.' Helena stroked her forehead gently. 'I'm dying, I know I don't have long, I was waiting until you came home, because I need you to do something for me.'

'Anything Nanny, just say the word and it's done,' she whispered softly.

A long thin arm stretched shakily towards the dresser.

'Top middle drawer, my diaries, I want you to have them. The entries in June 1940 and then on will interest you most, the ones previous, maybe not. You must take them now, I don't want that Jack Taylor to get his hands on them, do you hear me child?'

Helena looked puzzled. 'Jack! Why would Jack want your diaries?'

Panic flashed across the old woman's face and she grasped Helena hand. 'Just keep them away from him, please.'

Helena stroked Nanny's hand soothingly. 'I will, I promise, don't worry.'

The old woman sighed, as though a great load had lifted from her. 'You'll understand when you read them.'

Her arm fell beside her with a thump. She coughed painfully, licked her lips and asked for a sip of water. Her thirst quenched, she nodded gratefully to Helena. 'There is also a box I want you to have. It's in the wardrobe. Everything is in there - your life.' Helena furrowed her brow. 'Forgive me Helena. Forgive me when I have gone.'

'Forgive you? Whatever for? I love you Nanny, you've been wonderful, more like a mother,' she said, whispering the latter.

'The contents of the box are what a mother would give to you on your wedding day. The box is my gift to you. The diaries, well, they are also a gift, they are important to you though you don't realise it yet.' Her eyes flickered and she was quiet for a moment. 'I need to sleep now. You can take the things, but don't open them until I am gone. Will you promise me that?'

'I promise Nanny.' With that, the old woman closed her eyes. Helena sat with the woman who had nurtured and cared for her since she was born. No-one else came into the room, though they all knew death was imminent. Helena couldn't make up her mind if they were leaving her to be with the woman she really loved, or that they all just didn't care. At eleven-twenty-six, Nanny Charlotte took her final painful breath. Helena held her hand to the end. She cried until she was empty inside, then at one-forty she rang for the doctor and a funeral director. As she waited for them to arrive, she gently opened the middle top drawer and gathered an armful of diaries to her breast. She carried them to her room and hid them in her own wardrobe. She then took the box from Nanny's wardrobe, and placed it with the diaries. She stood for a moment, then took a suitcase down from her cupboard and moved them all into that. She zipped it up and locked it, though she knew not why, maybe to secure her life that Nanny had so preciously looked after.

Helena woke her parents just as the doctor arrived, and for a couple of hours there were comings and goings. Even Jack the gardener had got up and was milling around the house as copious amounts of coffee was being consumed. By three-thirty, the house was once again quiet. Helena took one last look at Nanny's bedroom before retiring herself. She lay awake for some time - her mind would not be still. Why had Nanny been so emphatic about Jack not seeing the diaries? Suddenly a noise punctured the stillness of the night. Perhaps someone was using the bathroom, but no, this was a quiet, embarrassed sort of noise. Helena rose and wrapped her robe about her. She opened the bedroom door and listened. Everywhere was silent, as she turned to return to her bedroom, a flash of light from under Nanny's door caught her eye.

Suddenly the door opened, and Helena moved back into the shadows. It was Jack, the flashlight was turned off, but Helena would know the slightly hunched back figure anywhere. She watched as he slipped down the stairs and out into the kitchen, when she heard the back door click shut, she made her way towards her Nanny's room. With only the moon for light, she noted the dresser drawers were not closed properly and the wardrobe was slightly ajar.

Helena shivered, whatever he was looking for, was locked safely in a suitcase under her bed, of that she was sure.

*

Helena had been very busy, what with work commitments and funeral arrangements, so it was almost a week before she had time to look into the suitcase. The box contained several photos, mostly of Helena at Christmas and every birthday. It held a lock of her hair, taken after her first haircut, and all her milk teeth, which Helena had placed under her pillow in return for a shiny sixpence. There was her christening gown, her first nightdress and bootees. A piece of christening cake, hard and green now wrapped in a napkin, embossed with her name. Helena quickly placed this aside. There was her first school report, and several paper cuttings from the Craven Herald announcing her birth, and eighteenth birthday. At the very bottom was a hessian band, on which the words 'baby girl Pendarves' was written. Helena frowned, and thought this must have been put in by mistake. She flipped it over in her fingers and found on the back a date, fourteenth of June 1940, her birth date. She placed everything back in the box except the band. She flipped the lid of the suitcase and rummaged until she found the diary for 1940, she teased the pages open until she came to the entry June the 23rd.

The entry ran over the allocated space for that day, in fact it took up the whole of the page, but the words were clear and concise, it read:

Such strange goings on in the house this evening! Mrs Davenport has visited the nursery a good seven times this evening, checking the cot and the drawer of clothes, though she isn't due for another two weeks.

It's six pm, and cook is livid, dinner has been postponed for a couple of hours - she was hoping to go to the pictures tonight.

Mr Davenport has just driven away and Cook says Mr Davenport didn't call for the chauffeur - he wanted to drive himself.

Oh my lord! Dear diary, where do I start? The master has returned with Jack the gardener. They have brought a baby girl home this evening. I have no idea where she has come from, I was just handed the baby and told to care for her and keep my mouth shut.

The child can't be more than a week old and she had a band around her tiny wrist - I don't think anyone else has noticed it. The child belongs to a woman named Pendarves. When I questioned Jack, he quite angrily told me the mother was dead. His manner was quite threatening when he told me the baby is the mistresses and I was not to breathe a word otherwise. They have obviously adopted the child, but I have a strange feeling all is not as it should be.

What a night this is turning out to be, I'm absolutely flabbergasted. Mrs Davenport breezed into the dining room this evening as slim as a post. The pregnancy had been a false one. I heard the master on the telephone to his great aunt Helena telling her the news of the birth. It seems they are going to pass the child off as their own. I must say the child is adorable, poor mite, but Mrs Davenport didn't even want to say goodnight to her. I heard her and the master laughing and celebrating. The master was giving a toast, which was quite extraordinary, I didn't mean to eavesdrop, but he was speaking quite loudly. 'To Stone Field Manor,' he said, 'the house is ours now we are a family. We can laugh in the face of great aunt Helena and her stupid family clause. I'm damned if I was going to let my brother Henri inherit this pile, just because he managed to produce a brood. So, here's to, what's the child called again? Oh yes Helena.'

My dear diary, I am shocked, shocked to the core, everything is making sense now.

Helena sat on her bed aghast. She could not believe what she had just read. 'I'm adopted!' she said the word out loud.

*

As Jenna's wedding neared, Rachel began to think of Fiona all the time, she wondered if she was somewhere wondering what had happened to her real mother. She would be twenty now. Had she been happy with her adopted family? Had she found a nice steady man to love, and would she be married with a family of her own? Oh so many questions unanswered.

*

Helena stood in the drawing room, stone-faced, with her hands on her hips. 'Were you ever going to tell me?' she demanded.

Daphne Davenport lit her cigarette and inhaled deeply. 'Tell you what?' she said, with a note of exasperation. Daphne had no time for the girl, this cuckoo in the nest - as she always referred her to.

'That I'm adopted!'

Daphne felt a surge of panic. 'Don't be absurd. Of course you're not adopted.' She glanced furiously towards Cedric for assistance.

'Anyone want another drink?' Cedric enquired when he heard the ice chink against the glass as Daphne quickly drained her remains of her gin and tonic.

'I know I'm adopted, so you can stop lying to me.' Daphne's cheeks spotted pink as Helena watched her stub out her cigarette.

Cedric was visibly angry now. 'This is ridiculous, I don't know where you have got this notion from, but you can just stop this nonsense now. Look you're upsetting your mother.'

'I know I'm adopted, because Nanny left me her diaries.'

Cedric swallowed hard and ran his hand over his receding hair. 'You're not seriously going to believe the scribbling of an old woman. I would have credited you with more sense than that Helena.'

'As a matter of fact I do believe her, it's all there, documented. Every single thing that happened the night I arrived.'

Daphne had paled significantly. She placed her glass down on the table with trembling fingers and said with as much authority as she could muster. 'I'm not listening to any more of this rubbish, kindly leave the drawing room Helena. We don't want to listen to your ranting anymore, do we Cedric?'

'I quite agree,' he answered stiffly.

Refusing to be perturbed, Helena played her trump card and produced the tiny wrist band from her pocket. 'My birth band, it says, 'Baby girl Pendarves, fourteenth of June 1940'.'

Daphne emitted a low groan. As Cedric moved toward the fireplace, he picked up the poker and stabbed the coals several times. The air was thick with emotion.

'You brought me here for some kind of financial gain didn't you? It was something to do with this place.' Her eyes skimmed the opulent room. 'You certainly didn't want a child of your own that is clear. Not once have you taken any interest in my upbringing or emotional welfare.'

Cedric bristled with antipathy. 'Now you can stop right there young lady. You have wanted for nothing. You have had a good education, been clothed in the finest and well looked after.'

'I wanted a mothers love, but you never loved me,' she directed the allegation at Daphne. 'Neither of you wanted me did you?'

'Oh for God sake, tell her Cedric, she knows most of it already,' Daphne said, lighting another cigarette.

Helena looked to both of her parents in anticipation, but Cedric kept his back to her.

Presently Daphne sighed heavily and said, 'We were going to lose Stone Field Manor. Your Great Aunt Helena insisted that Stone Field was a family home, and even though your father was the eldest she made it clear that unless we produced a family, your Uncle Henri would have inherited it. Your father and I never wanted children, which caused a dilemma as you can imagine. Fortunately, she became very ill and was not expected to live, so I told her I was pregnant and she said we could stay. Unfortunately, she recovered and we were thrown into a predicament. We were too old to adopt through the normal channels, so it was providence that we were told that some fallen woman had given birth to a daughter and had conveniently died, so in the kindness of our hearts we adopted you.'

'You really are despicable aren't you?' Helena hissed.

'Don't you dare speak to me in that manner - you have done very well out of the situation. You could have ended up anywhere, but instead you had all the comforts a child could need. And what's more lady, you wouldn't be inheriting ten thousand pounds on your marriage if it wasn't for us securing this inheritance.'

Helena's eyes were full of scorn. 'I still think you're despicable.'

'Be that as it may, and you may well look at me like that, but if you breathe a single word of this to anyone, you will not receive a single penny of that money, do I make myself clear?'

'Perfectly,' Helena said, as she swept from the room.

*

Though March 1960 had started cold and dry, there was a great storm three days before Jenna's wedding. Trees were brought down on all lanes leading to Widecombe. With the high winds and the lower fields and village paths lying under water, Jenna despaired that she was ever going to make it to the church, but with a lot of hard work, the trees were pulled to the side of the road enough to drive a car through and thankfully the day of her wedding to David broke fine and warm. The ceremony passed off well, before the forty or so guests. Afterwards, everyone made their way down the lanes scattered with tree trunks to the reception which was held at Runstone Manor Farm. Because the front parlour was hardly big enough to accommodate such a large influx of guests, the kitchen came into its own and was laid out with food and drink. On the whole the party was a fine affair.

The happy couple were to honeymoon in Torquay, and a colourful procession of people stood at the gates to wave them off on their way. Some of the guests stayed on for another hour, then presently the house was empty and

Rachel felt very much alone in life. Her surrogate daughter had flown the nest, and she felt quite bewildered at the emotions which gripped at her heart.

Presently, she made a start on clearing the debris of the reception, and as she gathered the plates together it was then she noticed the pile of unopened letters on the kitchen windowsill, which someone had obviously picked off the doormat that morning and pushed to one side. She wiped her hands down her apron and began to open the mail. The first three were utility bills, the other was from Vera, which she sat down with a mug of coffee to read and digest with relish. Vera always wrote an amusing anecdote of life with her husband and three children. She always found something funny to say about almost anything they had done. It always cheered Rachel up. She popped the letter back in the envelope and made to get up when she noticed another letter she'd overlooked. Her heart almost stopped as she opened and read it. Just at that moment Jake breezed into the kitchen and Rachel quickly folded the letter and pushed it deep into the pocket of her apron. She pondered on it for the rest of the day, and then later that night, she unfolded the cover letter from the adoption contact register, then the accompanying letter. Great tears ran down her face as she read:

Dear Ms Pendarves,

My name is Helena Davenport. You will, I think, know me better as Fiona. First of all may I apologise for the intrusion this letter may cause.

I have recently received knowledge that I was adopted at birth, a matter which came to light via a member of our household staff. I was of course shocked at the revelation, and confronted my parents, they verified that I was adopted, but told me you had died shortly after my birth. They also informed me that my birth father was unknown, so that adoption was the best thing for me. On learning this news and after much heart searching I contacted the Adoption Contact Register to learn more about you and was informed that you are in fact alive and well and registered with them. I'm not sure if I can understand why you had to give me away, but you must have had your reasons, and as I have been well cared for, largely due to my loving Nanny, I do not in any way reprimand you for your actions. I had a good childhood, I am a very happy, contented and well adjusted person, and I can safely say I have never wanted for anything.

At first I never intended to make any contact with you, but after much soul searching, I feel compelled to write to you to tell you that I am to be married on August the 27th to a good and kind man, a little older than me, but we have many things in common. I don't want to alert my parents that I have found you, so consequently I won't tell them I have written to you, but as my birth mother I believe this is an occasion that you may want to witness. As you can appreciate I will not be able to offer you a formal invitation to the wedding, but if perhaps you would like to attend the church ceremony, you will be very welcome to do so. This of course must be done in secrecy, and I will not make any contact with you on the day, but if you do attend, please wear a red rose so that I know who you are.

Of course, I am not sure how you will react to this letter. You probably have a family of your own now and may not be able to attend the wedding. If this is the case then I respect and understand your wishes. If I do see you there, I will know that you are open to more contact and I will write to you again and maybe we can meet at a location convenient to you.

Yours truly

Helena Davenport (Fiona)

Wedding ceremony, Saturday 27th August 1960, @ Bolton Abbey Priory, North Yorkshire at 3:30 pm. No RSVP please.

Darkness had fallen before Rachel arrived at the grand Devonshire Hotel in Bolton Abbey. It had been a long journey, first by taxi, then train then taxi again. She'd been travelling for nigh on twelve hours, and was heartily exhausted by the time she crawled onto her hotel bed.

It had been more than twenty years since Rachel had set foot on Yorkshire soil, and in truth, had rather hoped that she would never return, but this visit was for a very special reason - a very special reason indeed. Twenty years ago, she lost her one and only child by means of an illegal adoption, tomorrow she would, albeit secretly, be reunited with that daughter. With this thought in her mind, she laid her head upon the goose down pillow, and drifted into a deep dreamless sleep. She slept solidly for nine hours, only to wake stiff and chilled atop of the satin quilted eiderdown at eight the next morning.

After a quick bath, Rachel dressed and made her way to breakfast. With a few hours to spare before the wedding at three-thirty that afternoon, she clutched a brochure of the area from the hotel lobby, and took herself off to explore some of the vast Duke of Devonshire's estate, in which the Devonshire Hotel was situated.

She sat outside the pavilion café in the morning sunshine with a cup of hot steaming coffee, and planned her short excursion. With time at a premium, she decided not to visit the infamous 'Strid' where the broad River Wharfe is funnelled into a narrow channel. She read in her brochure that the sides of the channel had been undercut to a depth of thirty feet, turning the usual gentle river into vicious white swirling waters, which, it stated, if you were foolhardy enough to attempt to jump across the deceptively narrow stones and fail to make it, you would be sucked into the underwater whirlpools. Apparently, the 'Strid' had claimed many lives over the years. Rachel shuddered, drank down the remains of her coffee and decided instead to make her way down towards the stepping stones, which crossed the River Wharfe, by the ancient ruins of the magnificent twelfth century Bolton Priory. Stated to be one of England's most beautiful ecclesiastical ruins, the Abbey was set in immaculate parkland. As she sat on the river bank and dipped her toes into the icy water, she read that the priory was once used by Augustinian monks. This made her think of Jake, who had been mystified by her sudden revelation that she was taking a holiday.

'A holiday?' he'd exclaimed, thumping his fists into his sides in mock horror. 'In all the twenty years you've been here at Runstone Manor Farm, I have never known you to take a single day off.'

'Then maybe it's time I did,' she answered, adding a simple smile.

Though he joked with her, Jake was indeed mystified by her behaviour, though he certainly didn't begrudge her a break if she wanted it. In fact no-one deserved it better than Rachel. It was just the strange way she had been acting most of the summer that troubled him. He had wondered secretly if she had found herself a gentleman friend and was planning a meeting with him, but she had never offered to tell him where she was going and Jake certainly was in no position to ask.

Rachel sat for an hour by the river, and then had walked up to the 'Valley of Desolation', which was aptly named. The devastation was made by a terrible thunderstorm over one hundred and fifty years ago, and it still had an eerie feeling to this day, but there was, in consolation, an impressive waterfall there, where Rachel sat for a while as the sun flooded the valley in a pale yellow hue. She marvelled at the splendour of the age old woodlands, fringed with bracken moor land, full of grouse and deer, and thought it to be a beautiful place for her daughter to start married life. 'I hope you will be happy, my long lost daughter,' she whispered softly into the warm morning breeze.

*

Rachel, dressed in a cornflower blue skirt suit with accompanying black court shoes and handbag, took her seat on a pew at the rear of the church. She glanced at her watch - fifteen minutes to go and already the church was almost full. Rachel sighed gently, all these people gathered here, were all known by her daughter.

The lady in the pew in front of Rachel was talking to a fellow guest. 'Oh Hilda haven't you met Helena's intended,' she said, with much authority. 'He's much older than her you know, but oh so handsome. Yes, she met him at work. Well, they do say fifty percent of women meet their husband-to-be at work nowadays. It wasn't like that in our day was it Hilda? Oh look, I think he's just arrived. My, what a dashing groom he is. How wonderful for Helena to have met him, for she is such a wonderful girl, very kind and thoughtful. She's an absolute credit to her parents. Oh look Hilda, he's taking his seat.'

Rachel looked up, but could only see a glimpse of the back of the grooms head. She sighed. All these people knew more about her little girl than she did - her own mother. Her eyes filled with tears at the lost years. Twenty years had passed, but the pain of losing her had never left her, it was just something she had learned to cope with. She blinked away the tears, and patted the red rose she had secured to the lapel of her suit, and opened the 'order of service' card which had been thrust into her hand by one of the ushers. She cursed herself, without her spectacles she found it difficult to read the gold emboss on the cream card. She snapped open the clasp on her bag, and lifted her spectacle case onto her lap, but was suddenly distracted as two male figures dressed in grey morning suits and gold waistcoats took their places at the altar. Rachel felt herself go suddenly cold.

As the two men stood at the alter sharing a nervous joke, Rachel's head involuntarily shook in denial as her eyes swept over the familiar frame of the man she had known and loved so many, many, years ago. No, she told herself, it could not be him. It was her imagination - it must be. She fumbled with her spectacles and picked up the 'Order of Service' card, and her eyes widened with disbelief. 'Oh my God!'

The card read:

Bolton Abby Priory

Marriage
of
Helena Jayne Davenport
&
Adam de Sousa
***

Saturday 27th August 1960
At
3.30 p.m.

With a sickness in the pit of her stomach, and her head spinning, Rachel glanced back at Adam. The church was full now, though guests were still arriving, and many were standing at the rear. The vicar, a short stocky bespectacled man, glided around, smiling at everyone he came into contact with. Rachel knew what she must do. She stood up, excused herself past the row of guests, and quickly made her way toward the entrance where the Reverend Henry Stockdale was stood awaiting the arrival of the bride.

'Excuse me Reverend.'

'Yes dear,' he replied, as she touched him lightly on the shoulder.

'I must speak with you urgently.'

The Reverend smiled softly. 'Of course, I will see you after the ceremony.'

'No, you don't understand.' Her voice was low. 'I must speak with you before the ceremony. They cannot marry.'

The reverend pursed his lips. 'Then you must speak up during the ceremony, if you feel there is a reason that they may not marry.'

'Oh God no, you must not let the marriage begin. They cannot marry, they are related you see. It would be incest.' The very word stuck in her throat. 'You must stop them from marrying.

There was a pause. 'What exactly are you saying?'

'I'm saying that Adam is Fiona's,' Rachel hesitated. 'I mean Helena's birth father. I am Helena's birth mother. It would be an incestuous match.'

The vicar bristled slightly. 'Madam I have known this family for many years and I can assure you that Helena is not adopted.'

'Be that as it may, but I can assure you, Helena is my birth daughter, so you must stop this wedding before it's too late.'

'May I have your name please?'

'Rachel Pendarves.'

There was a period of icy silence between them, before the Reverend Harry Stockdale instructed his verger to stall the bride from vacating the limousine, then ushered Rachel into the vestry. He closed the door and stood against it, his hands clasped tightly behind him.

'This is cruel Mrs Pendarves. Why have you waited until now to reveal this information? How could you do this? To wait until this poor girl is..' He glanced at his watch. '..five minutes from the happiest moment of her life.'

'Oh believe me.' Rachel sobbed. 'I had no idea she was to marry Adam. I haven't seen Helena since she was taken from me for adoption twenty years ago. The invitation to this wedding came out of the blue. It's meant to be a secret from her adopted parents. Oh, what are we going to do, I can't face her with this.'

'So, you are saying Helena is adopted? But I saw her birth certificate which clearly said she was a Davenport.'

'The adoption was illegal. My daughter was taken from me just after birth. The Davenports must have registered her in their name.'

'And you say Adam de Sousa is her father?'

'Yes,' she said meekly.

'These are serious allegations Mrs Pendarves. How can I be sure you are telling the truth?'

Rachel hands flew to her face. 'You must believe me, you must.'

He cleared his throat. 'Wait there.' A second later he was gone, and so too had Rachel. She stole away from the vestry, hid behind one of the ancient pillars which supported the great arched roof, while she watched the vicar walk towards Adam. His handsome face was smiling, just as she remembered from all those years ago. She had thought he was dead, killed in the war perhaps. But, here he was, very much alive and as strong and handsome as ever. He had changed little over the years, slightly greying at the temples perhaps, but the sight of him made her heart lurch and the longing ache within her which she had suppressed for years, welled up to choke her. She ripped the red rose from her lapel, and walked swiftly out of the church. The limousine was parked some twenty yards away, and Rachel moved quickly out of sight. She put her hand on the cold stone wall of the church to steady herself, her fingers trailed along the wall as though she was blind, as she stumbled towards the rear of the building and into the brilliant sunshine. She stood for a moment with her back to the wall and her face upturned to let the heat of the sun warm the chill in her body. Suddenly her eyes snapped open with a start. This was something she could not face with either Adam or Helena - she knew she must leave. So, as fast as her tight court shoes would let her, she ran away from the debris of what was left of her daughter's wedding.

*

The journey home was long and traumatic as she tried hard not to think of the unthinkable, but her fears would not let her questions rest. Had they consummated their relationship before marriage? For sure they must have. How on earth would they live with such shame? She started to cry, her shoulders heaving, and her fellow passengers looked on, but did not interfere. It crossed her mind that Adam would be arrested, but no, he didn't know, it was just too awful to comprehend. The sight of Adam, so imprinted in her mind, made her heart ache. Where on earth had he been all these years? Why had he never tried to find her? This would never have happened if he had returned to her. None of the heartache would have happened, if he had just returned home to her.

24

The wedding limousine arrived back at the Davenports residence a little sooner than expected, sending the staff into a frenzy of panic. Before the limousine came to a halt, Helena jumped from the vehicle, her wedding gown gathered up in her arms and tears running from her face. The housekeeper stood open-mouthed as Helena pushed past her. She snapped her head around just in time to see Helena disappear up the staircase. Mystified, she set her gaze upon Cedric Davenport as he alighted from the vehicle - he looked pale and pinched around the mouth.

'Whatever is it sir? What on earth has happened?' the housekeeper cried.

Cedric gestured to her not to ask as he swept by, he then followed Helena up the stairs. A moment later, an entourage of cars turned into the drive, it was clear then to the housekeeper, that there was to be no wedding that day.

*

Adam sat in the now empty church with his head in his hands. Try as he might, he could not comprehend what had just happened. Why hadn't Rachel told him about the child? Why did she not try to find him, and why had she not just stayed in Gweek where he could have found her? He could not comprehend why she would have had their baby sent for adoption. Did she not know how much he loved her? Did she really think that he wouldn't come looking for her as soon as he was able? And why did no- one in Gweek tell him, he'd been in contact with them. 'Why, why, why?' The last three words were uttered out loud.

'If I may speak with you Adam?'

Adam lifted his head to face the Reverend Henry Stockdale.

'This has been a terrible shock for you my son, and for the Davenports.'

'Poor, poor Helena,' Adam said, burying his face in his

hands again.

'Indeed, poor Helena,' he said, looking skywards. He placed his hand upon Adam's shoulder. 'I must ask you a very delicate question Adam?' Adam did not raise his head, so the Reverend continued. 'Was Helena pure today?' Adam looked up at the Reverend mournfully, but before he could answer the reverend asked, '…did you, consummate your relationship?'

Adam swallowed hard and shook his head. 'No, no we haven't.'

The Reverend sighed with relief. 'Praise god that she was keeping herself pure for the wedding night'.

Adam cleared his throat. 'Yes quite,' he said, shifting uncomfortably. Thank god this had only been a business arrangement he thought. The alternative would have been just appalling.

The Reverend smiled softly, mistaking Adam's reverie as guilt. 'We must both pray for forgiveness my son.'

Adam could sit no more. He stood up with a violent jerk, his eyes shining and fierce. He felt as though he had aged in the last hour. 'If you will excuse me Reverend, I must speak with Helena. And I am so sorry to bring this on you and your church.'

'Your apology is between you and your maker my son, I'll pray for you and Helena every night.'

Adam nodded a curt bow to the Reverend, turned on his heel and left.

A half hour later he pulled his car to a halt outside Stone Field Manor, and was let into the hall by a very frosty faced Housekeeper. 'If you care to step into the library, I shall inform Mr Davenport that you are here.'

'It's Helena I want to see,' Adam pleaded. The housekeeper nodded as she pulled the door shut.

A moment later, Cedric Davenport entered the room, Adam noted that Cedric looked like he felt, desolate. 'de Sousa,' his voice quivered a little.

'Mr Davenport.'

'Well, I don't know what to say to you, this has been a terrible day.'

'Indeed it has,' Adam said, forcing his voice to stay calm. 'I would like to see Helena if I may Sir.'

Davenport cleared his voice. 'Understandably Helena does not want to see you... ever again.' Adam lowered his eyes to the floor.

'You must know that this relationship cannot go on man?'

'Of course I do, I just want to see her. I need to speak with her. Apparently I'm her father!'

Davenport shook his head violently. 'It's out of the question. I think you need to go a very long way away from here, and very quickly. But first I want the truth.'

'The truth?' Adam looked puzzled. 'About what?'

'Helena says you have not been intimate with her. Is this true?'

'Of course it's true. Can you not believe your own... daughter,' he practically choked on the word

'I don't know what to think at the moment. Why had you never told us you had a child somewhere?'

'I didn't know. I swear this is the first I have heard about it.'

Cedric's drawn face grew harder. 'I wonder how many more brats have you sired and left with some poor unsuspecting wretch.'

Adam felt the anger well up. 'Now just you wait a minute. I am not the only one to blame in this affair. You never told me she was adopted.' Davenport coloured a little. 'If I had seen her birth certificate I would have known instantly that I was her father. I don't deny having a relationship with Rachel Pendarves, I loved her, but we lost touch during the war.'

'The name Pendarves wasn't on Helena's birth certificate.'

Adam was puzzled now. 'How come?'

Davenport moistened his lips. 'The adoption was not, err…' He paused for a moment. 'We did not go through the normal channels. It was a private transaction.'

Adam's eyes widened. 'You mean you paid for the child?'

'In short, yes.'

'Rachel sold you her baby?' he said incredulously. 'I don't believe it. Rachel would never do such a thing, you're lying!'

Davenport walked towards the fireplace. He was troubled by the affair and unsure how to continue the conversation, but continue he must. He turned to face Adam. 'We did not buy the child from the mother. In fact we never met her. We understood she had died following complications after the birth. My gardener was a relative of Mrs Pendarves, and an agreement was made that we would take on the child for a fixed amount of money. We believed the mother to be dead, so when the child came to us, we registered her in our own names.' He waved a hand dismissively. 'Oh yes I know, it was all very illegal, but we were desperate for a child. It was our only option.'

'So, how did Helena find out she was adopted if her birth certificate gave your own names?'

'Her nanny let it slip on her death bed.'

Adam raised his eyebrows. 'Well it's lucky that Nanny did tell her, isn't it?' he said angrily. 'So, tell me, how did she find out about Rachel?'

'She says she wrote to the adoption agency to look for information on her birth mother. Apparently there was a letter from Mrs Pendarves on the off chance Helena would try to find her. Helena wrote to her and invited her to the wedding, without our knowledge.'

Adam fizzed with anger. 'I could go to the police about this!'

Davenport's face looked set in stone. 'I think not de

Sousa. You have courted my daughter for the last six months, you may not have, as you both plead, consummated the relationship, but nevertheless, the police would find it very difficult to believe you.'

The two men squared each other up for a good few seconds, and then the silence was broken by Davenport. 'I think it would be best if you leave. We shall endeavour to cover up this mess, by saying the wedding was called off by both parties - irreconcilable differences. You, I suggest should leave the county. I'm sure with your profession you can work anywhere. This will also pave the way for Helena to return to the Gardendale veterinary practice and continue her career there.' Without further ado, Davenport rang the bell for the housekeeper. When the door opened, Davenport said, 'Please show Mr de Sousa out.'

Adam glared at Davenport for a second, and then marched out of the library after the housekeeper. As he sped off down the drive, Helena watched desolately from her bedroom window. When he was out of sight she collapsed in a crumpled heap on the floor and wept into the cloud of lace which was her wedding gown.

*

Jake was walking in from the fields when Rachel, looking pale and distressed, returned to Runstone Manor late the next day. She glanced up at him as he called out to her, she said nothing, but her eyes told everything. Rachel moved quickly through the door into the kitchen, nodding an acknowledgement to Jenna as she passed.

Noting her countenance, Jenna quickly closed the recipe book she was engrossed in, jumped from her chair and followed Rachel up the stairs. 'Rachel?' Jenna called out.

Rachel paused as she turned the handle of her bedroom door, then without looking round she whispered. 'Later Jenna, please.' Then she locked herself in her room for the rest of that day.

She sat on the thick eiderdown, silent and sick with

grief, for it was like a grief. She was mourning the death of an ideal, a fantasy, a rose coloured dream. Her minds eye vision of one day finding her beautiful daughter and the man she had loved and lost, had suddenly amalgamated into a very real, but unspeakable nightmare.

She hardly noticed the sun setting until there came a knock at her door.

It was Jake. 'Rachel, are you alright?' His knock got louder. 'Rachel?'

'Yes I'm all right Jake,' she said, her voice faltering.

'Well, I don't think you are.' He turned the handle, but the door was locked. 'Let me in.'

Rachel stood up and glanced at the mirror on the back of the door, her face was drawn and white like china. The fine lines around her mouth and eyes seemed more pronounced than usual. She watched as Jake turned the handle again and her stomach tightened.

'Rachel let me in!' His voice held a hint of panic.

'No, I'm alright Jake, honestly I am. I just need to be alone for a while. I'll see you in the morning.' She relaxed slightly when she heard him release the handle. A few moments passed before she heard his footsteps on the stairs, it was only then that she returned to where she sat on the warmth of the eiderdown and resumed her aching unimaginable grief.

When Jake returned from milking the next morning, there was still no sign of Rachel. He sat heavily at the kitchen table and rubbed the stubble on his chin. 'Something awful has happened to her, I just know it,' he said to Jenna.

Jenna turned from cooking the breakfast and saw the look of concern on his face. 'Well, did she say what?'

Jake's mouth was pinched with anguish as he shook his head. 'I think she went to meet a man you know. I think it was some kind of date or something, and it all went horribly wrong.'

'Are you saying, that you think she's been raped or something?'

'I don't know. I just don't know.' He was pacing the kitchen now. 'If I find out that someone has hurt her, I'll bloody well seek them out and kill them.' He punched his clenched fist into his palm.

Jenna was shocked at the outburst of passion in her normally placid brother.

'There'll be no need for that,' Rachel spoke gently. They both spun around at the sound of her voice. 'There is no man, and I haven't been hurt, not in the way you think anyway.'

Jake was shocked at her appearance, and pulled her into his arms. 'Then what is it that bothers you? Look at you. You're obviously in some kind of deep shock. Tell me what it is then we can help?'

Rachel shook her weary head. 'I can't tell you. I love you both dearly, but I just can't, it's too terrible, too private and too painful. Please let me deal with it my way.'

The next morning Rachel packed her bags again and left for Cornwall.

*

The sun blazed down on the surrounding fields of Bank Newton Grange, but Adam felt as cold as the grave as he sat in the fireside chair. He had eaten little since his return to the house two days ago, and slept fitfully where he sat. He looked around the house, which belonged to him now. His parents had bought the property just after the war. They had died within months of each other, some eighteen years ago, but he knew he could not stay here any longer. He had covered most of the furniture in thick dust sheets, the water, gas and phone had been turned off, and the windows throughout had been shuttered. His suitcase stood at the front door, but still he sat by the empty fire. He was just psyching himself to leave the house which had been in his family for the past nineteen years.

He had made a call to the estate agents first thing to let the house, and promised to drop the key into their office on his way. He glanced at the resignation letter on the writing desk - he would drop that through the door of the Gartondale Veterinary practice on the way. He wouldn't have to say goodbye to anyone, he would just leave, though he knew not where he was going at the moment.

He had sat and pondered all weekend about what had happened. He cast his mind back to the day he returned from Runstone after seeing Rachel all those years ago. She had seemed so happy in her marriage to the tall dark man by her side, and their union had been blessed with a child too. On his return to Yorkshire and still unfit to be of any use to the war effort, he'd become a gentleman farmer, keeping a small amount of livestock and leasing out the surrounding fields. After the war, with his parents dead, he sold the stock, let the house and drove back to Tuscany to ascertain the damage Hitler had done to the villa. He was overjoyed at first to find it untouched. It was only when he opened the front door that he found a gaping hole where the back of the house once stood. It took him eight long years to rebuild the villa and restore it to its former glory. He returned to Yorkshire in 1950, and with a need to do something useful with his life, he re-trained and joined the Veterinary practice in Gartondale. In the last twenty years he had never forgotten Rachel, she had, and always would be the love of his life and because of this he vowed never to marry. He laughed cynically as he thought of it now. It was a vow he kept until six months ago when Helena Davenport, the veterinary practice manager, had propositioned him. If truth be known he was attracted to her because she had so reminded him of Rachel. He shook his head at the irony. She was in fact her own flesh and blood - and his! He shuddered at the thought. 'Oh Rachel, Rachel,' he spoke out loud. 'To think you were within twenty yards of me, in the same church as I was about to marry my own daughter, what a reunion that was to be.' He dropped his head in his hands. 'Oh god, what am I to do?' He sighed deeply. He spoke a lot to god at the moment. He had no one else to speak to. No one would return his calls, not even the other partners in the practice. Most of the guests saw him leave his pew in the church that morning shortly before the wedding was cancelled, to all intent and purpose, everyone believed that he had changed his mind and called the wedding off. Thankfully no one would know the awful truth.

25

Rachel knocked quietly at Lizzy's door then waited a moment. Everything was so similar, though smaller, which was a little disorientating. She sighed, and knocked a little louder this time. A moment later she glanced through the window into the empty kitchen, she stepped back and noted all the windows were shut. Her bag felt heavy, as she lifted it to walk. It crossed her mind that Lizzy and Charlie might not live here anymore, after all, it had been twenty years since she had been to Gweek. This had been a stupid idea, to come all this way to see someone who she had lost contact with. Someone who had once been her best friend, but had not returned her letter all those years ago. How on earth did she expect someone, who she hadn't been in touch with for years, to fling her arms around her as if they had only been parted a week or so. No, this had been a bad idea. She would go immediately in case anyone recognised her. She quickened her pace, walking with such vigour towards the bus stop at the far end of the bridge that she was quite out of breath when she arrived. She studied the timetable and her heart sank, there wasn't another bus to Falmouth until five-fifteen, which was over two hours away. As she sat, she had time to reflect on life in Gweek, how she lost her lovely husband Alex, and the tragic death of Verity. That first Christmas she spent with Adam, and how wonderful he had made it for her. She thought of Vicos, which made her stand to look out down river, but there were no black swans to be seen, perhaps they were long dead she thought to herself. It was after all, a long time ago. There were voices now coming from The Black Swan, as Rachel stood and watched she saw a woman step out and walk down the steps. There was a strange frisson in the air. It was as though Lizzy knew that someone was watching her, very slowly she turned her head to stare at the woman on the bridge. Momentarily they paused, and then something made Lizzy walk towards her. As she neared the brow of the bridge, recognition and realisation took over, and Rachel abandoned her bag and began to run. Their reunion was intense, emotional and overwhelming for both women. They hugged and cried and hugged again for a good five minutes, until they finally broke away from each other, though still holding hands, the years peeled away, the estrangement forgotten, the friends were back together again.

Sitting in the farm kitchen, Lizzy listened intently to Rachel's story, giving her time to compose herself every time a bout of sobbing halted her narrative. She was shocked indeed at Rachel's revelations, and sorry that she had gone through all this, while being quite alone in the world. The latter part of the story was indeed quite shocking, but as Lizzy absorbed the tale she did not offer any comment on it - things needed to be found out first. She could see Rachel needed to get it all off her chest. It was truly awful to think that there might, just might, have been incest committed, but until Lizzy could think of a way of getting some verification on the matter, she would not pass judgment.

'Oh what am I to do Lizzy?' she cried.

Lizzy wrapped her arms around her. 'Nothing at the moment my luver,' Lizzy said, as she stroked Rachel's hair. 'It's best to do nothing until you have calmed down. We'll talk about it more tomorrow, when you've had a good sleep. At least you've shared your story, you are not alone with it anymore, things will seem easier now, trust me. Things may not be as bleak as they seem, things often aren't after careful consideration.'

'But, incest is incest, no matter how you look at it Lizzy,' Rachel said, more quietly, but with her eyes brimming with tears.

'Tomorrow, trust me, let's wait until tomorrow.'

'Lizzy.' Rachel paused for a moment 'I wasn't sure

whether to come to you or not.' Lizzy cocked her head, but said nothing. Rachel licked her lips nervously. 'You never answered my letters.'

'You never gave me your address you daft mare.' She laughed. 'I got your letter and Christmas card, and then a birthday card came, but still no bloody address.'

Rachel put her hand to her mouth. 'Oh my goodness, you're absolutely right, I didn't, did I?'

'I tried to find you believe me. I wrote to Widecombe post office to see if they could give me your address, but I never got an answer.'

Rachel pulled a face at the mention of the postmaster there. He was a disagreeable chap at the best of times. Even serving people was a chore he could well do without, so answering a letter would have been out of the question. Thankfully he was no longer with us.

'Oh Lizzy, to think that I thought you were angry with me all these years for upping and leaving like that.'

The women embraced. 'Never mind, we are back together again now. Come on, I have a hungry man to feed in an hour - do you want to help me cook?'

Rachel nodded warmly. 'Can I just ask you to please not tell anyone I'm here? I can't face anyone at the moment.'

'My lips are sealed.'

As the two friends worked together in the kitchen in Gweek, Runstone Manor Farm was about to receive an unexpected visitor.

*

The village of Runstone wore the same appearance it had done some nineteen years ago, as Adam stood beside Runstone Cross and looked down the lane towards Runstone Manor Farm. How very déjà-vu he thought to himself, though this time he would speak to Rachel. This time he would make his presence known to her. He could not bear to think of her thinking ill of him. He must tell her, that what she believed to have happened between him and Helena, had not.

At the door he pushed his fingers through his hair nervously, took a deep breath and knocked. The girl who answered was about the same age as Helena, this, he thought, must be Rachel's daughter. He studied her for a moment. She had a strong, enquiring face, beneath her short cropped hair but bore no resemblance to Rachel.

'Can I help you?' she asked pleasantly.

'Yes, hello.' He cleared his throat. 'I would like to speak with your mother if I may?' he said, punctuating his sentence with slightly embarrassed smiles.

The smile on Jenna's face faltered slightly. 'My Mother?' Her eyebrows furrowed slightly.

Adam nodded. 'If I may.'

Jenna held his gaze for a moment. 'Do you mean Rachel?'

'Yes.' Suddenly realising, he had mistaken who the girl was. 'I'm sorry I thought you were her daughter.'

Jenna allowed a smile to warm her face. 'Well, Rachel did in fact bring me up. My mother died when I was a baby, so yes I suppose she has been my mother. I'm sorry I didn't catch your name?'

'Oh sorry. It's de Sousa, Adam de Sousa.'

The name meant nothing to Jenna. 'I'm sorry Mr de Sousa, Rachel isn't here.'

A man's voice suddenly filtered through from the inside of the house. 'Who is it Jen?' As the man appeared, Adam recognised him to be the same one he had seen with Rachel so many years ago.

'I'm sorry to disturb you. My name is Adam de Sousa,' he said, holding out his hand to Jake. 'I was in fact looking for your wife Rachel, but this young lady says she is not in.'

Jake gave Adam a broad smile. 'Rachel's not my wife and no, she isn't here. Can I ask what your business is with her?'

'She's not your wife?' he said in astonishment.

Jake looked cautiously at Adam, and then answered, 'Never been married in my life, Rachel has, but she was widowed some twenty odd years ago. Who are you, and what do you want her for?' Jake's eyes narrowed and wondered if this de Sousa fellow had something to do with Rachel going away as suddenly as she did.

Adam was clearly puzzled by these revelations, and for a few seconds, could not answer Jake. His eyes began to fog at the realisation, that nineteen years ago he'd thrown away the opportunity of being reunited with her on the basis of an assumption.

Adam staggered slightly, and Jake grabbed his arm to steady him. 'I think you had better come inside,' he said, leading Adam into Rachel's cosy kitchen, which smelt of rich fruit cakes.

Jenna offered him a mug of tea and a slice of the cake, Adam refused the latter, but drank the steaming tea thirstily as Jake and Jenna looked on. Adam felt a little better as the tea refreshed him. 'I need to see Rachel on a very delicate personal matter. I would be very much obliged to you if you can tell me when she will be back?' He directed the question to Jake.

'Rachel's gone away, and I have a mind to think you have something to do with her going.'

Adam took a deep sigh. 'You may be correct in that assumption I'm afraid. When did she go?'

Jake chewed at his bottom lip before he answered, 'She left this morning. She went away first for the weekend, we don't know where, she never said, but she came back extremely distressed. I couldn't get any sense out of her. She just said that something terrible had happened, and she needed to speak with her friend back home.'

'Home?' Adam enquired.

Jake shrugged his shoulders. 'Wherever home is! I always thought this was her home!' he added perplexed.

Adam turned his face from them and stared out of the

window. Home must be Gweek he thought to himself.

'Are you going to tell us what has happened Mr de Sousa?' Jenna asked. 'We are naturally very worried about her.'

'I appreciate your concern,' Adam answered. 'All I can tell you is that Rachel was confronted with her past, a past she thought was dead and buried - a past that came to light in a most unfortunate way. Yes, she received a terrible shock, and that is why I must find her. She believes something that is not true. I must tell her the truth, otherwise it will destroy her, but I'm afraid that is all I am permitted to tell you.'

Both Jake and Jenna glanced at each other, at length Jake asked, 'Do you know where she might have gone then Mr de Sousa?'

'I can't be sure, but by what you have told me, I believe she's in Cornwall - Gweek to be precise.' Adam stood up and the chair grated across the stone floor. 'If you'll excuse me, I must go. I have imposed on you long enough. I am sorry I cannot be more forthcoming with information, but I thank you for your help and hospitality.'

Jake caught hold of Adam's sleeve. 'You'll be going to Cornwall then?' Adam nodded. 'Tell her, tell Rachel when you see her, that we miss her and want her to come back home. Will you tell her that Mr de Sousa? Will you tell our Rachel that?'

Adam smiled thinly. 'I will, when I find her.'

*

Jenna was in the back yard hanging washing the next afternoon, when she heard an almighty crash preceded by the squeal of brakes. She dropped the shirt and pegs and ran around the side of the building, to find the wreckage of a car, buried deep into the stone wall of the herb garden. Jake came rushing from the dairy and was first at the scene. The passenger was slumped over the wheel of her mini coupe, and as Jake opened the door, the smell of alcohol nearly knocked him down. With a short tug he pulled the woman from her seat and laid her down on the grass verge. Thankfully there were no signs of real damage, other than a small cut to her forehead, but what stunned both Jake and Jenna, was the uncanny likeness of this woman to their own Rachel.

26

It was early morning when Adam drove into the familiar village of Gweek, he had stayed overnight at Tavistock, and set off at first light. Gweek was as Adam remembered, a tranquil river village, sheltered from the hustle and bustle of the world around it. The tide was in, which in Adam's mind, made the village more beautiful. The great oaks which flanked the Helford, hung heavy and lush with leaf, and small colourful fishing vessels still lined the grassy moorings. It was as though everything in life was the same, when in reality everything was so very, very, different. Adam stood by the bridge, drinking in the ambiance, when his eye caught sight of something quite wonderful. A pair of black swans glided majestically into view, surely this was not Vicos and his mate, but then of course swans mated for life, and lived to quite an age. The sight raised a lump in his throat, as happier times ran through his mind. His mouth which had been set hard, smiled, something he had not done in a long time. There was no laughter or joy in an empty heart. This sight warmed his heart though, it was an omen, a sign that happiness could be found again, and here was the place to find it.

'Well, I'll be....'

A voice from behind shook Adam from his reverie, he turned swiftly to acknowledge the speaker, who was moving swiftly across the road towards him.

'Mr de Sousa.' Harry Blewett clamped his hand around Adam's. 'I can hardly believe my own eyes.'

It took Adam a few seconds to recognise the man standing before him. 'Oh my goodness, if it isn't my old friend Harry. How are you?' Adam shook his hand with vigour.

'I'm well thank you. Gosh, but it's good to see you again after all these years. How many will it be, twenty at least?'

Adam nodded. Noting how very different this fine young man was, from the quiet nervous Harry he used to know. He noted too, that his skin no longer wore the yellow pallor, nor was he suffering from the skin infection which blighted his younger days.

Harry gently caught Adam by the arm and beckoned him across the road. 'You must come and meet my family, Mr de Sousa,' Harry said.

'Adam laughed. 'I'll be delighted,' he said, 'but call me Adam for goodness sake Harry.'

Rebecca was making bread in the kitchen of River Cottage, and quickly wiped her flowery hands down her apron. 'It's a pleasure to meet you at last, do sit down and share a cup of tea with us.' She cleared a chair, which held a pile of freshly ironed linen for him to sit on. Adam was charmed by Rebecca, and in turn he met Harry's children. They could not impress upon him too much, how the gift of the house he had given to the village, had given them such an excellent start in life, and Adam was profoundly happy for them. An hour later, he took his leave of the grateful family who inhabited Granny Pascoe's cottage, with a promise to return for tea the very next day. Once outside, he looked towards The Black Swan Hotel. Apart from a new roof, it had not changed much over the years. He would take a look inside he decided. He would go to where it had all begun, in that extraordinary year before world war two broke out.

As he approached the front door step, he found the door to be shut, he parted the mass of pansies on the window box and peered through the window, the place was empty of people.

'Adam!' A woman's voice shouted behind him. Adam turned to find Emma by the shop doorway. She rushed across the road and hugged him as all long lost friends do, making Adam smile at her openness with him - a far cry from the shy awkward girl he took on as an employee so very long ago. She took him by the arm, and led him back across the road. 'Oh I'm so happy you have come back to us at last. You must come home to us. How long are you staying? It's so lovely to see you after all this time, how are you keeping? How did you get here? Have you been here long? You should have sent word, you must stay with us. Oh listen at me nattering on,' she said, letting go of his arm. 'You probably have your own plans.'

'Not really,' he answered brightly. 'No plans, but I would love to see Robin and the children. I must say Emma you have grown into a fine looking woman, marriage obviously suits you.' Her smile was broad and wide. 'I can't tell you how happy my life has been Adam, and it's all down to you.' Adam shook his head in denial. 'Yes it is I tell you, you made all this happen for me, you believed in me and showed me the way.' She linked arms with him as though it was the most natural thing in the world, and as they walked towards the bridge, she waved at Harry's youngest as he sat cleaning his shoes on the front step of Granny Pascoe's house. 'Have you seen Harry and his family?'

'Yes, earlier, it's wonderful to see them so happy as well.'

'Well, as I was saying it's all down to you.' As they turned into the lane towards Barleyfield Farm, she said, 'I trained to be a vet you know!'

'Emma, that's wonderful,' he said, squeezing her hand which clasped his arm.

'Yes, ten years now I've been practising, in Bray's old surgery, well, your old surgery I should say. Oh I love it Adam, everything has worked out so well. Anyway enough about me, what about you, are you married? Did you ever see Rachel again? She just vanished from here you know, no-one has seen hide nor hair of her these last twenty years. I think Mum received a letter from her a long time ago, but that was it.' Emma saw the look in Adam's eyes and bit her words. 'Sorry Adam, I didn't mean to stir up old memories, I didn't think.'

'No don't apologise, Emma, I came down to find Rachel actually, I had a feeling she would come here, but I'm obviously mistaken.'

'What made you think she was here? Are you still in touch?'

Adam shook his head sadly. 'No we're not. Oh goodness, it's such a long story - I don't know where to start. Something dreadful has happened Emma, and I came to explain to her, but it seems I have come on a wild goose chase.'

She examined his face, there were lines around his mouth and his face looked ashen. 'Well, I'm a good listener Adam, if you want to tell me about it. Sometimes a problem shared as they say.'

He laughed softly. 'You may hate me if I tell you,' he answered evenly.

She looked at him and smiled. 'Nothing is ever as bad as it seems you know.' They were at the back door of Barleyfield Farm, having made their way through the yard, busy with brown hens and snow white geese picking at the gravel. The heat of the day was fading. The sky now covered in pearl grey clouds, threatened rain. His face was devoid of expression as he bit his lip nervously. 'Very well,' he said, 'I'll tell you and Robin together, then you can make the judgment. I know I need to talk to someone, because it's eating me up, it's so dreadful.'

The reunion with Robin was a joyous occasion, and the three of them sat in the front parlour watching the rain run down the windows as they drunk brandy all afternoon. They laughed and swapped stories, though Adam did not tell his sad tale until after they had eaten a hearty dinner.

The children, Edwin who was eighteen, had gone out and Joanna, who was twelve, was now tucked up in bed. The brandy glasses were filled as Robin and Emma listened intently as Adam told them his painful story. He was racked with grief and could hardly speak the last sentence. 'Our relationship was never consummated I promise. It was purely a business transaction. Helena needed to marry to release her dowry, for want of a better word, and I agreed to it. She was going to use the money to buy a part share in the Gartondale Veterinary practice where we worked together. I was going to put up the rest of the money and we would have been business partners. To all intents and purposes we would have been a couple in names only. Helena knew my feelings about marriage, she knew I loved only one woman, but I never told her Rachel's name. Oh goodness, do you believe me?' His eyes watered. There was silence while Adam composed himself. He was filled with dread that his friends would denounce him. Presently he said, 'It all sound terrible doesn't it, I expect you hate me now for what I have done?'

They both smiled gently as they assured him that was not the case. Robin stood up and refilled all three glasses. He handed them out and raised his own towards Adam. 'How the Devil was you supposed to know she was your own flesh and blood? My friend, we're all human. Here's to your good health and happier times.' Adam's eyes watered again as they chinked their glasses.

The next morning though the weather was inclement, Robin and Adam walked with the dogs towards Penboa, to clear their aching heads. It was a luxury Robin indulged in regularly since regaining his sight some twenty years ago. The trees and fields were a constant wonder to him, as he believed at one time he would never see them again. He noted how quiet Adam was and wondered whether it was because of the emotion from the previous night, or the copious amounts of brandy he had consumed. As they turned back along the road to Gweek, the dogs went ahead splashing through the mud and rain.

'What are your plans Adam?' Robin's voice jarred Adam back to the present.

'I don't know. I think I'll go abroad and settle

somewhere. I need to get away.'

Robin shook his head. 'No my friend, first you must contact her, write to her, go and find her, however you do it you must tell her Adam.'

He nodded miserably. 'I know I must and I will. I can't live peacefully knowing that Rachel is somewhere in the world thinking so badly of me.'

*

While the men were out walking, Emma took herself down to The Black Swan to see her mother.

Lizzy was behind the bar washing the glasses after closing time. She had been back at The Black Swan part time almost eighteen years now - it was a job she had always enjoyed. When Lizzy heard the door open, she shouted, 'I'm sorry we're closed. Open again at seven.' As she turned to see her daughter enter, she smiled lovingly.

'We have a visitor at Barleyfield Mum, and you'll never guess in a million years who it is.'

Lizzy laughed. 'Go on surprise me?'

'Adam de Sousa.'

Lizzy felt her heart lurch. 'Adam de Sousa?' she repeated out loud. Her face looked pale and shocked.

'Yes, he's here looking for Rachel, he seemed to think she would be here.'

'Is he by God,' she said curtly. 'Well, he's about twenty years too late, don't you think.' Her harshness shocked Emma. This was quite out of character for her mother. 'If he was so desperate to find Rachel why didn't he follow the lead I gave him nineteen years ago, I told him where to find her then.'

'He did,' Emma said quickly.

Lizzy huffed.

'He did Mum, he told us all about it, he went and found her in Devon, but saw her with a man and child and assumed she was married with a family, so he left her be.'

'Married! Don't you think I would have told him she

was married? Do you really think I would have told him where she was, if she was married?' She laughed haughtily. 'Typical man, he just assumed it, because she was with another man. How little he knows Rachel,' she snapped. 'Do you know, after Alex, she loved only one man, and that was Adam de Sousa!'

'Mum, don't be so harsh on him, he loves her. You only know the half of it.'

'Oh I know more then you think, Emma my dear. Love, you say, look where his love got her? I've had Rachel here these past two days weeping like a baby on my shoulder. She is utterly distraught. You would not believe what she has told me. He broke her heart. She didn't know what to do, or where to find him. She ran away you know, because she was with child by him, and couldn't face the disgrace that comes of having a child out of wedlock. And then had the babe taken away from her, poor lamb, and now this,' she spat the words. '...this horror of a scenario you obviously know nothing about. This terrible thing he has done, you wouldn't be so quick to have him as a house guest if you knew what he had done Emma, I can tell you.'

'I do know Mum, that's why I came to speak to you. He has told us everything, and I mean everything.'

She stopped short in surprise. 'So, it's true what Rachel tells me?'

'Yes and no.'

Lizzy raised her eyebrows. 'Either it is or it isn't?'

'It's not as simple as that.'

Lizzy folded her arms. 'No, it never is.'

She relayed all Adam had told them the previous night. There was a momentary silence between them. 'I believe him Mum, and so should you. Is Rachel still here?'

Lizzy shook her head. 'She went back first thing this morning.'

'Damn it.' Emma sighed heavily. 'If only I'd known she was here. Why didn't you tell me?'

'She didn't want anyone to know, that's why.'

'Well, we've got to do something. They can't live with this hanging over them.'

27

Helena retched into the bowl by her bedside. The sickness had lasted for most of the night, and her stomach gave out a cavernous groan. Little by little, she was given sips of water by the person who sat in constant vigil by her bed, and as morning dawned, she opened her eyes to look upon the handsome face of her carer. He smiled kindly when he saw her eyes open and stood up, later appearing with two rounds of dry toast and a cup of weak tea.

An hour later, Helena appeared in the kitchen, looking pale and fragile. 'I say, you don't happen to have an aspirin do you, my head is splitting this morning.'

'I'm not bloody surprised.' Jenna laughed. 'You must have downed a whole bottle of whiskey to get yourself into such a state.'

'And a half a bottle of sherry,' Helena added sheepishly.

'You do realise you could have killed yourself or somebody else, driving in that state? It's a bloody good job PC Clements didn't find you, or you would have spent the night in the cells.'

Helena slumped down at the kitchen table and wept into her hands.

'Oh now, come on missy, nothing can be that bad can it? Here, drink this, it's good and strong. Rachel always says a good cup of tea heals all worries. As she spoke Jenna saw a familiar figure walking down the lane. 'Well, talk of the devil,' she said, wiping her hands on a tea cloth. 'Here comes Rachel now.'

As the kitchen door opened, Helena stood up quickly and in doing so knocked her chair from under her. The two women eyed each other with trepidation. Jenna was astounded at the mirror image the women portrayed.

'Fiona?' Rachel whispered, as her knees weakened beneath her.

'Mum?' she replied, the word tripped off her tongue so

naturally.

Jenna's jaw dropped open. 'Righty o, I'll leave you both to it,' she said, edging her way past them. 'I'll be outside somewhere, if you need me.'

The yard was full of hens plucking at the earth, and beyond the front garden, a gaggle of geese were basking in the morning sunshine. Jenna looked towards the pig field for Jake and took off like the wind in great excitement when she spotted him shaking the bucket of scraps into the pig trough.

In the kitchen Rachel had somehow managed to control her nerves. 'Fiona,' she said moving towards her daughter. 'I don't know what to say to you.'

'Helena, Mum, my name's Helena.' Her words preceded a soft warm smile.

'Yes,' Rachel whispered. 'Yes, I'm sorry, of course it is.' Her eyes gazed in awe upon this well bred woman who stood before her. Beneath her finely tailored trouser suit peeped scarlet stilettos, which appealed to her own sense of style. Inwardly, Rachel's heart felt as though it would burst with joy at their meeting, and she felt such a bond between them it frightened her.

Helena reached her hand out to Rachel. 'I need some answers Mum.'

'As do I, my darling child.'

*

Later that evening, Rachel sat in her bedroom, drained both physically and emotionally, but her heart sang with happiness, which kept her from sleeping.

Both women had sat in the front room that afternoon and had talked and wept, hugged and struggled to come to terms with the events which had torn them apart. They were now, quite unbelievably, on a level playing field. The years of loss and yearning had diminished in one emotional afternoon. She now had the daughter she had been so deprived of all these years, and Helena in turn had found the woman who had given her life. Now Rachel turned her thoughts to Adam.

Helena's narrative had revealed that there had been no dreadful act of incest, as she had at first thought. She had poured her heart out to Rachel about their relationship. Her words were going round and round her head.

'We didn't love each other mum, it was never like that,' Helena admitted.

'But why marry someone, when you know it isn't the right thing for you?' Rachel had asked in dismay.

Helena bit down on her lower lip. 'I'm ashamed to say our union was a simple business arrangement. Marrying seemed the only practical solution to our predicament.' She smiled coyly. 'We both worked in a large veterinary practice in Gartondale. There were three vets. Adam being the head vet, three nurses and I was practice manager. It was a large established practice, with stables at the rear and well equipped operating theatres, but unfortunately the owner of the building decided to sell at the end of this summer. We were given first option, but couldn't quite raise the money to buy. The owner had had an offer from an estate agency and it was almost a done deal, until I came up with an idea. Adam had the finances to cover half the price and I knew I was due some money that had been kept in trust for me by my long dead maiden Aunt Helena, which would make up the deficit. Unfortunately, my Aunt was a stickler for marriage and families, and I could only access the money on the day I married. Adam was apprehensive about the whole scenario, but I had no qualms about sinking all my money into the practice. It was profitable, I loved the job and I didn't want for anything.' She laughed softly. 'So that's what we decided and that's what we did. We only wanted a quiet registry office marriage with no frills or reception, but unfortunately Mother wouldn't allow it. She insisted that it was to be a grand affair, it was all for show really, to impress her cronies from her Bridge club. Granted, she didn't know of our arrangement, and to all intents and purposes, the marriage was legitimate, she did question Adam's age, but I just brushed the matter aside and told her quite blasé that age didn't matter when you were in love.' She paused for a moment. 'I was so shocked when the vicar told me that you believed Adam to be my father. I just flew back home and locked myself away for the rest of the weekend. I just kept thinking 'my god what if I had eventually fallen in love with him'. I mean, I always liked him, he was such good company, and we worked so closely with each other, well, these things happen sometime. Don't they?' She shuddered. 'If I hadn't invited you, we would never have known.'

'It's all right my darling. Thankfully nothing happened,' Rachel said, comforting her distraught daughter.

Eventually when the tears had subsided, Helena continued with her story. 'When I eventually left my room, I had a terrible row with my parents. My father told me in no uncertain terms that I was to forget about you and Adam if I wanted to continue living in the manner I had become accustomed to. He told me I was never to contact either of you again, and the matter would never be spoken of again. I promptly walked out of Stone Field Manor, leaving all my belongings, drove down to Devon, booked into the first hotel I could find and promptly drank myself into oblivion. The rest they say is history.'

'Well, my darling daughter, you can stay here for as long as you want. I don't ever want to be parted from you again.'

*

Rachel moved to the bed and sat on the soft candlewick eiderdown and sighed. It had turned out that life with the Davenports had been hardly ideal. Helena had been brought up by her nanny, and had had little or no interaction with her parents. She had been sent off to boarding school at the tender age of nine, where she received an excellent education, far better than Rachel could have afforded for her, but oh, it broke her heart to even think of such a notion. It seemed she had been given all the luxuries a child could want, except for one commodity, a mother's love. The latter angered Rachel. To think her daughter was taken from her, and given to someone who didn't really want her, was inconceivable. Helena had seen the hurt and confusion in Rachel's eyes, and showed her the entry from her nanny's journals, which documented why the Davenports had taken such drastic action. 'It was just greed,' Helena had told her.

Thunder rumbled in the distance, a storm was brewing, as Rachel went to close the bedroom window, she glanced at the box on the dressing table which Helena had given to her.

'This box belongs to you Mum,' Helena had said, as she placed it in her hands. 'It's for you to catch up on all the lost and stolen years. Nanny would have liked you to have it.'

She placed it on the bed. Someone had written on the lid 'Helena's Memory Box'. Her fingers traced the wording, and then she carefully removed the lid, and chose an envelope which was marked, Helena's first curl, she slipped the lock of dark downy hair into her palm, and wept.

*

Adam was at his writing desk in his bedroom at Barleyfield Farm. He had had a long emotional talk with Lizzy that afternoon, and was shocked at what he had learned. He had spent the whole afternoon sitting in his bedroom, looking out down the Helford River, trying to comprehend what Lizzy had told him. He was upset and agitated, Lizzy's words continued around his head like a merry-go-round. It was in this perturbed state that he decided he must write to Rachel. His letter to Rachel was simple;

Thursday 31st August

My darling Rachel,

I have just spoken to your good friend Lizzy and I beseech you to forgive me for all the hurt I have caused you, none of it was intentional and all of it is heartbreaking for me to comprehend. I appear to have left a trail of destruction in my wake, the latter events being incomparable. The shame I feel for agreeing to go ahead with the marriage to Helena is immeasurable, though God knows we did nothing improper. I need to see you so I can tell you my story, and I want you to know how very, very sorry I am. I hope you can forgive me for this terrible mess.

I am staying with Robin and Emma at Barleyfield Farm, but it is my intention to go abroad soon. I leave from Plymouth mid afternoon on Tuesday 5th September. I will be staying at the same hotel we stayed at before our trip to Tuscany. If you can find it in your heart to join me, meet me at our hotel at eleven, maybe we could sort things out. If you feel you cannot, I will go away and shall not hurt you any more my love.

I remain forever yours
Adam

*

Gales and torrential rain swept across the country, though the farm work at Runstone was relentless. The yard was thick with mud and debris from fallen branches, and the days seemed long and miserable, except perhaps for two particular people. The weather seemed not to dampen the spirits of Helena and Jake. Rachel watched with mild curiosity at the playful behaviour between them. Something was afoot, of that she was sure. On the second day of the gale, a tragedy shook the village of Runstone, when a tree fell across the lane to Widecombe in the early hours. Dick Simpson, the local postman, was walking to work when it happened. He was struck down and killed and wasn't found until seven-thirty, some three hours later. The whole village was in mourning for him, as Dick was a likeable character. He always had sweets for the children, and always had a smile and a cheery hello for everyone. He had delivered two babies in the village, when no other help was available, and alerted to the fact old Mrs Kendal's hadn't met him by her front door to pick up her post, he broke in and rescued her after she'd fallen down the stairs and broke her leg. He was much missed by the whole community. Consequently, Rachel did not receive her post until Tuesday 5th September; it had lain undetected in Dick's sack near to where he had fallen. The new postman had apologised for the delay and handed over two very damp letters for her.

The first she recognised as Lizzy's handwriting, and read it immediately, the second she slipped into her pocket for later.

Thursday 31st August
Dearest friend,

I spoke to Adam the day you left us, I had no idea he was in the village. He was staying with my Emma at Barleyfield. I have to tell you he is a broken man. You two must speak to each other and get this sorted. He loves you. Please phone either Adam at Barleyfield, Gweek 258, or me at home Gweek 394 or The Black Swan as soon as you get this, as I know Adam leaves the country next week. I don't know where he is going, he will not say, but for god sake get in touch. All my love Lizzy

Rachel glanced at her watch - it was ten thirty - just enough time before she had to start dinner she thought. She grabbed her coat and braved the weather to walk to Widecombe to use the phone. With great trepidation she dialled the operator for the number for Barleyfield, but the line was dead, she rang the operator and asked her to connect her to The Black Swan, only to be told that all the phone lines were down on the Lizard, due to the gales. 'Damn.' She hammered her fist against the phone box wall.

Helena noted that Rachel looked out of sorts when she returned, but when she asked, Rachel just shook her head, and dismissed it. After the dishes were cleared, and Helena and Jake were in deep conversation in the front parlour, Rachel placed two cups of coffee on the kitchen table and sat down with Jenna. There was a tinkle of laughter from the front parlour and the two women both raised their eyebrows in unison.

'I believe love is in the air,' Jenna whispered.

Rachel smiled for the first time that day. 'I think you're right. Maybe something wonderful will come out of this terrible mess after all,' she sighed.

Jenna reached over and placed her hand on Rachel's. 'I'm sure it will.'

Rachel's face beamed. 'I am very lucky, I have two wonderful daughters.'

'And we have a wonderful Mum.'

Rachel smiled and dropped her head to hide her watery eyes. She reached deep into her pocket for a handkerchief and found the other letter she had placed there and forgotten about.

The moan of despair which Rachel omitted as she read the letter startled Jenna so much it prickled the hairs on the back of her head. 'Goodness Rachel, whatever is it, are you ill?' she asked.

Rachel pushed her chair back making a loud scraping noise on the stone floor. She clutched the letter to her chest, glanced at the kitchen clock, it was quarter past one and cried, 'Oh no. Adam, no!' She threw the letter on the table and this time without picking up her coat, she ran like the wind to Widecombe for the second time that day. When she got there, someone was using the phone, she stood and shivered in the rain, then in a moment of madness she wrenched the door open and shouted to the woman using the phone that she needed the phone for an emergency. The woman immediately hung up and had hardly stepped out of the box before Rachel pushed past and grabbed the receiver. She quickly dialled the operator for the number of Harbour View Hotel, Plymouth, only to be told all phone lines were down. She replaced the receiver and wept uncontrollably. The woman who had been evicted from the phone box was still outside, partly to see if she could help in anyway, and partly hoping to hear what the emergency was all about. Hot tears mingled with the rain as they fell down her cheeks, as Rachel emerged from the box.

'Oh my, can I do anything to help?' The woman asked.

Rachel shook her head. 'No thank you,' she croaked. 'No-one can help.' She had hardly walked fifty yards before Jake pulled up in Helena's car. When Rachel had left, Jenna had run into the parlour with the letter. After reading it, Jake delegated all the immediate farm jobs, as he pulled his coat and shoes on.

She stood by the car and cried, but made no attempt to get in. Jake pushed his door open and ran around to her. 'Come on,' he said, taking her by the arm. In her emotional daze, she looked at him puzzled. 'Get in, you need to get some dry clothes on, or you'll catch your death of cold. Back at the farm, he led her inside and instructed her to get upstairs and change as quickly as she could, as they had a ferry to catch.'

'A ferry?' Jenna and Helena said in unison as they looked at each other.

'But, I don't know which one he is catching!' Rachel wailed as she ran upstairs

'Which one who's catching?' Helena asked, trying to follow what was happening.

'Never mind that for a minute, just go and hurry her up. We have to leave, we must make haste,' Jake urged.

'Leave. Where are you going Jake?' Jenna asked, as Rachel thundered down the stairs with Helena in hot pursuit. 'Jake, tell me where you're going?' She followed Rachel and Jake out into the rain.

'We're going to Plymouth. You and Jenna see to the cows will you? I'll be back as soon as possible.'

'Plymouth?' she repeated, as she watched them run to

the car.

On entering the kitchen Jenna passed her the letter which had been discarded on the floor. 'I think that explains everything.'

Helena's lips curled into a smile. 'I think we may have a happy ending to the story after all,' she exclaimed.

'What about a happy ending for you? Am I right in thinking there is a little love interest going on here with you and a certain brother of mine.'

'What a notion, whatever gave you that idea?' Helena answered playfully.

*

The journey to Plymouth that wet and stormy afternoon was the most frightening Rachel had ever been on. Rachel sat in quiet trepidation, as Jake pulled out all the stops to get her to the ferry terminal. Her heart soared as they approached the docks, and when they could drive no closer, Rachel leapt out of the car and ran towards the Harbour View Hotel opposite.

'I'm sorry madam, but Mr de Sousa has left, I believe he was catching a ferry,' the proprietor told her.

'Did he say where he was going?' she cried.

She shook her head apologetically.

Rachel raced towards the ferry terminal. There were a few people milling about, and Rachel made her way to the ticket desk. Breathlessly she asked, 'Has the ferry left?'

'Just missed it I'm afraid. No more ferries today madam, the last one left forty minutes ago. I can book you on for seven-thirty tomorrow morning if you wish,' he said, with his pen poised over the folded ticket book.

Her heart dropped as she looked out towards the sea. He had gone forever, and she did not know where.

'Madam?' The desk clerk jarred her from her reverie.

She looked up at him and shook her head. 'It's too late,' she said, her voice hardly audible. 'It's too late.' She turned away weeping.

Despondently, Jake started the car and they made their way back to their lives at Runstone Manor.

28

Helena had decided to take up the offer for her to stay indefinitely at Runstone Manor. She felt happy here, more so than she had ever felt with the Davenports. So without regrets, she wrote to inform them that she would not be coming back home.

When Rachel realised that her Uncle Jack Taylor worked as a gardener for the Davenports at Stone field Manor, everything began to make sense.

'He's still there you know,' Helena told her. 'He doesn't work as many hours. In fact he never did much work at all. I always wondered why my parents kept him on. Now I know it was to keep their secret safe.' Her mouth set hard. 'I disliked him immensely you know, always have done.'

Rachel laughed. 'You and me both.'

'He was always telling me off for playing in the garden. Nanny disliked him as well, though she tried hard not to show it.'

After much deliberation, about whether to let sleeping dogs lie, Rachel and Helena came to the conclusion that he should pay for what he had done, and though it meant serious consequences to the Davenports, Rachel reported Jack Taylor to the police, and this time her allegations were heard.

*

Life at Runstone Manor settled down once again, and Rachel put on a brave face each morning. But everyone who knew her could see she had lost her sparkle. Of all the things she had been through, this was the hardest to bear, knowing now that Adam was lost to her forever. She had written to Lizzy and explained their dash to catch Adam, but no one could throw any light on where he'd gone.

She asked Helena if he still had the Tuscan villa, and Helena stared at her blankly. 'He never mentioned a villa in Tuscany,' she answered, then suggested that he may have gone to Australia. He'd spoken of it once or twice to her, knowing that he would get a passage without any problem being in the veterinary profession. So Rachel resigned herself to a life once again without him. But there was one thing she was happy about, and that was the love that had grown between Jake and Helena. They planned an engagement at Christmas, and a very low key wedding in May.

*

It was November. The Tuscan sunset glowed warm and orange against the villa walls. Adam stood in the courtyard and looked out across the ploughed red fields and down the vast valley towards Florence. He was desolate, as he opened another bottle of ruby Chianti to dull the pain that throbbed in his heart. He sat amongst the fallen leaves, watching the sun go down. The wind was freshening and there was a chill in the air - a change in the weather he suspected. He pulled his jacket around his shoulders. He was tired and weary of life. The copious amount of alcohol made him sleepy. When the rain came, he slept on until his body shuddered with the cold and wet. He undressed to his shirt and lay on his bed in desolation. The next day the fever took hold.

Adam was found that morning by Massimo who was delivering bread to the villa. The door was ajar, and Adam was slumped on the floor of the kitchen. There was a broken glass and water lay in a pool by his hand. Massimo lifted him to his feet, noting Adam's skin was cold and clammy, there were high pink spots on his cheeks and his hair was stuck wet to his forehead. On first inspection Massimo knew not whether Adam was soaked in sweat or rain. He half dragged, half walked Adam up the stairs to a bedroom. He stripped him of his shirt and wrapped his hot shivering body in a cotton throw. He ran as fast as his bandy legs would carry him to the village, and soon the villa was staffed with many able hands to nurse him.

For two days the fever raged, Adam was stripped and washed with cool lavender water at regular intervals, only to be drenched in sweat within moments of being dressed. His mind would not be still, it bothered him that his work colleagues were damning him for incest. He tried to battle with them, and would shout out that he was innocent of their charges. He cried when Rachel stood by his bed and shook her head at him sadly, he reached out to grab her, but only found an old withered hand to hold, and the voice which accompanied it was foreign. He could see people moving around the room, then the place was empty and he was frightened. He felt he was drowning as water was poured into his mouth, he would spit and cough, but still they tried to drown him. He tried to crawl out of bed, he was hot and wanted to swim, to drown, to end it, but hands pinned him to the bed so that he gave up and sighed. He called to Rachel, and each time she came to him he felt a wet cold slap of cloth on his face. The villagers were distressed, the fever normally abated by the second day, but they were afraid and began to pray.

On the fourth day he woke to the sound of silence, no-one was shouting, the rain had ceased, and the room was empty, but for one person.

'Rachel,' he whispered. The figure rose and laid a cool hand on his cheek.

'Buongiorno, Adam, come stai?' Cara from the bakery asked.

'Buongiorno, Cara, bene grazie,' he replied adding a weak smile.

'Porto la zuppa (I bring soup),' she said, leaving the room.

*

As the New Year dawned, it brought with it the cold weather. For six solid nights penetrating frost whitened the fields at Runstone Manor Farm, until the mud in the yard set hard in dangerous icy ruts. No amount of wood on the fire seemed to take the chill off the house. Only the kitchen remained warm from the Aga. Wash day was excruciating on the hands, as Rachel, Helena and Jenna hauled armfuls of washing outside to hang out. It was bitter cold as Rachel pegged the last of the clothes on the line. She picked up her basket, straightened her back, and shivered at the cold white barren landscape. She ran inside to join the others, who were tidying away the soap and buckets. She glanced outside at the lines of washing flapping in the breeze, and wondered if they would dry, or if their efforts had been in vain. She bent to build up the fire, before preparing the dinner. For the first time in a long time, she did not look at the New Year as a new beginning. There was a dullness about her, her spirit seemed to have faded over the past few months and try as she might, she could not lift this feeling of loss which hung over her. As they all sat down to a dinner of chunky bread and homemade broth, she watched as Helena and Jake flirted playfully with each other. Jenna seemed to be blooming, and Rachel wondered if she and David were about to become parents. Jim and Samuel Barker ate and chatted noisily, whilst Tom and Martin, always the quiet ones, finished their meal long before the others. Suddenly, Rachel felt hot tears stab behind her lids, and she quickly looked down before anyone noticed.

'You okay Rachel?' Jenna asked. 'Are you crying?' Everyone stopped eating and looked at her.

Rachel flushed up to the roots of her hair. 'No of course not, it's the cold - it must have got in my eyes. They keep watering that's all.' She broke into a broad smile. A moment later they all returned to their meal and the incident was forgotten.

At three, Rachel checked the washing and found it stiff and stuck to the washing lines. She sighed as she tugged and broke half a dozen pegs as she wrenched the board-stiff clothes from the line. 'Oh God, where is the peg gypsy when you need her and running out of pegs,' she cursed to herself. Eventually, she walked with the stack of hard clothes into the kitchen where they immediately started to wilt back into a damp mass on the floor. Just as she finished hanging the washing in the back parlour, there was a knock at the door. Rachel was astounded as she wrenched the front door open. Zena the peg gypsy, a woman of tiny stature, no more than five feet tall and birdlike, stood in the vestibule, wrapped in an inadequate shawl against the biting cold. 'Pegs my love - sixpence a bundle?' she asked, as she pushed her basket towards Rachel.

'Gosh you must have read my mind today. Yes I'll take whatever you have. Come on in until I find my purse,' Rachel said, beckoning her into the kitchen.

'I have three bundles for you today my love,' Zena said.

As Rachel counted the coins into the old woman's hand, she noted how icy cold she was. 'But, you're frozen stiff,' she said alarmed. 'Come in and get warm for goodness sake.'

The old woman pulled the shawl closer to her breast and timidly walked towards the table. 'Take a seat by the fire and warm your bones, would you like a nice cup of tea to warm you.'

'No my love, I'll just warm my hands a bit, if that's alright.'

Rachel watched her for a moment, and then excused herself. 'I won't be a moment,' she said, as she rummaged through the kitchen drawer and produced a hat, gloves and scarf. 'Forgive me. This is not charity. I don't need these anymore and thought perhaps you could use them - you feel so cold.'

Zena looked up at Rachel, her eyes were yellow with age, and her skin was lined and furrowed like an old piece of leather. She smiled softly. 'I have gloves and a scarf in my van, but they got soaked in the snow, thank you I don't need these, but you are very kind.' She placed a bony hand over the garments. Rachel sat beside her at the fire and

Zena reached out and took Rachel's hand in hers.

She flipped the palm upwards. 'Do you believe?' she asked.

Rachel looked down at her hand. 'In fortune telling? No.'

'No matter my love, I shall look anyway.' She took her time, and glanced up twice, then traced her long brown finger across the lines on her palm. 'You bear much sorrow in your heart.' It was a statement rather than a question. 'But bad things have turned good, though in your case these changes take a great deal of time.' Rachel laughed gently. 'You have lost a great love.' She glanced up at Rachel.

'I lost my husband over twenty years ago.'

Without changing her countenance, Zena shook her head. 'It's more recent than that.' Rachel's head bent forwards and she could once again feel tears well. The old woman cupped her other hand over hers. 'All this sorrow is coming to an end you know? This year, you will find great happiness. Joy beyond belief - I promise you that. Even if you don't believe, this is your destiny. Dry your eyes pretty lady, and look forward now not backwards, your time is coming.'

Rachel looked at her darkly.

The old woman gave a broad toothless smile. 'Soon your eyes will sparkle with love.' She pushed the chair back, and pulled the shawl over her thin grey hair.

Rachel too rose from her chair and kissed the old woman warmly on the cheek. 'It is bitter cold out there, do you have far to go?'

'No my love, my van and Cassy my horse are just up the road.'

'Will you be warm enough? I have blankets if you need them.'

'I'll be fine my love, and so will you. I bid you goodnight.'

Darkness had fallen now. 'Careful as you go,' Rachel

called after her, as the old woman shuffled across the yard and waved without looking back.

By the time tea-time had arrived, Rachel found her mood to have lifted and her spirits soared. Even though she struggled to believe anything the old woman had said, her words seemed to have done the trick.

'We need to get more pegs Rachel,' Jenna said, as she began to fold the dry washing.

'It's funny you should say that, I bought three bundles today,' Rachel answered, looking about the kitchen for her purchases. 'Though I'm damned if I know what I've done with them, I could have sworn I put them on the dresser.'

'What are you looking for?' Jake asked, as he breezed through the door in his stocking feet.

Rachel moved various bits of paper and ornaments from the dresser. 'Pegs, I bought them from Zena the peg gypsy this afternoon.'

'Zena the peg gypsy?' Jake said in astonishment.

'Yes, she was here this afternoon.'

'She can't have been. It must have been another gypsy.'

Rachel looked at him incredulously. 'I know who I spoke with, and it was definitely Zena.'

Jake looked a little dismayed. 'Well, it must have been her ghost then, because P. C. Clements found her dead last week over by Widecombe. Old Charlie Winstone has taken her horse Cassy in, and her van is parked on his land.'

The smile fell from her face and Rachel felt her scalp prickle. 'Oh my God, I must be going mad.'

Jenna and Jake exchanged glances. 'Well, can we wait until we've had tea before we commit you to the lunatic asylum?' Jake quipped as he kissed her lightly on the cheek.

29

Adam sat huddled on the veranda, wrapped up from the cold by a thick woollen blanket. The landscape was beautiful even in January, and thankfully the sun held a little heat to warm his face. The fever had taken its toll on his body, and left him with a hacking cough, which the local doctor said would improve with two glasses of Chianti a day, bread and honey and warm sunshine.

He watched with interest as a stranger made his way up the dusty path towards the villa. Some minutes later a tall distinguished gentleman stood at the gate and waved.

'Hello there. May I come in?' he shouted.

Adam beckoned him forward. As he approached, he noted that he wore a suit of beige flannel and a trilby hat with a band of brown suede trim. His brown brogues were highly polished, though slightly dusty from the red earth.

Adam pulled the blanket from his legs and made to get up.

'No, please don't get up. Barclay Graham at your service,' he said, doffing his trilby. 'Massimo at the bakery told me there was an English gentleman here. I understand you have been ill. I trust your health is improving?'

Adam nodded a thank you.

'I'm looking to buy Casomi villa,' he said, pointing eastward with his long forefinger. 'Massimo said you could tell me what it's like to live here and if I should take the plunge.'

Adam smiled broadly. 'I recommend it. Here, take a glass of Chianti with me.'

'I don't mind if I do.'

Adam offered up the glass of ruby liquid. 'Your good health sir,'

'And yours, Mr err.'

'de Sousa. Adam de Sousa, but please call me Adam.'

He nodded. 'Barclay.'

'Welcome to Tuscany Barclay.'

'I thank you. I understand you have had the fever, I trust you are on the mend.'

Adam pulled the blanket back over his knees. 'Yes a couple of months ago now, it's just the residue cough that is left.'

Barclay smiled and cocked his head. 'Forgive me, but your spirits seem a little low, does something trouble you my friend?' Adam raised an inquisitive eyebrow. 'Oh I know, tell me I'm an interfering old bugger and I'll leave you alone, but if you want to talk, I'm at your service. If it's any consolation I am a troubled soul too, but mine is because I have lost the love of my life. I have been a widower for many years now.'

'I'm sorry.' Adam yielded to the old gentlemen

'Yes, so am I. It's very hard to live alone, after a wonderful marriage. Have you been married?'

'No.'

'I recommend it. Have you never contemplated marriage?'

'Oh I've contemplated it, nearly did it twice, but..' his voice trailed off.

'But?'

'No matter,' Adam said, sipping his drink.

'If you can mend whatever has happened in your life then I beseech you to do just that. I cannot mend my broken heart, but it doesn't stop me living, or enjoying the simple things in life.' He took a sip of wine and savoured it for a moment. 'But it is always better if you have someone to share these things with I think.'

'You're absolutely right,' Adam said, raising his glass. 'Unfortunately, the woman I love doesn't like me very much.'

'Has she said that?'

Adam looked down the valley to where Rachel and he had lain all those years ago. 'No,' he replied at length.

'Then mend it dear boy.' He reached for the bottle of wine. 'May I?'

'Be my guest,'

'I already am,' he grinned.

They drank until the sunset at four-fifteen, and then Barclay said his goodbyes, thanked Adam for his hospitality, and set off down the dusty track.

'Call again,' Adam shouted.

Barclay nodded, but that was the last he ever saw of him, and when Adam made inquiries at the bakery, Massimo knew nothing about any gentlemen called Barclay Graham or that Casomi Villa was for sale and said, 'You must be seeing things my friend.'

*

As summer approached, the Tuscan sun warmed the land and Adam began to feel stronger. He was lonely though, and longed for some English conversation. He could not get Barclay Graham out of his mind, which in turn, made him think of Rachel and whether their relationship could ever be mended. He decided to write to Robin and Emma. Maybe a trip to Cornwall would lift his spirits again.

*

As Robin read his letter, an idea came into his head. It would be the twenty-first anniversary of the Gweek midsummer dance on the twenty-first of June. Well, it would have been the twenty-second, but for the one year it was cancelled, when word got through on the twentieth of June 1940 that two of the Bray brothers had been killed in action. The whole village was in mourning for them and their families. Adam had instigated the first one, so who better to open this anniversary one. He dropped what he was doing and marched down to The Black Swan to put a proposal to Lizzy.

*

Rachel walked through the garden, drinking in the sweet early morning air. This being early summer, the gardens

279

were a blaze of colour, with an array of yellow and purple irises, pink dianthus, and sumptuous clematis which scrambled over the sunny back porch. She climbed the stile and began to walk to the top of the meadow. She stopped at the very top of the hill and leant heavily against the wall and looked down the path she had just ascended. The countryside looked beautiful. The trees were full of bud and were swaying in the breeze, sunlight winked periodically through their branches, and swallows swooped and cried gently in the sky. She smiled and closed her eyes, breathing in the warm air as though it were a life giving elixir.

She was gathering her thoughts before the wonderful day which lay ahead of her when a may bug landed on her back. They were harmless, but huge and very ugly and always made her shiver whenever she saw one. She let out a soft cry and as she turned to brush the bug away she saw Jake approaching. Without prompting, he brushed the bug from her cardigan.

'Thank you. I'm such a ninny when it comes to May bugs.' She found a stone to sit on and beckoned Jake to do the same. 'Well, it's going to be a lovely day for your wedding Jake, I wish your mum and dad were here.'

His voice turned soft. 'It's enough that you are here for Helena, for once you have your proper role to play in life. You will be the mother of the bride, but I must say you look more like sisters than mother and daughter. I shall have to be careful which one I make my vows to.' He laughed.

She broke into a broad smile. 'Everyone in the village thought we would get married when you returned to Runstone all those years ago you know, especially when the war ended.'

'I know, and believe me Rachel, I would have married you, but your heart belonged to another, I could see that.'

She turned swiftly. 'Was it apparent?' she asked softly.

'It was to me, yes.'

'Little happiness it brought me though,' she reflected.

'Ah well, it's never too late you know. Look at me, who would have thought an ex monk at my age would find someone as wonderful as your beautiful daughter to love? I'm a very lucky man, and I wish you too could be as happy. I'm just so sorry that it didn't work out for you and Adam.'

Rachel rose, gave him a grateful smile.

'I had hoped we could have found him to invite him to the wedding, and then maybe you could all settle your differences once and for all,' Jake said, as he brushed the grass and dust from the seat of his pants.

He saw the corner of her lip twist as she considered this.

'I too wish that could have been the case.' She sighed. 'But I don't believe Helena could face him at the moment. It's just a little too soon, which is understandable.'

He linked up his arm in hers. 'She will, one day, I'm sure of that. Oh here, there's a letter for you.' He plunged his hand deep into his pocket and passed the envelope to her. The handwriting was Lizzy's and she ripped it open with anticipation.

'Good news?'

'She's invited me down on the twentieth of June for the week,'

'That's nice, will you go?' he asked cheerily.

'I don't know we'll be very busy at that time,' she said dismissively.

'Nonsense Rachel, you will go, even if I have to pack your bag myself.'

Her face was radiant as she turned her smiling eyes onto him. 'Bully.'

He smiled wryly. 'Come on, we have a wedding to attend to first.'

30

Rachel placed the last of her bags by the kitchen door, confident that she could leave the farm in safe hands now there were two women to see to the running of the farm. She glanced outside to see Jake and Helena walking back from the cow shed. Their wedding had been a very small affair, but none the less a wonderful day. The Davenports had been told about the wedding, but not invited. A stiff letter had arrived from them stating that as she was marrying a farmer, she was marrying beneath her, and they wanted nothing more to do with her. Surprisingly this did not have any effect on Helena whatsoever, she knew where her true family was now and all they wanted was her happiness. The Davenports were pushed to the back of her mind and the wedding went ahead with her real mother at her side. Rachel smiled inwardly, and noted how happy Jake and Helena looked together - their hands always finding each other whenever they walked side by side, their fingers forever entwined. They were a joy to watch, and she was so proud of them. She glanced at the clock which said nine-thirty, checked her handbag for the keys to Helena's car which she had borrowed for the trip and the wedding photos to show Lizzy. Happy that everything was ready, she had just begun to gather her things up to leave when Jenna came in from gathering the eggs. She stared at her in concern. Jenna was as white as a sheet and was clutching her eight months gone swollen belly. 'Whatever is the matter? Is it the baby?' she said, as she shot to her side.

Jenna sat down clumsily at the kitchen table, knocking the basket of eggs over. 'I have a pain just here.' She rubbed her lower abdomen.

'Right, where's David?'

'He's gone to market. Oh Rachel is the baby coming early?'

'I don't know my love, come on let's get you to the

hospital.' She bundled her into the car, told Jake where she was going, and sped off down the lane towards Buckfastleigh. At the hospital, Jenna was undergoing numerous tests, while Rachel sat patiently in the corridor awaiting news. David arrived at four-fifteen, flustered and agitated. 'Where is she? Is she alright? What about the baby?'

Rachel stood up and held him. 'I don't know anything yet, but I'm sure she's alright, maybe they will let you in to see her, I'm not family so they won't tell me anything.'

David huffed. 'Not family! We'll see about that. Where did they take her?'

Rachel smiled at his indignation. 'You'll have to go and see the matron, second door on the right.'

'I'll be back in a minute, I'm sorry you've missed your trip because of this, but thank you for being with her.'

'Oh lord, I'd clean forgotten about going down to Cornwall, what with all the panic. Do you have some money for the phone? I had better ring Lizzy.'

David emptied his pocket of coins and gave it all to Rachel.

'I'll be back in a tick,' she said.

*

Lizzy took the call from Rachel and she in turn called through to Barleyfield. 'All the best laid plans eh,' she said, as she relayed Rachel's apology for not coming down. 'Is Adam here yet?'

Robin said that he was. 'I don't know Lizzy. Will we ever get these two back together?'

'It's looking more and more unlikely, I think if Jenna has the baby, she won't come down at all,' she said sadly.

*

By eleven-thirty that evening Jenna was allowed to return home with Rachel and David to Runstone Manor farm. The pains had subsided, and mother and baby were okay, but not ready to meet each other as yet. There was a general concession that Rachel should still make the journey to Cornwall the next day, and would be kept informed should Jenna begin to experience any more pains. Very reluctantly she agreed and Rachel set off at midday. She took her time, and it was early evening by the time she pulled into Lizzy's yard. She knocked on the door and entered, but the place was deserted. She put her bags on the kitchen table and called out, but there was no response. She cursed under her breath. She should have sent word to Lizzy that she was coming.

Rachel knew the house well, and made for the bathroom to freshen up. She helped herself to a cup of tea, knowing full well that Lizzy would want her to do just that. She was tired and weary with travelling, and with a warm drink inside her and a comfy chair, she soon closed her eyes and slept. It was eight-fifty when she woke, and still no-one was about. She quickly brushed her teeth, combed her hair and stepped out into the warm evening air. There was a strong perfume of honeysuckle as she made her way down the lane towards The Black Swan, and as she approached she could hear music coming from Charlie's barn. She suddenly realised it was midsummer, and remembered when they had held the first dance in the barn. The memory also invoked the unwelcome image of Sam Blewett forcing her to dance. She shuddered at the thought of him, and had been relieved to learn from Lizzy that he had died in prison some fifteen years ago. As she approached, the music got louder. A noisy horde of teenagers made the building reverberate along with a band, which was playing a Swinging Blue Jeans song, 'Hippy, Hippy Shake'. The dance floor was jumping, as she elbowed her way past the crowds of people and looked about for Lizzy and Charlie. In the distance she spotted Emma, but there were too many people in her way to get to her. The band stopped playing and she turned towards the bar which was throng with people. Robin's voice came over the microphone, welcoming everyone to the annual Gweek midsummer dance. Rachel was still fighting her way to the bar as Robin announced a very special guest who had come all the way from Italy to open proceedings tonight. He held the microphone to Adam, who was making a 'please don't make me do that' face. 'Please give a warm welcome to the man who started the midsummer dance, back in 1939, Mr Adam de Sousa.'

Rachel stopped dead in her tracks. She could not turn towards the stage because of the crush of people. She could hear his voice and began to struggle back out of the crowd. His voice, his lovely dulcet tone, rang out from the microphone, but Rachel could hardly take in what he said. When she finally freed herself from the masses, her head was spinning, and her heart was in her throat as she looked up at the man she had loved for nigh on twenty-two years. As Adam spoke to the audience, his eyes swept over the heads of the people, stopping abruptly when he saw her face. He faltered for a moment. His eyes could not believe what he saw. The audience began to murmur impatiently. Robin frowned at his friend and nudged him to speak, so Adam cleared his voice and continued. 'I now have the pleasure of opening this, the twenty-first Gweek midsummer dance. Enjoy the night everybody.'

The band struck up and belted out a Rolling Stone's song. Rachel watched as Adam disappeared from the stage, her heart was pounding at the anticipation of the reunion. She waited and waited, but he did not come to her side, eventually her heart sank at the realisation that Adam had no intention of coming to see her, and she turned and ran back out of the barn doors.

Robin too had spotted Rachel and told Emma to rush and find Lizzy. As Rachel left, the three of them followed swiftly behind. They were worried their plan was about to backfire and were just about to call out when they were stopped in their tracks. 'Just a minute, I think all is not lost,' Lizzy whispered.

There were tears in her eyes as Rachel walked blindly towards the bridge, but before she could get there, a voice as soft and warm as melted chocolate called out her name. She took a deep breath and stopped short as Adam stepped out of the shadows. She turned towards him as he moved closer. Tenderly, he reached out for her hand and she met his with hers.

'Rachel, my beautiful Rachel,' his voice penetrated the silence of the night.

'Oh god Adam, I can't believe this.' Her voice sounded fragile, and then she began to sob uncontrollably as she fell into his arms.

'You better believe it my love' he said warmly. 'We've waited long enough.'

'When you didn't come to me inside the barn, I thought you didn't want to see me.'

'No my love, I didn't want our reunion to be in front of all those prying eyes. Come, let's go and sit for a moment, I have a lot to explain.'

She vigorously shook her head. 'You have nothing to explain to me Adam. Lizzy has told me why you didn't come back, and Helena has told me everything else.'

He was shocked at the mention of Helena's name. He led her towards the seat on the green and they sat down. The moonlight glinted romantically on the high tide. Two black swans glided elegantly and majestically across the moonlit river, bowing their long willowy necks deep into the water to feed. They came parallel to where Rachel and Adam were seated, slowed to a halt and made a burbling sound as though to greet them.

At length he said darkly, 'So you've seen Helena?'

'Yes, she lives with me now, in fact our daughter married Jake four weeks ago.'

Adam faltered. 'Our daughter! All these years and I had no idea I had a daughter,' Adam's voice was filled with sadness.

There was a sudden tightness in her stomach, her heart began to race. 'I'm sorry Adam, you must think me a terrible mother, because Helena was adopted, but I..'

He pressed his finger to her lips. 'It looks like Lizzy has been our guardian angel. She has told me the story about her adoption, and my heart wept for you my darling. To have had to go through all that on your own, it is inconceivable for me to imagine the pain you have gone through. All I wanted for you was to make you happy, but my legacy to you has been only heartbreak.'

She started to cry again, her shoulders heaving. 'I try only to remember the good times Adam.' She sobbed noisily 'They have pulled me through the bad times. I have never forgotten you. I have always loved you.'

'As I have you my darling wonderful Rachel.' As he tenderly kissed her wet cheek, he moved to kneel at her feet. She felt her heart race, knowing instinctively what he was about to propose. 'Darling Rachel, this may be twenty-two years late, but do you remember I was just about to say something to you when poor Verity burst in on us that fateful day.'

Rachel cast her mind back to the last time she had been in Adam's arms. 'I remember,' she said softly.

'Well I shall say it now. Rachel, will you come with me? Will you stay by my side forever more? Will you love me and cherish me, as I do you? And will you do me the honour of becoming my wife?'

Her face was radiant as she turned her smiling eyes onto him. 'With all my heart my darling Adam, I will.'

There was a ripple of applause from the bridge as Adam and Rachel turned from their embrace in startled astonishment to find Robin, Emma, Lizzy Charlie and Harry clapping their hands in happiness.

Adam laughed. 'I should have known that I can't do anything in this village without everyone knowing about it.'

Lizzy shouted, 'It took us long enough to get you both

back together, we're not going to miss out on the best bit.'

They all laughed together.

'Come on you love birds,' Robin beckoned. 'I think a celebration is called for and I may just have a couple of bottles of champagne cooling in the fridge.'

Very gently, Adam pulled Rachel to her feet and their embrace peeled away the years.

Mr de Sousa's Legacy

ABOUT THE AUTHOR

Ann E Brockbank was born in Yorkshire. Her inspiration comes from holidays and retreats in stunning locations in Greece, Italy and Cornwall. When she is not travelling, Ann lives with her artist partner on the beautiful banks of the Helford River in Cornwall. This novel is her first.

For news and updates follow Ann E Brockbank

on

Twitter @AnnEBrockbank1
Facebook.com/Ann-E-Brockbank-Author

Thank you for reading this novel.
If you enjoyed it, please feel free to review this book on Amazon or Goodreads

97809916R00174

Made in the USA
Columbia, SC
20 June 2018